've# Shadow of the West

A Story of Divided Berlin

SARAH BROTHERHOOD CHAPMAN

Black Rose Writing | Texas

©2023 by Sarah Brotherhood Chapman
All rights reserved. No part of this book may be reproduced, stored in a retrieval system or transmitted in any form or by any means without the prior written permission of the publishers, except by a reviewer who may quote brief passages in a review to be printed in a newspaper, magazine or journal.

The author grants the final approval for this literary material.

First printing

This is a work of fiction. Names, characters, businesses, places, events, and incidents are either the products of the author's imagination or used in a fictitious manner. Any resemblance to actual persons, living or dead, or actual events is purely coincidental.

ISBN: 978-1-68513-178-4
PUBLISHED BY BLACK ROSE WRITING
www.blackrosewriting.com

Printed in the United States of America
Suggested Retail Price (SRP) $22.95

Shadow of the West is printed in Minion Pro

*As a planet-friendly publisher, Black Rose Writing does its best to eliminate unnecessary waste to reduce paper usage and energy costs, while never compromising the reading experience. As a result, the final word count vs. page count may not meet common expectations.

To my three precious marvels,

Nicholas, Nancy, and Harrison

who weathered rootlessness

to enrich the world with their unique perspectives;

to my late, brother Nathaniel,

forever a resource;

and to Oliver Richter

who can finally come over to my house.

The Division of Germany and Berlin

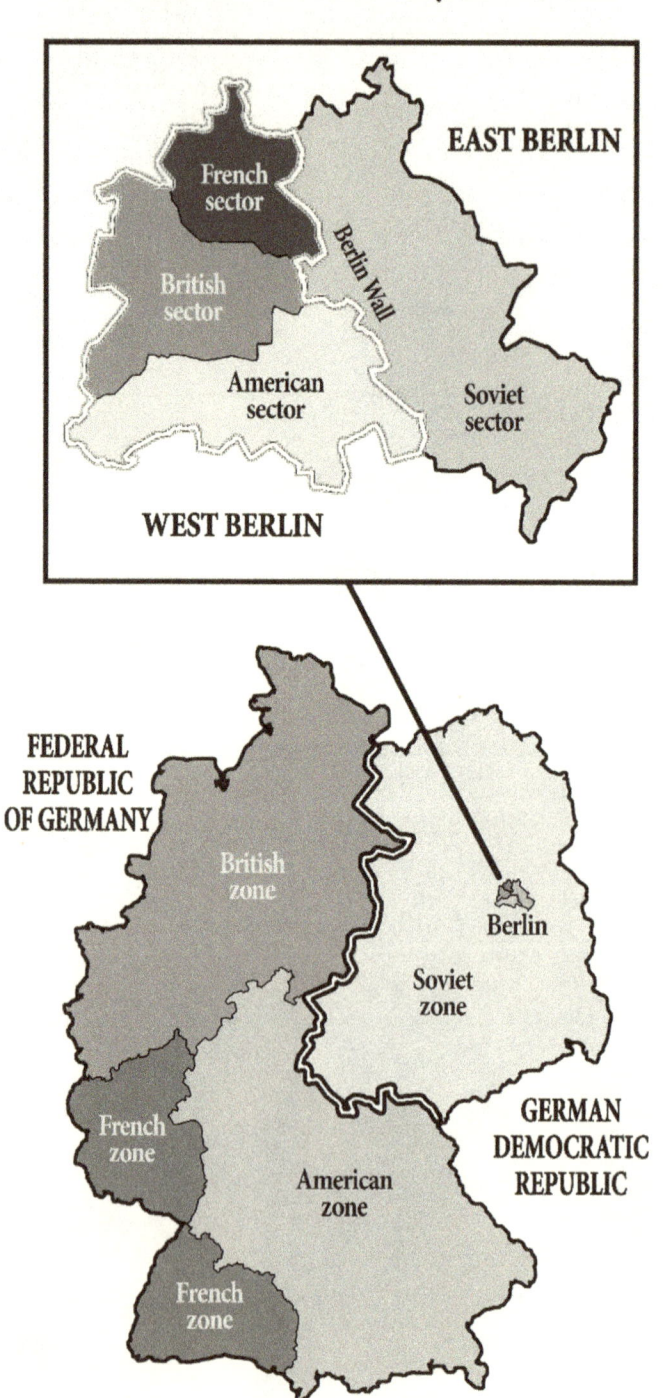

Shadow of the West

1

West Berlin, August 1977

A bell pierced the stillness, rattling me where I sat, alone in a row of orange-molded chairs. Doors burst open. Students spilled into the hallway filling it with a cacophony of chatter, laughter, and jostling, slamming metal locker doors. A basketball bounced and darted between a pack of maroon-and-white, Berlin Bear jackets with graduating years stitched across the chests—77, 78, 79.

The bouncing drew near. I leapt from where I'd been instructed to sit to conceal my new-kid face in a glass-fronted shelf full of trophies. The glass offered a convenient reflection, so when the ball bounced and ricocheted into a direct trajectory toward my head, I ducked and covered, bracing for splintering shards, pain, and even worse: embarrassment.

But, a mere centimeter from my nose, the orange meteor stopped. I peered up to a hand palming the ball—and on up, to a tousled, copper mop shrouding the eyes of a freckled face. It stretched into a sheepish grin. Other faces appeared, shadowing me with unabashed curiosity.

"Yo, man, sorry 'bout that!"

The pack began to stir as a matronly woman with a muss of gray hair brushed the boys aside. She, too, ogled down at me for a moment, then turned away with a tsk of disdain, shaking her head. "Another bounce," she declared, "and that ball will be confiscated!" Her threat dissipated into the din while the copper mop mimicked her retreating hips.

Turning back, he reached down to help me to my feet before spinning the ball to the tip of his index finger where it pirouetted, the rest of the world at a standstill. Whipping it around to nestle in the crook of his arm, he declared, "Raymond N. Bowen the third. Call me Ray. You're new?"

"Not Rainbow?" It jumped right out of my mouth before I could stop it. Ray frowned as his pack-mates began whistling *Somewhere Over the Rainbow*, then shoved each one in turn as he introduced them.

"Lance! Flex! Tricks! Meet—" He paused, turning back to me.

"Kate."

"Hey, Kate." It was the one called Tricks. Startling, sea-green eyes twinkled down at me between strands of sweaty hair. "Don't mind Rainbow. He's harmless," he began, laughing as Ray punched him in the arm, "long as he's fed regularly."

A flush rushed to my face just as the bell erupted again. The pack waved, merging into the ebbing sea of students streaming back to class. Voices beseeched order. Doors slammed, muting the sounds behind them. The empty lobby tingled with a vibrant hush. A familiar, hollow loneliness crept through me: recognition of the hurdle between now and being a part of that crowd, making friends, a new life here. I sat back down and closed my eyes to conjure up the city as I'd seen it flying in the night before. An island of freedom, surrounded by a wall. Walled-in freedom?

Berlin American High School was airy and modern compared with my last school in The Hague. I pictured my old school, its heavy, stone walls and barred windows—we students had been proud of its dubious legacy as a prison in the Middle Ages. I imagined all my friends gathering out front after homeroom, clutching *friets met mayo* in greasy paper cones, laughing, chatting: Jennie, Kim, Annette, Merete, Jon and Carol….

Without me.

I gazed down at the blue phallus on the side of my Adidas sneaker—the remains of a footprint Jennie's fist dipped in paint had made—her fingerprints the toes. *Phallus.* Jennie would've love that. We would've laughed until we cried. My smile froze: I was wearing sweatpants with *Jack's sweater*—baggy, beige, and enormous. I'd swiped it while helping him move into his new dorm room. In my morning lethargy, apparently I'd reached for *cozy*. Was I *begging* for invisibility? I ached for a chance to run home and change, skip past this awkward, new kid stage. Any semblance of confidence I was pretending to have deteriorated like a tooth in Coke.

Vacation in the States: over. Life in Holland: gone. I was starting a new school—a new life—in West Berlin—without Jack. And, staying in the States long enough to take my dear big brother to college had meant starting my junior year a week late. Saying goodbye to him had been agonizing—his brave smile shrinking to a pinprick as we drove off, Mom sniffling up front, Dad gripping her hand between the seats. As soon as we turned the corner, I'd thrown myself down to sob beneath my book. I pictured Jack waking to that life-sized, black-fisted Batman his new roommate Marvin had tacked up—on the ceiling. POW! WHAM! Imagine seeing *that* first thing every day.

And, as if a week wasn't already late enough, I'd slept through my alarm. After hours of staring at the ceiling and thrashing like a washed-up tuna—*boom*—I'd crashed. Out cold. That's jet lag. Even after sprinting the whole way, I was late for my first day.

A body descended into the orange chair beside me with a waft of *Charlie* perfume. Purple and green striped socks bunched into worn clogs beneath white painter's pants: obviously, this was someone straight from the States. I looked back down at my outfit and winced.

Down the hall, Miss Nolan, the school secretary, emerged from her office and strode towards us, her high heels clicking louder as she neared. She handed us each a slip of paper. "Here you go. Katherine Benton, and Amy Carson. Your locker combinations. Follow me, please. Introduce yourselves!"

We stood to follow but ignored her other command. Amy Carson towered over me by a whole foot—most people did—looking like she'd walked straight out of *Seventeen* magazine. I toddled along in Jack's big sweater, an ambulating tent. Amy's black hair swayed across her back like a curtain of shiny, smooth satin. Mine looked more like trampled shag carpeting.

Amy stared straight ahead, her locker combination crumpled in her fist. Either she was too shy to make friends or else she'd already deemed me unworthy. The silence gnawed at me. No way would I talk first. No way.

"So, incidentally, I'm Kate. I'm guessing, you're new here, too?"

At that very moment, my sneaker decided to kiss the vinyl after which followed eight seconds punctuated with at least as many "oh-my-god's" from me: First, I pitched forward, my arms flailing like kayak oars. Next—a nanosecond from impact—I caught myself. Third, I straightened, regained composure. Fourth, relief swept over me, but my hand was gripping Amy's arm. Fifth, I yanked it away, knocking her bag from her shoulder to the floor. Sixth, I bent to pick it up but in the process, dropped my bag. Seventh, I handed mine to her, hefting hers onto my shoulder before I noticed my error and, then, during the eighth second, I hurriedly switched them back.

Puffing from the exertion, I finally stopped moving and stared at Amy. She burst out laughing. "Walk much?"

That was the first thing Amy Carson ever said to me.

"Amy? Your English class."

Giggling, we rushed to catch up with Miss Nolan who was waiting by an open door. Amy flashed me a nervous shrug and stepped inside, sacrificing herself to a multitude of curious eyes. Miss Nolan ducked in after her concluding, belatedly, that it would be nice to introduce Amy instead of just tossing her into the lion's den. I waited alone in the echoey hall like an obedient hound, lost without Amy who had said a total of two words to me.

A moment later, Miss Nolan was back, whispering as she closed the door behind her. "Amy wanted me to ask if you'd wait for her by the door to the cafeteria at lunchtime." She placed an arm around my shoulder with a little squeeze. "That's nice, isn't it?"

The sudden outpouring of empathy—I wondered if I looked like I was about to cry. Which was ridiculous.

Through Government—taught by that anti-bouncing-in-the-halls frizzy-haired lady whose name was impossible to remember—and Algebra taught by a UFO fanatic, I kept to myself, counting the minutes until lunch. I worried Amy wouldn't show, but as I neared the cafeteria, there she was, smiling and waving above a cluster of heads. Ease settled over me. All it takes is one friend.

Now Amy was downright chatty, bombarding me with questions, mostly about moving all over the world, about life in The Hague, having a big brother—because she had no siblings. But when I pressed her for her story, she just rolled her eyes. "Believe me. Most interesting thing I've done up till now is move here."

Her dad, I managed to squeeze out of her, was a U.S. diplomat like mine. At least I didn't have to explain the quick basics: that a U.S. diplomat represented our government abroad and worked in our embassy based in the capital city of a foreign country that also had an embassy in Washington, D.C. Unlike me, Amy hadn't moved around the world with her dad. Her parents had divorced when she was tiny, and she'd lived with her mom and sometimes her mom's mom (whom she called Enid) until moving here.

When I asked her why—why she'd suddenly moved—she shrugged and said, "It was just a funky idea I had, and my dad said it was cool with him. You could say my mom and I needed a break from each other." She bit into her sandwich. "I might leave if it's too weird."

Leave? She could *choose?* I stared, dumbfounded, as the bell began its hideous, already familiar, clang. "Hey, where do you live?" I shouted, hoping it was near me in the American Sector.

"In the East," she shouted back—the moment the bell stopped ringing.

I rubbed my ear. "The *East?!* East Berlin? Like, the other side of the *Wall?* Why didn't you say so? That's so trippy!"

She shook her head. "It's a *drag.* I might as well live on the dark side of the moon."

2

East Berlin, August 1977

With a shiver, Anika willed away the gray cloud of thought hovering like a bully. She pulled the worn, wool sweater her mother had knit over her nightgown and plodded down the hall. The sweater carried her mother's essence, a reminder to stay courageous. When her mother's soul had abandoned her sick, tormented body, the message had been so clear: the worst that can happen is death—the inevitability that meets everyone—so why let fear guide us in life?

She paused beside her parents' room, inhaling memories of when it brought certain comfort, worth the cold stab of emptiness that followed. The door to her brothers' room stood ajar, propped open with one of Stefan's old slippers. Anika leaned into the semidarkness, envious of her little brother Michael's peaceful slumber undulating beneath the duvet. Next to him, Stefan's bedspread lay taut, a barren plain. Anika hastened on to the kitchen.

The gas beneath the kettle flared, settling into a steady, persistent hiss. Anika's lids grew heavy, her focus blurred. The cloud returned. With a jolt, she grabbed a mug from the shelf, a strainer from the drawer, the tin of tea next to the stove, and focused: tea leaves into the sieve, hot water until they float.... She steadied herself, her breathing. No point in dwelling on what might have been. Nor dreading what will be.

Closing the front door quietly behind her, Anika imagined Michael stirring into the morning alone, readying himself for his job at the news kiosk, grateful for any work at all, here in the land where "unemployment did not exist." The notion made her lip curl. They had laughed at the irony of *him* selling State propaganda.

Her footsteps echoed as she trudged down the empty street. Before she was given the early shift, she and Michael could at least have breakfast together. She ached for togetherness, for family bustle, the commotion—all she had taken for granted when they'd had it. Michael—the baby, the golden boy, once cosseted by them all—had been short-changed the most. She swallowed, setting her jaw against that torrent of thought.

It was still dark when she arrived at the tram stop. A dim streetlamp buzzed overhead and she shifted from foot to foot against the chill. Early hours seemed to magnify the void born the moment their mother had died. At least hers had been a natural death—unlike Stefan's. Not that they were unrelated.

It was losing their mother that had made Stefan so determined not to accept a life that required stooping to the whims of the State. Anika shivered. How she had begged him not to be rash, to seek serenity and complacency within, as the rest of them sought to do. But their mother's swift illness and death had revealed how tenuous life could be, and Stefan had resolved to pursue a life in freedom. If they'd shared their fears and dreads, rather than each coping in silent misery after her death, might they have thwarted his plan? Should she have noticed strange behavior in Stefan, been able to stop him?

She trembled less from the cold than from the rush of memory. The border police bursting through the door, suspending life in bleak oblivion one dark second before spinning into a whirl of unfathomable facts: Stefan had tried to escape. He'd been shot. Dead. The guard's lips, moist and red, spitting accusations: traitor to the State, betrayal. Father, dragged away in handcuffs. Michael and

Anika, left alone. They had not been allowed to see Stefan's body, there had been no funeral, the obituary had read only "killed in an accident". Nor were they dignified a word from—nor about—their father. Last month had marked a year of his imprisonment, time enough to become accustomed to, if not accept, their reality.

And now. The winter ahead filled her with dread.

Anika peered down the tracks, relieved to see an approaching light. As she clutched her coat across her chest, the cloud threatened. Not now. Not today. She attempted to shrug it off. The streetcar screeched to a halt. Tomorrow, she demanded, climbing aboard. But the moment she sat, the cloud descended.

3

That first week Amy and I met in the cafeteria every day. Lunch was a welcome break from the strain of those first days when your head spins from all the newness. We were content to sit by ourselves at a table by the entrance and made no attempt to get to know anyone else.

The last person I thought would be the key to our social introduction was Nadia, whom I'd met in chemistry my first day. She'd seemed nice, if a tad *out there*. Then today, she'd become my lab partner, and I couldn't wait to tell Amy all about it.

We grabbed our usual table and sat down, opening our paper bags of lunch. I began right away, "Hey, remember I told you about Nadia? The dramatic one? Well, get ready. She wants to introduce us to her friends. Mr. Sennett made her my lab partner today. So, listen to this. After he explained to the class about the lab, I turned to her—you know, to get started—but she just stared at me—breathlessly, blinking in this weird way. I mean—you'd think we'd been tasked to do an *assassination* or something!" Amy laughed, popping a handful of chips into her mouth. "And then—*all serious*— she says," my eyes bore into Amy's for effect, "'I have to confess something.' Then she dug her *nails* into my *wrist* and said," I grabbed Amy's wrist and stared into her eyes before tossing back imaginary hair and lowering my voice. "'I am *categorically*. Miserable. At chemistry.'" I dropped Amy's wrist, grabbing a handful of chips. "Seriously. What am I supposed to say to that?" Amy grinned, leaning on her elbows for more. We munched together for a moment before I continued.

"So, anyway, I did the *entire* lab on my own—while she *babbled*. Everyone was giving me sympathetic looks. She literally never shut up. '*Chemistry* doesn't matter to *me* because *I'm* heading to *Broadway* the moment we graduate!'" Amy began to choke with giggles, which just egged me on. "Honestly?" I asserted, "I *can* see her on Broadway. Her voice has amplitude. And she's striking—in that Elizabeth Taylor sort of way—know what I mean? *Gigantic* blue eyes, and *big*, black hair…" My hands were waving above my head demonstrating Nadia's majesty when, above us—as though my gestures had painted her into being—came the very voice I'd been mimicking.

"*There* you are!"

And there *she* was. I dropped my arms and bit my lip. Amy stifled a giggle.

"I'm *so glad* I found you! *Come*. I'm going to introduce you to the *best* people in the school. Right *now*."

Amy and I stood on command and began to waddle behind Nadia like ducklings braving the big pond for the first time. We wove between tables and chairs alive with the unleashed anarchy of lunchtime, until, on the far side of the cafeteria, Nadia stopped. And sitting there, among three others, was none other than the cute basketball player, Tricks.

"Everyone? As promised. Here. They. Are." Nadia's arms were draped around Amy's shoulders. "This is—" She paused and looked at me with a trace of panic. "Am-uh-Amelia?"

"Just 'Amy'," I clarified, with a sheepish glance toward Amy. I'd already told her a little about Amy, not to sound like I had no friends.

"Amy!" Nadia's eyes grew round and darted left and right. She deepened her voice, as though imparting classified information. "Amy's never lived abroad before, but *now*—she lives in the *East!*"

Amy darted me a look of betrayal while Nadia turned to me. "And *this* is Kate. I told you, I absolutely do not know what I would do without her. She is *brilliant*. Kate has lived *every*where in the world and knows absolutely *every*thing. She's going to save me from failing chemistry, I *swear*. To. *God.*" I rolled my eyes and scrunched my nose. They had to know Nadia exaggerated.

"Kate, Amy. Meet Molly, Will, and Rick. The best friends anyone could have. In the entire. Universe."

Tricks—Rick—smiled at me. "Oh, Nadia. Kate and I go waaay back." My face burned.

"What? Really? How on earth—?!" Nadia glanced from me to Rick.

Molly sat ramrod straight, eyeing us all like a director accruing notes for a scene. She had golden-brown skin, just a shade lighter than her curly hair, jammed unceremoniously beneath a plastic headband. "Oh, dear, Nadia, did Rick meet someone before *you*?" She scooted her chair over and patted the empty one next to her so Amy could sit.

Since he'd remembered me, I had the guts to settle next to Rick—who was disarmingly clueless of his slaying powers. Before biting into my peanut butter sandwich, I asked him what brought him to Berlin, hoping to chew—and watch—while he talked.

"Dad's a colonel at BB," he said with a shrug, referring to the Berlin Brigade. Among the military brats, I'd noticed it was common to mention rank. "You military?" he asked—too soon. I shook my head, working peanut butter from the roof of my mouth.

"Nope. Dad's a diplomat." Being a diplomat's kid set you apart here, though I still didn't get just why. It hadn't meant much in The Hague where there was no military. "He works at RIAS." I assumed he knew about the Radio in the American Sector, the station that broadcast truth to the news-starved East.

"A dip brat, eh? Cool!"

Rick explained that, no, he wasn't on the basketball team. He just shot hoops with the guys now and then. And no one else called him Tricks besides those guys. "I played last year but, honestly? I'm no good and don't miss it. Much happier running." He paused. "Hey, do you run?"

"Run? Well, sure, who doesn't run? If I'm late or being chased…or walking alone, spacing out," I smiled. My friends in The Hague had made fun of me. "When my thoughts start to go fast? So do my legs." I gave up on the peanut butter and grabbed my apple, penetrating the skin with a pop.

"So, you're a natural."

"A natural *pony*—way too little to race. I'd have to take triple the number of steps you take. And—I can't run long distances."

"Sure. At first. You'll quickly learn how fast you can turn those little steps over and build stamina. Seriously. You should think about joining. Coach Kilner's cool—serious, but basically just wants everyone in the world to love running. And the girls' team needs more girls. Whaddya say?"

I cowered. I'd never been on a sports team in my life and I'd only just arrived. My approach was to hang back, get a feel for a place before joining anything. But, well. *Rick* was asking me. So I shrugged a maybe, just to humor him and see his green eyes squint into a smile.

"Will's our fastest runner. Talk about a natural." Rick nodded towards Will who'd kept on eating, off in his own world, letting his friends deal with us newbies. "Even if his dad's a *civilian*." Rick chuckled. Will's father was a pilot for Pan Am, he explained, the only American airline allowed to fly into West Berlin. He sighed loudly, pretending to whisper an aside. "My daily challenge is *tolerating* Will."

Will, his eyes still on his sandwich, nodded. "Yeah, right. Try tolerating Rick's daily *tolerance*." His voice was mellow yet weighty. Something inside of me sat up.

Rick laughed, leaning back—then leapt to his feet as though his chair had caught fire. "Damn! I'm 'sposed to meet Chuckie! He's gonna help me finish my lab before class. Sennett's all over my ass. Need a genius to figure out what I did with my data." He tapped me on the head. "Should transfer to *your* class," then leaned over to pound the center of the table. "Gotta scram. Great to meet you two! Later."

I watched his receding figure maneuver the cafeteria with the grace of a gallant steed. Across the table, Amy bounced her eyebrows up and down, grinning, before turning back to her conversation with Molly and Nadia. I chomped my apple, feeling left out.

Will wadded up the remains of his lunch and cocked his head at the empty space between us. I knew I should slide over, but a sudden attack of shyness glued my feet to the floor. When I didn't move, Will dragged his chair over instead.

"Rick make you cough up your life story?" he asked, his dark eyes locking onto mine. "He'd make a great secret agent—can get most anything out of anyone."

With a quiet calm, he began to ask simple things—where I came from, where else we'd lived, sibling questions—but it felt as though with only a few data points, he pegged me down to my freckles, as though he could see right through my cool school veneer. I felt naked, yet oddly not exposed. There was something about how he listened. Exactly who would make a great secret agent, I wondered.

"I'm suffering from 'only child syndrome' now," I lamented after telling him about leaving Jack in the States.

Will was the youngest of *seven* kids, the only one to come to Berlin two years ago from Seattle. "So I, too, suffer from only child syndrome." He grinned, then became serious, thoughtful. "But, you're doing OK?"

What a question. My thoughts swarmed like drunk gnats, unable to coalesce, to match his sincerity. But his calm was contagious, infusing me with a kind of truth serum. "Well, I miss The Hague, of course. But, meeting Amy right away was amazing. I'm waiting for that point where, because I'm equally invested here, there's no going back. Know what I mean? Moving can suck. It hurts. But the alternative—staying in one place? That would be like—like going to the zoo and seeing only the hippos? I dunno. It's hard, but, somehow, it's all worth it."

He cocked his head, as if tuning into the source of my voice inside my head and nodded slowly. "Yeah. Challenges create stories." He sat back, shifting his focus beyond me. I took in his pine green sweater tufted with snags, the narrow band of white t-shirt between it and his tan neck. His gaze was that of an alert, lone wolf watching from his lair, detached from the throbbing, turbulent, teenaged blood and natural rhythm of human conversation around us. The sun glanced off his unblinking, chocolate eyes in golden daggers. As the cafeteria melee faded to a distant hum, I closed my eyes, imagining my fingers gliding through his dark, tangled, unruly waves. Hair not unlike my own, I realized, opening my eyes. Amy was grinning at me, Molly and Nadia in animated discussion, leaning first forward then back to converse around her.

The bell jangled and student zombies lurched into motion, rising, gathering lunch remains. When we stood, my head came up only to Will's sternum. He smiled down at me, and placed a hand on my shoulder.

"Friday. Catch you later?" He lifted a strand of hair from my cheek and held it a moment before dropping it, nodding as though I'd answered his question, then ambled off, alone, somehow, in the crowd.

"See ya, Will!" Molly and Nadia crooned after him. He raised a hand without turning.

"So. Glad. I found you two!" Nadia blew us kisses then linked elbows with Molly, and, together, they strolled away.

Amy tried to nudge me out of my stupor. "Hey! So...you and Rick hit it off, huh? Or was it you and Will?" She laughed, pushing me along. "Seriously, seems like you and Will were on another planet." A chair fell into our path because of two guys boxing. Amy deftly steered me around it, pulling me aside. "Kate, listen. I have to tell you..." she hesitated.

"What?" Her tone jerked me back. Suddenly we had gossip?

"Well, Molly told me—in a little side whisper, you know?—that Nadia is madly in love with Will. So, yeah, I guess I got that 'tread carefully' vibe from her on the Will front?" She stopped walking to face me.

"Oh." My mind went blank. "I mean, we were just talking. Not like it was...*some*thing. Whatever." I fought a twinge of shame, confusion.

"Right." Amy studied my reaction before shrugging it off. "Sure. I mean, it's not like I see glowing embers or anything." She laughed. "For real? I almost feel sorry for Nadia, like she's miscast Will in her play—know what I mean? You'd think she'd know better. But, still, we're new to the scene so, I guess...."

"Yeah, OK. I *get* it." I said, then grabbed her arm and faced her. "Amy. He is *intense*."

She blinked back at me, sensing trouble. I dropped her arm. "Seriously, Amy. Not an issue." I changed gears. "They're nice, huh? Eclectic group. So! Do we have new friends? Hey—you wanna spend the night?" I hadn't even planned to ask.

"Seriously? I'd love to! I'll call my dad from Nolan's office. Molly said they're all meeting at the Outpost Theater to see *Annie Hall*."

"See *who*?" My heart thumped but I refused to examine why.

"Is Holland under a rock? It's a *movie*. Woody Allen's latest? I saw it with Alex in the States before I left."

"Cool." Alex was her boyfriend. I had no idea who Woody Allen was and didn't care what we saw. That afternoon, I didn't think of The Hague once.

4

By mid-afternoon, Michael's stomach was growling. He'd skipped breakfast; what few rations they had in their pantry were meagre and odd. A can of tuna (that would be dinner). A remnant of a loaf of bread, a day old. Some dried peas. He stretched, acknowledging his own laziness. What could he make from that stuff? Anika was better at food alchemy. But it would be a challenge, even for her. Maybe they'd get another mystery basket at the door. Why it irritated his sister to have a secret benefactor made no sense to him, though they both knew it had to be that strange relative.

He checked his watch, wondering if she'd already prepared for their evening meal. Half four. Two more hours before she'd be home from the clinic. It felt like an exceptionally long day. The kiosk had been in worse shambles than usual when he'd arrived, as if Ingo had either been dancing wildly or in a drunken brawl on his early morning shift. But Michael took it in stride. Ingo was a *safe* work partner and that was worth a lot. Anyway, tidying gave him something to do while he was there. Since he had to be there, he may as well be organizing all the propaganda—to show off our nation's remarkable news! He chuckled. He'd have earned a shiny red star in grade school with that mindset.

A man wearing a suit at least five sizes too big, strode toward the window. It looked downright clownish, but Michael knew better than to laugh. He brought his arm across his face, as though to wipe sweat from his upper lip, but really, it was to hide his smile. He imagined the man dressing in front of the mirror in the morning. What did he see? Did he think the suit fit him? Michael hoped so.

"Good afternoon." Michael posed, ready to help, but the man ignored him, seemed interested only in reading headlines.

"No drinks?" The man queried after a few moments without looking up.

"None left," Michael replied. "I'm sorry." They'd run out last Friday. The man began to turn away, his trouser hems catching beneath the heels of his shoes, then hesitated.

"Do you have news on that RAF kidnapping? Of the Nazi capitalist pig Schleyer?"

The slur rolled thoughtlessly off his tongue, instantly putting Michael on guard. He reached for a *Berliner Zeitung*, pulling one out of a stack. "Here. Long article. Front page."

The man dropped coins into Michael's hand and snatched the paper, poring over it as he walked away. Now a part of Michael wanted to tell him he looked like a fool. He certainly thought like one. The Red Army Faction, the West German militants, were not to be applauded. Violence, Michael thought, counting the money as he dropped it into the tray, must never be glorified. Their methods delegitimized all their ideals. But he knew better than to express his thoughts out loud—it was dangerous enough to engage them.

He crouched on the low wooden stool to read the Berliner Zeitung himself. Each day, he chose one of the more outlandish stories to take to Anika. With the the radio up for cover, they would read it together and laugh at the transparency of the propaganda. How people could not see through it was a mystery to them; their father had taught them early to question the source of everything. These days, with all the artists disappearing after the slightest non-conformist comment—killed, arrested or fleeing to the West, who knew where they went?—it was imperative to keep quiet. No one could be trusted anymore. They had few friends (not to mention family members) left. Old friends brought more frustration than anything else since—to protect yourself—you now had to presume they, too, had turned informant. The best of friendships had been poisoned.

Michael studied the headlines. There was a story praising the magnificent plans of the Free German Youth's upcoming parade to celebrate sixty years since the Russian Revolution in 1917. "The Stronger our Socialism, the stronger our freedoms!" it began. Not even remotely interesting. There was a comparison of literacy in the GDR to other countries. Nah—just made up numbers, not funny. Anika needed humor.

With that thought came the niggling feeling that there was something wrong, something that Anika was not telling him. The thought slid like a cube of ice down a hot ramp, from his mind to his gut. Was it about their father? Or Anika herself? His body shuddered, as if tickled by a malicious ghost.

Neues Deutschland had a story about the coffee crisis. Michael skimmed it: Coffee had become too expensive to import from the West…the East had to save their store of West Marks for petroleum, also in crisis…yes, yes, not news. It had been months since he and Anika had been able to afford coffee. They had no *Westie* relatives to provide for them. He yawned. A coffee right now wouldn't hurt. Rather than waste money on outrageous prices of imports that serve only to fortify capitalism and greed, the State had created a new drink. Michael leaned in. A new drink?! Forget coffee, the article said. Now the good people of the GDR will drink *Misch Kaffee*, mixed coffee. Coffee combined with…Michael scanned ahead. But they never mentioned what the other ingredients were. Of course. But drink it they would! Solidarity! He laughed and reached into his pocket to pay for the paper. Anika would enjoy this one. A hot, patriotic drink.

5

By October, Berlin felt more and more like home, and the thought of The Hague became less of a yearning and more a gauge of how much more I'd gained than lost by moving. Letters to friends in The Hague were easier to write now that I had some things to say, and getting letters, even from Jennie, didn't hurt so much. Instead, I was eager for friends to visit so I could show off my new life.

Walking to school took less than half an hour door to door, faster if I half-ran, which I usually ended up doing. The headquarters of the Berlin Brigade, the U.S. Mission (what would be an embassy if we were in a normal capital city), the schools, the PX and Commissary were all nearby. It was essentially an American neighborhood tucked inside a German one. I often wondered what it felt like for native Berliners. Did they *feel* occupied? Dad would say, "They feel safe because of us." If we Allies gave up on them, the USSR would overtake the whole city.

My bedroom was at the top of a spiral staircase located in a wing on the opposite end from my parents' ground floor bedroom. It had high ceilings sloping down to dormer windows overlooking a back garden full of fruit trees and rose gardens. Little steps led up to my own, quirky, triangular-shaped bathroom with a massive, claw-footed tub and a round, stained-glass window. It was the best bedroom I'd ever had.

Thinking of Jack in his squishy dorm room with that bizarro Marvin made me feel slightly spoiled, especially since "Jack's room," the little one across the hall from mine that Jack had yet to see, had become Amy's. If she stayed over weekend nights, Amy could sleep on the extra bed in my room. But during the week—Mom allowed her to stay only two school nights per week, especially if she was planning to stay over the weekend, too, which she usually did—she had to sleep in Jack's room to keep us from chatting all night. Amy would've moved right in with us, but Mom worried about Amy wanting to stay at our house all the time—instead of spending time with her father.

"Max doesn't care," I insisted. Amy called her dad Max.

"Do we know that? Isn't she in Berlin to get to know him?"

The truth was, I didn't know. However close we'd become, Amy still hadn't told me much. I found myself defending her without really knowing why. She just complained about how much she missed when she took the embassy van home right after school every day, and that, what with the hassle of the checkpoint and all, going home on her own was a royal pain and took forever. I commiserated as though I knew what she meant, though I had yet to cross over, even once.

I had only seen the Wall accidentally. A couple of times, Mom and I had gotten lost driving home from somewhere and the road had dead-ended into a solid block of concrete extending to the right and left as far as we could see. Mom would exclaim, "Oops! The Wall! Guess we *did* go wrong!" and we'd turn around.

When I was younger, I thought the Iron Curtain was a giant, wavy, gunmetal divide, rising a mile from the earth, visible from outer space. Learning that there was no *real* iron curtain, Jack had teased me about my 'naive literalness' while Dad had seized the opportunity to teach me about metaphors. So, then to find out that the Berlin Wall was, in fact, an actual, concrete wall, I was struck by the builders' lack of resourcefulness. Why resort to the real thing when a metaphor could suffice?

Thirteen feet high, rounded at the top to make it difficult to grab ahold of when trying to escape, the Wall had seemed silly in its unsophisticated simplicity, a solution a kid might have come up with—not adults. Every few meters along its expanse rose forty-foot towers with guards surveying the Death Strip below.

Since the Wall's first crude, middle-of-the-night construction on August 13, 1961, it had been engineered and enhanced until it was the efficient, lethal human deterrent that it was now. In some stretches, as wide as a hundred and sixty meters, a strip had been cleared, equipped with trenches, trip wires, dog runs, fences, and criss-crossed cement barricades. At night, the Death Strip gleamed under spotlights as bright as day.

Not that I'd seen any of that yet—I'd only read about it. From the West all you could see was a wall. Maybe that was what had shocked me the most. You could drive up to it, touch it. Even paint graffiti on it. Look up to the towers and see the two armed guards, machine guns poised to shoot anyone trying to escape from the East. Many died trying.

The Wall surrounded us, blocking out the rest of the world—yet we were the ones who could come and go at will. What existed on the other side was hard to fathom—and no one liked to think too much about it. Life in the West went on as it would have anywhere—except for the occasional bomb exploding or the barrage of rifle fire rattling in the distance—training, demonstrations of might—a reminder that we were in military occupied zones: French, British, American, and Soviet. We felt safe and ignored the explosions. Most of our parents dealt with the Cold War daily in some manner or another, but we kids rarely gave the Wall much thought—nor life on the other side. Like teenagers anywhere, we were too preoccupied with our own lives.

Tomorrow was the last day to join the cross country team. I didn't want to if Amy didn't. She was sprawled across the bed in Jack's room reading the latest *Cosmopolitan*.

"Come on, Amy, it's easy. Anyone can run. The guys are cute, and we'll get to go on the Duty Train…"

"Told you: I don't run, Katie."

"That's ridiculous, like saying you don't breathe. It's not a skill, it's a—ah—a *discipline*. So what if we lose every race? We'll get in shape, have some good laughs…"

"Stop, Kate. Answer is no. I don't *want* to." She rolled over and began to read the advice column out loud. "*My boyfriend has never seen me without make-up and…*"

She could be exasperating. "OK. Forget it."

"You should do it."

"Don't want to without you."

Amy rolled over and gave me a stern look. "If you don't, you'll regret it and I'll be the reason you didn't and then you'll resent me and that'll ruin our friendship. So, now that I think about it, you have to." The *Cosmo* rose between us. "You run all the time anyway. Maybe this way, you'll get it out of your system so that when I'm walking with you, I don't have to keep reining you in like some spooked mare." She propped herself higher on the pillow, raised the magazine in front of her face again, and mumbled, "You need a life without me. In case I decide to leave."

It was something she said from time to time, and I hated it. As if Berlin was just an experiment she could quit whenever she wanted.

6

"Anika," Michael began, unsure how to approach this. He took a deep breath. "You're not telling me something." He glanced at her walking beside him. She kept her eyes on the sidewalk in front of her.

After dinner, they frequently went for a stroll. It was the best time to talk about things—since their situation forced them to assume their house was bugged. That had seemed like an overly paranoid notion before Stefan was killed and they'd lost their father inside the black hole of the system. Not anymore.

Anika said nothing for a beat too long before exclaiming with too much emphasis, "Oh? No, not at all, sweetheart. You know I tell you everything. We—we are a team."

Unconvinced, Michael fell silent. He knew there was no point in arguing with her. If there was something he should know, she would tell him. For now, it was important to go along with her. He tugged his pants up to his waist but in three steps they'd slid back down around his thin hips. He kept forgetting to put on Stefan's old belt. Just then, a car slowed almost to a full stop a few meters past them. A shiny, black Lada. But as soon as they approached, it took off again.

"What was *that* all about?" Michael mused as the hard-to-come-by Russian-made car turned a corner up ahead. He tried to quell his suspicions by shrugging it off as perhaps someone about to ask them directions, or perhaps mistaking them for someone they knew, when, beside him, Anika twitched and wriggled, as if she'd walked into a spider's web. "Anika? What is it, Anika?"

"Oh, nothing, Michael, I promise you. I'm just chilly. Let's go on home, shall we?"

Michael's disquiet grew. He was not making it up.

7

Practices often took place in the *Grünewald*, a park behind the school where we ran around the *Krumme Lanke*, a lake surrounded by a three kilometer path that snaked through trees. West Berlin had beautiful parks—there was some good stuff on our side of the Wall. Endurance runs were my favorite, when the boys' and girls' teams ran together. Knowing I'd see Will at practice made the day brighter from the moment I stepped into school in the morning. When the varsity teams had to run extra and we didn't finish together, I'd wait for them to get back so we could walk home together. Rick lived on the way to my house and Will, just beyond. That gave me four natural minutes to be alone with Will. I'd tucked away my feelings and kept a cool, casual demeanor—fooling even Amy who'd stopped mentioning Will as anything but a friend.

Rick and Will sometimes slowed to run alongside me, until Coach Kilner ran up to say, "C'mon, guys! Puuuush it!" and I'd step up my pace to stay with them until I couldn't anymore. But it quickly made me faster. That was when Tanya and Marny began giving me grief. The two of them ran their own internal race, perpetually competing for second and third behind impossible-to-beat Odele.

Odele happened to be a star, a Berlin treasure, a legend among all the DOD schools in Germany—our Israeli gazelle who disappeared from sight the moment the gun went off. When Odele was in a race, the only question was, who would come in second. Tanya and Marny didn't care, as long as it was one of them—and the other was right behind.

They were tall, dark, regal, and inseparable friends. Tanya wore her hair in a perfect aura-radiating afro. She had almond-shaped, black eyes surrounded by thick lashes. Marny's braids curtained her neck, weighed down by beads that clicked as she ran. A jade pendant tied with leather lay flat between her collar bones. I was in awe of their seemingly effortless strides and watched closely as they ran, side by side, legs in perfect sync. Over time, their pace began to feel right for me, so I began to fall in alongside them, two of my steps to one of theirs. They never spoke to me, but their dirty looks had to be all my imagination.

Then one day before practice, I was pulling my running clothes from my bag when Marny and Tanya stopped talking. No one else was in the locker room. They were staring, their eyes narrow. I pulled off my jeans and stepped into my shorts, befuddled worry edging my mind.

Marny's beads clacked like machine-gun fire as she elbowed Tanya. "Mmm," she murmured. "Mm-mm." Her gaze grew sinister as she approached. She reached out and shoved. Hard. I fell backwards into the lockers, my shorts dropping to my shins.

"Hey!" I cried, bewildered.

"White skin 'n bones. Tanya! Com'ere. Look at this." Marny was poking my ribs. It only tickled, but that was beside the point. *"Just bones, I'm telling you!"*

"You are sooo right—I *swear*!" Tanya began to poke too, with glee.

They pinched and prodded me as though scrutinizing a washed up sea creature. My fruitless batting back only made them laugh. Soon any move I made generated squeals of delight. Then Marny lifted me off the ground, jiggling me like a piggy bank until my shorts dropped from my ankles. "Look at this! Doesn't weigh nuthin'!" When she released her grip, I dropped to the ground, unhurt—yet hurt.

The two of them could barely breathe through their giggling, watching me scramble, struggling to untwist my pants. They were doubled over, clutching each other in hysterics. I yanked up my shorts and lurched to escape just as the door opened. It was Odele. She stopped cold, hands on hips.

I seized the moment to push past Tanya and Marny. "Glad to be so entertaining," I muttered, my fury melding with shame.

Odele caught up with me outside. "They're threatened by you. Don't take it too hard, OK? They're all right. It's been a while since anyone came so close to them." I shrugged, pretending I wasn't remotely bothered—and as soon as I saw Will and Rick, I beelined toward them for comfort—and status: they were universally beloved.

Tanya and Marny started calling me the Bleached Stickbug and poked me when I ran too close. I tried to ignore them, hiding behind the guys and Odele whenever possible. Once, Tanya stuck out her foot, and ran ahead, laughing while I brushed mud off my knees and tried not to cry. When I saw Marny in the hallway between class, she'd go out of her way to bump into me and then keep going, laughing riotously.

Rick said they just had a strange sense of humor, but I failed to see anything funny. Amy called it "light bullying", said I should just stay away. Will said he was sure that, if I could hang in there, they'd get to know me and it would all work out. He said to pace with them, but from a ways back, just to focus on my time. I wanted to quit but knew that would just make me look pathetic.

Fridays, we had to run timed sprints up the *Teufelsberg*, a mountain created from Berlin's accumulated rubble piled up after World War II. It meant "Devil's Mountain," and practices up its steep side were legendary. But I liked them—uphill was my specialty.

It was grueling all right, but of the three timed runs, I beat Marny twice.

After practice one Friday, Rick's mom had picked him up for a doctor's appointment, so Will and I walked home alone. Beside him, my tummy felt funny all of a sudden, my movements jerky, my arms too gangly, like the part of my brain that controlled me needed oiling. Even talking felt awkward.

"Man, you sprinted up that *Teufelsberg* without even breaking a sweat," Will said, exaggerating. "Marny and Tanya have good reason to worry. Don't quit."

"Hah. *Teufelsberg* is torture. I dig the symbolism, though, you know? Our generation suffering atop the ruins of the last." We were at the corner by my house.

Will chuckled. "Yeah. Lest we forget." He shifted from foot to foot, strangely twitchy, for him. "Do we have practice tomorrow?"

"It's Thursday. Why wouldn't we?"

"Oh, right," he laughed. I'd never known him to act so peculiar—as if he'd caught what I had. We stared at a passing car, as though it told us something.

"What time is it? So dark already."

He checked his watch. "Five." Practice always ended at 4:30.

"Where'd you get the watch?" It wasn't new.

"PX. It has a timer." He shrugged flicking his wrist, then glanced up at the windows to my room. "Is Amy there?"

"Nope. She went home in the van."

We batted around running strategies until we ran out and the streetlights began to glow. I leaned against the hood of a shiny black BMW. "Mmm, cozy," I said, laying my cheek against the metal. "Still warm."

He palmed my cheek and nodded, then jumped atop the glistening hood, patting the spot beside him. We swiveled to lean side by side against the windshield, legs stretched out across the warm hood, the engine ticking below. When a car passed, I pressed my face behind Will's shoulder.

"Think they can't see you, ostrich?" he teased.

We spoke little as the sky darkened and stars emerged, one by one. The car's warmth dissipated. My heart trembled like a baby bird's, alert. If only time would stop. I turned to look at him, just as he faced me. Our lips had barely touched—maybe it was only our breath commingling—when a metal door in the brick wall beside the car began to creak open. We froze for a split second, then flew from the hood, each of us landing on opposite sides of the car as a man emerged from the gate, tapping the brim of his hat.

"*Guten Abend!*" Keys jangling, the man unlocked the door to his BMW and got in. I stood aside, waving at Will who, grinning, backed into the street before trotting off into the shadows. As the BMW roared away, I wanted to call Will back, but he'd disappeared. I leaned against the wall, heart pounding, already worried that I'd only imagined the near kiss.

8

Anika kept her back to the door to feel more secure as she rummaged through her bag. She shook it, fished out the jingle of keys, and selected one from the bunch to unlock the large, metal door to the clinic, her hands trembling. Once inside, she locked it again behind her to feel safe until it was time to open for the others. With a deep breath, she then unlocked an inner door to the waiting area.

Thus began her round of unlocking doors to doctors' offices, rooms with diagnostic machines, and screening rooms, switching on lights as she went. The clinic seemed to yawn awake, neon buzzing. Finally, she took off her coat and hung it on the rack near her desk in the front room.

When patients entered the clinic, her desk was the first they saw. It was her job to take names and update information, and type out legions of forms with carbon paper between copies to register new people. After sending a patient to the waiting room, she stuck the forms in files for the doctors. She performed these duties between answering the incessantly ringing telephone, making appointments and scribbling messages on a memo pad to be carried to recipients as soon as possible.

After patients had been seen, nurses handed files to Frieda whose desk was behind Anika's. Anika was ever aware of Frieda's eyes on the back of her head, piercing her scalp with judgment. Across from Frieda's, Mina's desk was seldom occupied as she, a nurse, called patients to be seen, walking them to examining rooms where she weighed them, took their vitals, and instructed them to strip after tossing them a thin, cotton sheet.

The three women worked in close proximity, but they were not close. Anika knew better than to try to become friends. Work was work and should not become social. To allow it to be was fraught with peril. Still, their working relationship was civil, and for that, she was grateful.

With a gasp at the time, Anika remembered the ribbon in her typewriter. It had been almost too faint to read the type on the original yesterday and both doctors Schmidt and Hesse had complained. Panic rising, she glanced at the clock. Five minutes. She should have done it yesterday before leaving, but she'd been too anxious to get home to Michael. Rushing, she tugged open her drawer and searched, relieved when fingers met a box the right size. She sighed, grateful for small miracles. No need to wait and ask that nasty Gertrude to accompany her on a trip to the supply room—the one key they did not trust her with.

She lifted the top of the typewriter and tugged to dislodge the old ribbon from the brackets holding it flush against the platen. Grasping only the spools, trying not to touch the ribbon or the metal arms caked with old ink, she yanked it free. Almost done—she began to relax. As she pried open the box that held the new ribbon, there was a banging on the front door. She had forgotten to unlock it.

Anika rushed to it and, cringing, twisted the knob. If it was a doctor, she would hear about it. Holding her breath, she pulled open the door and came face to face with Frieda, a cigarette pinched between blood-red lips pouting in annoyance. She took one last puff and yanked it out between gloved fingers as she pushed Anika aside.

"What is with you and locking that door? If you're here already, just leave it open! What are you afraid of, anyway?" She marched over to her desk, dropping her bag on top, her smoking cigarette into an ashtray. She pulled a fresh carton of f6's from her desk drawer, expertly tore it open, lit another cigarette and squashed the butt of the old one. All this before taking off her gloves, she then stood there eyeing Anika, smoke snaking around her.

Anika stared back in dumb fascination until, with a start, she remembered her task and rushed to her desk. Replacing the top of the typewriter, she noticed black smudges on the casing. Despite her caution, her fingertips were black with ink. She looked up as Mina entered with two other nurses, laughing, marching past Anika without so much as a nod. Everyone began to enter at once, the inner door banging shut after each until Anika ran over and—something else she'd forgotten to do—jammed the doorstopper beneath it to be removed at 8 o'clock sharp, before the first patient arrived. She still had to pull files from the back room. But—she blinked down at her smudged fingers—she needed to clean her hands.

She stood rooted, addled, her breaths short and shallow, her hands flicking the air. The dread began to engulf her; for a horrible moment she thought she might burst into tears. Instead, nausea hit her, and she beelined for the toilet.

By the time she returned, Mina had dropped the pile of yesterday's patients' files on her desk. Anika scooped it up and rushed to the file room. It was Mina's job to file them, but ever since Anika had managed to get the morning shift, she had assumed as many jobs as she could to seem indispensable, terrified of being put back on afternoons; and Mina had quickly come to expect Anika to do her work for her.

Anika hurried back to her desk. Now all she had to do was insert carbon sheets between layers of forms and she'd be ready for her first patient. She sat, glanced at the clock—7:59—and jumped up again to release the inner door from its jam as an elderly man, his arm in a sling, pushed through. Anika slipped back behind her desk—Frieda's disdainful smirk not lost on her—just as the man neared. With dismay, only then did she remember that the forms were not prepared.

9

On a crisp, fall day, summer a fading memory, our house buzzed with the familiar signs of transitions: the smell of cardboard and paper, the screech of knives slicing open packing tape, the air tinged with promise. Boxes shipped from The Hague—leaving our home there the empty cavern it had been before our boxes had arrived from Moscow—would now transform another empty house into a home here in Berlin, ending another long period of limbo. Life would finally settle—until time to move again.

I'd been at it since we got home from school, ripping open boxes, piling things to put away in my room. Earlier, Amy had found my guitar, tuned it, and had been strumming away in her own world, cross-legged atop my giant *kilim* pillow made from a traditional Turkish grain sack.

"You gonna help?" Annoyed, I dumped a stack of albums down next to her. She ignored me but leaned over to flick through the albums. I began to unpack noisily, grunting and dropping things with a thump, ignoring Amy right back—until I caught her about to plug my stereo into the 220 wall socket with only a plug adapter.

"Stop!" I shouted. "It'll blow!" and snatched the plug from her hand. "It's *110*, Amy." I rolled my eyes and sent her downstairs for a transformer. Ignorant American, I muttered. What was eating her, anyway?

She returned, dropping the heavy metal box on the floor with a groan, then plunked right back down and picked up the guitar. Not angry, just *Amy*. I knew what we needed. I dropped the books in my arms in front of the empty bookshelf and began to set up the stereo. Turning the volume way up, I dropped the needle down. *Helplessly Hoping* blotted out everything else. Amy finally looked up, back from Mars.

Except—Dad was hollering up the stairs. "Kaaaatieee!" I ran out to lean over the railing. "Whew. You don't make it easy, Kiki, having to compete with all that music! Phone call, honey. A boy. Military line."

Kicking aside an empty box blocking the stairs, I slid down the bannister, hoping said "boy" hadn't heard my father who met me, shirtsleeves rolled up, boxcutter in one hand, receiver pressed against his chest with the other.

"Fellow named Rick. Your beau, or Amy's?" He held the receiver just out of reach, teasing for an answer.

"Good grief, Dad." I jumped up and snatched the receiver from him.

The modern, plastic push-button phone was an internal line for U.S. military and diplomatic families. The other phone, an old-timey, black metal phone with a shiny bronze dial, was the German line. The two sat side by side on a desk in an alcove outside the kitchen. We were trained to always answer the military line with: "Hello. This phone is not secure," which, before long, rolled out: "Lothusfunznotskur!"

"Kiki? It's me, a boy. Your *beau*...?" I squirmed.

"That was Rick, Amy," I said, catching my breath after bounding back upstairs. "We're going to *Das Klo*. Remember—that bar Rick's been talking about?" Again, she was far away, fingering some difficult chord, despite *CSN* playing loudly in the background.

"Hey! Earth to Amy!" I waved my hands in front of her face.

"OK." She bit her lip while she strummed.

I wondered what went on inside that head of hers. Most of the time, she seemed perfectly content—downright chipper—but then in a heartbeat, she would be as accessible as the planet Pluto until, just as quickly, she'd be over it. As a result, we never got to the bottom of anything: any attempt I made to investigate, Amy deftly stifled.

"I'm just wearing what I'm wearing," I sighed, stuffing my baggy t-shirt into my jeans to dress it up, focusing on looking disinterested around Will in front of the gang. But I was excited—about seeing him and going down to the hub of the West's famous nightlife, the *Kurfürstendamm*. At night, the *Gedächtniskirche*—a bombed out church intentionally left in ruins to remember the war's devastation—would be lit up, jagged and stark against the night sky, all the modern neon lights pulsing around it.

"Oh, no, Kate." Amy dropped the guitar, jumping into action. "No." Turning to a newly unpacked pile of clothes on my bed, she held up items one by one before tossing them aside. I cringed knowing they were all wrong for Berlin's night scene, not that I really had a clue what *right* looked like.

"Don't bother. There's nothing *there*." I threw myself backwards onto the bed. I hated clothes. Hated worrying about the way I looked. I was never in one place long enough to get it right.

"Wait—this? This is cute." Amy said, not without a tinge of surprise. It was the white peasant top with green stitching I'd bought with Jennie at the street market in Amsterdam last spring. I blinked, feeling the tender spot in my heart for my old life. Amy tossed it at me.

"That's a summer thing." That much, I knew.

"It'll work. We'll layer it."

I pulled off my t-shirt and took the top from her. She stood back, head cocked, waiting. "Tuck it in." She nodded with approval. "Perfect. Casually hip."

"Thank heavens for that," I sneered, secretly grateful for any fashion advice I could get, realizing, though, that I'd freeze. "I'll just put a turtleneck under it."

"Bathroom," Amy pointed. Finally, I thought, she's back on earth. "Enough tomboy stuff. Tonight, you're wearing make-up. I think it's time for Will to see you're a *girl* who likes *boys*."

"What? Will and I are *friends*, Amy. That's it. You know that."

"Sigh. What's he gotta do, Kate? Preen his feathers?" She wiggled her tail on the steps to the bathroom. "A mating dance?"

"Don't be absurd."

"Sit." She banged down the toilet seat cover and pointed. I sat while she rummaged through her makeup. I didn't own any. Even Mom only wore the stuff when she dressed up for black tie occasions, like the annual Marine Corps Ball.

"We're just going to a bar, Amy."

She bent down, whipping her thick hair over her shoulder. It slinked right back, like a cliché shampoo commercial. "Let's see. Blue?...yeah...to match your eyes...a little smoky, not too bright..." she tilted my face up to glide the soft brush across my eyelids. Again and again.

"Enough," I mumbled through her hand clenching my jaw. What would Will think?

"Hush. Hold still. Now. A little mascara..." Amy's own, perfectly caked lashes flickered close to mine. She could pull it off. But I feared looking like a kid playing dress up. The wand loomed dangerously close. I squeezed my eyes closed. "Open!" Amy snapped, whipping her hair back again. The wand jabbed the air. "It's about moderation. The last thing we want is call attention to the make-up *itself*—contrary to what all these peacocks at Berlin American High School think."

"Pea-*hens*," I corrected.

She blinked down at me. "You get my drift." I didn't, really. She leaned back to eyeball me, then pulled me over to look in the mirror. "Perfect."

My blue eyes, surrounded by a fringe of black lashes, jumped off my face. I was secretly pleased but dreaded calling attention to myself. "You don't think I look like a harlot? A lady of the night?" I wiped at the blue with my fingertips. "Or worse—like I got into Mommy's make-up?" She yanked my hand from my face and tossed me a hairbrush. My choppy waves bounced back the moment the brush passed through. I failed to see the point.

"You look *pretty*. Feminine. Like you care about your looks, and, maybe, care about *some*one. Poor Will. A little hint from you wouldn't hurt, Kate."

Had she forgotten all about the Nadia issue?

Amy pulled her Andean poncho—all the rage in the States, apparently—over her head, then bent over until the ends of her hair swept the floor before flicking back up, each strand falling freshly into place to frame her face perfectly. Zipping up a pair of fringed moccasin boots, she stood, ready.

"Let's go." She turned and bolted down the stairs.

I stepped into my clogs—they brought me up to almost normal height—and snatched Jack's heavy, wool sweater from the back of a chair before following her. Now she was almost too chipper, I thought, shouting goodbye to my parents before slamming the front door shut behind me while squirming my way into Jack's warm, cozy sweater. It fell down to just above my knees. Snuggly. I followed the familiar trail of *Charlie* perfume down the walk.

At the gate, Amy turned back and smacked her forehead. "Oh, my god, Kate! *What* are you wearing?"

"What." I pushed past her. "Come on. We're late."

10

Amy, Molly, Rick, Will and I emerged from the *U-Bahn* after a quick debate about whether to transfer at *Fehrbellinerplatz*. We'd decided to walk from the Ku-damm and skip the transfer. Rick got his bearings, surveying the area like a tracker in the Kalahari. "This way!"

A downtown bustle had replaced our familiar *Dahlem* suburb calm. Reflections of kaleidoscopic lights twinkled in fresh puddles: we'd missed a shower.

Following Rick, we melded into the Ku-damm's streaming chic: ankle-length fur coats alongside umbrellas tapping in syncopation with the clip clip of stiletto heels, perfumes blending with cigarette smoke in the wet night air. Spiffy Mercedes pulled up outside nightclubs throbbing with life, dislodging VIPs who parted crowds jammed in doorways awaiting entry. West Berliners, they said, perpetually aware of the Soviets at their threshold, had a knack for partying every night like there was no tomorrow.

"Don't you love it?" Molly cried, a skip in her step, her eyes twinkling. Prep had gone into her evening, too: eyeliner, blush, her hair straightened. She was wearing fashionable, knee-high black-leather boots I'd never seen her in before. Molly, it occurred to me, seemed happier without Nadia around. Yet usually, she opted to go with Nadia and her mother to some avant-garde, trendy nightclub or disco—where none of us would dare to go—instead of hanging out with us. The weird thing was that, without her mother, Nadia wasn't allowed downtown.

"I wonder what all this looks and sounds like from the other side," I mused to no one in particular. I pictured a cartoon image of stars and music notes bursting above a wall.

"Partying must help drown out the thought of families and friends trapped over there," Will mused, suddenly beside me. I looked up and nodded, my heart fluttering. We hung back, letting Molly, Rick and Amy trot ahead.

Wednesday's closeness returned, daring me to believe in the near-kiss again. I'd been afraid to tell Amy about it, fearing its insignificance would be exposed in the telling. We'd sat on a car together, so what? Will's scruffy, black high-tops squeaked alongside my clogs' clomping against the wet pavement: one squeak to one and a half clomps. Ahead, pinpricks of moisture dangled in the air, silhouetted by streetlights. Amy was animated, bouncing between Rick and Molly, the poncho batwings when she raised her arms.

"Think West Berliners feel guilty living so lavishly?" I wondered, knowing Will wouldn't think it strange.

"Maybe. But no good comes from both sides being repressed."

"It's like the East is the West's shadow. Know what I mean? I want to go over, see for myself. Amy tells me nothing besides 'it's boring'."

"Maybe it is."

"Well, still. I wanna see what that means." I snuck a peek to see if I could guess what was going through his mind. Our eyes met, and I tripped over a cobblestone.

"Whoa!" Will grabbed me, clutching my arm. "How can you walk in those things," he teased, his laugh soft and gentle.

"Oh, you know me—a slave to fashion," I joked, trying to stave off embarrassment. Both my ankle—and cheeks—were on fire. Up ahead, Rick hollered at us to move it.

"Hold your horses!" I yelled back, relieved at the distraction. Will took my elbow and we quickened our pace, the ends of his blue scarf rippling behind him like a wake.

"Rick must get frustrated with us insolent troops," I noted after we'd slowed again and he'd had to call, again. Everyone talked about how Rick was destined for West Point. "He sure is *star* quality."

"Three. Minimum," Will agreed, grinning as we turned down a little road called *Nestorstrasse*. A red awning with white, balloon-letters that spelled out *Das Klo* fluttered over a large picture window. Rick was pumping his fist in triumph. He'd been trying to get us to come to this place for weeks.

"This is it!" he said as we walked up. Inside the window, in glistening white porcelain, was a toilet. It was choked with lush, green vines like from a scene in Sleeping Beauty.

"A toilet?" Amy gave me a questioning look. Had no one told her what *Das Klo* meant?

Rick held the door wide for us to walk through to an area bordered with floor to ceiling terrariums bathed in a lime-green light. As my eyes began to adjust, I noticed movement and bent low to peer through the glass. A few inches from my nose a miniature, golden-eyed dragon, its tiny, green hands curled around twigs, slowly crawled forward.

"Ew!" Molly lurched backwards.

"An iguana," Will whispered, his hand resting on my back. He smelled like a magical blend of Irish Spring and orange-flavored Life Savers. I felt giddy.

"Breathtaking," I murmured, standing to fill my lungs. Will probably thought I meant the lizard.

Votive candles twinkled from tables with Persian rugs for tablecloths, a crisp, white toilet paper roll gracing the center of each. Amy waited for me to scooch down the bench to the corner next to

Will before sitting next to me. I was aware of Molly's keen gaze and knew she planned to report everything to Nadia, though she pretended not to be looking and grabbed the toilet roll.

"Whatever you do, don't squeeze the Charmin," she joked.

"You mean like this?" Rick snatched it from her, giving it a squeeze before unrolling it across the table toward Will who let it unroll back, the paper forming a criss-crossing trail—until Molly intervened to restore dignity.

"Need-only basis," she declared, carefully re-rolling it and plunking it back down on the table.

Das Klo worked hard to reflect its name. The barstools were toilet seats. Posters displayed illustrated lists of rules for when and how to sit on a *klo*, how best to puke into one. Arrows all over pointed toward the restrooms. One poster of a stick figure on a toilet read, *Warnung! Zum reisen braucht man Schuhe, zum scheißen braucht man Ruhe*—to travel man needs shoes, to shit a man needs calm. Yet, despite the prevalence of scatological references, the warm candlelight and all the lush greenery nestled in the walls made the place downright cozy.

Between poop-oriented stuff, a hodgepodge of artifacts covered the walls. Dented copper bowls, faded wooden signs, ivory dice. Will eyed an old bicycle with tireless, dented rims hanging behind our heads. I'd read how, during the war, they'd had to resort to riding on bare metal rims once tires had worn away.

"Too bad this bike can't tell its story," Will said, barely touching the threadbare American flag draped across the seat. Next to it in a grainy black and white photograph, a smiling pilot leaned against a U.S. military plane.

"Hey! That's The Candy Bomber," I realized, twisting to get a better look. I'd just read about him.

At the end of World War II, when Germany was divided among the four occupying forces, the capital city—Berlin—happened to lie in the Soviet quadrant of Germany so, it, too was divided and occupied by the four forces. The Russians did not like the fact that this meant other occupying forces would be inside their territory. But the French, British, and Americans declared they would remain in Berlin unless the Soviets pulled out, too.

The Russians had no intention of leaving, and eventually, they decided to force the issue by cutting off West Berlin, shutting down all roads and railways through their territory to West Germany. They hoped, essentially, to deprive Berlin of food and supplies so that the Allies would have no choice but to abandon the city to the Russians. The Soviet Blockade would starve them out.

But the Western Allies refused to leave. Instead, they dug in with great support from native West Berliners. If they couldn't use roads, they'd use the air.

The Berlin Airlift was considered the first big crisis of the Cold War. From June of 1948 through May 1949, American and British planes flew around the clock, taking off and landing every three minutes—every thirty seconds during the most frenzied times—carrying tons of food, clothing, fuel, and medical supplies to keep the city alive. Berliners scrimped and saved, turning every little piece of land—even median strips—into gardens to grow food. They'd rather starve to death—and nearly did—than be ruled by the communists. Ultimately, the Soviets recognized their determination and that the Blockade was only serving to solidify the resolve to stay, so they ended it.

I told Will how I'd been reading about the Airlift on our back porch one day when my mom called me over. She was by our rose garden, chatting with our elderly, prim and intimidating neighbor whose gray hair was always tightly coiled in a braided bun, her back as straight as an iron rod. But up close, I saw that her eyes smiled softly. "Frau Werner, this is my daughter, Kate." I curtseyed, as I'd been taught back in German kindergarten.

"Call me Ursula," she'd insisted. And later, when we were seated in her sunny salon sipping tea from delicate, china cups, the bouquet of our pink roses carefully arranged in a vase on the coffee table, Ursula noticed the Airlift book I'd placed on the sofa beside me.

"Ah. How I remember that year, standing at the end of the runway with the other children, waiting for *"Onkel Wackelflügel...."* When her eyes misted over, I tried to imagine the images flitting through her mind. She'd been there.

Col. Gail Halvorsen was an American Air Force pilot. He related how one day, he'd handed out a couple of sticks of gum to a crowd of hungry, grimy children who'd gathered near the runway to watch the planes take off and land. Instead of fighting over what little there was, the children had torn the gum into many tiny pieces to share. That inspired Col. Halvorsen with an idea. He called it "Operation Little Vittles." Fashioning parachutes out of handkerchiefs, he'd attached candy to them and dropped them from the plane. Before long, people all over the USA were sending him—and now other pilots, too—parachutes and candy. Just after take-off, Halvorsen would dip his airplane's wings as a signal, and then down floated the tiny parachutes to the children. He became known as The Candy Bomber.

"We *Kinder* waited for him to *wackel* his wings," Ursula told me, her face beaming with the memory, her flat hand tilting from side to side. "Like so. And then we knew!" Her hands cupped and floated, imitating the candy-filled parachutes fluttering down through the air.

"She got all teary-eyed," I told Will next to me. He'd been listening, his head tilted toward me. "She made the Airlift feel so real." I sighed. "She's living history."

Will smiled. "Wonder what we'll talk about when we're that old?"

11

"Hey, what're you two discussing down there?" Rick was shouting over the music as his arm shot up to catch the passing waitress whose black t-shirt had a graphic of a snake curling out of a toilet. Beneath it was written, "*Aufsssss Klo, geht'sss lossssss*" —It all happensssss on the toilet. It sounded better in German-snake.

"*Hier zum ersten Mal?*" She asked, grinning.

I responded when no one else did. It was weird to be the new kid, yet the one who spoke the language best. I'd learned German from our nanny and attending Kindergarten when we lived in Garmisch. Living in the American sector, it was easy to get by without learning German, so many kids didn't bother. "*Ja,*" I told the waitress. It was probably obvious that it was our first time there.

"*Möchten Sie unser traditionelles Begrüßungsgetränk probieren?*" The waitress asked sweetly, clicking her pen. Maybe I should have read into her strange smile.

I translated to poll the others. "Who wants to try their traditional welcome drink?" The waitress counted hands and disappeared. A moment later, she placed four shot glasses down in front of us—for all but Amy who never touched alcohol.

"*Prosit!*" we toasted, clinking the tiny glasses together, then in unison, froze. The liquid was a thick, dark red, eerily reminiscent of blood.

"*Na, Also!*" The waitress encouraged, miming gulping it down. "*Auf einem Schluck—Hop!*"

We tossed them back. Hot lava, seared lips, tongue, throat, on down, inch by inch. No one spoke. Brimming, blinking eyes said it all. Amy cast her gaze around the table, her arms crossed righteously in front of her as, one by one, we began to gasp and cough.

"Holy smokes!" Rick managed, gasping through sputters. "What *was* that!?"

"Alcoholic Tabasco?" Molly proclaimed, hoarse. Tears oozed between her eyelashes, her hands clutching her throat.

Will sucked in air beside me. He rasped, "need beer."

"Oh my god, your faces," Amy cried, rolling her eyes. "Pathetic."

The waitress appeared. "*Herzliches Willkommen!*" she laughed when we begged for water. The guys ordered beers and Molly and I each a glass of red wine. Amy got a Coke.

"Aside from the burn, that was kinda *lecker*," Rick declared, after downing a glass of water. "Cheers! Hey, Amy don't you know coke will rot your teeth? You ought to try an *Erdinger*. Much healthier."

My heart sank as I turned to Amy, waiting for her mood to shrivel. She hated any attention to the fact that she didn't drink. She stared, frowning at her glass, stirring up bubbles with her straw. Oblivious, Rick was gathering a pile of beer coasters and stacking them on the edge of the table. With a flick of the back of his fingers, he whipped the whole stack into the air and caught them mid flip. My mind scrambled for a way to change the subject. His proud grin faded when he looked around to see that his stunt had failed to elicit even one smile.

"Hey, Amy, tell us about your neighborhood—in the East," Will prompted. Not for the first time, I wanted to hug him.

Amy stopped up the end of her straw with her finger to carry the contents to her mouth. We watched and waited as she muddled through her internal struggle. She repeated the move again before dunking the straw back into her glass, crossing her arms in front of her. "OK. I'll tell you. Take the West, turn off three-fourths of the lights, dim what's left. Subtract two-thirds of the people, add decades of black scuzz everywhere and a few ugly, modern, square buildings. Add some giant propaganda posters everywhere. Close restaurants at ten—they run out of food anyway. And—take away all cars besides a few rickety *Trabants*...." *Trabants* were the most common car made in the GDR, the butt of many a joke in the West. "In short, it's quiet, dirty, and boring. And *way too serious*." She sucked the end of her straw again. "Oh, and someone is always *listening*. Or—you have to assume so, anyway." She rolled her eyes.

Molly piped up. "You know Aydin from Turkey? He lives over there. He's in my German class. Anyway, he told me he was playing soccer in the streets and kicked the ball into a *Trabi*—no really—*into!* It went right through the door. I mean, *literally* made a *hole* in the car."

Rick shrugged. "Course it's going to be a crappy car: State-made. Communism. No competition, no incentive to make anything better." He was parroting Mr. Bluem, everyone's favorite government teacher. He took a swig of beer and wiped the froth from his mouth. "Sounds depressing."

I nodded. "My dad thinks that ultimately the *economy* will fail and that will bring down the whole Soviet Bloc."

I desperately wanted to cross over to see it for myself. With my diplomatic passport, I—unlike the others—could even spend the night. But anytime I suggested we spend a weekend over there, Amy mentioned something going on over here that we'd miss. I sipped my wine, once again wondering if there was something she was hiding.

Rick flicked a nut at Will before popping one in his mouth. "I just wanna get a Soviet belt buckle," he said.

It was a rite of passage. With a few West Marks and maybe a pack of Marlboros, guys could procure a soldier's belt buckle. Mostly, it was bragging rights, how daring they'd had to be—hiding in a smoky office at the border, or behind a tree in the East, what they got away with trading for it.

Will shrugged, tossing a nut back at Rick. "Pan Am discourages employees' families from even going over—they're afraid we'll get detained. The military would come looking for you guys, but we'd just be left to rot in a cold cell somewhere." He settled back, closer than he had been, and draped an arm on the back of the bench behind me. I looked over to see if Molly had noticed.

Amy swept her hair up into an impressive pile on top of her head, then let go, letting it tumble down around her shoulders, a sign she was coming out of her slump. "Anyway," she declared with a grin, "I've pretty much moved into Kate's house. When Jack comes home, he can have that little maid's room off the kitchen. He won't mind, will he, Katie?"

"Does he have a choice?" I laughed, relieved she was back. But I was thinking: It's my turn to go to *your* house.

12

From the bathroom, Anika heard the kitchen door open and shut, Michael returning from work. She splashed her face with cold water and pinched her cheeks for color before walking out to greet him. Another wave of nausea loomed at the idea of having to eat dinner, but eat she must, so as not to make Michael worry that something was amiss.

As she reheated the schnitzel on the stove, Michael fell in alongside her, setting the table with comforting sounds of clinking forks, heavy plates hitting the table. She tried to relax. Dinner tonight was good, too. The latest basket had contained fresh veal from the butcher. She'd breaded it and made schnitzel to go with a potato salad—which even had mustard in it. Maybe Michael would finally gain some weight. All those stressful, lean months following their father's arrest, before they'd gotten jobs. Before the baskets. She tried to be appreciative. She was. Yet, she wasn't.

"Anika? You heard from Marcus! How is he?" Michael, clearly ravenous, dumped a massive portion of the potatoes on his plate before looking up at her. He no doubt was anticipating glee over news from her boyfriend who—a conscientious objector—was doing his obligatory military service as a *Bausoldat*. They did construction for the military, never held a gun.

Anika chided herself for leaving his letter on the counter. She used to live for letters from Marcus. She would drop everything and write back that very day. Until she'd stopped altogether. This letter was frantic, worried, upset. What could she say? That all their dreams were lost? That he was writing to someone who no longer existed? The letter had arrived that afternoon, Marcus' handwriting as familiar as her own. For a brief moment, she had felt that old joy, excited anticipation before tearing it open—a flicker—until the present flooded back, flattening the momentary wrinkle in time. The letter was pure, innocent; she'd dropped it from her loathsome, vile hands. She had to spare him. She simply could not write back.

Michael stared at her, waiting to hear the news. She could not talk about Marcus. Not without crying, and how would she explain that? A bite of veal rolled in her mouth like wood pulp. She grabbed her glass of water to wash it down.

"He's fine, fine. Two months down, sixteen to go." She placed her glass back down and managed to take up her fork. Michael blinked back at her. She knew he was trying to read what was going on with her odd behavior, knew she would have to explain. But, not yet. Oh, not now.

13

Rick and Will had gotten ahead of us, laughing, kidding around. Amy was grilling Molly about Lavinia, Nadia's quirky mother. I trotted quietly alongside lost in thoughts about Will—worried he was nowhere near as gone over me as I was over him. Maybe I needed to wake up. And what about Nadia? Molly was sleeping over tonight, too, so I'd have to squelch my angst until later when Amy and I were alone. She'd know what to do with this complicated relationship stuff.

The sound of glass breaking brought me back to earth. There was a shout, scuffles, grunts. Amy, Molly, and I froze in our tracks. Ahead, the boys' silhouettes merged into a black, writhing monster in the drizzly mist—not playing; they were *fighting*. The number of arms and legs—the *heads*—didn't add up. It made no sense.

We ran ahead only to stop short at Will's blue scarf lying crumpled on the wet pavement amid sparkling shards of glass— remains of the beer stein Rick had swiped for his collection. In front of us, Rick's arms were full, not of Will, but of somebody else, the guy's arms flailing, punching the air, his white shirt untucked, his black tie swinging like a pendulum.

Rick held tight until the man stopped resisting, moaned, went limp. He loosened his hold, easing the guy down to the ground. A sound like a sob emerged, more anguish than pain.

Only then did I notice Will, in the shadows behind Rick, bent over, his face in his hands.

"Will?"

He turned his head to look at me, his face smeared with blood. More streamed from his nose. "Will!" I grabbed his arm. He stood to blot his nose with his sleeve, but the flow remained steady. I reached up to pinch it just below the bridge, as Jack used to do when he was prone to nose bleeds, but he winced and pulled away, tried tilting his head back, then forward to cough, black drops splattering the pavement.

"Oh my god, Will." I was blabbing, digging fruitlessly in my pockets for something to stanch the blood. The scarf—but it was covered in glass shards, no matter how much I shook it. Will reached a hand to calm me. Amy and Molly just stared, their hands covering their own noses.

The man was propped up against Rick's legs, slumped over like a discarded marionette. His tux, smeared with puddle water, glistened like a wet seal. After glancing up and down the street, Rick reached beneath the man's armpits and dragged him to the safety of the sidewalk, his heels leaving parallel tracks on the wet tarmac. Rick tucked him next to the side of a building and stood back.

"Have we calmed down now, *mein Herr*?" He asked, panting slightly.

All of us stood staring down at the stranger as he groaned, his head lolling to one side. I reached a trembling arm around Will's waist, burying my face in his sweater that was wet with rain or blood, or both. Then the man began to gag and I spun away, pulling Will with me. The others followed like zombies and we shuffled off, leaving the repulsive retching behind.

"He was possessed," Rick muttered, shaking his head in disbelief. The instant we turned the corner, the incident felt impossible, as though it had happened in a different dimension and if we turned back, no one would be there. "Came out of nowhere—fists flying." Rick was rambling, unconsciously reenacting the episode: Will had caught a punch full on. Hard. In the face. When the man reeled, that's when Rick had grabbed him. Dropped his glass. It had happened so quickly, he still couldn't fathom why.

"Must've been drunk," Molly said, "off his ass."

Will was still bleeding, trying in vain to blot the flow with a sodden sleeve.

"Hey, guys, stop a sec?" I urged. But Will shook his head and waved for us to keep going, so we ambled on down the dark, empty street.

"That tux? Those shoes? He was no bum." Rick seemed compelled to make sense of it all.

I couldn't think about the man. "Guys? Will's nose is broken. We need ice or—*something.*"

"Kate, I'm *fine.*" Will insisted. He withdrew his fist for a second, but when a stream trailed down his lips to drip from his chin, he yanked an already blood-drenched sleeve out from beneath his sweater to find a drier spot higher up. "Damn."

Turning another corner, we saw lights—a café bustling with late-night coffee drinkers and I bolted past surprised occupants at a table near the door and tugged fistfuls of napkins from a holder. Back outside, I handed them to Will who winked at me from behind the wad that filled instantly with blood.

"Maybe it *is* broken," Rick said.

"Shouldn't we call the *Polizei*? What if the guy gets mugged while he's lying there?" Molly fretted. I winced. Forget about the guy. What about Will?

"We have no more responsibility for what happens to that guy now than we did before he came outta nowhere to jump us. Unless Will wants to call the *Polizei* to press charges or something?" Rick turned toward Will, who shook his head. "OK. Then I say we just get out of here."

Amy hadn't uttered a word since we came upon the fight. Her head was hunched into her shoulders, arms crossed tight beneath her poncho. I nudged her. "You OK?" She looked at me and nodded. I was unconvinced and gave her a quick squeeze.

Rick got more napkins, reported that the cafe didn't have ice. No surprise, ice in drinks wasn't a German thing. We stood in the shadows, away from streetlights exposing us to gawking passersby and waited. Finally, the bleeding subsided, and we ambled on toward the U-Bahn, dazed and weary, longing to be home.

On the train, Will's dried blood drew stares. His eyes were puffy. What else could it be from but fighting? *Americans*, they seemed to be saying. They get away with murder. We kept our gazes low and didn't speak until we got off and walked to my house where the boys offered faint goodbyes. When I handed Will his filthy scarf, I reached up to palm his blood-caked cheek. He moved my palm for a moment against his lips and kissed it.

The front light had been left on for us. As Amy and Molly tiptoed upstairs, I turned down the hall to Mom and Dad's room where the door was ajar and whispered into the blackness sealed tight by the wooden *Rollläden*. Mom would be half asleep, half waiting for me to get home. I felt for the edge of the bed and knelt next to her, my heart bursting with love, Dad's slumber rumbling beside her.

"Mama?"

"Hi, sweetie," she whispered back. "Everything OK?" She reached up, feeling for my face in the dark.

"Yep, fine, Mama." I kissed her cheek and lay my head on her blanketed warmth, wishing all life's problems could be solved like this.

"Sweet dreams!" she murmured sleepily as I shut the door behind me.

A yellow arc of light from the bathroom dissected my room. Molly was curled up in the single bed between the gables, Amy facing the wall in my double bed, neither one talking. Any other night, I'd have wondered if they'd had some kind of quarrel, but not tonight.

I brushed my teeth picturing Will washing away the blood. Despite the twisted ending, the evening had compounded my feelings for him and—his kiss on my palm—I did believe he had them for me. Smiling in the dark, I climbed in next to Amy, snuggling down on my back. A shadow from a passing car moved across the ceiling, trailed by Amy's finger dive-bombing my nose.

Startled, I jumped, then whispered so as not to wake Molly. "Thought you were asleep."

"Nope."

"You OK?"

"Why wouldn't I be?"

"Because. Come *on*."

"*I* didn't get punched in the face."

Typical Amy. But this time, I pushed back. "You don't have to tell me *what*, but *something* else was eating you out there. God. Don't *lie*," I hissed.

Amy took a deep breath. "OK."

"Not now, not ever. I never lie to you."

"OK. I won't."

Of course, now she might just not tell me anything—that, after all, wouldn't be lying. Still, somehow my pushback felt like a tiny notch into impenetrable Amy. But I couldn't press on, not now, not with Molly here. I turned on my side, my thoughts swimming into slumber.

"Kate?" Amy whispered.

"Hm?" I managed, drowsily.

"Look, I trust you. OK? I'm just not…ready. Once I tell you, it'll be, well, a burden—a secret—because, you can't tell anyone."

My mind jerked back into focus. So she *was* hiding something. And she knew I knew it.

"OK."

"I know you're there. For me."

"Well, sure, I mean, come on. You're there for me, too," I paused, realizing I needed affirmation. "Right?"

"Of course I am—like *you'd* ever need *me*." Then, she whispered directly into my ear. "You and Will are so damn cute. I can't stand it!"

I turned to her in the dark, wide awake now. "Oh, Amy, I can't stop thinking about him. All that blood! He was so chill—I was a mess! He's so—"

Molly's voice interjected. "Hey, I hear you guys, y'know. And I'm feeling left out!"

I swallowed in the dark, guilt prickling my senses, imagining Nadia crying from a broken heart, hating me forever. "Get over here, Molly!"

"Shove over." Molly squeezed in next to me. "Listen," she said, her tone matter-of-fact, "Kate, the static between you and Will is so thick, it's like—like standing in an electrical storm."

"Seriously," Amy laughed, "zzzzzzt!" She writhed like she was being electrocuted.

Molly laughed, too. I braced myself for the imminent lecture on Nadia's feelings. "Yeah," I gulped. "But. *Nadia.*"

"Nadia?" Molly jolted next to me. "What *about* her?"

"I mean, if—for the sake of argument—Will really does—if we—it's just that—I—" Wait. What had Molly just said?

"Whoa, Kate." Molly put her hand on my arm in the dark. "You guys. You've *got* to keep up! Will is *yesterday's* crush. *News Flash*: Tim Brennan? Yeah, that senior hunk? He smiled at Nadia last week, all sweaty and sexy after football practice—and now—*thump thump*"—Molly's fist pumped against her heart—"she can't *sleep*. In fact, just the other day she said, 'Molly? We have to push Kate and Will together. It's so obvious to me—why isn't it to them?'"

My mind was spinning. Why hadn't Molly *said* anything?

"Golly, Miss Molly! *Now* you tell us?" Amy grabbed her pillow and jumped to her feet. I snuggled down and buried my face. Besieged with pillow blows and giggles above me, stepped on and kneed, I felt like I was floating above the whole world.

14

They had finished eating what little there was before Anika found the nerve. She stood to dial in music from an approved radio station to be safe and then, one hand on his shoulder, she leaned over to whisper into her brother's ear. She recounted only the facts, the chronology of the incident, sparing him details. He pressed his hands against his eyes as if to block it out, his body tensing beneath her hand.

Anika sat back and waited for what would come. Michael's hair still shimmered in soft, golden tufts as it always had. But now, beneath it, a muscular jaw prickled with a yellow stubble. When had he become a man? Anika quelled a rising panic at the passing of time, warm memories repressed by constant fear and dread.

"We have jobs because of him. Good jobs, food…" Anika attempted. Lame comfort; it served more to underscore the extent of their entrapment. She could feel the churning inside her brother's mind. When his hands fell from his face, Michael stared in powerless desperation at his sister.

She closed her eyes, longing for the tranquility of their youth. But instead, what came to her was a tableau of the moment it had ended: She, at fifteen, laden with a heartache unlike anything she'd known before gazing at Michael, small, only ten, framed in the doorway to their parent's room, eyes blinking into the stifling bleakness. His hair tousled, hands and knees smeared with dirt from playing in the yard. Behind him, Stefan's hand gently pressing Michael forward, coaxing him in. Next to Anika their father lay hunched over what had been their Mama—her impoverished, inanimate, empty body.

She'd inhaled, but never released the breath, as though it had impelled her soul to flight, sent it soaring, free of her terrestrial bond. Anika had felt a confusion—how was this an ending? Why had they fought it so long when death was the solution? Weeks of torment and suffering—Mama clinging to what no longer could be called life—death had brought release from all of it. Anika had floated on a cloud of glorious relief—until slamming into reality, a new, bleak landscape: a world without her Mama.

It was Michael's tears of incomprehension and woeful disorientation that had stirred Anika into action. With single-minded dedication, Michael became her mission. When he cried, she held and comforted him, encouraging him to laugh at life's quirks, as their mother had. When their father's weeping woke her, Anika would tiptoe down the hall to close the door to the boys' room, softly, protecting Michael from that inconsolable grief. And Anika had rushed to shelter him when Stefan raged his frustrations with a world he could not countenance: his grim future, the pressures to conform that stifled his very being.

Five years had passed since that night that began with a banging on the front door. The uniformed men, the ensuing blur of terror. Stefan dead. Shot while attempting to escape over the Wall. Treason. Their father, already so fragile, crumbling in shock. Screams—Anika's own—pleading for it not to be true, begging the guards to release their father. The door slamming. Then silence, but for their whimpering, as she and Michael clutched one another, bodies quaking. Stefan had been erased from their lives without so much as a body to prove it; their father, too, gone.

Since then, Michael had propped her up. How he had managed to maintain his natural, trusting optimism, she could not fathom. She gazed at him now, suspecting it had been his indomitable, loving spirit holding her up all along—not the other way round. And now, more than ever, she needed him.

"Apparently," Michael said, softly, "he has given you more than just a job." His cheek muscles tensed. He did not mean to be snide; simply stated fact.

"Yes," Anika sighed, bone weary, desperate to escape into sleep.

Michael reached his arms around her shoulders. "We will get through this."

In a trance, Anika watched as her brother washed, dried, stacked the dishes on the shelf. Time would pass. Yes. They would get through it. But who would she be, after? Already, she was a different person. Michael, his hands kneading a towel, turned to face her, his eyes still wild with the weight of her confession. Her stomach knotted. Should she have lied, said she'd had feelings for the man, let Michael think that that monster brought her comfort, romance? No. Impossible. Michael was no fool, no longer a child. Even if the truth destroyed any shred of innocence Michael may have had left, she would not lie.

"Anika," he began, his forearm muscles engaging as the towel twisted between them. "This does not define you. He cannot break your spirit unless you let him. Don't let him. Do not give him that triumph. Promise me."

Anika nodded as a tear hit a faded sunflower beneath her, as though she was watering it. Or, that's what the little girl would have thought, the one who'd sat, entranced, watching her mama neatly knot-stitch the black seeds between the yellow petals.

Michael had a point. She had the choice not to let what he had done define her, break her. But—what of the other life she had to contend with, half-monster, half-her?

15

Since the partition of Germany in 1945, a Duty Train rolled through communist East Germany to the West every night: one to Frankfurt the other, Bremerhaven, returning to Berlin the following evening. American military, diplomats, and dependents rode for free. As did students who attended Berlin American High School when traveling for a school event. Each passenger had to obtain a military-issued Flag Order to ride, to be scrutinized by Soviet soldiers at several checkpoints along the way. Military Police rode to ensure no Soviet or East German ever boarded. No one was allowed on or off the train until it arrived at its destination.

The Duty Train was there on its designated track, a massive hunk of dormant, kinetic energy, when Dad dropped me at the *Bahnhof*. Coach Kilner, chatting with the train commander on the platform, waved me over and checked my Flag Orders against my military-issued ID and passport. They were looking for any tiny discrepancy the Soviets might use as an excuse to detain the train.

A cluster of maroon-and-white track suits matching mine gathered nearby. I sensed their excitement, but stood apart, my gym-bag swinging from hip to hip, my eyes on the entrance to the platform, willing the next person that emerged to be Will. Riding the

Duty Train for the first time was exciting, but I couldn't even think about the race itself. Will would calm me.

"We board in five!" Kilner announced. Panic rising, I spun around and almost shouted that we had to wait, but then, there was Rick. I flung my arms around him. "Rick! Thank goodness!"

"Hah, nice to see you, too!" He laughed.

"Where's Will?" I tried to sound merely curious.

"Not here yet?" he asked, glancing around. "Weird. He's rarely late. He'll show," he added, with an encouraging pat.

When Kilner ordered us to board, I grabbed Rick's arm in a panic as we lined up. The MP checked us off his list, gave us each a compartment number. I climbed aboard, trying to convince myself that the trip was about the race, not about being with Will. But that only increased my race jitters.

Rick went left into another train car with the guys; I to the right with the girls, down the narrow hallway lined with windows on one side and sliding doors to compartments on the other. Each compartment had a curtained window to the outside, flanked by two sets of bunks, already made up with tightly tucked crisp sheets and wool blankets. I was the first to arrive and chose a top bunk, tossing my bag up before climbing the ladder.

I lay on my stomach peering out, combing the platform. The door slid open and Marny and Tanya entered, whipping their bags onto the bunks opposite mine. My sagging mood wilted altogether. No Will *and* I was rooming with these two? I couldn't believe my luck.

Marny, walkman headphones covering her ears and bopping to a cool beat only she could hear, jutted her chin up at me. I nodded back, propping my legs up the wall in an attempt to look chill.

Odele heaved a bag onto the bunk beneath mine. I waved, relieved to see her. "Hey." The door slid open again and Cheryl and Briana entered, just to hang. Outside, the train puffed, anticipating our imminent departure. I didn't want to go. Not without Will.

"Yeah, girl! You know it!" Tanya hooted, punching Marny who flopped onto the bottom bunk in conspiratorial hysterics. They were laughing at me, I knew it—and then I saw why. Tanya, lying on her bunk across from me was mirroring my every move. When I rolled onto my side, so did she. I let a leg hang over. So did she. Marny was choking with laughter. She knew I knew she knew, which only made it worse.

"All Aboooard!" The bellow was followed by a slamming and locking of doors, the hefty train lurching with a groan and a screech of steel. My heart sank. Will had missed it. I ached to rewind to our cozy kitchen where I'd spent the morning baking Mom a birthday cake, where I could relax, just be me. I wished I hadn't joined this team. Wished I'd never moved to Berlin.

"We'll celebrate Sunday after you get back," Mom had assured me as I presented my frosted masterpiece decked with chocolate-covered almonds.

"Who says there'll be anything left by then?" Dad had teased, trailing a finger through left-over icing in the bowl.

I rolled toward the wall, annoyed with my social anxiety, allowing myself to lower my expectations; it'd only been three months and it took six minimum to suddenly realize you didn't have that new-kid angst anymore. I knew this. But knowing doesn't suddenly take away the unsettled gut feeling. I held my breath before letting it go slowly, closing my eyes. And there, in my mind, I saw Mark, Jack's best friend in The Hague who'd taught Jack and me to meditate to calm our nerves. I'd gone along with the hippy-dippy stuff because Mark was cute and paying attention to me. But I'd never really considered that it might work.

Pulling myself into into a cross-legged position, I sat up straight, eyes closed and inhaled deeply, held it for the count of five, then exhaled, slowly, controlled. In my mind, I repeated the mantra "I am calm." Then, I did it again, counting, focusing on the air leaving my nose, trying to believe the words in my head. It seemed to be working. I kept at it, so focused, I didn't realize a hush had descended over the compartment.

"Girl!" Tanya was shaking my knee. "What *are* you, some kinda Buddha?" Everyone burst out laughing.

The moment I opened my eyes, Tanya's pillow flew at me. "Dang, Stickbug! You as white as they come."

Briana, antisocial by choice, glanced up before returning to her magazine. I admired her cool indifference to what people thought of her and, with that thought, pathetically, I wondered what she thought of me. But her coolness endowed me with a burst of courage and I tossed the pillow right back at Tanya.

"What about Briana? She's is as skinny as I am!"

"Yeah? So what?" Tanya asked.

"Well, I don't hear you calling *her* Stickbug."

Marny shrugged. "She wouldn't like it."

"Hm." I leaned forward from the bunk. "Well, for the record, neither do I!"

Marny pretended to mull it over. "You don't? Well, why didn't you *say* so?" She rolled backwards gasping with laughter before sitting bolt upright. "Dayam, Tanya, now what're we gonna call her?"

"My *name* is Kate. You could start with that. Once we're tight, I might tolerate Katie."

Everyone laughed. (Well, not Briana. She kept reading; she was above all this silliness.) I smiled, too. It *was* silly.

"Guys!" Odele jumped up from her bunk to root around in her duffel bag like an addict seeking a fix. "I almost forgot!" She held up a package the size of a deck of cards wrapped with a bow, before flinging it towards Cheryl. "Happy Birthday, lady!"

"Hey, it's my mom's birthday, too!" It just flew out of my mouth. I braced for the taunts.

Instead, Cheryl jumped up, shrieking with glee. "A present?—I *love* presents!" She tore into it, then tugged at the plastic packaging around maroon and white striped terrycloth headbands. Pulling both over her head, she jumped from the bunk, and began to sing a cheer. "HEY, maroon and white, na, na, *naa*, na, na!" I joined in, along with everyone else, even Briana. "Berlin is dy-na-mite, na, na, *naa*, na, na…"

So when the door slid open, it took me a moment to notice.

"What the hell is goin' *on* in here?" It was Rick's grinning head poking into the room. He looked up at me, winked, and pushed the door all the way open. There, next to him, was Will. My heart and mind triple-flipped down to the floor to smack him on the lips with sheer joy, while the rest of me gripped the edge of the bunk in shock.

Wolfie, then Andy and Dennis, pushed in past Rick and Will, passing out bottles of cold Berliner Pilsners. With one foot on the middle rung of the ladder, Will whipped himself up to sit beside me landing a piercing smooch right on my ear.

"Hey!" I shook him with a mix of relief and frustration. "Damn it, Will! Where *were* you? I seriously thought you'd missed the train."

He shook his head, shouting over the mushrooming hullabaloo below us. "Forgot my running shoes. Anything else, OK—but not my sneakers. Cut it real close."

The volume was up on the boombox, the small floorspace pulsating like a crowded disco. Rick shouted up, "Did he tell you, Kate? How I had to pull him up while he ran alongside the train as we pulled out?" He pointed at Will, his arm flexed shoulder height, biceps on display. "Lucky I had my spinach today, man." At that, Marny pulled Rick away, hands on his hips, syncing them with hers. Next second, Cheryl yanked him back crying, "It's *my* birthday, lady!" and Rick began to bop around with her, oblivious to the pounding beat. Beyond them, sheltered in the shade of the upper bunk, Briana was lying alongside Wolfie, faces close—the opposite of chill now, I thought, knowing the feeling.

"You know it's only thanks to Rick that I was born at all, right?" Will joked, his lips close so I could hear. "I got there with thirty seconds to spare, but Kilner was pretty steamed. The MP had to calm him down." He threw his hands up. "It's OK. I'll make it up to him tomorrow."

What with all my social angst, I'd forgotten to worry about the race. At his mention of it, the nerves in my gut threatened to resurface. But then the drumbeat to *Brick House* set the place in motion and I dropped back into the moment. A good song—*and* Will next to me. There must have been twelve of us in that compartment, dancing, cuddling, hanging off the ladder. And after several, impromptu, "Happy Birthday" cheers to Cheryl, Marny suddenly tossed in, "And a Happy Birthday to Stickbug's mommy!"

I just laughed, wondering why I ever let anything bother me.

When the song ended, bodies crammed onto the bottom bunks. Marny, in her white-girl-voice, asked. "So, what did you get Mother for her birthday, Stick? Maybe, a Dior scarf?" The music stopped. Someone fiddled with the cassette.

"Um, funny story, actually." I smiled. The story could go either way in this crowd, I thought. But I was going to risk telling it. "You know those Sweet Earth perfumes at the PX? They come in a little jar—you know what I'm talking about. Well, so, that's what I got her, this cute little jar of jasmine scent. Or at least *thought* I did. The cashier wrapped it for me, so when Mom opened it and sniffed and looked at it, giving me this weird look, I wondered, what the heck? Did she not like the smell? And then, she, my Mom, started to *giggle*. Because," I paused, "apparently, those cute little Sweet Earth perfumes look a lot like—and what I actually bought," I looked right at Marny. "was a cute little jar," I took a deep breath, "of afro sheen." An eternity of silence fell. My cheeks began to burn. Just when everything had been going so well.

But then, Tanya and Marny began to howl. "*Afro sheen*?" They were choking, gasping for air, railing with my ignorance, and before long, they were wielding a comb, palming a few African beads, some tiny rubber bands. Time I got educated, they said. I was about to be schooled. Right now.

I learned how to fluff Tanya's hair into a perfect afro, and how to braid it starting from the top where the comb parted the sections, how to keep the braid tight to the scalp. I was good at it, getting fast, and learning a whole new vocabulary along with it: *kinky, nappy, cucabug....* I repeated that one. *"Cucabug."* It was fun to say. Tanya did my hair, too, which they claimed was harder to work with. They tied the ends of two little braids with beads. They said it'd bring me luck tomorrow. I smiled: Tanya and Marny, *wishing me luck*.

An MP slid the door open with a bang. Beer bottles vanished behind backs and pillows. "Approaching Potsdam! Alpha Bravo!" he bellowed, moving on down the car. "Window shades must be closed for the remainder of the night! No eye contact with any Soviets or East Germans!" Odele reached over to close the curtain against the newly fallen night. Bottles reemerged, final swallows drained. A moment later, Kilner ordered teammates back to their own compartments.

"Killner the killjoy," Rick sighed after everyone else had left. He was leaning against the open door, the train rumbling below. Next to me, Will lay his head on my shoulder, his arm around my waist. Sleep seemed to beckon with the steady rocking. I wanted to topple down and pull Will beside me.

"Nobody sleeps on the train, anyway," Marny yawned, "with all that stopping and starting all night long. Might as well let us unwind a little longer before the race. We'd probably run better that way."

"Yeah, those screeching brakes..." Odele caught Marny's yawn as she switched off the bright overhead light, collapsing back onto her bunk. The nightlight bathed the room in a dusty blue glow. On cue, the train squealed and slowed.

"Mmhmm," Tanya murmured, descending her ladder. "We'd relax, all right—like afro sheen on a cucabug!"

Everyone giggled, including me, happy to be here. My nose burrowed into Will's messy hair as the train jerked to a stop. Outside, whistles blew, orders flew in German, and, just below our window, voices murmured in Russian as a beam of light flitted against the shade.

"What're they looking for?" I wondered, leaning across Will to pull the curtain aside.

"Stowaways, mostly," Will said, gently pulling my hand away.

"Just wanted to peek."

"Don't give them the satisfaction that we're even curious," Rick advised from the doorway. "This is the long stop where we change locomotives to an East German one that'll take us through the East. Once we hit West Germany, we change engines again." He looked up at Will. "Do I have to drag you out of here?"

Halfway down the ladder, Will paused to turn to me. "Dream you can fly. OK?" He cuffed a bead, grinned, and leaned in to kiss me on my cheek, his eyes melting into mine for one magical second.

"Cucabug's got a boyfriend!" Tanya teased as soon as the door was shut.

We decided to go two-by-two to the bathroom. I wriggled out of my jeans and bra beneath my t-shirt and stuffed legs into sweatpants before plodding down the hall to brush my teeth with Odele. Back in my bunk, when I closed my eyes, my mind flew to Will. Compared with Amy, I was a novice with this boyfriend stuff.

"That doesn't count," she'd said after I'd told her my first—and only—kisses had been playing spin the bottle in Moscow at the Anglo-American School behind bushes in the playground.

"Why not? It *was* the first time I kissed a boy."

"Your first *real* kiss. You know, with someone you really *liked*."

Her first real kiss was with some guy she'd worked with one summer at a pancake house as a busboy—bus*girl*—and he was a waiter. She was thirteen and he was twenty-two. She'd flirted with him constantly, never expecting him to pay any attention to her. One day when she was out by the dumpster behind the restaurant smashing up boxes, he'd come out for a smoke and said, "'Hey, girl, you know I'm too old for you.'" His laughter had infuriated her.

"So I leaned in and pulled his face right up to mine and kissed him. I had no idea what I was doing." But Amy said it counted all right, "cause *he* sure knew what he was doing."

The story gave me the creeps, though I didn't say so. I couldn't judge. That American life—where once school got out you got summer jobs at burger joints or pancake houses, or mowed grass on fenceless lawns—was as alien to me as the word *diplomat* was to most American kids. The only summer jobs we could get were at the embassy—which could be fun, if a little weird, working where your dad worked.

Amy met Alex selling popcorn at a movie theater. They'd started sleeping together before she left. I'd tried not to act shocked or overly curious when she told me. When she asked about *my* boyfriend history, at first I thought about making something up, afraid she wouldn't want to be friends with a total novice. But then our friendship wouldn't be honest, and what was the point in that?

The whole pressure to lose your virginity perplexed me. What was the rush? Some people had sex just to get it over with. Or lied to save face. I wasn't hung up on waiting for marriage or anything, just wanted to wait for that worthy someone with whom the first time would actually be memorable. *Transcendent* rather than cringeworthy. I refused to be embarrassed about that. So, when Amy asked, I'd come clean.

"When it comes to sex, Amy, I am a *tabula rasa*."

"A *what*?"

"A clean slate. The very picture of virtuosity." She stared back, still not getting it. "Geez, Amy, I'm trying to say that I've had *no sexual experience*. What. So. Ever."

"Oh," Amy exclaimed, finally getting it. "Well. *That's* about to change."

Maybe I hadn't had a lot of *that* kind of experience, I thought, as the train rolled through enemy territory, but I knew the *world* better than Amy. Between the two of us, we had plenty covered.

16

The morning had started cold and drizzly and I'd been in no mood to run. Will had sensed it, held my shoulders, crouching low so we were eye to eye. "OK, Katie. Focus in. Just you and the path," his voice soothing. "Breathe with the rhythm of your steps. You got this."

A steady rain had begun to fall as the gun went off, as if it had shot a hole in a cloud. Over the first mile, I settled into my rhythm, two steps for each breath: in-in, out-out, my two beads clicking in time, mud squelching below. I fell in behind Marny, matching her pace. In the damp, pine saturated woods, the path narrowed, forcing us to contend for space. A Hahn Hawk shoved me and I fell back. I focused in, regaining my tempo.

Odele had bounded ahead at the start, racing only against her own best time. A mix of Bad Kreuznach Bear Kats' blue and gold, Bitburg Barons' blue and white, and Hahn Hawks' green and gold, trailed her lead like a colorful Chinese dragon. Bobbing just ahead, I glimpsed Marny and Tanya's maroon-and-white. The path widened as the course climbed a steep hill. I shortened my steps but kept the same tempo and began to pass the slowing pack. My lungs heaved into the climb but I soon realized I could take Tanya, maybe even

Marny. At the top, the course swept down to the flat of the football field—and the finish. Tanya glanced at me with surprise as I passed. She picked up her pace but not enough. Entering the football field exploding with cheers, my energy surged. Marny and I were neck and neck. I gained on her. She pumped hard and caught up. My lungs screamed. "Yes, Kate! You're flying!" It was Will's voice, rising above the others. My legs numb, I managed a final, painful push just as Marny lurched forward, too, finishing a fraction of a second before me.

Arms enveloped, lifted me, spinning me in the air. "You were *sensational*, Kate! I knew you had it in you!" Will was laughing, hugging me. "You're such a compact, deceptive little powerhouse! Our new secret weapon!" When he set me down, the world did not stop whirling. I blinked for something—anything—to come into focus. The grass rolled below me like an emerald sea as I felt lips pressing against mine as I teetered, swayed. And then, green turned to black.

"*Katie?*" Will's voice came from far away. Cold, moist grass tickled my face. Hands rocked my shoulders, fingers dug beneath me, wrapped around, lifted me: Will, warm and steady. He clutched me to his chest like a pile of laundry. I tried to open my eyes, but even the gray sky blinded, and I turned, burying my face in his heavenly, sweaty, chest. He lay me on the ground again, the grass wet, the cheering more distant now. I squinted, trying to focus.

I'd ruined it. My first real kiss.

"Kate? Kate?" Will was stroking my cheeks. "You all right? I'm going to get Coach Kilner." He knelt beside me. "Actually, maybe you'd better sit up. Put your head between your knees." He guided me into position. I looked down at the green cave between my legs. Will had kissed me.

"I'll get you some juice. A banana? Just water?" He prodded gently, concerned. "Kate?"

I looked up, smiling. "It's your fault, Will." I paused. "You took my breath away."

"*My* fault, huh? Nothing to do with that breakneck pace you broke into at the end there?" He grinned down, his expression relaxing, then hugged me to him. "You scared me," he whispered.

"What if we, um, try that again?" I looked away, wondering where my boldness had come from. Will laughed and lifted my chin. Gazing at me with that startling intensity, his eyes sparkling with *this* moment. He neared until our eyelashes touched, tickling, and then, for the second time that day, the earth fell away. But this time, I floated above it.

"Yo! Knock! Knock! Cucabug?" Mortified, I untangled myself from Will and blinked up into Marny's contour against the gray sky. "Girl, I gotta say! Thought I was gonna have to *trip* you *up* at the end there—know what I'm sayin'?!" She stuck her leg out to make sure I got the picture. "For real, girl. For a rookie? Amazing run." She punched me in the arm as I scrambled to my feet, peeling my shorts away from where they were stuck to my legs. "Seriously," Marny continued. "You *almost* made me work for it."

I punched her back. "Yeah? Hey, I *let* you win this time. Don't get too cocky!"

"Uh huh. Sure, li'l cucabug. I'm scared. *Real* scared." She wrapped her arms around herself and pretended to quake as she walked off, laughing.

I was shivering too, but for real. Will whipped off his jacket, wrapping it around me as we wandered back toward the finish line just in time to see Cheryl run across. I cheered, shouting at the top of my lungs, heart and soul, dancing and yelling "*Ber-lin! Ber-lin!*", fists punching the air. Will wrapped his arms around my shoulders behind me filling me with a contentment that felt like a strange, new source of power.

Later, hair still damp from showering, Will and I boarded a downtown bus in our Berlin team tracksuits (as per school policy). Rick had gone on ahead with some Bad K guys after Coach Kilner threatened us with slow, torturous death if we weren't back at the school gym by 1630 sharp to board the bus for the hour-long ride to the Frankfurt *Bahnhof*.

"Will, we *have* to see the famous bridge." Dad had read to me from *Foder's Guide* in preparation for the trip, all about Bad Kreuznach, with its "old-world quaintness" and "vestiges of the past." *The medieval, spa town, snuggled against the banks of the Nahe River in Germany's Rheinland-Pfalz area,* the book informed, *was one of the lucky towns that had come through WWII unscathed.* The photos were beautiful. I peered out the window of the bus as we neared a meandering river.

"Lunch first? I'm starving." Will bent down to kiss me right in front of an elderly woman gripping netted grocery bags, staring with distinct disapproval. I was one of *those* kids now, I thought, relieved when our stop came and we hopped off. Americans creating any kind of spectacle made me cringe; I could hear Dad's voice: *Like it or not, your behavior represents our entire nation.*

Off the bus, we followed the directions the Bad K runners had given to find "the *Kneipe* with the best wurst and beer in all of Deutschland." Clouds passed quickly in front of the sun, taunting us with intermittent warmth as we wandered down picturesque streets and alleyways so narrow the jutting upper floors nearly touched. We strolled past windows crowded with exquisite displays of chocolates, antiques, and outrageous hats, and then there was the *Kneipe,* too soon.

The air inside was dense with a blend of cigarettes and sizzling bratwurst. "Over there," Will said, pointing to a table in the back packed with runners—including Rick—waving us over. Will clutched my hand as we wove between tables. I held tight, not at all ready to share him with anyone else.

"Hey, guys! Here." Rick coaxed me into his chair while he foraged for two more. A frizzy-haired guy in Bad K colors next to me slouched over a hefty stein of beer. Long, skinny legs were sticking up like a giant cricket, poking into my space.

He held out his hand. "Jim."

"Hi, I'm Kate."

I chose the moment he jammed his wurst into his mouth to ask him how his race had gone. He chomped, nodding until he swallowed. "Pretty good, broke my record—*the* record," he said with a smile and humble shrug, wiping mustard from his cheek. This was The Jim. Jim was to the boys what Odele was to the girls. The reigning champ.

"Course I knew the course. Hometown advantage." He shrugged again, washing the conversation down with beer, also in record time. I worked my knee out from beneath his.

Will was leaning away from me, talking to a guy on the far side of Rick. I nudged him, combing the place for a *Kellnerin*. "Hungry?"

Will leapt up and disappeared into the smoke, returning a moment later. "Ordered us each a *Bratwurst* and a beer. Hope that's OK?" Beneath the table, he reached for my hand and lay it atop his thigh, keeping his hand on mine.

"Quite a *trip* coming on the Duty Train, huh?" Jim was saying between giant bites of bratwurst. "I mean, *besides* literally," he chuckled. "Been on it twice. Pretty cool. Definitely trippy. But hard to sleep. Exhausting before a meet. Went to the East once, got a Soviet belt buckle. Seriously trippy. Living there, you must go over a lot?"

The waitress placed a frothy beer in front of me followed by a plate heaped with sauerkraut and a glistening wurst snaked with yellow mustard. My knife sliced into the skin, releasing a burst of steam. "Actually," I admitted, wondering where Amy was right now, "I just moved there this year and have not gone once. But I have a friend who lives in the East."

"She *lives* over there? American?" Jim sounded dubious.

I explained how an American Embassy had to be in the capital, and the East Germans claimed Berlin *was* their capital. "At the same time, it's still the occupied Soviet Sector, but, *diplomatically*, we recognize it as the capital city of the German Democratic Republic—

a kind of Cold War compromise to keep peace. So, yeah, my friend, whose father is posted to East Germany, has to live over there."

Jim's brow furrowed. I'd lost him.

"Definitely a trippy place," he said, nodding, facing his near-empty beer stein.

I gave up on Jim, annoyed. He should *want* to understand this stuff. Rick and his Bad K buddy were in a deep discussion about Pelé retiring. Next to me, Will was quiet, sipping his beer. I couldn't tell if he was listening.

I wanted to get out of there. "Hey," I whispered to him. "Wanna go soon?"

Will bounced up, digging in his pocket. "Hey, Rick, take care of Katie and me?" He passed a crumpled wad of Deutsch Marks to Rick and swigged a final gulp of beer, shaking his head at my handful of cash. "No, it's good, let's go."

I waved at Jim as Will guided me out. Jim raised his eyebrows before hunching back over his glass.

"Phew!" Will said when we were back in fresh air and sunshine. "That was semi-torturous—you sitting there, falling in love with Jim Cunningham."

"Oh, yeah?"

"Not to mention, he beat me by three seconds today. But then, if he won you, too? *That* would hurt." All of a sudden, there was this potential to hurt—or be hurt. It was scary, but I didn't want it to stop.

We wandered back through the old town till we found the medieval bridge arching across the river. Crooked, medieval houses rose from the center, teetering over the water, supported only by toothpick-thin wooden supports. It looked like a fairytale book illustration.

"Oh, it's gorgeous!" I pulled Will to the middle where we stared down over the railing as a wooden boat floated beneath, a couple of ducks bobbing in its gentle wake. "I think we've been zapped back in time. Look. Nothing tells you it's 1977. "

Will nodded. "1977? What's trig? What's chemistry? What's pressure? I'm a local shepherd, just me and my sheep."

"Yeah. Meanwhile, I can imagine my chores as a woman while you lie in the shade nibbling wild grass." I shoved him, because he was born a man, but relished when he pulled me close for the same reason. A cloud drifted, exposing the sun. I blinked down into the river watching an eddy choreograph a twig's pirouette, drawing Will's arms around me.

"Feels good to be out of Berlin," he murmured.

"It's always there, in the back of your mind, isn't it? That walled-in feeling." A cloud blocked the sun, a soft breeze made the surface of the water ripple. "I *have* to get over there," I continued. "To the East. I hate not being able to picture it, hate that my view of Berlin ends at the Wall."

"Our city *does* end at the Wall, Kate. What do you expect to see over there? Not sure I want to see it—I'd rather stay ignorant of their reality." He shook his head. "A *Wall*—blocking people from most of the world. I don't know how they stand it." He spun me around to face him. "I bet if *you* were stuck over there? *You'd* find a way to scale that Wall and get the hell out." He smiled and kissed the top of my head.

It was an attempt to lighten things up, compliment my spunk, but I wasn't ready to go there. It didn't just depend on personality, who managed to escape. I started to argue, but Will bent down and kissed me until I reached for his shoulders and jumped, wrapping my legs around his waist so we were face to face where I could stroke his black eye, now a rainbow of colors, and marvel how far we'd come from that rainy night we went to *Das Klo*.

"Whoa, we're late!" Will dropped me to the ground. Grabbing my hand, we started to run. But my legs were jelly from the race, and I lagged. Will motioned for me to climb onto his back. He piggy-backed me all the way to the bus stop where he set me down, laughing. There was no bus in sight. Will checked his watch again. "We'll make it," he said, peering down the street again.

"Until I moved to Berlin, I can't say I ever thought about my freedom," I said, Will's quip about me escaping from the East still rattling. I couldn't let it go. "Not *really*. I mean, did you?"

"Maybe that's the thing about freedom. If you have it, you don't think about it. Like water to a fish."

"Well, I think about it a lot now. Maybe that's why I want to understand what it's really like over there. Imagine wondering if you should risk your *life* to live somewhere else. How would you know how to decide that?"

Will gazed down the road as a bus approached. He looked down at me, shaking his head. "I can't imagine. Nor do I want to. There's nothing *we* can do about it, Kate."

The bus edged the curb, the doors pumped open. We climbed on, stamped our tickets, and walked toward the middle where I leaned against a window. Will grasped the strap overhead, the sun lower now, covering his face in a rosy glow. I absorbed the moment, then moved back to making my fuzzy point. "It just feels like a duty, somehow, to learn about life there. So we appreciate what we have here more."

Will placed a hand on my shoulder. "OK, Kate. You go and see. I'm not going to stop you."

17

Back on the Duty Train twenty hours later felt like weeks had passed. This time I grabbed the bottom bunk and plunked down while the others settled in around me. My body was exhausted, but my brain buzzed, teeming with thoughts of Will.

Odele tossed her stuff on the bunk above. I smiled, proud to be friends with a star. She'd come in first overall, naturally. And somehow, I'd run my best time ever. The day played in a loop, over and over in my head

It was *deja vu*: most of the team filed into our compartment, the music cranking. But this time, we were relaxed, buoyant, content with our third place overall win. Coach Kilner knocked and waved through the window.

"Come on in, Coach! Join the party!" Someone slid the door open.

"At Marienborn, you head back to your compartments. Deal?" He shut the door, making a peace sign through the window.

Briana yanked Rick up to dance, shocking everyone including Wolfie who was scrutinizing her every move. Rick must've sensed his eyes on him, because he sank back down on my bunk, feigning exhaustion. Will and I had squeezed into a corner, his arm around the small of my back. When his hand ventured beneath my sweatshirt onto bare skin, I shivered, snuggling into him.

"It must be hard for Rick. Everyone being in love with him," I said into Will's ear, trying not to obsess over his hand's every blissful movement. "And he acts like he loves everyone right back. But—who does he *really* like?" Will's reply was drowned out by the party. Instead of repeating himself, he thumbed toward the door.

Outside, the corridor was only marginally more peaceful. I commiserated with anyone else riding the train. Will and I leaned into a window, the shades already drawn, daylight all but gone.

"I was saying," Will explained, "about Rick. Love would be too much of a distraction. He's completely focused on West Point."

"Yeah? You know him better than anyone."

"Maybe. He's kind of an enigma." I knew he was only half joking. "I worry about him."

"That's how I feel about Amy. It bothers me."

"Why?"

"I *want* to be a good friend, but, it's like she won't let me in. So it's hard to know *how*."

"You're a good friend for not forcing her."

"She's hiding something. Maybe I'm not enough of a friend."

"No, you *care*. Enough to give her time."

The train slowed and an MP marched down the corridor barking, "Helm*stedt*! Checkpoint *Alpha*!" We were approaching the border where they switched locomotives for the ride back through the East.

Kilner strolled down the corridor behind the MP and winked at Will and me. "Think they're ready for their bedtime story?" He slid the door open to break up the party to a chorus of groans.

Will bent to whisper into my ear. "Third door down. I'm on the bottom bunk. Kilner crashes hard and the MPs play poker in their car. If you want." He kissed my cheek, then added, "*Only* if you want. No pressure."

My mind raced. If I said I'd come, what was I agreeing to? Did Will expect more than I wanted to give? And if I said no, was that really what I wanted?—or what I thought I should want? What if I got caught?

Will seemed to sense my predicament. He quickly shook his head. "Hey. Sorry, Kate. I don't mean to—you don't—"

All it took was his acknowledgment to ease my mind. "OK," I said.

"Sweet dreams, then. See you in the morning: 'Orange juice, coffee, maaaarble cake!?'"

I laughed at his impersonation of the train vendor, but grabbed him back. "*Will*," I whispered, tugging him down to where I could reach his ear, "I meant: I'll come."

Without waiting for his response, I turned and rushed into the now quiet compartment. Tanya was stashing empty beer bottles into her bag to dispose of later, soft music tinkling from her boombox. I grabbed my duffel from the baggage space, and sat with it on the edge of the bunk. What had I just committed myself to?

The train groaned and began to gather momentum, rolling into Soviet territory. Marny and Tanya returned from the WC, switched off the music and settled into their bunks. Odele and I went next. Wriggling down beneath the crisp sheets and tight wool blankets, I wished I could tell Will I'd changed my mind, though I knew I didn't have to—he'd understand if I just didn't show. That thought then made me want to be with him all over again.

I'd play it by ear. I'd wait until we started up again after the next time the train stopped, after everyone was lulled back to sleep. Then, *if* I was still awake, I'd head for the bathroom. From there, *if* it felt safe and I had the nerve to cross through to Will's train car, I'd go. If not, I'd just come back. That settled, I fell asleep.

Screeching brakes woke me. The train lurched to a stop. In the sudden stillness, flashlight beams flitted through the curtain. I blinked into the blue glow, listening to the eerie mumble of Russian voices, picturing soldiers sliding mirrors beneath the train, stowaways clinging to its underbelly in desperation. What if they found someone? I swallowed hard. A mere window divided our high school drama from Cold War reality.

I was wide-awake. My heart began to pound. Across the way, Tanya was snoring, her arm drooping over the side of the bunk, swaying with the roll of the train. As soon as it regained a rhythmic tempo, I stood, stocking-footed, and reached for the door handle. Opening it would be noisy. I counted to three.

"Goin' somewhere, Cucabug?" I glanced back. Odele was on her elbow on the top bunk, a circle of light glowing beneath her blanket. She grinned, pushing it aside to reveal a mini-flashlight and a book. "I can never sleep after a race." She held the flashlight to her chin and made the Scream face, then crossed her eyes and ducked back down beneath her blanket.

"Just gotta pee," I whispered, sliding the door shut behind me.

Squinting in the bright light of the empty corridor, I padded toward the back of the train and ducked inside the restroom, straddling a suspicious puddle on the floor. The tracks whizzed past in a dizzying blur through the toilet hole. Lingering there was pointless—and unappealing. I peeked out. Still empty. I darted. At the door between the cars, I paused to peer through, saw no one, and pushed it open, stepping into a rush of noise and cold air. What, I wondered, did the East Germans think about this untouchable iron snake of freedom that sped through every day?

The window into the second compartment was open, its curtain dancing with the rumbling movement. It was where Coach Kilner and the teacher chaperone, Mr. Horton, were sleeping. I felt stupid, ashamed—no longer daring. This wasn't worth getting kicked off the team. Yet I'd gotten this far—and Will would make it all right. I ducked and dashed.

My eyes struggled to adjust to the darkness as I slid the door shut behind me, inhaling the boys' musk. The lumps in the beds all looked alike. Where'd Will say he was? I stifled a giggle. Something seized my knee. I jumped, slapping my hand to my mouth.

"Hey!" Will's whisper came from the low bunk on my right. There was a stirring—the other guys, pretending they didn't know I was there, or tuning in because I was. I scrambled over Will to lie next to the wall. When Will rolled over, my eyes struggled to make sense of his shadowy expression.

"You mad woman! What time is it?" His voice was soft and tender. He seemed surprised, which made me a little embarrassed. Maybe he'd rather sleep?

"Odele thinks I just went to pee, so I gotta go right back."

"OK. Well, I'm happy you came." Will propped his head on his elbow and I traced the veins that bulged from his forearm. He slid his other hand behind my head and I waited to be drawn in close for a kiss. Instead, he stared through the dimness, his hair in peaks where it had been smashed against the pillow, his face ghoulish in the blue-light. His hand nestled behind my back to pull me toward him. Then, it slipped beneath my sweatshirt.

I swallowed hard. In the end, I'd taken my bra off. Who goes to bed in a bra? Then I'd put it back on. It was too suggestive to come here with it off. Then, at the last second, I'd taken it off again, telling myself I was overthinking things. Now I regretted not thinking it through. What was he thinking? I buried my face in his chest, mortified, begging my heart to slow down.

He kissed the nape of my neck then stopped and paused, waiting for a sign. I breathed into my longing, reaching my hands behind his neck, pushing a leg between his, my heart pounding strong enough to derail the train. We kissed, exploring more and more of what we had already begun to learn about each other. When he pulled back to control his breathing, his urges, I felt a thrill, a new kind of power, and pulled him back. His fingertips drew ticklish circles on my belly at the pace of a drugged snail, my torso infinitely long. A kaleidoscope swirled in my head, blurring the reason vying for attention. Be smart. Stop before too late.

What was too late? That was the point. Like freedom—you didn't know until you lost it. I giggled. I was confused, clueless. "Will," I forced a whisper and moved his hand to my face, kissing it. "Shouldn't we—I—I think we need to—slow down?"

"OK." He hugged me, untangling his legs from from mine and propped himself on his elbow. A surge of emotion washed over me—my fears of having to enforce limits respected—just like that. He spoke softly, hesitantly, breathing through the blue glow. "You're right—you're right." He was so—eyes squeezed shut, I lifted my sweatshirt above my belly and pressed his face into it. A soft moan escaped as his lips and tongue cultivated my skin, ever so gently. The kaleidoscope returned, the colors pulsating, the train rhythmic, my heart, my body in sync. When I guided Will's face up to my lips aching for a kiss, the door slid open. A wedge of light spread through the compartment, casting the shadow of Coach Kilner.

Will flung his body over mine, like a soldier on a hand grenade, smashing his pillow over my face. Pinned in the stuffy blackness, I imagined the whole scene and—fueled by mortification—was overcome with giggles. Will squeezed my thigh to shush me.

"Everything OK, Coach?" Rick's voice came from across the way, sleepy and muffled. Will seized the moment to shift his body and tug the blanket across me.

"Yep, yep, just doin' a head-count." Kilner murmured. I felt a cold wave of panic. Had the coach already noticed my empty bed? "All good here, boys. Sorry to wake you." The door slid shut with a thud.

"Holy crap, that was close!" Rick whispered, laughing. "You two lucked out! Yeah, you're welcome."

"Thanks, man. Nice save." Will yanked the pillow from my face. "Still alive down there? You almost blew it with your giggling!" He smashed it back down.

I wriggled upright, tugging down my sweatshirt. "Man, how am I going to get back?" I fluffed up my mussed hair. "Think he's already discovered me missing? I'm in deep kimchi."

"That was strange. He's never done that before," Will said, puzzled. He sat up, banging his head on the top bunk.

"What do I *do*?" I felt desperate, alone in my predicament.

Will pondered a second, rubbing his head. "I'll cover for you." He pulled me up, leaving no time to second-guess him. He peered behind the door shade. "All clear! Now. Let's go."

"Night Rick!" It occurred to me with chagrin, that I didn't even know who else was in there, who else knew about my little exploit.

From his top bunk, Rick patted my head as I slipped out behind Will. We ducked and darted to the door into the next car. Peering through, there was Kilner, his back to us, just exiting one compartment and heading on—toward mine—where he'd find out I wasn't in there. And, if we passed through the cars now, he'd hear—and look—and I'd be caught. I was screwed.

"Stay behind me, Kate." Will spurred me into action. "We gotta move fast. When we pass the toilet, you duck inside. By the time Kilner turns around, you have to be in there. OK? Count to ten, then come out. I'll deal with him while you head to your room—sleepy, like you just got up to pee!" Will's voice was an urgent whisper. I knew how funny this would be in retrospect—but not if I got caught.

"What will you say?!" I couldn't think of anything plausible.

"I'll think of something. Let's go—before he turns around!"

We pushed through the car doors, Will shielding me, and then I peeled off into the WC, straddling that same puddle. I counted to eleven because it was luckier than ten and then slowly opened the door to peek. Will was in what looked to be deep conversation with Kilner whose back was to me. Now or never. I feigned a drowsy stumble back to my compartment, giving them a sleepy wave as I innocently slid the door open. Kilner glanced up and gave me an unsuspecting nod, while Will continued murmuring, intent on whatever he was saying. I released a deep breath into the dark, climbing under my covers with relief and a smile.

"How's Will?" Odele's long braid dangled down as she peeked from above.

"Holy smokes, Odele! You scared me. Can't you asleep?"

"Coach came in—twice—all worried cause you weren't here! I told him you'd gone to pee. You're back just in time, cause, *man,* I don't know what his beef is. He was all flustered when he came in, like he'd seen a ghost."

"Was he mad?"

"No, more, like, upset."

"Thanks, Odele. I owe you one." I reached up and rang her braid.

She pulled her head back but then returned. "Hope it was worth it." She made a kissing noise then pressed, "*Was* it?"

"*So* worth it," I sighed, snuggling down, my face flushing in the dark. She could take that any way she liked.

In the middle of the night, I woke to the clipped footsteps of an MP in the corridor, the brakes screeching. We slowed to a stop again somewhere in the Soviet zone. Scooting down to the end of the bunk near the window, I mashed my cheek against the wall to peer through a crack between the curtain and the glass. Below our window, two Soviet soldiers wearing long uniform coats and fur hats stood smoking, conversing in hushed Russian, rifles slung across their shoulders. They looked not much older than we. When one turned to look up at the window, I jerked my face away and steadied the swaying curtain.

After school the next day, I regaled Amy with the great train adventure, until she was writhing on the floor of my room in hysterics. "It's like a *Monty Python* scene! What *did* Will tell Kilner?"

"He told him he'd had a nightmare. Sweet, huh?" Will had pretended to run to the coach like a scared child—for me. "He told Kilner it had been about Russians breaking through the doors, boarding the train and kidnapping all of us. Brilliant, right? But get this! Kilner said he'd had a nightmare, too, about Russians getting on the train! That's why he got up to check on everyone—because his dream had been so disturbing."

Amy shook her head in disbelief. "Glad you had fun. Meanwhile, I was utterly bored." She rolled her eyes eastward. "Over there. I even finished my book report."

"We'll make up for it next weekend."

"Yeah—how 'bout *Quasimodo*?" It was our favorite place to go dancing.

"I have a better idea. Amy Carson, no ifs ands or buts, you and I are finally going to spend the whole weekend together—in the *East*."

18

Anika sat with her hands in her lap facing a bowl of steaming, thick, brown stew. Such a meal was not to be taken for granted, but the smell alone made her gag.

"Eat," he commanded, reaching over to tap her bowl with his spoon from across the small table. He shoveled a heaping bite into his own mouth and chewed. A glistening line of grease oozed between thin lips, the muscles in his cheeks pulsing. He grabbed his glass of water and swallowed in noisy gulps before banging it down leaving a lip-smudge around the rim, his eyes on her.

She breathed through a wave of nausea, cold sweat spreading from between her eyes to the back of her jaw. She filled her spoon, but when his little finger delved to explore a back molar, emerging with a smack, she dropped it, letting it sink into the gravy.

He leaned in. "You have nothing to worry about—as long as you do what I say." Those words—again. "Need I repeat that I have great influence in 'certain areas,' shall we say? Ah, for example, the department of prisons! If you truly love your father and want to see him again—how lucky you are to have me on your side." He tittered like a madman. "Of course," he continued, "if you are stupid enough to think you can go to the authorities, they will not only assume you are a liar, but—let's just say—your family's abominable reputation will suffer even more. I have many ideas," he clucked, bringing the back of his hand across his lips. His voice droned on and on. Anika imagined the table knife in front of her possessed, flying up of its own accord, piercing his skin, slicing cleanly through that throbbing artery in his neck, blood spurting, that voice ceasing forever, mid-word.

The first time she'd seen Herr Klein was at her mother's funeral, when only Anika, Michael, her father, and Stefan remained standing, huddled around the muddy pile that marked the fresh grave, a steady rain having discouraged mourners from lingering. Finally turning away, their father had gently urged his drenched children, "Come now." Anika, her arms folded around her little brother's shoulders, had felt paralyzed, lacking the courage to begin the rest of her life without their mother. But when the raindrops had tripled in size and Michael tugged at her, she'd allowed him to lead her away.

Her face low against the downpour, Anika had not noticed them at first, not until, at their car, she'd glanced up. There, through the curtain of rain, standing beneath a large, black umbrella, she'd made out the figures of a man and a woman. She didn't recognize them, but then others at the funeral were also unknown to her, acquaintances of her parents. Pressing Michael into the car ahead of her, curious, she'd turned back for a second look. The man had stared with a piercing, knowing smile; the woman beside him, had remained expressionless. Anika had hurried into the car and slammed the door.

She spooned her stew, the memory insisting: his penetrating gaze, the woman's skin phantasmal against her black clothing. Her eyes had seemed not to register—as though she were blind. What did the woman really know about this man, her husband? Was it possible she knew nothing of this? Or did she know exactly who he was?

The tiny Trabant had chugged into life, rain pelting the thin roof. The extra space inside had felt wrong: until losing Mama, a family drive always included a cozy squeeze.

"Who is that strange couple?" Stefan had asked. Struggling to extract the small wheels from the muddy lane that meandered through the cemetery, their father had not responded at once.

"Ah, strange, indeed," he'd said at last. "The woman is Trudi, your mother's cousin from Dresden—your great-uncle Theo's daughter." Anika remembered feeling a surge of anger: suddenly strange relatives from her mother's family inhabited her world, yet her mother did not? "As a young teenager, Trudi struggled, mentally. She disappeared. No one spoke of her. We never learned details—until, over a decade later—we received an invitation. To a wedding. Her wedding."

Their father's voice had been edged with his own surprise at seeing the couple, and Anika had wondered at his sudden loquaciousness; he'd been so withdrawn since their mother had passed. "The wedding came as a shock. Klein is his name, her husband: Karl Klein. Theo told your mother that he was important—with the government." Father's expression in the rear-view mirror revealed consternation. "He works for the Stasi. And so, we—your mother and I—were wary of any association with them. We found it odd that they invited us to their wedding. But *not* attending might have drawn more attention. After the civil ceremony, there was a painful, stilted reception—everyone toasting the wealth and health of the State and so on, on and on. Ridiculous. We kept to ourselves. How desperate your mother and I were to get out of there."

Father had grown silent, the Trabi sputtering, whirring through puddles, wipers straining to keep up with the torrent. Yet the children had known he wasn't finished and indeed, when he resumed, his voice sounded different, almost snide—uncharacteristic of him. Anika had felt a prickle of fear that their kind—saintly, even—father might turn bitter without their mother. "After the newlyweds left in their shiny, black Lada"—the car she'd seen at the funeral, Anika had realized—"a small man who had been standing in a corner during the toasts, marched up to us and handed us a key."

The wipers had flicked back and forth like a metronome, pacing time, while they'd waited for him to continue. Anika had watched through the rearview mirror, his eyes staring front, his mind on that strange wedding day on this, the day he buried his wife. When his words came, they were laced with cynicism. "Ever wonder how we—of all families—were allowed a Trabant? Well. That is how." He'd let that sink in. "We had never even considered applying. Certainly, we were grateful. People wait years for a Trabant." Only now was it clear to Anika, the burden he must have known then that he was imparting on his children.

Stefan had muttered a low, drawn out, "Ahh," as if everything had become clear. Anika was grateful when little Michael had asked, "But *why*, Papa?"

"You see, children, the gift came with two messages, clear and simple: 'We have all the power,' and, 'We are watching you.' After we were given the car, my job was taken away. Coincidence? No. Work would not be provided unless I joined the Party. I refused, began to sell my pottery—ironically, creating my own private business. It has kept us alive, if barely, but not in favor. They tolerate it, but, any day, that privilege, too, can be yanked away. With one false move. In the meantime, we have a car." His words had hung over them like the drone of a wasps' nest, but they had never spoken of it again.

As children, Anika and her brothers had grown accustomed to being ostracized when, one by one, they'd refused to become members of the communist youth organization, the Freie Deutsche Jugend, and made no secret of their Christian faith. As a result, they were denied the opportunity to take the Abitur, the big exam before university, so higher education was never an option. On her own, Anika had taught herself to type, but had no proper certification. Even now, at twenty-one—Michael, seventeen—they, like their father, had been denied State-sanctioned authorization to work. And as if life hadn't been precarious enough, they now had to own the disgrace of their brother who had attempted escape, his death brought on "by his selfishness," their father imprisoned for raising a child disobedient to the State.

The next time she'd seen Herr Klein was eight days after Stefan died. She and Michael had been alone, terrified, torn with grief, and struggling to come to terms with their situation, unsure where to turn for help—when there came a banging on their front door.

And then Klein and their mother's cousin had barged in without a word, pushing past Anika into the kitchen, as though they owned the place. Trudi's skeletal, white hand had trembled as she pulled out a chair—like a starving vampire, Anika remembers thinking with a shiver. Herr Klein, by contrast, had exuded vitality—thriving, it seemed, *on her*. He'd taken charge as if summoned to answer their cries for help, whipping off hat and gloves with a flourish to present a great basket teeming with scarcities—chocolate, oranges, sugar, sticks of cinnamon, real coffee—things impossible to find, even at an Intershop, the State-run store where purchasing required western currency.

Accepting the gift had sickened Anika, but she'd remembered Father's warning: as with the Trabant, turning it down was not an option. They'd stayed at the kitchen table, Trudi silent, barely breathing, Anika repressing an impulse to touch her, to determine whether her skin held the warmth of life. Through his incessant babbling, boasting about himself, Herr Klein's eyes had darted up and down Anika with the same penetrating gaze that had unsettled her at the cemetery. She'd found herself with no recourse but to look away in perplexed shame until he growled, poking a finger into her shoulder.

"It is time you began working, now that your father is tucked away for his own good. Tomorrow morning. Report to the polyclinic in Lichtenberg. Receptionist. The position requires very little skill." He'd flicked at her head as though to demonstrate its hollowness. "Nine o'clock. Report to Dr. Schmidt. Do not be late." And, just like that, their problems had been solved. And yet.

Of course, Anika would come to recognize the timing of the couple's visit as completely intentional, but back then, she was still naive. The job had served her well for a year, kept them from starving. Klein had provided work, too, for Michael, at the kiosk. There had even been moments when Anika had wondered if perhaps they'd misjudged the hearts of their odd relatives.

She pressed her spoon through the sludge in front of her, bracing as the cloud descended, enveloping her with flashes, lightning stabs of her nightmare. Then it returned, in full, as if happening *now*. She was powerless to stop it.

> *Sunday evening: She and Michael are reading in the living room, one at each end of the couch, legs overlapped in the middle. Anika does not hear the knock, but Michael rises, walks to door. There, on the ground outside, a basket, full of goodies. They peer into the dark, see no one, but hear the peal of tires scraping away from the curb. The basket is identical to the one from Klein from the year before, packed with treats so rare, they could never have found them. Together, they carry it into the kitchen, pleased, disconcerted. Why? Why now?*
>
> *The following Wednesday: She is alone at the clinic. Everyone else has left. It is her job to lock up. She likes this time, appreciates the routine, the solitude, before walking to the streetcar in the warm, clear, evening air, home to the dinner Michael has prepared. She hums, tidies her desk, files patients' records. Ready. She grabs her keys, her coat. The door to the clinic opens. A man walks in.*
>
> *Fear immobilizes her like a block of ice. Now, she comprehends with a stab of clarity, I am to pay.* "Herr Klein."

"Anika." He seems to read her mind, takes her keys from her hand, locks the door behind him. He draws near until Anika is overwhelmed by his cologne, her eyes on his chest, rising, falling, too close. When he speaks, his voice is dead, inhuman. Anika's body refuses to respond to her command to run. For a fleeting, hopeful moment, she tries to wake herself. But, this is no nightmare; this day was coming. Had she not known, been living in dread of it? The wait was over; there was an ironic trace of relief in that.

"I saved you and your brother. You owe me." He flings his coat to the top of her desk, scattering her neat stacks. Forms float mockingly to the ground. He pushes her into an examination room—a room she herself had prepped for the next day, crisp, clean paper stretched across vinyl awaiting the next patient. He pushes her face into it, pins her head—where it stays while he shreds her dignity, distinctions between pain, shame, and survival blur; he changes her, forever.

Even after he releases her, Anika cannot move. Her cheek is stuck to crumpled paper with a mixture of sweat, saliva, and tears, though she cannot remember crying. The paper's peaks and valleys loom before her eyes—if only she could become tiny, find a place to hide among them. He—matter-of-fact, instructive, a disinterested teacher—is still there, behind her, but his voice comes from some distance, drifting, in and out. "your life itself depends on your silence." He grunts. There is a soughing of wool, a quick zip. The disturbed air sends a chill to her damp legs. "Our arrangement will last until I get what I want. I will return. If you are not here, I will have to come to your home—but that would doubtlessly be uncomfortable for your brother?" He snorts. "Auf wiedersehen."

She clings to a bat, flits, darts in and out of a cave, terrified to let go. For how long? Seconds, an hour? Then the paper mountains are crushed by a giant hand. Hers. She wiggles her fingers, reconnects to her body, orders it to rise. Dizzy, she clutches the table for balance, listens, holds her breath as the front door bangs shut. Her body convulses with pain and relief.

Cold linoleum slaps her bare thighs as she hits the floor. Next to her lies a pink, twisted rosebud: her panties. She wipes her eyes, registers salt on her lips, does not trust the silence; she is alert, a terror-driven, predator-sensing rabbit. The moon is framed by the window, the branch of a linden gently sways across it. The soft beauty does not make sense.

The memory ended with a lurch, Anika sitting motionless, numb, across from her perpetrator who seemed to be gloating with pride. There had been successive visits, always preceded by a basket at the door. How she'd lived in dread of the knock. "Another basket!" Michael would say, his delight blind to her petrified silence. "Why do you suppose he does this? Do you think it has to do with Papa? Does he feel guilty? What do you think, Anika? I suppose we shouldn't complain."

"Don't worry about it, Michael. I'm sure it has nothing to do with Papa." That, at least, she knew.

And then, triumphant, Klein had won. She had prayed to God for it not to be, contemplated throwing herself down stairs, beating her belly. Murder, yes, even that. But no action could undo what was. The constant revulsion—like a stench from an inaccessible source—was better, at least, than those clinic visits. She moved as a hollow shell through life—though now, she was anything but.

She pushed her spoon through the stew, no longer steaming. Her voice quivered despite her will to maintain an air of indifference.

"So, what happens now?" she asked, hating to give him the satisfaction of revealing her terror.

Klein leaned across the table, too close, too fast. She cringed, fists clenched in her lap, fingernails piercing her palms. He mocked her, dripping acid on her soul. "*Now what?* Simple. You will be silent. You will eat, sleep, stay healthy, until my baby is born. Then, you may carry on with your wayward, useless life. Any trouble, ever, I will swiftly have you arrested for being an *Andersdekende*, a critic of the State." His fists clenched on the table, his eyes steel, locked onto hers. "This baby—*my* baby—will bring much adulation to me and Trudi. After all, we will be offering a home to a bastard waif, so it can be raised decently, properly."

He sat back, running his tongue across his front teeth. A fist opened, fingertips rolling on the tablecloth, tapping out time, her life. Anika could muster only a glare, hoping it concealed the soul shriveling inside her.

He yawned, exposing thick silver molars. "You should be pleased, not ungrateful. Think of Trudi, your own dead mother's cousin. She will be a perfect mother, raise the baby as a consummate servant of the State. This is your opportunity to redeem yourself, make amends for all you have done to compromise your nation." He tapped at her tepid bowl. "Now eat. If you do not cooperate, I cannot be responsible for your fate. Eat."

19

Will tried to hide his disappointment that I'd be gone all weekend, while I downplayed my enthusiasm. We savored the little time alone together after practice, the few minutes when he walked me home once Rick peeled off toward his house.

Finally it was Friday. Amy and I left Rick and Will hanging out on the wall in front of the school making their own plans for the evening. A peck on Will's cheek was all my shyness could muster in front of the others before we took off for my house—and I regretted it as I jammed some clothes into a bag. But then, when we went outside to wait for Max, there, leaning against a tree across the street peeling bark from a stick, was Will. With a flick, he tossed the stick aside and ambled over. Grinning, he hugged Amy first, then pulled me aside for a deep kiss that made my knees wobble. His whisper in my ear made me tremble. "Be safe." And then he walked away. Amy caught me swiping at my eyes.

"Whoa. You two have it bad. One tiny weekend apart and it's all a weepy drama? You'd think the world was about to change forever!"

She laughed, but I couldn't shake the strange feeling that it was.

With a screech of tires, Max pulled up to the curb and we climbed in back. The door had barely closed before he tore off, jerking the car left and right to the beat of a German pop song. We laughed, shrieking encouragement until Amy reached in front to change the station to AFN.

"Reasons!" she cried, cranking up the volume. We sang at the top of our lungs, "*...the reasons that we're he-ee-re...*" Max howled along like a wild hyena until Amy punched him to stop. "*The reasons that we fear, our feelings won't disappear...*" I shivered, the words sticking in my throat, Will farther and farther away.

At Checkpoint Charlie, we drove past the little hut, American flag fluttering above it, and the sign that said: ALLIED CHECKPOINT. YOU ARE LEAVING THE AMERICAN SECTOR in English, Russian, French, and German. An MP emerged from the hut, then turned away.

"Why's he ignoring us?" I wondered aloud.

"He saw our East German diplomatic plates. We have nothing to do with the U.S. military," Max explained.

The U.S. military was in charge of the American Sector. Max's license plates showed that he represented the U.S. in East Berlin, which, in this case, was the recognized capital of the GDR. Max and Amy could cross at any of the checkpoints, but with me, they had to go through Charlie. And I was allowed to cross in their car only because I, too, had diplomatic status. Will couldn't. Rick couldn't. It was confusing, but I was starting to get it. I handed my diplomatic passport to Max. He and Amy each held special IDs issued by the East German government indicating their affiliation with the U.S. Embassy in the East.

Guards armed with rifles glared down from a cement tower looming over us. "Kalashnikovs," Max commented, rolling down his window and peering up. An East German guard approached, his own rifle draped over his shoulder. He compared faces with photos on our IDs before handing back Amy and Max's, but walked off and disappeared into a little shack with my passport.

"Should I go with him?" I asked, vaguely remembering a rule about never letting your passport out of your sight.

"Nah. He'll just stamp it," Max explained, "—and no doubt write down all your data, so they can start a brand new Stasi file on you." He winked at me in the rearview mirror. When the guard returned my passport, he winked at me too, making the whole thing feel like some warped, adult game. The barrier rose and Max put the car in gear. As we passed, a couple of Soviet guards glanced up. We weren't their concern, either.

"Are the East Germans allowed to search our car?"

"Nope. They're careful with this new diplomatic arrangement we've made with them. We don't search their officials coming into the West either."

I knew Max was referring to the 1972 Quadripartite Agreement that the four occupying powers had created to benefit each side in some way: the West had gained the right for its citizens and the occupying forces to cross over to the East to visit relatives and friends, and to drive between West Berlin and West Germany through the GDR on the Helmstedt-Berlin Autobahn where your activity was questioned if you drove too fast (you'd been speeding) or too slow (you'd stopped along the way to spy). The Agreement allowed for recognition of the German Democratic Republic as a state—separate from West Germany—which made diplomatic relations possible.

"The downside of the Quadripartite Agreement is that the Federal Republic of Germany essentially gave up any hope of reunification," Dad had explained to me. "In a sense, we're acknowledging that the Wall is here to stay. But now West Germans can cross over, they can visit and bring things to families in the East including hard currency. That boosts the East's struggling economy, which also improves life for those stuck over there."

Even though the Western allies considered East Berlin to be the Soviet Sector, for practical reasons, when the U.S. opened an embassy in 1974, East Berlin had become both: the *de facto* capital of the GDR *and* the Soviet Sector—just depending on the situation, whether it involved the military or diplomats. So, when crossing over as a diplomat, I was essentially recognizing East Berlin as the capital of the GDR. I could talk to and deal with the East German guards. But if I went in our car—with its military license plates—I had to use my military-issued Flag Pass, not my diplomatic passport. In that case, I would be following military rules, entering the *Soviet Sector*. I would not recognize East German guards, because, according to the military, they didn't "exist"; the Soviets were in charge.

"It's crazy," I murmured, my head buzzing, as we drove through the Wall.

Once in the East, Max slowed down. Everything did. The narrow streets seemed empty. The massive, ornate, pre-war architecture was so covered with black grime, it seemed to disappear into the past next to the new, quickly constructed, block Soviet buildings. We passed a church, walled off and left to decompose. I couldn't shake the feeling that time had stopped somewhere back in the 50s.

"Glad you've got a playmate tonight, kiddo. Afraid I'm gonna be late," Max announced.

"So? What else is new." Amy shrugged, gazing out her window, annoyed or completely unconcerned; I couldn't tell which. At least he tried to be fun. She didn't make it easy.

"Kate, has Amy explained about the ears in our walls?"

"She lived in Moscow, Max. She knows all about bugs."

"Oh," Max replied, clearly disappointed. "Hey, Kate, know how you know when the Stasi has put a new bug in your house?"

I played along. "No, how?"

"You get a new cupboard."

I laughed. Amy rolled her eyes. "Oh my God. That's such a bad joke."

Max dropped us in front of a giant cinderblock house identical to all the others on the street. "They built this street specifically for diplomats," Amy explained as he drove away. "At least it's tree-lined." A row of struggling, waist-high saplings had been spaced down an otherwise barren sidewalk. "Pretty sad, huh? Come on." I followed her up the driveway to steps leading to the front door.

20

"Anika? Anika Streil? Oh! It is you!"

A short, red-headed woman was waving frantically, darting between cars to cross the street. Anika's mind scrambled to place her. Her walk, her legs—impossibly knock-kneed and pigeon-toed at the same time—jogged Anika's memory of mocking grade school boys. And—oh, that squeaky voice. Brigitta.

"How long it's been!" Brigitta squealed, wrapping her arms around Anika's neck, kissing her on both cheeks.

"*Hallo*, Brigitta. Yes, it has been some time, hasn't it?" People really don't change, Anika thought. Brigitta, who had never been her friend, seemed overly excited to see her. Anika pulled herself up, conscious of her belly. "Three—four—years?" She calculated quickly. Everything was either before or after Stefan's death. She wondered what Brigitta knew.

"Oh, too long! Tell me! How are you?" Brigitta's hand patted Anika's shoulder making Anika's guard go up. Brigitta's mannerisms were not normal.

"I'm afraid I can't chat now, Brigitta, but it has been very nice to see you." Anika slipped from beneath Brigitta's hand, but the hand reached out and grabbed her wrist—too tightly.

"We must have tea!" she pressed. "What time do you normally finish at the clinic?"

Anika froze. She hadn't mentioned where she worked. Wrenching away her wrist, she turned on her heel. "I'm sorry, Brigitta. I'm late!"

Back at work, Anika lingered in the restroom studying her reflection in the mirror as she washed her hands. Dark shadows beneath her eyes sank into wan cheeks, her hair dull and flat against her scalp. She smirked—where was that healthy glow they spoke about? If anything, she'd aged way beyond her twenty-one years, her youth stolen, to create a baby she did not want who would be seized from her anyway. Her soul would never heal. What's more, she'd have to live with the knowledge that her child was being raised in a poisonous household, its father a monster.

Anika yanked at the towel hanging on a hook beside the sink, popping the suction, causing the hook to fall to the floor. She was groping in the dark beneath the sink, her hands searching for the hook, when the door to the restroom opened. She rose quickly, too quickly, grabbing the edge of the sink as the room swirled. From the doorway, Mina frowned at her before sauntering directly into a stall, without so much as a nod. Anika moistened the hook and smashed it back onto the tile.

What had she ever done to them? she wondered, hurrying back to her desk to the pile of forms waiting for her. The clinic buzzed with mid-afternoon activity. Surrounded by people, yet so alone. She knew her co-workers—not nice to begin with—were talking behind her back. Did they know? If so, how?

Her encounter with Brigitta had been no accident, she was certain of it. She trusted no one, assumed everyone to be informers for the Stasi. *Inoffiziele Mitarbeiter*—'unofficial collaborators'—the euphemism they gave their rats. It was no secret that the Stasi had enough eyes for everyone—the IMs even watched each other. Ever since Stefan's death and their father's imprisonment, they had to assume prying eyes were everywhere. But—the chance encounters, the note-scribbling, passed slips of paper—*were* they for the Stasi? Or were her co-workers working for Herr Klein, reporting to him directly? But he worked for the Stasi, anyway, so she supposed it made little difference.

She could trust only Michael. He, too, was afraid. She could see it in his eyes, the silent terror simmering within. Sweet Michael. Last night, he'd come home with fresh oranges—he'd stood in line for two hours for them—for her. He'd refused to eat even one. She needed them to stay healthy, he'd insisted.

She wanted to assure him that everything would be all right; instead, she kept quiet to downplay her fears, walling herself in. She did not tell Michael of the deep, dark dread perpetually gnawing at her insides like an insatiable, burrowing worm, nor of the nightmares that woke her bathed in hot shame. She could not pray. She feared even God—from whom she could not hide her desire that the half-formed baby inside her shrivel up and disappear. She longed for her mother like never before, craved her counsel. Anyone's. But there was no one.

"Fräulein?" A veined hand was tapping gently on her desk. Anika looked up into a drawn, lined face and blinked away the moisture pooling in her eyes. With a forced smile, she took the paper the old woman held out to her. Everyone had worries, she remembered.

"Entschuldigung, Frau Holzhaus, I'm sorry. Please, have a seat." At least it was Friday.

21

Once inside, we headed straight upstairs. Amy flicked on the overhead light in her room, flooding it with a cold fluorescent glow, illuminating a bed, a bureau, and a bedside table with a lamp. Embassy furniture, same as ours. Aside from a couple familiar school texts and notebooks piled on the bureau, there was nothing else—no personal touches revealing anything more about Amy. I switched on the lamp, then turned the overhead off, in an attempt to soften the ambience.

"Boring, huh?" Amy was eyeing me. I shrugged as if the thought had never crossed my mind. Pity would infuriate her. "Everything I brought fits in there." She kicked a suitcase stashed beneath the bed. "Good for a quick getaway—catch my drift?"

I didn't respond. Sometimes it felt like I didn't know Amy at all.

"Let's do our homework," she suggested, flinging her bag onto the bed to take out books and binders, "get it out of the way." I nodded as if I thought that was a brilliant plan—and precisely the reason I'd come all the way over here. Heading downstairs, she turned to face me. "Oh, yeah, and keep in mind," she cupped her ear with one hand and waved an index finger all around: they were listening.

"Gotcha," I whispered.

In our apartment in Moscow, we used to find little disc-shaped bugs hidden beneath furniture. Mom would sigh and say, "leave them alone—or else they'll just break in tomorrow to replace them."

"Have you found any...?" I made a little circle with my thumb and index fingers.

Amy shook her head. "Nope." Technology must have improved since my last police state.

Soon we were sprawled on the living room floor with East German TV playing in the background to make it harder to hear us. We divvied up trig problems: even for me, odd for Amy, but then she decided to do her German instead, while I was there to help. Schoolwork felt familiar, a bridge to the real world.

"Did you see Nadia pawing Will today?" I asked, attempting chit chat. Nadia had been driving me nuts. "Every time I turn around, she's got some excuse to grab him." The minute Nadia'd found out about Will and me, she'd started acting interested in him again, bringing up all these things they'd done together before I got there. It was constant, little inside jokes between the two of them. Will was as annoyed as I was. "I mean, Molly tried to tell her—"

"She's manipulating." Amy interrupted.

"Molly? It's not like Nadia listens to her. And anyway—,"

"Not *Molly*. Nadia. *Nadia* manipulates *Molly*."

"I think Molly *loves* being bossed around by Nadia. But, I agree, it's gross, what Molly puts up with."

"Yeah, but why? It's obvious, if you think about it." Amy stared at me as if expecting a response. I merely shrugged. What was she getting at? She sighed loudly, as though exasperated by my denseness. "Molly's completely in love with Nadia. And Nadia takes advantage of it."

I laughed but Amy looked me straight in the eye. "I'm not *joking*, Kate." She flicked her pencil against her notebook and stared back at me.

I frowned, confused. Where had this attitude come from? "What do you mean by in *love*?"

"Oh, come on, Kate. Molly adores, worships—is *totally in love with*—Nadia. It's obvious." She turned back to her German workbook. As far as she was concerned, the discussion was over. I wanted to understand, but she had closed all lines of questioning.

"It's *Ein*, not *eine*," I pointed to her notebook. "*Das Kind*, so it has to be *ein Kind* here."

"Thanks," Amy said, tersely, and erased the 'e'.

I chewed my pencil eraser, picturing Molly gazing at Nadia, wondering just what Amy meant. "Love," I needed to clarify, "you mean—more than like a *friend*?"

Amy blinked up at me. "It's not that weird, you know."

It felt like a test. I had no frame of reference for this discussion and wasn't altogether sure I knew what we were talking about.

"Well, so what? It's pointless—if Nadia isn't in love *back*."

Amy slouched over her German, refusing to talk. If she didn't want to discuss it, fine. Why had she brought it up? I plotted numbers on a graph, thinking coming over was a mistake if Amy was going to be in weird-mode the whole time. My heart emitted a little pang: I could have stayed in the West with Will.

A few awkward minutes of silence later, Amy sat up. I kept my focus on my graph, hoping she was about to apologize. She shoved her German aside, stretching and yawning. "Let's make dinner." She bounced up and strode to the kitchen where she opened and slammed shut cupboards and the fridge before announcing dinner had to be spaghetti. In stony silence, she filled a pot with water and banged it on the stove. I added a pinch of salt, and she barked that I'd added too much. That was it. I stomped into the living room and sat down in a pout. There was no point in dealing with her when she was like this.

Then I noticed the stereo and a shelf of albums. I picked out a couple to play in a stack, turned up the volume, and wandered toward the kitchen as the music burst through the air. Amy was grinning. She was back, as if the music had freed her from her own mind. We chatted, danced, and sang our way through the dinner preparations, then filled our plates to eat in the dining room.

As we sat, plates heaped and steaming in front of us, forks midair, everything went dark. And quiet. The electricity was off. Amy stumbled into the kitchen, scrounging in drawers until she found a box of matches, lighting one after another to find a candle, cursing when the matches burned down to her fingers.

"Just light the stove," I suggested. It's what we did when the electricity went off. "It'll put off some light."

We carried our plates to the little kitchen table to sit in the flickering glow of the flames. It felt like an eerie, parallel universe, silent but for the gentle hiss of gas.

"Think Helmut can still hear us?" I whispered.

"Good question! Do his *ears* need electricity?" Amy whispered back.

"I bet he can hear us loud and clear." The quiet magnified every sound.

We began to perform for Helmut. I slurped my noodles and smacked my lips, hoping to torment the eavesdropper. Amy followed suit. We conversed in beeps and squawks until, like boneless aliens, we slid beneath the table into our cosmic den. Amy maintained a low drone to my rhythmic tongue clicks. We grew louder, yowled mournful wails and screeches until, picturing Helmut wrenching the headset from his head, we collapsed into uncontrollable laughter, and then the electricity returned and the world exploded into color, the song resuming from where it had stopped. Still on our backs, we air-danced like disco-bugs until flopping flat, breathless, and climbed back onto our chairs to eat. After the dishes were done, Amy nudged me, pointing toward the front door. Grabbing jackets and sneakers, we tip-toed out of the house, leaving Helmut behind to question the sudden silence.

22

"This is the most fun I've had over here," Amy said as we bounced down the steps to the driveway. "Correction: the *only* fun I've had."

"Where's Max?" I asked, catching my breath after we'd spontaneously sprinted halfway down the road. It felt good.

"The embassy, I guess. Who cares?" she said, tugging my sleeve. "This way, I'll show you a little park I've been to a couple of times."

"Alone?"

"Yeah—who else?" She kicked a rock down the path and ran after it—then kicked it again, hard. It disappeared into the shadows. "It's the best thing about Max, though."

"What?"

"That he leaves me alone."

"A lot?" I asked, treading carefully. Not one car had passed by and our voices echoed in the streets. It felt like we were alone in the city.

"Yep. A lot. Sometimes I wonder if he's avoiding me. I think I freak him out. I mean, we don't even know each other. It's weird to live with a man you don't know. It's not like when I was little and used to stay with him overnight and we'd go to McDonald's and a Disney movie." She laughed. "But I don't mind being alone. The alternative—if he hovered all the time?—*that* would be worse." She laughed again, but I failed to see what was so funny, though now I got why she was at our house all the time.

"I'd be lonely," I admitted.

"Hah!" She grabbed a clump of dead leaves off a tree and tossed them at me. "It's just boring over here. Like I've been telling you."

"Will your mom ever come visit? I mean, would that be weird—with Max?" I dug crunchy leaf bits out of my hair.

"Not a chance."

We turned a corner. It was only around nine o'clock, but felt like two in the morning. Where was everybody?

"Even if—anyway, she won't. Basically, she *can't*." When Amy stopped to zip up her jacket, I waited for her to explain. But, zipper at chin, she walked on without a word.

"*Why*, Amy?" It came out so quietly—for a moment I hoped she hadn't heard. We walked on but now the silence bore down like a heavy weight. I'd broken my rule not to push, to give her time. Then, she spoke.

"You want to know *all about me*, Kate?" She stopped to face me. It felt like a punch in the gut. I nodded. It was the truth. I *did* want to know all about her. We couldn't pretend to be this close with some big secret between us. Her eyes were black and darting.

"OK." She crossed her arms and sighed. "My mom's a drunk. She lost her job, then our apartment—so I *had* to come and live with my dad."

A drunk? Her *mom*? It sounded so ugly, the way she'd said it. I'd contemplated a dozen different scenarios, but never this. Her shame burned next to me, and I understood why she hadn't wanted to tell me. I wasn't sure I wanted to know more. But it wasn't her fault—I wasn't even sure it was anyone's fault—or if fault even mattered.

I stood there like an idiot—couldn't think what to say—until she threw her hands up and walked off at a fast clip. I rushed to catch up. She stared straight ahead, arms swinging.

"*Amy*," I pleaded, remembering what Will had said. It wasn't being nosy if I *cared*. This wasn't about whether or not I wanted to know. She *needed* to tell me, for me to understand. "I may not be helpful, I know that. But, I can try. I want to know—what you've been through."

She stopped marching and faced me, both of us panting. Her eyes narrowed with an intensity I'd never seen in her before. "That night? With the drunk man?" Clearly her mind had been racing as fast as her feet because then it all burst out, like an opened balloon zig zagging around a room. "Katie, I've seen my *mom* like that. Not violent like that, no—but, yeah, *that drunk*. Falling over, puking, passing out...." She took off again, fast. I scurried along. The road went downhill, and her story tumbled out as if propelled by the tilt of the earth.

"I was still little when Max came back from Vietnam. I think I was five. By then, Sylvia was living with us—I don't know what my mom *thought* was going to happen—but anyway, when he came back, she said he was a different guy. And when she said he was different? I thought she meant actually the *wrong* guy—like they'd sent the wrong *dad* home. She and Sylvia used to laugh about that." Amy slowed, gazing into her past. "My earliest memories of Max are of this silent man who sat on the couch making Mom uncomfortable. Sylvia was gone—and I missed her. She was my other *mom*, you know?" She inhaled a couple of deep breaths. "And then one day, *Max* was gone. The living room seemed bigger. I learned the word 'divorce'. And, Sylvia moved back."

I listened hard, trying to follow, all the while thinking: finally, Amy, finally. She began to walk again, but calmer, her narrative matching her pace.

"For years, things were great. It was just Sylvia and my mom and me and we were happy. We went camping and played *Parcheesi* and *Chutes and Ladders*, and cooked and danced together—until..." Amy took a deep breath, her eyes closing. "Sylvia got sick. I was twelve, almost thirteen. Mom took care of her, but she got worse. It was awful. Eventually, Mom sent me to stay with Enid. And then one day, Enid told me, Sylvia was dead." At 'dead', Amy stopped walking and looked away.

I whispered, "What was it?"

"Cancer. It took six months." She shivered, then went on. "I moved home—but it wasn't the same. My *mom* wasn't the same. She was sad—broken. She cried all the time. But, sometimes, when she drank? She would even laugh—so, she drank. I poured her drinks. I thought it made her better." Amy pondered that a moment, shaking her head as if only now recognizing the absurdity. "But of course we also knew it was bad so we kept it secret—did all kinds of shit to fool people. Our secret. It was fun. For a while."

Amy veered off the road toward a bench in a little green patch surrounded by trees where we sat. I closed my eyes, frightened by her story. Would knowing it change who I thought Amy was? What a stupid thing to think.

"Eventually," Amy continued, "she lost her job selling houses. I worked after school and in summers, but never made enough. The landlord gave us time to get our act together, but we couldn't do it, and ultimately, he kicked us out."

The sound of a car jerked us back to the present. A *Volkspolizei*, blue light whirling, pulled up to the curb. Two East German policemen climbed out and strode over to where we sat, the light pulsing against their uniforms: one tall and skinny with a big nose and pointy Adam's apple, the other short, with a baby face and bucteeth. Rocky and Bullwinkle.

They asked why we were out so late. Late? I replied we were just out for a stroll and a chat.

Amy tugged at my sleeve. "What're they saying?"

They demanded identification. We had none. I said we didn't think to carry IDs just to go for a walk. Rocky said it was too late to be out walking and we had to have IDs at all times. I glanced at his watch: 9:30 on a Friday night, but I knew better than to argue.

Amy was still tugging at my jacket. "Apparently, we're supposed to have our IDs," I explained, then turned back to the cops. "*Wir gehen sofort nach Hause.*" Back to Amy, I said, "I told them we'd go home. Come on. Let's go."

"*Aufstehen,*" Bullwinkle barked.

"He said stand up." I nudged Amy.

"*Mitkommen!*" Rocky ordered.

Amy and I stared at each other in a panic. Come with them? Where were they going to take us? It felt wrong in all kinds of ways to follow two men into a car, even if they were police. But what choice did we have? We climbed in the back. Bullwinkle slammed the door. There was the crackle of a radio inside and a woman's voice nattering incoherently between clicks and beeps. Rocky started the car.

I imagined our destination: a dark cell with a dim lightbulb hanging from a wire, hands tied behind us, maybe to a chair, maybe blindfolded. Interrogation. How long would we hold out? What if they tortured us until we talked? About what? What did we even know? I swallowed. We were clutching each other, trembling, our heads bent together. No one would ever know what had happened to us.

"Should we demand to see a Soviet officer?" I whispered. If I'd come as a military person, that would be the protocol; but, no, I'd come as a diplomat. That meant we had to deal with the East Germans.

"If we get one call, I'll call the embassy," Amy offered.

"*If,*" I gulped. Images from Solzhenitsyn's *Gulag Archipelago* swirled in my head.

The car stopped. We looked up. Bullwinkle opened the back door. It took us a moment to register: we were in front of Amy's house.

"*Raus. Das nächste Mal: Ausweis mitbringen! Und keine Nachtspaziergänge!*" He shoved us in the direction of the house, his command to bring IDs with us next time still ringing in my ears. "*Guten nacht!*" he called out, not unkindly.

We scurried up the steps to the front door. Amy's hand shook. She fumbled the key, dropped it, picked it up, and dropped it again as though directed by Hitchcock. Finally managing to get the door open, we darted inside. I turned to wave as if to new friends, then slammed the door behind us, blood pounding in my ears.

"What the *hell*?" Amy squealed in the dark and only then did it register that she'd been repeating that since we got to the door. "I mean what did we do *wrong*? Is it breaking the law to go out for a little *walk*?" She turned indignant. "See? It's creepy over here! I *hate* it."

"Is there a curfew? Someone should have told us." I shook my head. "Honestly? I bet they were driving around bored, and Bullwinkle said to Rocky, '"How 'bout we scare the crap out of these American kids?"' That's when it hit me. "Whoa. *Amy!*" I grabbed her arm.

"What?" She jumped, still skittish.

"*We* didn't tell them where we lived! So, how—?"

"Ew, you're right! They know where I live!" We clutched each other, whimpering.

Amy double-locked the front door and we rushed to brush teeth and get in pajamas, hopping through the chilly air to snuggle under the blanket. Silent, pondering our recent adventure, we both stared through the dark at the ceiling. But then Amy muttered, "Rocky and Bullwinkle?" and we laughed until our stomachs hurt.

"I'm glad you came, Katie. You were right. I needed you to see this, to know what it's like. The weirdness is actually fun when you're here."

"Yeah, me, too. I needed to picture this, your other life." I snuggled down sleepily, happy I'd come.

But Amy needed to talk, picking up right where she'd left off in the park, so I perked up, all ears. "We were evicted, had a week to get out. Mom had no plan at all, just cried and cried. I called Enid, and she met me after I got off work—this was last summer—took me to her house, sat me down, and we talked."

Was Helmut taking notes? I wondered.

"Enid had known all along—about the drinking. Guess we hadn't been fooling everyone after all. And by the time Enid took me home, Mom was sloshed. She lost it, started screaming—furious her mom was there, furious that I'd brought her. A glass crashed on the floor—vodka and shards, everywhere. She screamed when I tried to clean it up. She shouted that Enid was just pretending to care, that she'd never accepted her for who she was. On and on." Amy caught her breath. "Enid took it all calmly, listened, said we had to make a plan. She's a tough lady." Amy explained. "Somehow, watching one of mom's rages through Enid's eyes—with her there—I saw things differently. The more she screamed, the calmer I got. I felt..." she paused.

"Like you weren't alone anymore?" I offered.

"Exactly."

We lay quiet for a few moments until she continued, more relaxed. Was she relieved to have told me?

Enid found a rehab facility. Her mom went, was there now. Amy moved in with Enid again. When she heard Max was posted to Berlin, she'd come up with the idea of going to live with him. "I needed to get away, Max said fine, and—yeah, the rest is history."

"How long is her rehab?"

"Ninety days."

"And you've been here..."

"She's more than halfway through."

I stared into the dark. She didn't have to say it. She was planning to leave when her mother got out of rehab. "What happens—when you go back?"

"Alex and I talked about getting our own place once he graduates and I turn eighteen in May."

Living with her boyfriend. It seemed crazy to me—the responsibility, the weight of it all. She seemed so much older than me. Too old. I didn't envy her at all.

"Kate?" Amy asked. "I know it's a burden, but…"

"No burden, Amy." I knew what she wanted. "I won't tell a soul."

Amy turned toward the wall. "Man, I'm exhausted. Aren't you?" She yawned loudly and then bellowed into the darkness, making me jump. "*Gute nacht, Gottfried!*"

"*Ja! Gute nacht, Gottfried!*" I echoed, settling onto my side. I felt closer to Amy than ever, and she was going to leave. "Hey! When did *Helmut* turn into *Gottfried*?"

We giggled, and quickly dozed off. Sometime in the night, I woke to the key in the front door. I listened as Max went to his room, shutting the door behind him, and thought of how, when my parents came home, no matter how late, Mom would stick her head into my room and call out softly, "We're home, sweetheart!" and only then would I fall into a deep, safe slumber.

23

Anika listened to the thump and whir of the pottery wheel in the tiny room adjacent to hers, and in her half-awake state, imagined her father's expert hands working to transform an amorphous lump of clay into a smooth, graceful vessel. His hobby had become his livelihood after his license to practice law was revoked when he refused to join the Communist party. The irony, of course, was that the punishment forced him into making a living privately, contrary to communist principles. Like a good capitalist.

When they were big enough, their father had taught her and Michael to throw clay, too. Anika had never stuck with it. Her brother, though, had cultivated his skills over the years and eventually, Anika couldn't distinguish Michael's rhythm from her father's; now, of course, it could only be Michael. She shivered a sympathetic prison chill and reached for her blanket.

Lately, she'd detected a flutter, as if a spider roamed inside her. She pictured it: black and evil, thriving on her flesh. Michael had grown protective, hovering, looking for ways to ease her load. He meant well, but his efforts overwhelmed hers to forget. She wondered if it had been a mistake to tell him; perhaps she should have suffered alone, sparing him her torment a little longer. But time had given her no choice. Soon, it would be obvious.

She'd have to lie, develop a story. Klein would get what he wanted, then leave her alone. He'd have to, she thought, because forever, she will know his secret, the true identity of his child. That realization gave her a modicum of control.

But never could she go back to who she had been. She ached for Marcus, for their innocent longings, the tender dreams they'd had, the promises they'd made. Hard enough to have had to wait until his return from his service. But now, *that* Anika, the one he'd known, no longer existed.

The whirring of the wheel ceased. Michael would come soon, asking her what he could do to help. She closed her eyes and pretended to sleep.

24

Max was in the living room holding a mug and the *International Herald Tribune,* just like my dad would be on a Sunday morning. I began a polite greeting, but Amy pulled me into the kitchen, an index finger to her lips. She poured what was left of cold coffee into a pot with some milk to heat it up. When the flame whooshed and hissed, we looked at each other and laughed, without needing to say a word.

We left the house after breakfast letting the front door bang shut behind us. "See ya, Max!" If Max so much as grunted a reply to Amy's farewell, I missed it.

"Not a morning person, huh?" I offered, putting up my hood. Now it wasn't so hard to picture him on the couch, back from Vietnam.

"Nope," she agreed, hopping over a puddle on the sidewalk.

It was cold and rainy. We'd been tempted to stay cozy at home, but were on a mission to explore her city, and the idea of Helmut or Gottfried or whoever eavesdropping motivated us to get out. Our first destination: the spa at the Metropol Hotel, an extravagance we'd never consider in the West.

The newly opened Metropol would not have been particularly remarkable in the West. But here, it stood out like a jewel in a sandbox, meant to attract businessmen and diplomats and anyone else who could pay with hard currency to help the East's struggling economy—which meant it was off-limits to the majority of the people who lived here.

The moment we hopped off the S-Bahn, the drizzle turned into a drenching downpour. We dashed past the doorman, where the concierge greeted us dripping and shivering in a spit-shined lobby. After paying a laughably small amount of western currency for use of the spa for the whole day, we followed a bellhop to the elevator. It opened to a tell-tale waft of chlorine leading to a glass door. Beyond it, a turquoise pool shimmered next to a steaming hot tub. We had the whole place to ourselves.

Sinking beneath the hot foam and steam, we massaged our feet and backs against jet streams, the roar gurgling in our ears. Floating weightlessly, we bobbed and drifted through the bubbles until the heat was too much. Then we climbed out to rush over to the pool, our bare feet slapping the tiles, careful not to slip. The cool water took our breath away, and we thrashed through a few laps to warm up. We filled our lungs and tested how far we could swim in one breath. And then, shivering, we padded back to the hot tub and sank back in. We sang songs underwater until we grew dizzy and hot, got out to quench our thirst from a faucet in the ladies' room, dove back into the pool, then went back to the hot tub. The downpour outside formed crystal bars on the large windows, encaging us in dreamy luxury.

I was facedown in the jacuzzi floating, eyes open to a frothy underworld, when a torpedo and trail of bubbles split the surface. Then another—and another and another: we were being dive-bombed by legs. I gasped and came up for air just as Amy surfaced, her hair snaking in the foam. She rolled her eyes and dove right back down.

There were two young men, clearly amused. Something about their confident demeanor convinced me they were from the West, and, anyway, the spa was only accessible with hard currency.

Curious, I draped my arms over the side behind me and slipped down into the water leaving just my eyes above the surface, closing them, trying to act indifferent to their presence, peeking through my lashes. The balding one had eyes that twinkled and a mischievous smile, the other, a comma of blond bangs that drooped across his forehead, high cheeks beneath sharply defined eyes that drew me in—a hypnotic beauty that made me uneasy and mesmerized at the same time. One of his eyes was a pale, piercing blue, the other, almost black. His lips slowly pressed into a tight smile. He knew I was peeking.

Embarrassed, I dunked beneath the surface, and in the bubbly fog, it hit me. I sputtered, pushed back up through the foam. Swiping water from my eyes, I spun around, looking for Amy. She was lolling on her back like a drowned Ophelia, arms and torso bobbing on the surface.

The blonde grinned and leaned in to speak over the gurgling. "What brings you two here?" That voice. I became lightheaded, dizzy. "You do speak English, yes? *Oder Deutsch, vielleicht?*"

He laughed, tossing back his head. I wanted to explode, managing only a nod despite desperate pleas to the universe for something brilliant to say. Amy's head rolled up like a surfacing mermaid, but after a drowsy look of disdain, she dove right back beneath the bubbles.

"You—you're..." But I held off, as if saying his name would make him disappear like reaching for a dream.

His eyes sparkled. He smiled and winked. My heart was beating like a hummingbird's. "Horrific weather, isn't it? Perfect day for a jacuzzi. Alas, Brian and I only have time for a quick dip. Lovely to meet you." And with that, out they climbed, water streaming between taut muscles, grabbing towels from lounge chairs and whipping them around their shoulders. They waved back at me and turned to go.

My jaw dangled in the water. Bubbles tickled my nose. "Wait!" I cried, my arm shooting up through the foam. "It was really, really cool to meet you!" What a dumb thing to say. Then they were gone, soft laughter trailing behind them. I wobbled in the jet streams. "Oh. My. God."

Amy gurgled to the surface. "They're gone? Good. Were you *talking* to them?"

"Amy. Did you *see* who that was?" I was weak with awe.

"*Who?*" Amy demanded, annoyed.

"You didn't *see*—," I turned from where I stared at the door, still stunned, "who that *was?*"

Amy pinched her nose and dunked her head backwards, her hair wriggling across the surface like Medusa's snakes. "Just *tell* me!" she demanded, impatient.

She was going to regret her aloofness.

"David Bowie. David bloody Bowie. *David Bowie!* I swear. Here. In a hot tub. With us." I fainted into the bubbles.

Amy grabbed me. "No *way.*" She looked toward the door. "Holy crap. You think?"

"I know."

She sank beneath the froth, rising with a sputter. "You're *sure?*"

I nodded.

"We were in a *hot tub* with *David Bowie*?!"

I laughed. "Yeah. And you didn't even know it!"

Later, alone in the hotel restaurant, we ordered borscht—the only thing available on the hotel's extensive menu—with Coca Cola—at the insistence of a swarm of waiters who "knew" what Americans liked. Self-conscious beneath the scrutiny of a bored, excessive staff, we gobbled down our food between glances toward the door hoping for a sign of David and Brian—who had to be Brian Eno. But none came. We paid, pulled our hoods over our damp hair, and headed back out into the cold and wet.

Staring into bars of rain, the drab of East Berlin felt even heavier after our luxurious interlude, but it was a relief to be away from the slew of gawking waiters.

"Those guys were doing important work," Amy commented, "watching us eat."

"Indeed! No unemployment in East Germany!"

"A job for everyone!"

I responded with a coke belch. Amy countered with an even longer one. A second later, brilliant veins of lightning flashed across the sky followed by an earth-shaking cloudburst. We squealed and ran out into the rain, laughing.

25

The bittersweet significance of the day hung silently between them as Michael and Anika went about their Sunday morning. When together they began to hang the laundry over a rope that pulled out from a wall in the warmed kitchen, Anika announced, "I have the ingredients for a small cake. I want to make it this afternoon. What will you do?" She tilted her head, hoping she already knew.

"I'll give you one guess." Michael winked at her.

Anika's heart ached with love. She nodded, smiled. "You're all right, going alone?"

"I am." Michael lowered his eyes, avoiding Anika's gaze. "I will imagine he is with me."

As far back as he could remember, whenever Michael asked, "Papa, what do you want for your birthday?" his father would respond with, "I'd like you to take me to the Pergamon Museum." Every year, Michael's gift to his father was an excursion to the museum. At first it was thrilling, made little Michael feel grown up to go anywhere alone with his Papa. There were, admittedly, a couple of years where Michael found the museum trips to be slightly boring, not that he ever would've admitted this to his father. But the last time his father and he had gone to the Pergamon—his father's birthday before he was arrested—the trip to the museum had utterly transported Michael. Maybe it was his age, a sign that his brain had passed a threshold of understanding, because, suddenly, it seemed his father had so many fascinating facts and stories to tell about pottery and ceramic styles, techniques, archeological wisdom, ancient histories—that Michael had suggested they go back the very next week to see more. As he worked on his own pottery-making skills, so much of what his father taught him came back to inspire him. Last year had been too dismal to think about going without him on his birthday, but this year, Michael had decided that there was no better way to honor their father, imprisoned in a cell somewhere, than to go to the very place he'd go were he free.

By early afternoon, it was pouring outside. Anika rose from the couch where she had been reading their father's book of 19th Century poetry, imagining his contemplative expression responding to his favorite verses. Michael was dozing in his wingback chair, a book open, pages flailing in his lap. She wandered into the kitchen to assemble the simple cake, debating whether to nudge her brother, wake him before it got too late. Opening the back door to check the weather, the air whipped through the rain falling in thick cords, nipping at her face before she quickly shut it. She decided against waking Michael, though she did worry that he may feel disappointed in himself if he didn't go, despite the elements.

Anika was pouring cake batter into a pan, thinking how her mood matched the weather, when a bright flash of lightning made her look up. Not two seconds later, the house shook with a loud clap of thunder. Anika dropped the bowl right into the pan full of batter, then reached for a distant spatula to clean it off, dripping batter along the way. "Super," she snapped aloud.

"That thunder made me jump out of my skin," Michael said, walking into the kitchen rubbing his eyes. Just as Anika had a half hour ago, he, too, gazed outside, then shut the door with a groan. "Rain or not, I need to go soon. I had a dream about Papa. He was telling me something about the Pergamon Altar, how I needed to check the damage done there during the war," Michael mused as he sat to tie his shoes, still drowsy from his nap.

"I'm happy you're still planning to go. If the rain stops, I'd like to get out for some fresh air. Meet me under the clock? How about 5:30?"

"Sounds good," Michael called out as he pulled his jacket over his head to dash through the rain toward the bus. Anika frowned, seeing his scarf and warm sweater still hanging from the hook. Guess he'll learn the hard way, she supposed, realizing she was beginning to sound like their mother.

26

Though the bad weather made the trip to the Pergamon more inviting, Amy said just walking into a museum made her instantly sleepy and I admitted I had a hard time getting excited about glass shelves full of numbered rows of glued vases. But the moment we entered the Pergamon Museum, we were awestruck by a long hallway of turquoise, lapis-blue, and gold-glazed brick walls: the reconstruction of a Babylonian road. We strolled to the far end to gaze up at the towering Ishtar Gate, emblazoned with lions and dragons.

"Pretty impressive," Amy said, both of us stretching our necks to admire the massive structure that nearly touched the ceiling. The next moment, I was on the ground, sprawled flat amongst a forest of legs. Someone had pushed me, hard. Amy blinked down, bewildered.

"That was no accident," I snapped, as she pulled me up. No one in the crowd snickered or looked guilty. There was nothing to do but rub the filth from my palms and plod on. But our mood had begun to sour. People were staring, judging. We felt unwelcome. Was it because we were from the West? Was it that obvious? Shuffling along with the crowd, the air felt thick and stifling. We peeled off our damp jackets and draped them over our arms. Just as I was telling Amy how my wrist hurt, a beady-eyed guard grabbed that very wrist and yanked me aside, glaring as he pointed to a sign—*Garderobe*. His shove toward the back of the line snaking beneath it was far from gentle.

"I gather it's mandatory to check one's garments," I growled when Amy joined me. "Subtle, huh?"

After what felt like forever, a coat-check girl whose grouchy countenance mirrored ours—the mood was contagious—took our jackets and handed us plastic numbers. We rammed them into our pockets.

"*That's* a year of our lives we'll never get back, huh?" Amy grinned as she spun around to walk backwards, her palms pressed together at her heart, head sliding side-to-side—her Indian dance that never failed to make me laugh. Steering her around a stationary clump of people, instead, we both ran into a rope, nearly tripping over it and each other. The rope encircled a carved stone façade laced with intricate detail.

"*Mashatta Fassade, Jordan, 8 v.u.Z.*" Amy read the label over my shoulder. "What's 'v-u-z'?"

"Stands for *"vor unserer Zeitrechnung"*—which literally means 'before our time calculations'. It's their way of saying BC. They don't want to use BC because, you know, Before *Christ?* No religion, remember?" Amy looked puzzled. I thought about it. "Yeah, kind of ridiculous if you think about it because they're using the same time line—so, in fact, they *are* measuring time from the birth of Christ."

Amy stared at me. "How do you *know* this stuff? You should be my tour guide." She grinned. "Go on." She crossed her arms and knit her eyebrows. "I'm listening."

I fluffed my hair and cleared my throat, stretching out an arm, the back of my hand grazing the ancient carving like a hostess on a game show. "Archae-*ah*-logists buh-*lieve* this *deli*cate carving was done by two—" It wasn't clear where the southern accent had emerged from, but it seemed to fit. A couple turned to stare. Amy nodded with a feigned sober expression, goading me on. "—*two* un*us*ually talented *slaves* of ancient Jordan." We caught flashes of disapproval which only encouraged us.

The more serious everything—and everyone—seemed, the more we cracked up. We couldn't stop laughing, that stomach-aching kind of laughter that made you bend in half—until, Amy, looking beyond me, croaked, "Run, Kate! Run!" and grabbed me just as a guard emerged through the crowd, stomping toward us, fit to be tied. We dodged him, slipping through a doorway, Amy clutching my arm, slinking between people like a snake through grass. We stopped only when blocked by a massive, two-storied, ancient portico.

"*Roman Market Gate of Miletus,*" I translated, gasping for air. "Man, look how lucky they were." I pointed to the top that nearly touched the ceiling. "It fits *perfectly* in here."

It took Amy a moment to get my joke, but then, we lost it all over again, bending over, guts full of laughter. Again, a guard beelined toward us. And again, we darted—beneath the ancient gate into yet another gigantic room where we were blocked by the *Great Altar of Pergama.*

"Pergama. Like the name of the museum!" Amy exclaimed. The hysterics returned.

"I can't look at you," I groaned, a hand on my stomach. I was sweating, desperate for fresh air.

We meandered toward the roped-off front of the giant altar, where steps led to a three-sided, columned portico. The base was carved with scenes of battles between Olympian gods and giants: naked mortals bound with serpents contorted in fear; winged gods on the backs of lions, shields and swords raised in triumph. I took in the scenes, avoiding Amy's gaze, shoving bangs off my sweaty forehead. The marble looked smooth and cool and I reached out to rest my hot palm against the rippled abdomen of a Greek god.

The slap made my head spin. "*Nicht anfassen!*" Don't touch! A tiny guard, her face pinched in rage beneath her billed cap, lifted her hand to slap me again, shaking from self-restraint.

My cheek stung. Words of protest amassed in my mouth. But in trying to form a cohesive defense, all at once I saw us through their eyes: we, who were free to know both worlds, to compare, to judge. Entitled, spoiled. I curbed my outrage. To them, we'd been disrespectful. And yet.

A circle of onlookers grew. I rubbed my burning cheek, facing off with the guard, wondering what to do, when Amy pushed me aside, enraged, her hands in tight fists. "*Hey, lady!* Lighten up!" She towered over the elfin woman. I tried to pull her away, but she shook me off. "What the *hell*, Kate? She *slapped* you!"

More guards were closing in. We were becoming a spectacle. "*Amy*," I urged, tugging her arm, "let's *go*."

But Amy stood her ground, wresting her arm from my grip. I'd never seen her so furious. "Kate! She can't just *hit* you." A murmur coursed through the crowd, judging. An angry mob was the last thing we needed.

"Forget it, Amy." I pleaded. "We have to go. *Now*." Scanning overhead, I found the nearest *Ausfahrt* sign glowing red, and pushed through the throng, Amy in tow, toward the exit. We were trailed by an entourage of guards. "*Wir gehen! Wir gehen!* We're going, already…." I muttered. I could hear snatches of German phrases from the gawkers, like 'they need to learn to behave,' and '*schlechte Kinderstube*'—bad upbringing—that buzzed in my ears.

My shoulders rounded with shame, my mind spinning with the now familiar turmoil: What to do if detained? How long can they keep us? Would anyone come looking for us? At what point was I supposed to demand to see a Soviet officer? I was here as a diplomat, so, no Soviets—we recognized the East Germans.… Nearing the exit, I expected to be blocked, but, instead, the guards seemed to be making dang sure we left.

Outside in the chilly air, we gasped, resisting the urge to bolt, walking swiftly, skittering between the museum buildings, trying to remember how we'd gotten there. When we saw the bridge across the River Spree, we bolted to the other side. Only once we were there, did I loosen my grip on Amy's arm. She sputtered, stomping around, livid. "That *bitch!*" She roared. "I mean—what just happened?" She looked at me, bewildered, angry—and scared.

I was angry, too. At her. "Man, Amy! You know we were an inch from being *detained?*" I wanted to shake her. "What *was* all that—what were you planning to do? Beat her up? Change the way they think? Persuade them to run out and tear down the Wall singing Hallelujah? They had a *point*—we weren't exactly acting like circumspect, model Americans in there. We're the *outsiders* over here." I crossed my arms, exasperated.

She glared back at me. "You're yelling at *me?* I was defending you! She *slapped you in the face!* You're an American *diplomat* kid! Seriously, what did we *do*? *Laugh?*—touch *marble?* Is that such a crime? What the hell?" She shook her head, stomped away, then stomped right back. "I *hate* it over here. This place is so messed up. And—and—you're yelling at *me?*"

I refused to look at her but, she had a point, too. Why *were* we fighting each other? This place *was* messed up. Amy stared over the wall, down into the river. I leaned against a tree and watched a couple of pigeons peck at a chunk of bread. One would steal it from the other and walk away, head bobbing until the other stole it back. The bread broke into clumps, then crumbs. I glanced up and caught Amy wiping her face with the back of her hand. My heart filled with regret.

"Amy?" She turned around. I held up a peace sign.

"Hey," she said—as though nothing had happened. She hadn't been crying after all, maybe hadn't even noticed our tiff. "It stopped raining! Look, clear skies."

Thin, gray clouds raced above us, exposing a dusky sky. Temperatures had dropped and the air felt heavy and biting, as if it might even snow. I shivered. So, we were to move on, no discussion of what had just happened, Amy-style. I took it in stride, resigned, jamming icy hands into my jean pockets; maybe, this was how she'd learned to cope.

My fingers curled around a piece of plastic. The moment I pulled it out, Amy held up hers. Our coats. We'd left without them. "No wonder we're so cold!" Our laughter puffed in clouds between us, until we stared back across the bridge.

"I cannot believe we have to go back there!" Amy groaned, kicking the wall beside her. "What if they don't let us in?" Her eyes narrowed. "Hey." I followed her gaze.

Someone was marching with distinct purpose, heading directly toward *us*. His beige jacket flapped as he strode, his hands rammed into typical East German, knock-off jeans—stiff, waist and crotch too high (it was clear why real Levi's were a hot, black market commodity). But he had a graceful gait, as if his legs only pretended to touch down, like an angel playing human, his long, yellow hair rippling with each step.

He smiled as he approached, his eyes gentle, seeking, instantly disarming. "*Guten Tag,* I am Michael." Mee—kha—yel, the German pronunciation pure velvet compared with the English. We shook hands, introduced ourselves.

"I was in the museum—*ja?*" he pointed behind him. "*So,* I saw what has happened." Despite the accent, he seemed comfortable in English.

His eyes filled with concern. "Your face—it is OK?" He touched my cheek with a finger, gingerly turning my head side to side. I was hoping for telltale welts, to justify our behavior.

"I'm fine," I assured him. "I shouldn't have touched the marble. It was disrespectful."

"Uh, yeah, but I still think that guard over-reacted just a *teeny* bit," Amy insisted, starting right back up again. "Honestly, I think she was *psycho!*"

"Amy," I pressed, embarrassed by her lack of cultural sensitivity.

Michael nodded with a look of consternation. The streetlights came on just then, sparkling inside his round eyes. "I looked to find you…to apologize. It is not the proper way to treat guests."

"Your English is very good," Amy noted, her tone slightly less offensive.

"*Danke.*" He laughed. "I mean, thank you. I am teaching it to—me. To myself? Ach, it is not so good." His laugh was easy, gentle.

"*Besser als unsere Deutsch!*" I said, appreciating his efforts. I couldn't take my eyes off him.

"*Ach! Du sprichst aber gut Deutsch!*" he replied, not that I'd said enough to warrant the compliment. In his own language, he was even more beautiful.

"Hallooo…? 'Scuse me, guys, sorry, but, uh, mein Deutsch is nicht zo goot! You're going to have to parlay in Anglay for me, I'm afraid," Amy complained.

Michael laughed. "I am happy to practice my English. You—you are Americans?" He sounded hopeful. We nodded. "Ah," he mused, "I envy you your freedoms," referencing a basic human right as if chatting about the weather. "I am sure it is strange for you here." It struck me how we *could* experience how it was here, while he could only dream what our world might be like, a world a mere walk and a hideous, thirteen-foot man-made barrier away from where we stood. I looked down, unsure what to say.

"Anyway, look what we just found." Amy held up her coat check ticket. "We have to go back," she shrugged, gesturing toward the museum.

Michael slapped his head, grasping our predicament at once, and reached for the tickets. "I will get your coats. It is OK? Wait here. I will return, soon." With that, he took off, his long legs gliding over the earth. We stared as he floated back across the bridge. A fog had descended, obscuring the far end, and soon, Michael disappeared altogether.

"Whoa," Amy whispered.

"Yeah. An angel interested in practicing his English…or, a spy for the Stasi?" I turned to Amy. "But talk about cute."

Wrapping her arms around herself, she hopped in place to get warm. "Exactly what does *Stasi* mean, anyway?"

"*Staatssicherheit*. State Security. It's their internal secret police—primarily for spying on their own people," I explained through chattering teeth.

"Can't help but think of the Nazi *SS*."

"They recruit normal, everyday citizens to spy on others. That's why the whole society is so paranoid. No one trusts anyone. It's not crazy to suspect this guy."

Amy giggled. "An angel spy."

"Definitely something." I said dreamily, both enthralled and disturbed by my emotions. "Something one could grow to love."

"Whoa, sister, wake up! Remember your darling Will?"

"Lord, I just meant he's *dreamy*."

"Uhh, actually, what you said was, 'I could love that.'" Amy was enjoying this. She released an exaggerated sigh. "Poor Will. Competing," she cocked her head, "with a spy for the *Lord*."

"OK, knock it off."

"Anyway, I worship him, too, for going back there for us."

"No kidding. Hope he hurries! I'm f-f-f-f-freezing." Remembering the long line at the *Garderobe* made me shiver even more. "Hey, did you have anything incriminating in your jacket pockets?"

"Like what?"

"I don't know. Phone numbers, addresses—Top Secret documents?" I grinned. "Seriously—what would they want from us?"

"A pack of western cigarettes? All he'll find is nasty East German gum." Amy grabbed my arm and pointed. Michael had emerged from the cloud, holding our jackets aloft in triumph.

I zipped up tight and on an impulse, leaned over to hug Michael, my cheek brushing against his golden mane. "Thank you, thank you!"

"My pleasure," Michael replied, beaming, maybe even blushing a bit.

"Good grief," Amy grunted. Her zipper had caught halfway.

Michael and I waited, watching her struggle. Next to me, his breath came in quick puffs. He had his sleeves pulled down over his hands—he looked cold. Had he planned badly or did he not own a winter jacket? If he were poor, would that make him *more* likely to become a spy? Or maybe he was poor because he refused to cooperate with the State—so definitely *not* a spy? And maybe he wasn't poor at all because there weren't any poor people over here—theoretically; of course that was ridiculous. Most likely, I decided, he was just a typical guy. Mom was forever haranguing Jack about going out in the wrong clothes.

"Got it." Amy looked up with a sheepish grin as she slid the zipper to her chin and released her hair from where it was trapped beneath her hood. "So! What's the plan?" she asked, both of them looking to me. They looked celestial in the lamplight, both of them. I felt like the lone mortal on Mount Olympus.

"I must meet my sister at Alexanderplatz. Maybe—you can walk with me? She would be happy to meet you," Michael suggested.

It would be fully dark soon. We needed to get back, especially after our encounter with Rocky and Bullwinkle the night before. On the other hand, we couldn't just walk away now and never see this guy again after what he'd done for us.

Amy had no qualms. "Sure! We have time. Right, Kate?"

Amy and Michael started off while I held back, needing to think. But about what, I wasn't sure. Mid-stride Amy turned around and whispered, "You want to, right?" I nodded and she gave me a conspiratorial wink, always looking out for me when it came to guys. I chuckled to myself. Was it her goal in life to get me *laid*? For a fleeting second, I wondered if losing my virginity in East Berlin would even count back in the West—as if this was a parallel dimension, and when I went back, no time would have gone by.

27

We passed a poster on a column shouting at us: "*Aufmerksam! Rucksichtsvol! Diszipliniert! Ich Bin Dabei!*"—Attentive! Considerate! Disciplined! I am with you! These propaganda posters always seemed to be shouting. The Russian anti-U.S. posters—they'd shouted, too. Jack had bought some from Moscow as souvenirs—one with the Statue of Liberty, her head dangling sideways, opening from a hinge in her neck from which Ku Klux Klanners like a stream of ghosts—each with a torch aloft, just like Lady Liberty's—flew. Another was a painting that at first glance appeared to be an American flag, but, close up, the red stripes were bloody trails, coming from American fighter jets. *Americans out of Vietnam!*, it read, in Russian. So far, the East German ones seemed more direct, less clever, like a younger brother trying too hard to impress an older.

Were we really about to meet Michael's sister? What if—when he ran back to the museum—he'd found a phone and called someone higher up who would *pose* as a sister? Or, was it more likely that we were the first Americans he'd ever met, and he just wanted to practice his English—and he actually had a sister? I guessed him to be our age, maybe a little older.

Amy was chatting too loudly, typical of people who aren't used to talking to foreigners—as if Michael were deaf, not just German—explaining that her father worked at the American Embassy. Course, if Michael was Stasi, he already knew that. But when I caught up with them and Michael turned to smile at me—with such a genuine, kind smile—it was harder and harder to perpetuate the Stasi informant notion.

The avenue opened onto Alexanderplatz, and Michael slowed and squinted, scanning the dark-clothed individuals crisscrossing the open square, heads bowed against the chilly wind. For a big city on a weekend, it seemed empty. I tried to pinpoint the difference between it and a similar square in the West. There was an underlying tension here, a foreboding feeling, like everyone knew they were being watched. Or was I making that up?

Michael returned the wave of a woman standing beneath what looked like a giant, one-legged robot, and we headed towards her. She looked a little older than Michael, hair a bit darker—butterscotch to his lemon—but doubtlessly related. Her shapeless black coat hung loosely from her; a navy blue scarf was knotted '50s style beneath her chin. (The only women wearing scarves these days in the West were GI wives covering up curlers while shopping at the PX.) She seemed to have just walked out of an old black and white photograph, like the ones of the Wall going up in 1961, the year I was born. If Michael was around our age, he wouldn't remember that, but his sister might, I thought, as she leaned in to give him a peck on his cheek. As he introduced us, she tilted her head to catch our names. Hers was Anika.

"I am happy to meet you," she said, in comfortable English. Her eyes were her brother's, large, round, the same startling shade of indigo, but deeper set, imparting a more intense expression. Her hand was thin and cold when I shook it. "You are American," she said, not a question; anyway, Michael had just told her we were. She held my hand a moment longer than necessary and I thought I felt it tremble. Her smile was genuine, gracious, almost fragile. The last thing they are is spies, I concluded, once and for all.

Amy's voice echoed across the square, explaining again how she lived in the East but went to school in the West. She may as well have been belting out the Star-Spangled Banner, I thought, looking around to see who might be listening, mentally imploring her to hush. I wandered off a few paces to examine the bizarre structure we were standing beneath, a cement cylinder crowned with a spinning model of the galaxy; the golden numbers, I realized, rotated to align with local times in cities listed beneath and above the numbers. I walked around it, reading the place names: Accra, Amsterdam, Rome.... Istanbul, Honolulu, Edmonton, the Galapagos, Kuwait, Cairo.... A world clock. The perversity of it hit me. Was it someone's idea of a taunt?—advertising the time in cities inaccessible to the very population wandering past? Michael appeared beside me, pointing to a city on the clock. New York. "I am sorry, but you can't get there from here." I stared at him, confused, until a guilty grin spread across his face. Oh, God, it occurred to me—he was making fun of it. I coughed out a strained chuckle.

As Michael and I wandered back, I prodded Amy, "Hey, shouldn't we go? Your father's probably wondering where we are."

Amy rolled her eyes, "I doubt it. But, yeah, guess we should."

Michael asked if we'd like to meet there the next day for coffee, under the *Weltzeituhr,* the world clock, at one o'clock. We agreed. I figured I could make my way to Checkpoint Charlie from there, and then grab the U-Bahn to get home once on the other side. As we headed off toward the S-Bahn, I glanced over my shoulder and caught Michael doing the same. He smiled and waved. I was happy we had a plan to meet the next day.

28

Even after they got home, Michael was still talking about meeting the two American girls. Anika couldn't remember when she'd last seen him so animated, gesticulating and acting out, describing in vivid detail the scene he'd come upon in the Pergamon. His indignation at the way the guards had treated the girls seemed almost personal, as if he himself had been slapped, as if seeing things through the eyes of outsiders had given him a new perspective, woken a dormant outrage. Anika felt the edges of a familiar worry begin to creep into her psyche.

"It's one thing," Michael continued, as they hung their coats on hooks inside the kitchen door, "for us to endure this rigid system, to live this lie that it is all for the greater good. But when the rest of the world is allowed to see how controlled—how pathetic—we as individuals must be, when foreigners are treated like us—?" He slapped his hands to his face, drawing them back through his hair. "I—I don't know. It was mortifying." Michael plopped into a chair at the table, finally spent.

"Michael," Anika began, choosing her words carefully, "you know how dangerous this line of thinking can be. We are helpless against the system. If we fight it more than we already do, if we make waves, we will lose. We must find peace within ourselves, you know this. You know we are in a particularly vulnerable place—you know." She did not need to mention their father in prison, or their brother—what his own outrage had wrought. She left the rest unsaid, staring in despair at her sweet brother coming alive.

"I know. Of course, I know. But—there is something else, something else that I felt today." Michael looked into her eyes and smiled. "Their friendship—how they talked and laughed—all without worry, without fear of watching what they said. It was—refreshing. Kate—the cute, the little one?—she is very bright. There is a lot going on in that little head of hers. I wanted to hear it, all of it. I felt a—a connection to her, Anika. And Amy, she has such a guileless sense of herself—and—such beauty! It was their closeness, the honesty. I don't know. I can't describe it."

Anika pulled out a chair next to him and sat, taking his hands in hers. Their isolation felt unbearable, desolate. He was young, so attractive. He should be meeting girls, having dates, but instead, they lived apart, paranoid, with an inherent fear of others—and others wanted nothing to do with them. The *Junge Gemeinde* group, a community of like-minded young people they met with, was meant to be enriching, but even there, she'd observed how he kept to himself, guarded his privacy. Maybe these American girls could help loosen him up, just a bit, rekindle in him the value of—the need for—human connection. But was that wise—or dangerous? Where would it lead?

"Meet them tomorrow, Michael, and have fun—and it will be wonderful practice for your English. I won't go. It is my day off and I want to rest. But, please, please, do not get any ideas—do not," she gazed into his face, searching for the right words, "expect them to free you. We are coping and must continue to bide our time, toe the line. For now. Papa's life requires it."

"Don't worry," Michael insisted. "I'm not Stefan." He sat back, a shadow crossing his face momentarily until he seemed to shake off a memory, allowing a broad smile to brighten his countenance. "But I might try to persuade Kate to marry me and stay in the East forever. What could possibly stop her?"

They both laughed.

29

The clunky, old streetcar rumbled to a stop and we climbed aboard, fishing in our pockets for the fare. The dim light and wooden interior felt cozy after the cold but I sensed gazes turning our way, to stare at *the girls from over there*. The conductor, hunched over a counter behind the driver, flicked our weightless East Marks into a hole as the car jolted forward.

It was practically empty. A middle-aged couple was staring right at us, no shame. There was a girl about our age wearing a scarf like Anika's, a book in her hands— but she, too, was watching us; and an old lady with a worn, leather pocketbook balanced on her skinny lap. Her eyes locked onto mine, a grimace in her smile—or smile in her grimace? I couldn't decide which. Amy pulled me toward a seat near the front and I sank down onto the smoothly worn bench next to her, wondering about the old woman's history. It brought a pang of longing for Will as I calculated: say she was 80, she'd have been our age in 1914. Before the *first* world war. I glanced back and she smiled again.

"What are you contemplating, Plato?" Amy asked with a nudge.

"Nothing," I sighed, then turned to her. "Michael and Anika—a lot going on there, huh? For one thing, I'm not at all sure Anika liked that we were there. Know what I mean? She seemed nervous—scared, somehow. Did you get that sense?" Amy shrugged. "That's why I thought we should leave. This way, we give her an out, in case she doesn't want to come tomorrow—and I bet she doesn't. But—what would that tell us? I mean, if she *doesn't* come, does that make it *more* likely they're spies? Or, if she *does* come, it tells us...well, nothing. I guess. Never mind." I rubbed my palms across my face.

Amy laughed. "Listen to you. Good grief! You don't really think they're spies, do you? Like this was all some kind of set up? Really?" Amy's voice rose with that assured boldness that stood out over here. It made me self-conscious.

I shushed her, my fingers to my lips, and spoke quietly into her ear, wondering if the old lady thought us rude or crass, the sting on my cheek burning again with the memory of our earlier shame. "Well, the security guys at the Mission told us they think up to a *third* of the population over here works as informants for the Stasi. That's one in three!" I paused to let that sink in. "So, we have to be suspicious. Think about it—why was Michael at the museum by himself? Not that it's a crime to go to a museum by yourself, I guess. But isn't it a little weird—for a teenage guy?"

The tram bumped over the old tracks. "A rainy Sunday—what *else* is there to do over here?" Amy insisted. She was right. We had no idea what was normal here. "He seems like a typical guy. After all, we are exotic, foreign chicks—magnets to any guy. He no doubt mistook us for famous models. Can't blame him."

"True. One famous covergirl, anyway," I pointed at her, "and her frumpy side-kick." I pointed at myself. "Probably thought I was your personal attendant."

"Katie! Hush! You really don't realize how adorable you are, do you? It's *nuts*." She shouldered me so hard, I almost fell into the aisle. "When we're together, I feel like the Jolly Green Giant next to cute, dainty Tinker Bell."

"*Really?* Well, I feel like a scrawny, shaggy stray next to a pedigree show-dog."

"Oh, man, it's a good thing you're so teeny because—with your personality—any bigger would be totally unmanageable."

"OK, OK, knock off all the 'beautiful on the inside' compliments. I know my place. I'm cool with it."

Amy slapped her forehead and laughed, leaning back against the window to face me. "Hang on, Katie," she said, leaning over. "You *do* have red marks! Look, two fingers, right here and here. God. You're so lucky I intervened before that loon knocked you flat."

"Yeah, I should have just let you clock her." I rolled my eyes.

"*Clock* her? Katie-honey—for your outdated information—*no* one says that nowadays. But yeah, I was dying to *sock* her."

"Man. *Then* where might we be now—instead of heading home to dinner, with a cute date for tomorrow?"

Amy laughed. "But really. You as a tour guide? Oh, man, I was *dying*." She attempted to imitate me but her southern accent was so bad, we collapsed into giggles all over again, bumping heads, which resulted in another paroxysm of all-consuming hysterics and gasping for breath.

So when the bony hand clutched the back of the seat in front of me, it took me a moment to ride the wave of laughter before I could comprehend: it belonged to the old lady. She was swaying and quaking with the effort it took to maintain her balance against the lurching streetcar. And then, she leaned over—so close, I could smell cheap face powder, could see the micro-movements of her bulging irises, darting back and forth in their veined, yellow plasma beds. I shrank away, bracing for her reproach, another slap, more shame.

She spoke, her voice thin and tinny, like crinkling aluminum foil. there was only a vague tinge of a German accent. "Watching you fills me with memories of when I was your age. Before the wars, before the Wall." Her face was lined with a map of her life, the years she'd witnessed, all she'd endured. Moisture gathered in the bottom of her eyes. "You have reminded me of wonder." She smiled. "Keep laughing. For us, all of us."

Then, her skeletal hand reached for the rope over the window, her tiny purse dangling from her thin wrist. She tugged on the rope, signaling a stop. We bumped and rumbled together a moment longer, until the brakes squeaked, the tram slowed, stopped with a final lurch, and the old lady shuffled away, the driver patiently waiting for her to descend, down the few steps, that same hand white-knuckling the railing. At the bottom, she moved off, alone, into the night.

30

Amy, mid-yammering about how much she hated winter, stopped talking. I followed her gaze. Michael was already there, leaning against the metal pillar, his hair luminous, even within the shade of the *Weltzeituhr*. He was staring off into space, one leg crossed over the other, hands plunged into his pockets.

"Oh my god! He came." It wasn't so much that I was surprised he'd come, as amazed he existed at all. Everything about yesterday felt surreal. "No Anika," I noted. "Told you."

Michael lit up when he saw us and kissed our cold cheeks. There was a moment when our eyes met that I felt myself drawn into him, as though pushed by an insistent, invisible force. For a moment, it felt as if our bodies were touching—a feeling more than physical, almost *spiritual,* our energetic fields coalescing with a metaphysical hum. The feeling passed as quickly as it had come. I looked away, my face blushing hot. Who *was* this guy?

"Hope you haven't been waiting long?" I muttered, for something to say. He was rubbing his palms together, already cold, and I knew he had. He was wearing the same jacket as yesterday, hardly sufficient.

"*Nein, nein,*" Michael protested, "Coffee?" he asked, brightly.

"Anything hot!" Amy agreed, taking one of his proffered arms while I took the other. He led us in the direction of the Museum Island, explaining that Anika sent her greetings and apologies. She was tired—but she'd laughed, he recounted, when he told her the story of the nasty guard who had brought us together.

Above us, the sun peeked out between clouds and I blinked up to warm my face. The city's trademark television transmission tower—the *Fernsehturm*—a giant needle piercing a silver golf ball at its top, loomed over us. The West called it 'The Pope's Revenge' because when the sun reflected off the ball, the shape of the cross emerged—and there was nothing the anti-religious Communists could do about it. Sure enough: a distinct cross was shining down over East Berlin right now.

Michael leaned over. "*Die Rache des Papstes,*" he whispered, eyeing me to see if I'd understood. Had he read my mind? I laughed, surprised. They called it that here, too.

Just past Alexanderplatz, we wandered down a side street to stairs to a below-ground entrance. There was no sign above, just a crudely painted *Café am Alexanderplatz* on a frosted glass door. Michael held it open as we passed through, expecting the typical cozy cafe bustle; instead, harsh neon lights buzzed over an odd stillness, the air heavy with stale cigarette smoke. The floor was unpainted cement, the walls lined with worn, Formica-topped tables with metal folding chairs. It reminded me of a church basement—where tomorrow, the room might be rearranged, chairs stacked in a corner for a square dance, or arranged in a circle for an AA meeting. There were no other customers. Michael seemed to think nothing of it. Amy passed me a dubious look.

At the end of one table, plucked straight from an old Route 66 roadside diner and as incongruous as a tulip in a desert, sat an honest-to-goodness jukebox. Amy saw it the moment I did. "Check *this* out!" she exclaimed, plunking down beside it. "Think it works?" I grabbed the chair next to hers, wondering at its provenance.

Michael, smiling at her enthusiasm, settled across from us. "Yes, it works," he said. "It is why I come here."

"Some serious Golden Oldies," Amy murmured, already flipping through while digging into her pocket for change. She dropped an East Mark into the slot. A whir, a buzz, and a click later, Pete Seeger flooded the air, transforming the atmosphere, bolstering us, a glimmer of the West bursting through—as though through a crack in the Wall. *"If I had a hammer...."* I wondered if Pete's workingman lyrics appealed to the communists' glorification of the proletariat, allowing his songs to pass the anti-western censors.

In the back, a door swung open. A hefty waitress shuffled to our table, slapped a menu down, then stood and stared, eyeing us like trespassers, tapping her pen against a wad of paper, her cheeks puffing with impatience. With lowered eyes, I took in her grimy apron stretched across a black skirt in a losing battle to grow with her, her thick, gray stockings sagging at her knees, feet jammed into plastic slippers flattened by relentless time and weight.

With a shiver, I remembered the scary babushka in our apartment building in Moscow, the one who guarded the attic and shouted insults in Russian, bombarding us Western kids with peanut shells whenever we dared each other to climb the last flight of stairs for a stealthy peek at her. One day, the door had been open, only the babushka's wide derrière visible as she leaned inside. And, behind her, we could see men with headphones, giant tape recorders in front of them, listening to our lives in the apartments below.

Amy and I glanced at the menu, slightly peckish after only toast that morning. The waitress smacked her lips announcing, *"Hier gibt's nur Suppe,"* her *gibt's* a *yip's* in the East Berlin dialect.

I blinked, confused. Why, then, had she bothered giving us a menu? "So, it's soup—or no soup," I told Amy. *"Nein, danke,"* I said, deciding for both of us.

Michael held up his thumb, index, and middle finger, indicating three. *"Drei Kaffee,"* he ordered, *"bitte."*

The waitress scribbled on her pad, eyeballs darting up and down beneath tightly knit eyebrows. Three coffees, I thought—what on earth was she writing? The song ended, a heavy silence descended, severing us from the rest of the world once again. And she was still scrawling. I covered my mouth to stifle a giggle, feeling Amy already trembling next to me. Finally, jamming pen and pad into her apron pocket, the waitress shuffled away, back to where she'd come from. The moment the door swung shut behind her, we lost it. Michael grinned at our laughter, thankfully not offended by it.

"Maybe we stink!" Amy joked, smelling her pits.

Michael's gaze elsewhere, turned back, confused. "What? We sting?" he asked. "*Wie eine Biene*?" He turned to me for clarification.

Now I was confused. "Like a bee?" It took me a moment. "Oh, no, not *sting*—"

"*Stink*," Amy repeated, emphasizing the k, again, mockingly sniffing her armpit, then pinching her nose.

I giggled at Michael's focus—so intense. I could relate—knew the feeling of how your mind scrambled to interpret a foreign language.

Amy was flapping her hand at an imaginary stench. "*Stiiink?*"

Michael nodded. "Ja, ja, OK, *stinken*, nicht *stechen*!"

We were all laughing when the waitress whipped the door open like an outlaw entering a saloon and lumbered over carrying a small tray. One by one, she slammed cups onto the table, coffee sloshing into saucers, her eyes boring into us, as if our cheer was improper, which, of course, only made everything funnier. It was just like at the museum, but this time, Michael made it all right.

"Maybe we make her work too hard," Michael said, after she disappeared, wiping his eyes from laughing. "So! How do you know each other? From America? Or here?"

"We met here—well, in *West* Berlin—at school." Amy replied, wrapping her hands around her warm cup.

"Ah, it is a school for Americans?"

We nodded. He turned to me. "Your father is also diplomat?"

"He is a diplomat, yes, at the U.S. Mission in the West—the Mission in the American Sector?" I grabbed my cup and sipped, unsure what he knew or what to say about a place off-limits to him. The coffee hit my tongue with a bitter tanginess unlike any coffee I'd ever tasted. My throat shut on instinct, afraid to let the liquid pass. It sat in a hot pool on my tongue, my lips pressed tight, eyes watering and darting, desperate for a place to spit. Poison. Were we being poisoned?

Amy was lifting her cup. I shook my head with vigor and pointed, but Amy, her eyebrows knit, only stared at me over the rim of her cup. I had to warn her! I tried, "Mm-mm!" swallowing in the process, the poison snaking down my throat. "Amy, no!"

Black liquid was already spurting from Amy's lips, right back into the cup. "*Ech*. That is *disgusting!*"

With zero deference to cultural sensitivity, Amy had saved herself from certain death. Meanwhile, the poison was surging through my body. I waited for pain, for death, my eyes scanning life for the last time, taking in Michael's beauty, his puzzled expression. Could he have been in on it? Had we been lured here to die? Even on the threshold of death, I refused to believe it. The waitress. Of course!

Amy was leaning over the table, coffee dripping from her chin. As Michael handed her his cloth handkerchief, he slapped his forehead. "Ach, *klar!* I should have warned you," he said. "This is *Mischkaffee*. Erich Honecker's new drink." His fingers combing his flaxen locks, he rushed to explain. "Coffee is—how do you say—in crisis? So, now we must drink this, a mix—*Chicoree, Rüben und Roggen*—I don't know how—the English?" He looked to me for help.

I was trying to process all of it. Not a murder plot; instead, the communist party leader *made* them drink this? I wasn't sure which notion was more absurd.

"We call it 'Instant Erich,'" he chuckled. "Not so tasty, but you get used to it." He raised his cup and took a hearty gulp, swallowing with a sympathetic grimace.

I raised my cup, willing to give it another try, to be polite. If Michael had to drink it, so could I. But one whiff of the noxious scent and I gave up, dropping the cup back to the saucer. "What is in it? *Roggen?*—that's rye, I think—and chicory, OK, but—what else?"

"*Rüben*: it is dark—like blood—a vegetable—in *borscht?*"

"Beets!?" My least favorite vegetable. I pushed my cup away, abandoning any hope of becoming a diplomat. No wonder it had made me gag.

Amy pushed hers away, too. "Beets in coffee? Who even *thinks* of that? For a second, I thought you were poisoning us!"

"God, Amy!" I punched her playfully. Silly girl.

Amy scrounged for change. I emptied my pockets into her palm and she poked another East Mark through the slot. This time, it was Loretta Lynn whose voice drifted over from home. Amy and I sang along, exaggerating the country twang. "*...cause you ain't woman enough to take my man...*" Michael grinned, tapping his fingers on the table.

Before the song even finished, Amy was flipping through for another, which suited me—the less we had to endure the silences between, the better. I turned to Michael. "How old are you, Michael? Are you in school?"

"I am eighteen years old. No, after I finished my polytechnic, I studied with my father. It is not usual. My family—" Michael stopped mid-sentence, took a deep breath. "We are not popular, you might say, with the State," he shrugged. "Now, I work as salesman, at a kiosk. It is an easy job." He snickered. "I sell lies and propaganda." That raw, East German humor, again.

"What did your father teach you?"

"*Keramiker?*" He mimed the outlines of a vase with his hands.

"Ceramics." I was impressed and wanted to know more, but his thoughts seemed to have drifted far away.

"Have you heard about the *Junge Gemeinde*?" He'd switched gears.

We shook our heads. "'Young community'?" I asked, uncertain.

"*Ja, genau.* It is a group, based on *evangelische* values." We looked blank so he tried a different tack. "You know the *FDJ*?" He said the letters in German: eff-day-yot.

I nodded—Amy looked at me, surprised. "It's the *Freie Deutsche Jugend.*" I explained to her. "It's their Communist Youth organization, like their version of scouts."

Michael nodded. "I refused to join. My family believes it is a—" He scrounged for the right word, glancing toward the kitchen door. "*Ja*, a *tool*. For the State. You understand? This is how they…" he grappled again.

"Brainwash people?" I offered.

"*Ja, ja, genau, Gehirnwäsche.* But, *die Junge Gemeinde*—we talk about philosophy, religious ideas, listen to music—sometimes even Western music. So," he paused, smiling, "I would be happy if you come to a meeting. It might be interesting for you."

I wasn't sure what to say. My mind said *no way*, but, those huge, pleading eyes.… "Sure, we'd love to!" How bad could it be?

"Ach, wonderful! So. I will expect you. Our next meeting is November, always the first Saturday. May I telephone you?"

"Can you?" I wondered how hard it was for him to call the West.

"The kiosk has a telephone. My working companion is *teilnahmsvoll.*"

I didn't know why it mattered that his co-worker was sympathetic. "Amy, why don't you give him your number, since you live over here?"

"That would be easier," Michael agreed.

I rummaged in my jacket pocket until I found a pen and paper. But Amy brushed them away. "I don't know it," she muttered, flipping through songs. I couldn't tell if she was afraid to give it, annoyed that I'd suggested it, or really just into the jukebox.

Michael shifted awkwardly. Scribbling my own number on the scrap of paper, I pushed it across the table. He smiled, nodded thanks, and folded it into his pocket. Amy missed the whole transaction. We'd have to talk about this later. It couldn't be bad for *us*, I decided; if anything, it was dangerous for Michael.

"So—your father—he's a ceramicist?" I asked, digging into my pockets and dumping all the change I had into into Amy's begging palm.

"He is, but," he lowered his voice, leaning in with a heavy sigh, "he is in prison."

Prison? All I could do was stare back at him.

"Why?" Amy, tuning in all of a sudden with a fistful of coins, asked for me.

Michael paused, eyeing us before sitting back, shaking his head. "For *Gedanken*—thoughts—against the State. A *Regimekritiker*." He slumped, his focus beyond us while his hand tapped a spoon against his saucer. When he looked back, he seemed to be begging one of us to say something.

One thing was clear, I decided, once and for all: Michael was as fond of his government as I was of beets. I decided to change the topic. "And Anika? Where does she work?"

Michael seemed relieved: a question he could handle. "She has a job in a polyclinic. Office work. She is lucky to have this job." Something about his tone—was it edged in sarcasm? I had the distinct sense that there were multiple dimensions of complexity over here that we could not begin to comprehend.

"But doesn't the government promise everyone a job? 'Zero unemployment' and all that?" I was genuinely curious how he stood with this proclamation by his government.

Dad had explained it to me like this: "Imagine a heavy snowfall," he'd said, "—you could get a snowplow—and let *one* guy drive it, clean up the snow in a few minutes. *Or*, you could send a *thousand* people out with spoons, day after day, never really getting the job done, but, well, they'd all be *employed*."

Michael said nothing. He stirred his cold coffee, watching the eddy formed when he removed the spoon.

"Play something," I urged Amy who was just staring at him.

"How about *Fleetwood Mac*?" Michael asked. It came out Fleet-vut Mahk and took me a moment to comprehend.

"*Fleetwood Mac*?" It was one thing to be listening to golden oldies, but Michael knew *Fleetwood Mac*? That surprised me.

Amy rolled through the options. "Um…. Nope. No Fleetwood Mac."

"Of course not," Michael grinned. "It was my joke." I laughed, too, starting to catch onto this East German humor. "I listen to Western stations on the radio. At night, I get very good reception. I also listen to your Western propaganda on RIAS." Michael winked at me.

I wondered what he'd think if he knew that my dad happened to work at the Radio in the American Sector that was blasted across the GDR to deliver real world news, hoping to counter the false reports and propaganda. Tuning in over here was dangerous, but many did, secretly.

"Do you know the song *Dreams*? It is my favorite song from Fleet-vut Mahk." Michael leaned in, lowering his voice. "It is a song about freedom."

"Freedom?" I'd thought of it as a song about a couple breaking up. *Now, here you go again, you say, you want your freedom. Well who am I to keep you down?* The lyrics rolled through my mind. "Yeah, OK, I guess it is about freedom."

"There is freedom in a society, but also freedom we give to each other." Michael became serious, his voice soft and steady. "A society that does not allow you to be yourself—it is like—" he mimed a noose tightening around his neck. "But, we can also do this to each other, and this can kill our dreams." His eyes settled on mine. "When dreams die, I think we cannot love—or live." I swallowed, nodding at his earnestness. "*Na, ja,*" Michael continued, leaning back with a sigh, "I also like very much the *Crosby, Stills & Nash*, and the *Rolling Stones*. Do you know them?"

"Uh, *yeah!*" Amy blurted, like who didn't?—then checked her attitude. "I mean, well, they're very big in the West." She listed the

CSN songs we'd been practicing on the guitar. Michael knew them all.

When Johnny Cash began to sing, Michael drummed his fingers on the table, pressing his ear to the speaker to catch the lyrics. I wondered how we'd come upon such an unusual guy. He'd clearly had to forge his own path over here—where the pressure to do the opposite was so great.

Catching a whiff of Honecker's nasty, patriotic drink, I shoved the cups to the end of the table, even this move feeling like an act of rebellion. Until now, my notion of life in the East had been simplified into two categories: people trying to escape, or those ratting on those trying to escape. But the reality was that people just got on with life like anywhere else, adapting to the limitations, making choices day by day. Clearly, Michael's family had chosen a life in defiance of the repressive system, to live true to themselves—and they'd suffered for it. His father—in prison for his thoughts! Listening to Western music, attending *Junge Gemeinde* meetings, even hanging out with the likes of us—Michael did it, despite the fact that it could make his life more difficult, lead to trouble. Would I be that brave?

The three of us turned as the door to the cafe opened with a blast of cold air. Two men, each in long, black coats slammed the door behind them. At that moment, the song ended, and the silence froze us in a momentary, icy tableau. Of all the empty tables, the men chose the one next to ours, scraping chairs across the cement floor as they sat. One who had a tight, bald head and scarred cheek let his legs sprawl into the aisle between our tables. He crossed his arms, a grin spreading across his face as he stared at Michael. The other, with a crew cut and thick, black glasses, slapped his palms against the table, mumbling something about the waitress, glancing impatiently toward the kitchen door.

Michael's eyes were blinking excessively, as though churning over options in his mind, any trace of good humor drained from his face. Amy and I stayed quiet, braced to take our cue from Michael. My gut was screaming: Get Out.

The waitress butted through the swinging door, holding aloft a tray steaming with soup. Giggling like a coquettish schoolgirl, she shifted deeply, hip to hip, as she gently placed a steaming bowl in front of each man.

"*Wie viel für den Kaffee?*" Michael called out as she turned back toward the kitchen. But she just plowed on, ignoring him, causing the men to chortle like playground bullies. Michael leaned back, reaching into his pockets. Amy and I quickly dug out wadded East Mark bills and tossed them onto the table. Michael dropped down some coins, handing our cash back. "It is too much," he mumbled, motioning for us to go. We grabbed our jackets and bags and climbed over the legs blocking the aisle. But as Michael passed, the bald guy reached up to stop him.

"Let's go, Amy," I urged, pushing her toward the door. We ran out and up the outside steps. Not a moment later, Michael surfaced, looking shaken.

"Who were those guys?" Amy asked, eyeing first Michael and then me—as if I knew anything.

Michael sank his hands into his pockets and shrugged, shifting anxiously from foot to foot. "They are colleagues of…a relative…a man who—*ach*, we do not like him. But don't worry. It is no problem."

"What did he say to you?" I asked, sensing danger, a little surprised by my urge to protect Michael.

"He—he asked after my sister," he said, eyeing his watch. It was evident he needed to go.

I held out my hand. "Hope we see you again." His sparkle had been replaced by a resignation so oppressive, it frightened me.

"I hope so, too, yes." He took my hand, then pulled me in for a gentle kiss on each cheek and did the same to Amy. My face warmed as he strode away, head down, hands jammed in his pockets.

"Kate—your tram!" Amy cried. She hugged, then pushed me toward the waiting streetcar. Pulling my shoulder strap over my head, I bolted. Behind me, Amy was shouting, "Call the second you get home!"

I grabbed a seat near the front and peered out. Amy was waving and flapping her arms, a version of the crazy bug dance we'd done on the floor of her kitchen. I waved back, a lump forming in my throat, even though I'd see her at school the very next day.

At the stop nearest Checkpoint Charlie, I jumped off, quelling my desire to run. Max's directions were in my pocket—drawn on a scrap of paper that morning—a comfort, better than asking an East Berliner: "Excuse me, which way to the exit?"—but I hoped not to have to pull them out. Afraid to appear hesitant or anything but entitled to leave, I marched straight into the checkpoint, thoughts swirling through my head, my hand clutching my diplomatic passport. I had nothing to worry about, I told myself. But another voice asked, why? Why should it be so easy for me?

By the time I entered the shack, dusk had fallen. A kerosene heater glowed and hissed in a corner. A guard stood to switch on lights, as though I was the first customer of the evening. Another guard rose from his stool and took my passport, asking if I'd had a good time. Had I broken any boy's heart while there? Both guards chuckled.

"*Vielleicht,*" maybe, I said, warily, unsure whether or not I was supposed to think it all funny. The guard winked at me as he stamped my passport, said he didn't doubt that I'd broken at least one heart.

And then I walked right through the Wall. In the West, the American Military Police ignored me. I guessed there was nothing to indicate I wasn't just another West German back from a day's visit with relatives on the other side. Walking to the U-Bahn, the streetlights seemed brighter, life bustling with familiar sounds at the right decibels; my heart calmed while my pulse quickened to sync with the faster beat of the free world. Everything made sense again.

Mom was in the kitchen, humming to a song on the radio. Before I even said hello, I tossed my bag on the stairs and dialed Amy's number, the familiar breathing in the background when she picked up.

"Hey! You home?"

"Yep. Over two hours, but I made it! You OK? Max home?"

"Soon."

"OK. School tomorrow?"

"Yep. Monday. Ugh."

"Yeah." Neither one of us wanted to sign off just yet, but talking on the phone wasn't satisfying either, considering.

"Well, OK, then. Hey, it's the last week of your running job!" It was how Amy referred to cross country practices.

"Yep."

"Finally." She paused. "Hey, Kate. Glad you came over."

"Me, too." So much had transpired, I couldn't believe it had been only two days.

"Bye, and—*Auf wiedersehen, Helmut!*"

"See you tomorrow, Amy. *Tschüß, Heinrich!*"

I waited for the dial tone, then began to dial Will's number to tell him about the weekend, as promised. But halfway, I stopped, replaced the receiver, and went to greet Mom in the kitchen.

31

Anika passed the heavy bag with the potatoes to Michael, bracing against the wind. When they turned the corner toward home, tiny pinpricks of icy drizzle pierced their faces.

"What should I say if someone asks me?" Michael's head was low as he leaned into a gust, his voice gentle but serious. "It is beginning to show, Anika."

Had Anika felt less weary, she might have raged. Instead, sarcasm took over. "Don't worry, dear. It is arranged, down to the very sentence I must repeat: 'I am a surrogate as a favor for a relative. It is a business arrangement. I am having a baby purely for the money—a greedy woman with no moral qualms.' Oh, and I must also add, 'The baby is to be raised and educated in a good family with strong, State values.'"

"Who would believe that coming from us? You are no puppet."

Anika winced, the rise to self-loathing swift these days. "He doesn't care—don't you understand—if people don't believe me. Anyway, what am I—if not a puppet—Michael?"

"What are you!?" Michael hissed with a rare fury. "A victim, trapped!"

Anika wanted to be neither a puppet nor a victim. Nor did she want Michael to become bitter. She knew he wanted her to let him fight this man, do something, anything; knew he felt inadequate, pathetic. But he had to know as well as she did that it was pointless. She began to tremble. They were both trapped. What had they become? It was too much. She clutched her belly, bent over. Michael dropped the potatoes and caught her. He held her tight saying nothing, waiting, patient, as she quaked against him.

When her sobbing finally slowed, she looked up, her face flushed, eyes red. Her voice came out odd, controlled. "Michael, do you remember—how his wife stood next to him—that day at mother's graveside?" Anika pulled herself up, gaining strength. Michael stepped back, unsure what to make of this mood shift.

"Remember? The day we buried Mama. The two of them, side by side, under an umbrella? Vampires. The way he looked at me. That was the very moment he began to hone his fangs for my blood."

Michael pulled her behind a pillar plastered with propaganda posters."Shh, Anika. Anika, it will be all right, please." His eyes were round with fear, aware of their vulnerability, afraid of his sister's tone. Klein needed no justification to lock her up.

Anika seemed possessed, quoting Klein, mimicking his voice, his manipulative words. "You will put up no fuss—unless, of course, you and your brother truly want to share your father's experience." When she turned and walked away, Michael rushed to follow her. He grabbed the heavy bag of potatoes, swinging it fast, intending to drape it over a shoulder; instead, it rammed hard against her belly.

"Oh! Anika! I'm sorry." He dropped the bag, his hands on her shoulders. "Your baby! Are you all right?"

Anika stared up at him as though waking from a deep sleep, her hands cradling her bulge. "My baby." She murmured. "*My* baby. Michael. He can't have it."

Michael shook his head, confused. "Anika. What? You *know* you can't—you must—"

"What I know, Michael, is that I must find a home for my baby." She was nodding with certainty. "We will hide it, hide my child from that monster."

"Anika, think. We can't! It's too dangerous. Not just for the baby. What would he do to you? to us? Anika—think of Papa!" Michael was frantic.

"Once the baby is safe, I'll turn myself in, I'll admit that I know, only I, but I will never reveal where the baby is. They can lock me up, torture me—but I'll survive because I'll be at peace, knowing my baby is safe—from him." Anika was babbling, walking, her speed mounting with her determination. Michael trotted alongside, the potatoes ramming his knees with each step. Only after they entered their yard, did she stop, in front of the mound rising from the center—their father's kiln.

Michael implored her. "Anika, Anika, please. Be realistic—you are not making sense. You must give the baby to him. It's not your fault. It's just what has to be. There is no other choice." He grabbed her arms, his face contorted. "He will kill you. Do you hear me? Please, Anika, listen!" Out of desperation, he switched tactics. "The baby—whether you like it or not—is half his." He couldn't look at her. It was cruel—she knew he knew it. "Let him have it, Anika. Put an end to this. Please. It is the only way." His eyes brimmed with tears.

Anika's resolve dissipated. Her knees buckled, she dropped to the packed dirt and began to cry again. She wept for the helpless baby developing inside her, for the hideous life awaiting it; she cried for her mother, her father, for Stefan, for the way life used to be, for her shame, for the God who had abandoned them. She cried because they would never know comfort again.

32

Amy was munching on her sandwich, watching the scene across the table. Molly and Nadia were making fun of Rick, something he'd said in class, while Rick protested with loud indignation. They were all laughing. And here was Will, making his way through the cafeteria toward the table. Just another day at school, but somehow, everything felt different. I felt different.

"Hey, how was your weekend exploring the East?" Will pulled out the chair next to me, a hand on my shoulder. "Got a plan to tear down the Wall?"

Molly, Rick, and Nadia stopped talking and tuned in, expectant. The silence grew, felt like a balloon about to pop. I smiled at him, but no words formed in my mouth.

Amy dropped her sandwich. "Just guess. Guess who we met. In a hot tub." I breathed a sigh of relief and let her tell the story.

That whole week, I avoided Will. On Saturday, I ran my best time at our final, home tournament, making third place on the team, beating Tanya by a nose. Will met me at the finish and swung me around with a hug, but I pulled away to cheer for other team members crossing the line. Without a word, Will picked up on my distance and gave me space. No one had time to go out, with exams looming, homework and term papers piling up. Time to hunker down, I told myself, nothing more; but instinct told me to tuck my wings in close, to protect my confused heart. Things were not the same.

As usual, high school life carried on without a moment's thought to the world behind the Wall. But whenever I was alone: brushing my teeth, standing in the shower, in bed at night, walking to school, Michael invaded my thoughts. I heard his gentle, pensive voice, felt his shimmering, golden hair, saw his disarming, purple eyes. I thought of his German, how he articulated so I could easily follow. I thought how unfair it was that he would never visit here, that his world was so limited, and of the courage and resilience it took to live within those limitations. I thought, too, of Anika, how her cold, thin hand had trembled in mine.

Two weeks passed, and I'd still not spoken to Will alone. I told myself it was fine, that he and I were fine, that space between us was healthy, normal, part of getting to know one another. But niggling in my mind was an urgency, the sense that there was something important to contend with, before I could be with Will again.

Michael buzzed inside me, unshakeable, constant, that inexplicable force I'd felt beside him drawing me to him, even from afar. Reuniting with him became an obsession, as though normal life could not continue until I saw him again; yet the harder I tried to understand this compulsion, the less I understood it. There was no way to get in touch with Michael, anyway. So I never spoke about it, not even to Amy. I couldn't explain it, even to myself.

Wednesday, into the third week of not speaking to Will, Amy went off after school to the library to study with a girl from her history class before coming over later, so I began to walk home alone. As I cut across the field near Clayallee, I heard a distant, familiar voice calling my name. I froze where I stood, trying to stanch my panic. Will. I waited. But when he caught up to me, he said nothing. We started walking, side by side, as we had so many times before—

before the weekend in the East. This walk that I used to never want to end: now, it felt interminable, a heavy, awkward slog.

We had approached the end of the field before Will began to speak, his voice steady, no hint of anger, but insistent. "You owe me nothing, Kate. OK? Don't worry about anything."

I knew that wasn't true. But I couldn't think. Maybe, if I told him about the weekend, about all that had happened from the moment we got to Amy's house until after we said goodbye to Michael at the cafe, then, maybe, *he'd* figure it out—for me, too. And then, I was talking, about the evening in the park after curfew, about the incident at the museum, the old lady on the tram, about Michael, his family, how brave they are, how he listens to forbidden western music, likes to philosophize, think his own mind; I told Will about the *Mischkaffe,* about the scary men at the cafe. I only left out the part about Bowie in the hot tub because he'd already heard it, and Amy's story, which was not to be shared. And as I spoke, I kept thinking, now, now, he'll understand, he'll help me understand.

When I finally stopped talking, I looked up. Now he had the whole story. He would comprehend my turmoil, we would finally talk things out. On the corner by my house, we stopped to face each other. Above us, clouds coagulated, forming dark, ominous blobs. Will's head was high, eyes distant. He said nothing, just stood there, staring over my head. I swallowed hard.

Comprehension dawned in a flash: He was hurt—I had hurt him. My body twitched with the urge to dash, my throat knotting, a vise tightening in my chest. This was Will, *my* Will. What was I putting him through? Why? What did I expect from him? I couldn't even explain it to myself. I bit my lip, looked up at the threatening sky. I missed Holland. I hated Berlin. A fat raindrop hit me between the eyes.

Will shifted his weight, letting out a weary sigh. "Honestly? I don't get it. That's your explanation for your sudden cold shoulder? OK—things are bad over there. It was hard to bear. I get that. The East is a stifling police state, its entire population *imprisoned*, forced to live a twisted lie about sacrificing themselves for a nebulous utopia. Yeah, we knew that, it sucks. I just can't see what *that* has to do with *us*. Am I supposed to be reading between the lines? I don't think that's my place. If there's more, you'll have to tell me."

I stared down. Polka-dot drops were decorating the sidewalk. The harder I thought, the more logic evaded me. The heavens opened, the dots bled together. My tears would be camouflaged at least. "You missed my point," I muttered, knowing I was on thin ground, since I knew I was incapable of explaining further.

"Did I?" His voice sounded unlike him, filled with a combination of fury and exasperation. I'd pushed him to this. "Maybe I'm incapable of comprehending, or just lack compassion—or, maybe you've decided you don't really want me to understand, don't care that I don't—or—OK, yeah, maybe none of this is the point. Then— what *is*, Kate?" He turned skyward, blinking into the rain that was now a deluge, swiping wet hair from his eyes.

I felt stiff, like the Tin Man in the rain. Even my jaw wouldn't move. The guilt rose in my throat and began to choke me. And then Will was turning and walking away, breaking into his easy lope. I stared after him, my books soaking in my arms until, numb with more than cold, I plodded toward our gate. When Amy walked into my room an hour later, I was still lying on the carpet, wet and shivering, staring up at the ugly light fixture on the ceiling that looked like a dangling boob.

"Good grief, what's with you?" She dropped her books on top of the bureau and sat on my bed, nudging me with her paisley-socked foot. "I saw Will run up to you." She tugged a blanket off the bed and tossed it over me. "Talk."

The warmth from the blanket soothed my vocal cords, sore from crying. "I told him pretty much everything that happened over there—the museum, meeting Michael, the cafe."

"And…he's jealous."

"No, he's not. He has no reason to be. That's not *it*."

Amy shifted down to the floor, peering over me to stare right into my eyes. "Oh, really? Seriously, Kate, it's time we talked about this. I fell in love with Michael as much as you did. He's a *god*. But it wasn't the same with you, no matter what you're telling yourself. Will senses it. The truth is, Katie-kins, you're only good at hiding your feelings from yourself."

I sat up. "Oh, come *on,* Amy!" It *wasn't* about Michael. Amy had been there. Didn't she get it? "I described it all to him—what it's like over there—and he was so—I don't know—belligerently *dismissive*..." I stopped, wondering if that was true, or if what Amy said had any merit. "I swear, I don't get it. But I do know that Will ended it. Totally. Finished. *Finito. Fertig.*" I filled my lungs to soften the blow. "Romance aborted. Never meant to be." I began to whimper, rubbing the butt of my hands into my eyes. Truth was, I'd sabotaged the relationship. But why?

"Listen to me. Whatever happens," Amy pressed, "Will is totally into you. Remember that. And don't be a *bitch*. Be kind. And, Kate? You need to do a deep dive, in there." She poked a finger toward my heart.

But the more I sought a way out of my funk, the more confused I became. I slept restlessly, woke tired and glum, dragged myself to school in dread of seeing anyone but Amy. We all sat together; the chill between Will and me was not lost on anyone but no one mentioned it. Amy talked more than usual, to make up for my silent brooding. Everything sounded superficial and trivial to me, not that I'd gotten past even the shallow end on my deep dive.

One day, Nadia and Molly sidled up to me in the hallway. "Kate, sweetie," Nadia said in her dripping-pity voice, wrapping her arms around me for a squeeze, "So, I was wondering—I mean, how sad for your relationship to end before it ever even *began!* Do you want *me* to talk to Will for you?" She was loving every second of this role.

I grit my teeth, wriggling out of her grasp. "No, Nadia. I don't. Thanks."

Molly pulled her away. "C'mon, Nadia. I think they can handle this themselves." She threw me a sympathetic eye roll and mouthed "sorry" as if her unruly puppy had leapt on me.

At the end of the month, Amy tried to talk me into going to a Halloween party at Becky's house. Becky, a senior, lived near Rick and her dad was Rick's dad's commanding officer. Normally, we'd have leapt at the opportunity, but I wasn't in the mood. "Halloween is a silly American holiday that I've never celebrated," I argued, knowing it was lame. "Why start now?"

"Cut it out. You know that's idiotic." Amy put on a long, flowing skirt. She tucked her hair beneath an emerald green, diaphanous scarf. She put on cheap bangles piled to her elbows, lined her eyes in black and added a mole on her chin. While I watched, hating myself, she transformed herself into an exotic, bewitching fortune teller. "You can still go, you know," she implored one last time. "Grab a sheet—as a toga or a ghost."

I cried all evening, wondering what I was hoping to gain, why everything seemed so inaccessible and bleak. Later, I heard voices outside and peered out from behind a curtain at the window at the top of the stairs. Amy was laughing, holding onto Rick's arm, coming through our gate. Dennis and Wolfie peeled off and were waving goodbye from the street. Amy looked up, saw me, and waved. But I ducked back, afraid Rick would see me, hiding like Boo Radley.

Amy stomped up the stairs and walked past me, heading straight to Jack's room. But at the door, she stopped and turned to face me. "Whatever's going on, Kate? Snap the hell out of it. It sucks. For all of us." She slammed the door shut behind her.

33

Ingo leaned out from the window of the kiosk and waved when he saw Michael approach. Not just a hand wave but an entire arm wave, his arm arcing overhead, torso along for the ride. His smile was as open and genuine as a child's, incongruous on a middle-aged man with a paunch.

Michael waved back, trying to match Ingo's indomitable enthusiasm. Since the day they began working together, Michael had made a study of every move, every word the guy said and not once did he suspect Ingo was a Stasi informant.

If anything, Michael felt he had to rein *Ingo* in. Like when Ingo told jokes—too loudly—jokes that could be interpreted as anti-state agitation, jokes that could get him arrested if overheard by the wrong guy—or the listener, if by chance the kiosk was bugged. It made Michael think he should wonder why Ingo thought *Michael* was safe to talk to. Was he goading him, trying to get him to open up—so that they he could report him for his nonconformity? You could never be too careful.

But Michael's gut feeling told him that Ingo was safe, on their side, that he had Ingo's credo pegged: Do your bit, ask for nothing, keep your head down, keep things simple. To Michael, Ingo was a man who had intentionally taken a job that was beneath him, where he could look a part without feeling it.

Ingo was manager of the kiosk and if Michael ever wanted to use the phone, he had to ask Ingo. And now, he wanted to call Kate. In the West. It would be monitored, but in theory, Ingo could cover for him, come up with some scenario to explain, an emergency, maybe. But Michael had to be wary, even more so after meeting Kate and Amy. He knew Klein could use anything against them, make things even worse for Anika. Klein. The sheer thought of him made Michael clench in fury.

"Good *morning*, Michael! A beautiful, autumn day!" The side door yawned open, revealing the broad figure of Ingo.

"It's *afternoon*, Ingo! That's why I'm here. I have the afternoon shift, remember?" Michael teased. The kerosene heater glowed from the corner near where Ingo stood, illuminating his shins with an eerie red. Michael hung his jacket on the hook behind the door while surveying the damage wrought by Ingo's bumbling presence. Relatively little. Must mean he'd had a slow day. "How's business?"

"Well, now that depends," Ingo instructed, grinning. "If you are a capitalist, you will think business is bad. On the other hand, as a true communist—what does it matter? I've had a luxurious morning, sitting here napping undisturbed for the past two hours. And now—the sun is out!" He leaned back against the wall and took out his pack of tobacco. Mid-roll, he eyed Michael with a coy look. "Know the one about Honecker on a sunny day?"

Michael braced himself. Another political joke. Should he laugh? Act disgusted? He busied himself with what little tidying he could find, hiding his grin, pretending not to pay attention. Ingo told a good joke.

"One sunny morning, our esteemed Chairman, Erich Honecker greets the day, 'Good morning, Mr. Sun!' and the sun replies immediately, 'Good morning, Mr. Chairman!' That afternoon, the sun, still out, Mr. Honecker peers out the window again. 'Good afternoon, Mr. Sun!' The sun responds, 'Good afternoon, Mr.

Chairman!' By evening, the sky is a glorious salmon pink, our sun, beginning to dip low on the horizon. Erich cries out, 'Good evening, Mr. Sun!' But this time, the sun does not reply. Erich tries again. Nothing. Mr. Honecker is upset. He leans far out of the window now and calls out once more, indignant. 'Why do you not return my greeting, Mr. Sun?' And all at once, the sun begins to laugh, the sky swirling in quivering, glorious color—and then, the sun says, 'Listen, man! I'm in the West now. You can *kiss my ass*!'" Ingo dissolved into hearty laughter, his paunch jiggling, his eyes tearing up. He looked up as if to remember the gods and feigned a serious tone. "Awful joke! So disrespectful. I don't even get it." Still chuckling, he donned his coat and hat, preparing to depart for the day.

Michael began to wring his hands. He had to call Kate. He was determined to see her again, couldn't get her out of his mind. She was quick, smart—she listened, seemed to connect with him. There was something about her, being with Kate had filled him with hope. Possibility. He couldn't explain it. And if he didn't call her, he'd never see her again. He had to risk it. The burning question flew from of his mouth. "Eh, Ingo, would it be possible to use the phone? To call the West, I mean. Just to—" He realized his mistake mid-sentence and bit his lip.

Ingo broke in with an air of nonchalance, "Oh, yeah—your sick, old auntie over there? You've told me all about her, remember? Sure, sure, call anytime. Hope she's feels better soon." He winked, snatched a newspaper and tucked it under his arm. With a finger to his lips, he waved, and then was gone.

34

I sat contentedly alone, humming to AFN songs on the radio, writing my English essay at the kitchen table. Mom and Dad were at a diplomatic reception. Amy had gone home after school for a change. I knew she was mad at me, but I pushed the thought from my mind and focused on my homework. When the German phone began to ring, I didn't want to answer it. Whoever it was could call back. Chances were, it wasn't for me anyway, as most friends called on the military phone. Except for Will.

The ringing stopped and I focused again on my essay told from the point of view of a French fry on the floor of the cafeteria. When it began ringing again, I fretted that it might be important, for Dad, so I put my pen down, forcing myself to the phone.

"Hello?"

"*Katie?*" My heart slammed into my chest wall. The German pronunciation, Kah-tee, his voice. "*Ja, Tante Katie, hier ist Michael.*"

"Michael!" My voice came out pinched, a whisper. He spoke only in German and called me his aunt. I caught on, immediately.

"How are you, Auntie?" he said, his words flowing, as if to another native speaker. I paid close attention. "I wanted to remind you. Your appointment, you remember? It will be next Saturday—

three o'clock. Meet where you did before, *OK*? Half three. Try not to be more than fifteen minutes late. Someone will be there to help you." Before I said a word, he hung up.

I stared at the phone, an inanimate clump of black plastic, cable, and metal wires that had just carried Michael's voice to me. I scribbled the time on the blotter pad before I forgot, and then, heart racing, pushed aside a pile of bills to reveal where Amy's number was scribbled. We called so rarely, I didn't know it by heart. My index finger was dragging the heavy dial around for the final number when I paused and banged the receiver back into its cradle. What was I thinking? We couldn't talk about this on the phone.

Back in the kitchen—forget homework—I turned up the radio, hoping the music would calm me. Reaching inside the freezer, I grabbed a tub of ice cream, then shouldered the door shut, grabbing a bowl and a spoon. A creamy wave curled around the scoop. Obviously, it was an invitation to his meeting. We couldn't go. It might be dangerous, what did we know? As the icy sphere slid from the spoon, Stevie Nicks' husky voice broke through my thoughts. I froze. *Dreams.* Michael's favorite song. And just like that I knew: we *had* to go.

The next morning, I left home early and was at school before I realized I was running, book bag pounding against my side. The van from the East wasn't in the parking lot yet so I knew I'd gotten there before Amy. I waited just inside the front doors, my nose pressed against the window. Buses pulled up and emptied. Kids flowed in.

"Hey, Cucabug!" Marny slapped my palm and walked on. I turned back to watch for the van that carried the few kids from the East. When it finally pulled up, the back door slid open and out they stumbled, sleepy after their long ride. The moment an eighth grader with pigtails and glasses pushed through the glass door, I grabbed her.

"Hey, Linda." I tried to sound blasé. "Know where Amy is?"

"Um, she's sick or something," she said, twisting a pigtail. "Her dad came out and told the driver she wasn't coming." She shrugged a half smile, hitched her bag up onto her shoulder, and bounded off to greet someone.

My mind raced through reasons Amy might skip school. She'd seemed fine yesterday. She'd turned in her term paper for history, finished her chem lab, didn't have PE—which she hated. Max had come out to the van? Usually, he was at work by the time Amy left, so, maybe she *was* sick.

I moped around all day, hiding from everyone. Instead of going to the cafeteria at lunch, I wandered outside and loitered behind the gym with the smokers, pretending to be very involved with my apple, desperate for the day to end. The moment I got home, I called Amy. She picked up right away. "*Amy!*" I must've sounded frantic.

"Hey, Kate. I'm fine… It's…well, my mom called, early, like midnight her time? I had to talk to her—then I missed the van. Max had some meeting and couldn't take me, so I just ended up staying home."

"Your mom called?" Above my head, a sword dangled by a thread.

"Yep. She's out, Katie. Doing great. Man, she sounded so good!" Her voice wobbled. Her mom's voice must have jiggled open her tight lock.

I swallowed, twisting the phone cord around my fingers. Amy's previous life was no longer a story about her past. It was her *now*. And it didn't include me. Be happy for her, I told myself, a lump forming in my throat. "That's great, Amy! Where is she?"

"At Enid's. She sounded happy. I mean, like they know it's one day at a time and all that—but…" I waited for her to continue. The line was so quiet, even Helmut seemed to be holding his breath, but I knew Amy was there, holding off saying what she had to say.

"Amy? It's OK." I tried to sound chipper. "She needs you, wants you back." For a split second, I hoped I was wrong. "Right?"

"Yeah." The sword fell. I bowed my head, choking back tears.

When she finally spoke, she was crying, too. "But, Kate, I told her I can't leave—not *right* away. School gets out December 14th. That's over a month—six weeks. But. Yeah. It's gonna suck."

I hated that Helmut could hear us crying and wanted to hang up. "Listen, Amy, you're coming to school tomorrow, right? Can you stay over? We've got to talk about something."

"What? Yeah, sure, sure, see you tomorrow." She hung up.

I lingered on the line a moment, listening for Helmut's breathing. There it was, an eerie, telltale *pooooh*. He was puffing a cigarette. I waited, wanting him to hang up before me, but he waited, too.

"Screw you, Helmut." I slammed the receiver into the cradle.

The next day, the specter of loneliness hovered everywhere I went, even with Amy who felt like a ghost who could disappear at will. Between classes, I found myself standing at my open locker staring at a pile of notebooks, incapable of remembering which class I had next. I peered down the bustling hallway. Will was standing at his locker and glanced up at the same moment. We mustered a civil nod before both turning away. I stuck my head into my locker and sank my face into smelly PE clothes to stifle a sob. Everything sucked.

"Amy, honey, I hear you weren't feeling well?" Mom passed a bowl of potatoes to me as Amy dished a hearty helping of broccoli onto her plate.

"Um, yeah. Actually, I wasn't sick." I looked up, surprised. I'd told Mom she'd stayed home with a cold yesterday. Keeping her secret had become so second nature, a part of me wanted to shush her.

"My mother called and I missed the van. I had to talk to her." She passed the broccoli to Dad, continuing as though she'd rehearsed what she needed to say. "See, I moved over here to live with Max—until Mom got well. And, now she's better. So…." She looked at me, maybe wondering what I'd told them. I looked back with a blank expression as if to show that's what they knew: nothing.

"Oh! Was she unwell, sweetheart? Well, goodness, I'm glad to hear she's better." Mom stole a glance at me. I offered her the same, blank look. "Oh, my!" Mom cried, when it hit her. "Does this mean you're leaving, Amy?" Her voice was gentle.

"Yeah. At the end of the semester."

"Oh," Mom sighed. I looked away before she could meet my eyes, my tears just waiting for a reason to gush. "We'll miss you, dear. But you two will keep in touch. True friendships do not die with distance if they are nourished now and then—and Kate's an avid letter-writer. You, too, Amy?" Mom's voice was upbeat. When you moved as often as we did, letters were like glue holding the pieces of our lives together. For years we'd made Sunday evening letter-writing time.

"Honestly?" Amy grimaced. "I've never written a letter in my life." We all laughed, though I didn't think it funny. She'd better start.

"Well, now you'll have to." Mom winked at me, with a knowing smile.

Finally, after helping with the dishes, we retreated to my room. All day, I'd wanted to talk to Amy alone, but there'd been no time. As soon as we got there, Amy closed the door and turned to me, her arms locked across her chest. Here it comes, I thought, not really knowing what *it* was.

"Listen, Kate. I know I shouldn't say this, but I'm going to anyway. The whole gang is upset because of you and Will. Right now, I'm some sort of a bridge, linking you to them. But once I'm gone, it'll be up to you. And you're gonna *need* them." She gave me a stern look. "Before I go. You gotta fix things."

It had been ages since the gang had come over to hang out and do homework or sit around and sing while I played guitar, Nadia belting louder than all of us put together, or to play Monopoly which I hated because it took so long so I'd sneakily give away all my money to hasten the end so we could grab a pizza and sangria at *Fra Diavolos* on Clayallee, or go dancing at *Quasimodo*. Forever—since we'd had a crepe from *Loretta's Garden* or even met up to get a curry wurst and beer at a *Schnell-Imbiss* before a movie at the Outpost. We ate lunch together at school, but there was a distinct us-and-them-ness going on.

It was true. I'd ruined things. And now, like salt in a wound, punishment, Amy was abandoning me. I tuned my guitar, feeling sorry for myself. "I guess that's why they say you shouldn't date friends."

Amy blinked at me. "Do *they*? So who should you date? Enemies? Kate. Look at me. Get this into your skull: Michael lives over there. He is not part of our lives. *You'll never see him again.*"

The guitar fell with a twang. *Michael.* I bounced to my feet. "Holy crap, Amy! I haven't told you!" I ran to put music on. She understood it was serious enough for background noise and waited until I plunked down crosslegged in front of her.

"*Guess* who called? Tuesday—I guess it was—evening. I couldn't tell you because—"

"*Who?*"

"Michael."

"What? Wait, *Michael?* No way—I mean, how could he?"

"Yeah. That's the other thing. I have a tiny confession to make. Nothing big—so don't get pissed, OK?"

"*Talk*, lady." Amy demanded. She sat poised atop the *kilim* pillow.

"Remember when we were in that cafe and you claimed you didn't know your phone number?"

"I wasn't making that up. I still don't know it." Her eyes narrowed. "What about it?"

"Well, so, when you were playing with the jukebox, I wrote down mine and gave it to him. I didn't tell you because I thought it might have been stupid and you weren't giving him yours because you thought it wasn't safe. I don't know. I never thought he'd call me over here, so I sort of forgot about it."

"*Seriously?* Why didn't you just tell me? Kate, sometimes—," She grunted, rolling her eyes before leaning over to shove me. "*Forgot* about it? Baloney-maloney! You've been *waiting* for him to call!" She shook her head. "It all makes sense now. OK, go on! What did he say?"

I told her his exact words, how quickly he'd hung up, and how, afterwards, I'd been sure there was no way we could ever go to a *Junge Gemeinde* meeting. I lowered my voice to deliver the next shock. "But, then, Amy? *Right* then? No lie. *Dreams* came on the radio."

"Whoa. No. Way."

"I know." I leaned in, dead serious. "We have to go."

Amy nodded. I knew she'd get it. "Yeah, I see what you're saying. I guess—if he invited us—it wouldn't be dangerous, would it?"

"If anything, it's dangerous for *him*," I said. "Inviting two Americans? It seems almost reckless on his part. Like he wants to stir up trouble."

"What about you, Kate? I'm worried…"

"Amy. It's not like that." She didn't argue with me.

We made a plan: we would sleep here Friday night and then head over Saturday morning, go to the meeting, and come back together to the West afterwards. We would tell no one. We didn't want anyone to try and talk us out of it.

"Kate," Amy paused, her face somber. "The fact that I'm leaving. That's gotta be secret, too." She was not into goodbyes. She'd leave over the break as though something had sprung up. That way, she reasoned, she wouldn't have to answer questions and she wouldn't have to make up a story to explain why. She made me promise I wouldn't say a word until after she'd left.

"You'll regret it, Amy. I should know—goodbyes serve a purpose. And anyway, *then* what am I going to tell them?"

"Tell them whatever you want." She dismissed my worry and looked straight at me. "Meantime, what are you going to do to fix things with the gang?"

35

Saturday morning, Amy and I rose early, resolved not to waste the day sleeping in and lounging around doing nothing, not to squander any of the time we had left together. There was a note from Mom on the kitchen counter:

Mornin' Katamy,
Dad and I are out—biking!! See you both at dinner? Have fun!
Love, Mom xx

"They're nuts," I said. "It's freezing out!"
"She's so so cute," Amy muttered, studying the note.
"She loves you. She'll miss you," I told her, pouring steaming water through a filter, dying for coffee. This waking early on a Saturday was nuts.
"She's got her act together. Up early, out biking with her man, dinner sorted.... I don't think my mom *ever*...."
"Your mom'll get there, Amy." I stumbled around getting mugs, warming milk, trying to wake up. She sat at the table, picking at a placemat. "Give her a chance, some *time*."

"For her sake, yeah, OK. But the days when I really needed her? They're past."

"Well, despite everything? You became an amazing person." I placed a steaming mug in front of her and sat. I didn't want to shut her down when she was talking about her mom, but needed to steer her away from this ditch. "And *that* person now will be there for *her*."

"She didn't exactly rise to her challenges, did she? I mean, y*our* parents, they've had their challenges—living in crazy places, moving all the time while raising kids—"

"C'mon. You can't compare our situations. Your mom loved you—*loves* you. That's what matters."

Amy snorted. "What good is love if you can't show it, don't feel it, don't even *know* it's there? No, she was an awful mom. *That's* the truth."

"Not *awful*—sad—had an addiction—"

"God, Kate! Can't you just—*appreciate* what you had—*have*?" She slammed her mug down and stormed out of the kitchen.

Sighing, I sipped my coffee, trying to decide if I was angry, hurt, or just exasperated and decided it was a mix. These last few weeks weren't going to be easy. We were a mess. Amy was nervous about leaving *and* I'd screwed up everything at school. Grabbing our mugs, I pushed backwards through the swinging door leading to the front hall. Amy was there, sitting by the telephones. She wiped her eyes, stared at her lap. I set her coffee down beside her.

"Let's make some pancakes and then get ready fast and go to Haus Am Checkpoint Charlie—to cheer up before we meet Michael." It was on our list of things she'd wanted to do before leaving Berlin.

"A museum of people killed at the Wall? Yeah, that'll cheer me up." She blinked through wet eyelashes and forced a smile.

The museum was jammed with cars, weird spherical subs, and diagrams of how people had contorted themselves to squeeze next to engines and gas tanks to escape. A series of photographs showed phases of the Wall from that first night on August 13, 1961. By morning, the Wall consisted only of rolls of barbed wire but swiftly became an ugly brick and mortar barrier; and finally, the thirteen-foot high, formidable contrivance it was now. A recent photograph—credited to the German Democratic Republic—showed a bird's-eye view of the ultimate construction: the Wall, Death Strip, lights, and towers. They were proud of it.

In the early days, you could look over the Wall. People could stand face to face on opposite sides—the lucky facing the unlucky. More photos showed everyday people the moment their lives changed: a soldier leaping over a giant coil of barbed wire, another dropping a little boy from East to West; one showed a woman midair, her skirt aloft, dropping from a building whose facade only was in the West. Below, arms stretched up to catch her.

In the center sat a minuscule car, like a chubby egg with wheels: a BMW Isetta. It's front—steering wheel and all—opened as a door. It was cute until we read it had been rigged so a third passenger—hard enough to imagine even two—could hide curled up next to the battery. Nine people snuck out in it before they were caught.

"Would you do it?" Amy asked, staring at the tiny car.

"If life were bad enough, I guess so." With a pang, my mind jumped from Will telling me he knew I would try to escape, to Michael, bravely making the best of an awful situation. I didn't know what to think.

Forgetting about the time it took to get through the checkpoint, it was only once we emerged in the East that we realized with a panic how late we were. Stashing our precious passports, Amy yanked me back as I started to break into a run. The clock read 14:25 when we got there. Twenty minutes late. Michael had said something about waiting fifteen minutes. We scoured the square. He was nowhere in sight.

"Shit, shit, shit. How could we have been so dumb?" I moaned. "He's going to think we didn't come, that we don't care."

"Ugh! German punctuality," Amy groaned.

"*Hallo?*" The voice made us jump, despite its gentleness. She seemed younger than she had before, her hair loose, falling softly around those deep, blue eyes. Her hands were clenched beneath her chin apologetically. "You remember me? I am, Anika, Michael's sister." Fragile. I thought, if I were to puff, she'd float away like a dandelion seed.

"Oh, Anika, we are glad to see you! We were late—" I began.

"No, no, but I am also late—afraid I would miss you! Michael went already to the meeting. He will be so happy you came." She beamed. "He has prepared a surprise."

After only two stops on the S-Bahn, we jumped off and walked a couple of blocks to catch a bus. Anika seemed shy, apologizing for her English, explaining that she and Michael had been allowed to study it in high school only as long as they maintained good marks in Russian. Conversation lagged, and eventually we just stared out the window. I wondered how far we were going.

"Here is Niederschönhausen," Anika offered, as though reading my mind. "We get off now." We walked a few blocks to a small house veined with bare ivy vines where Anika explained church services were held and their friend, the *Pfarrer*, pastor, lived upstairs. Around the far side mossy brick steps led to a basement door.

36

Michael's face lit up when he saw us, and he peeled himself away from a clump of people to introduce us to a white-haired man, the *Pfarrer*, who soon excused himself to go upstairs, saying he was leaving the basement to us young folk. The musky room was empty but for a few chairs in a circle and a table pushed up against a whitewashed wall. Meager light came from a bulb in the ceiling and a high, casement window all but obscured by dead weeds outside. Michael tugged us around, introducing us to everyone, eager as a kid with a frog in his pocket.

"Wow, what if we hadn't come?" I whispered to Amy.

Eventually, Amy and I grabbed chairs next to each other as the room fell silent. A guy with curly hair and glasses, a dead ringer for John Lennon, spoke first. He greeted everyone, then asked Michael to tell the group how he'd met us. Michael told the group that we'd accidentally left the museum without our coats, and that when he'd run into us, he'd offered to rescue them.

"Americans lost in the big city," he laughed, gently, turning to Amy. "Shall I say it again in English?" Amy shook her head, flashing me a look of mortification. I said not to worry, I'd do it, and then everyone waited patiently while I did.

Lennon began with words of prayer, and all heads bowed—except Amy's since she hadn't understood. She was day-dreaming out the dim casement window until I squeezed her hand. One look around and she dropped her head like a narcoleptic. Lennon expressed appreciation for our presence and Amy heard our names mentioned. Behind her curtain of hair, she crossed her eyes and made faces at me. *Please don't laugh*, I begged myself.

Everyone welcomed us, radiating warmth—until it came to one guy still wearing his coat, as if he wasn't wedded to staying. He could have been a poster child for the Third Reich, his short trimmed, blonde hair parted down the middle, his eyes steely blue. While everyone else smiled, he smirked. His name was Peter.

Someone uncorked a bottle of red wine and passed it around. Before taking a swig, each person tossed out a tribute—to friendship, understanding, truth, tolerance. In my focus to follow the German, I neglected to translate for Amy, so when the bottle came to her before me, she just scrunched her nose and faked taking a sip before passing it directly to me. I stared at the bottle trying to control the simmer of giggles about to boil over, knowing I had to toast *some*thing—but what? Everyone stared expectantly, but my mind went blank, my face burning, and I lifted the bottle before thinking things through.

"*Die Mauer muss weg!*" The Wall must fall. It was a protest cry, not a toast, graffitied all over the West. The group stared at their laps uncomfortably, hiding chuckles. I took a generous gulp and passed the bottle to the girl next to me, still fighting stifled giggles—knowing it would be awfully inappropriate to make fun of this.

Next to me, Amy had already succumbed, her head tucked, shoulders trembling in silent laughter. It seemed unfair that she had so much hair to hide behind. Desperately, I thought of puppies being hit by a car, worms inside my sweater. I pinched my nose to hold back a snort, my eyes watering, on the verge of running from the room, when Lennon made an announcement.

"*Nun hat der Michael eine Überraschung.*"

Nodding and smiling, Michael stood up and squeezed between chairs to head out the doorway leading upstairs.

"Where's he going?" Amy asked in a choked whisper.

"To get a surprise."

"Oh, god."

What had Anika said? Something about a surprise—for us?

Michael returned, each hand wrapped around the neck of an acoustic guitar, scratched and worn—but freshly strung, unclipped ends poking out every which-a-way. He handed one to me, one to Amy.

"Oh, man, no," Amy moaned, holding the guitar out from her as though it were a putrid, dead rat. "No way."

From the circle came a happy buzz of suspense. It was going to be more embarrassing *not* to sing. "I'm sure someone else can do better!" I offered, holding the guitar toward the center of the circle, waiting for a taker. No one so much as twitched.

"We want to hear *you—your* music!" Michael pleaded, dismayed by our resistance.

Peter spoke up, his voice dripping with sarcasm. "Ach, they do not want to play. Leave them." He waved us away as though dispelling pesky mosquitos, stretching out his legs to slouch into a satisfied smirk, clearly enjoying our discomfort.

Michael ignored him. "*Na ja*, OK. Then I will begin." With a grin, he took the guitar from me and painstakingly picked out a chord, then began a slow, straight strum. The guitar was completely out of tune, but he didn't seem to notice. He played and sang, but not at the same time and at each chord change, his brow furrowed with effort. It couldn't have been more adorable. He was singing a traditional German nursery song about little Hans braving the big world for the first time. Even I knew it.

"*Hänschen klein, Ging allein, In die weite Welt hinein…*" Everyone laughed and we all sang along—except for Peter whose smirk evolved into utter disgust. "*Stock und Hut, Steht ihm gut, Ist gar wohlgemut!*" Michael grinned, nodding encouragement, blurting the words between strums. He wiped his brow to a round of applause and asked me to explain how I knew the song. As I told them I'd gone to kindergarten in Garmisch—and had had a German nanny who sang to me, Michael handed the guitar back. Resigned, I began to tune it and grudgingly, Amy tuned the other one.

We started with *Blowin' in the Wind*, figuring it would be easy if they knew it, and sure enough, they joined in. Next, we tried "*If I had a Hammer.*" After that, starting to get into it, we attempted the tricky harmony of "*Helplessly Hoping.*" They tapped, clapped, and swayed. No one cared when we messed up, and soon, neither did we.

Tuning between songs, Amy leaned over. "*Dreams?*" she whispered. We had just figured it out the other day and it was still rusty, but I nodded. As we strummed the opening chords, I saw the recognition cross Michael's face, though he kept it subtle. Only we knew he knew the song; it was our shared secret. My cheeks grew warm as he leaned forward to listen. When we finished, there was a moment of suspended silence before the circle erupted into applause—except Peter, whose disdain was palpable.

As if the music had broken the ice, the group suddenly pelted us with questions—like where in America we were from, where we lived in Berlin, what school we attended. And compliments—on our jeans, my Adidas sneakers, Amy's poncho. Were they expensive? Were they American? We laughed, flustered by the strange attention. But then, the questions turned serious.

Someone asked what we thought about our freedom of speech, did we worry it could be dangerous? Luckily, we had just discussed this in Bluem's class, so Amy and I had an inkling of an intelligent response. We attempted to explain the difference between freedom of speech and intentionally hurting others; we tossed out words like libel, blackmail, and slander, attempting to clarify each, while translations murmured through the group for those who didn't understand.

"Here—to speak our mind is impossible without trouble." Lennon pushed his glasses up his nose, thought for a moment, then continued in German. "We are restricted in what we do, where we go—what we believe, even *think*." He stole a glance toward Peter, but went on. "We give up ourselves, for the State. Do you think this is an acceptable trade?" Expectant eyes fell on me.

Amy stared at the floor, not comprehending the German, but as I translated his question, her eyes widened and we stared at each other, unsure how to respond. I scrambled for a safe, logical line to toss out, but couldn't think of one. Judging or showing pity seemed wrong—imperious, even. Honesty, then, I had to speak from the heart. I took a deep breath.

"Well," I began, knowing I could only get this across in English, "I think that, ultimately, a society allowing for diverse thoughts and opinions is stronger, more interesting, more enriching—a kind of life worth living. No system is ever perfect; after all, humans create them, and not only are we all flawed, but each of us experiences the world through our own unique lenses. So how do you make a system that works for everyone? I'm not sure, but it has to be a system that, like ourselves, can grow—evolve with and embrace—our humanity. Maybe it's something that is *never* finished. A system shouldn't be carved into stone, it should evolve as we evolve. But, no, I *don't* believe that you get anywhere by forcing people to think the same." I paused. There were whispers, translations. "I guess we'd have to agree that our *humanity* should be nonnegotiable. Lose it, and you've lost everything. " I glanced around the room wondering if anything I'd said made any sense. "I mean, just *who* gets to tell everyone else what to think?"

My hands flew in the air with this last bit. Next to me, Amy whispered, "good one."

Peter's English was flawless. "Ah. This is the basic difference between our systems. You call it human to please yourself—instead of doing what is necessary to make the system function optimally—benefitting *all* humanity."

I met his gaze. "Does it ever, though?—And just who gets to define 'optimal'? And at what cost? I guess we have different notions of what it means to be human, humane."

"Your poverty, racism, people living in the margins—this is humane? Our government provides for a classless society, equal distribution—zero poverty," he hissed.

"*Sounds* nice—but is it working? No—! Why? Because *humans* are involved! How do you solve *that*? And, zero poverty, hah, what about poverty of the *mind*?" I snapped back, knowing I should rein myself in.

"A mind cannot function if the body is starving," he whipped.

"Why would it *need* to function in your one-size-fits-all fantasy society?" The discussion wasn't making me livid—but Peter's smug, superior attitude was. I glared at him, my heart thudding with ire. Amy put a hand on my arm to calm me.

Michael cleared his throat. "We appreciate your perspective," he said, in German. "It is an important reminder of our basic human values. How far is too far to go along with a government that denies us our individuality? At what point do we all lose what is important?"

I looked around the room, taking in the fundamental differences between our daily struggles—and our societies. How precarious it was to take things for granted. My mind drifted to that day in Bad Kreuznach when Will and I were on the bridge talking about how you could only appreciate what you had once you were aware of it. I longed for Will to understand what I was thinking, and then made a mental note of that longing—to examine it later.

"Do you think the Wall will *ever* come down?" That was Amy—ever bold. A low murmur rippled through the group, some shrugs, guarded chuckling. But no one responded. Until Peter—causing everyone to shift uncomfortably.

"Left to their own devices, people are weak, self-indulgent. Our State teaches us we are stronger together. The Wall keeps the decadence of the West out, allows us to be pure." His eyes darted between Amy and me. "The Wall is a necessity *because* of you."

The room fell silent until a tiny girl with long, greasy pigtails had the courage to respond to Peter's bluster. She sat on her hands, her short legs scissoring above the floor, scrunched down, her shoulders jutting up like two shields protecting her head. "Kate is right," she said, her voice shy and gentle. "Humanity must come first. Look at us. We are each so different." She gazed around the circle before sitting up brightly. "I think God made us different on purpose. It is not our place to question His plan."

Peter scoffed. "There is no God and there is no plan."

At that, Lennon bowed his head to recite a closing prayer. This time, Amy caught on and I kept my cool. It ended in a chorus of Amens, after which everyone got up, took turns shaking our hands thanking us for coming, and then walked out the door. Only Michael, Anika, and—to my dismay—Peter remained.

"It meant so much to Michael and me that you came," Anika whispered, hugging us. She took my hand and didn't let it go while she leaned over to whisper in Michael's ear. I was aware of Peter's interest in all of this, and of her disinterest in him. Then, with a final squeeze of my hand, Anika, too, left.

Amy and I jumped in to help Michael line chairs against one wall while Peter leaned against another, rolling paper around a wad of tobacco. When Michael dashed upstairs with the guitars, Peter dragged on his cigarette, staring at us with a righteous glare. It was all I could do to keep quiet, yearning for Michael to hurry back. And when Michael offered to walk us to the bus, Peter tagged along. We weren't going to get one second alone with Michael.

At the bus stop, Michael gestured toward a bench in a mud patch next to rusted monkey-bars dripping with rain. "Sit for a moment?" he suggested, wiping the bench with his handkerchief.

"Ah! Good idea." Peter sprawled across the dried half, leaving the rest for the three of us to squeeze onto together. After rolling another, he popped a cigarette between clenched teeth. "So!" Shreds of tobacco jiggled from the loose end. "You Americans continue to occupy West Berlin." He struck a match and inhaled, exhaling directly into my face. I waited for his point, blinking through smoke, wishing he would go. Wet had penetrated my one butt cheek gracing the bench, and damp air was seeping through my jacket. If Peter was staying, we might as well leave.

"And the Russians occupy the East," Amy retorted, calm and matter of fact. I wanted to clap.

Michael meanwhile sat in silence, gazing off with a detached expression, one arm gripping the back of the bench. Soft bangs obscured his eyes, and I almost reached out to brush them away, to clear my view. His silence could fill a library, I imagined, dying to be inside his head.

"Ach, this pathetic desire to go to the West," Peter scoffed, inhaling another lungful before tilting his head back to release a couple of smoke rings. He blew out the rest into Amy's face. "What for? Climb the Wall like an eager little rat—and then?" He eyed Michael with a sneer, "*If* you survive?—what will you find on the other side? Another wall! There's always another wall in the West: walls of class, race, greed...." He yawned. "Why bother?" He flicked the glowing butt through the air. It landed, smoking in the mud. "Why bother, when you can find fulfillment where you are?" With that, he bolted to his feet, nodded at Amy and me, tapped his forehead in a mock salute at Michael, and strolled off, chin high. My heart did a little jig watching him go, and we immediately scooted over, filling the space he'd left behind.

"Wow. What a donkey!" Amy declared, as soon as Peter was out of earshot.

"Yeah, man, I wanted to—" I shook my head; no response would have satisfied.

Michael shrugged. "We are lucky to be allowed these meetings, but each time, there is someone who comes we do not invite. Tonight, it was Peter." He shrugged again, taking it in stride. "I hope that you were able to enjoy, anyway? We were very happy to have you." He blew warm air into his hands, then clapped them together. "Now! Anika would be happy—she said to me—if you come for a visit. We are not far. But first, we had to make this boy," he snapped his fingers, "disappear." With a grin, he stood and offered each of us a hand. As we trailed him down the quiet, darkening street, I fought the creepy feeling that Peter was still watching us from somewhere. It seemed crazy how they just accepted him.

"Was that a typical meeting?" I asked, wondering how much our presence had changed things.

Michael pulled his hands inside his sleeves, the same thin jacket from before. "Sometimes, we discuss more—the Bible, philosophy, meanings, lessons for our life, you know? And sometimes we just share experiences." He paused a moment, then walked on. "The most important thing is for us to continue to come together. We must do so regularly, you understand?—not to lose this freedom—and to show we are not afraid." He turned to face us with a little bow. "Today, your singing was a present. *Danke*—it was *echt* cool."

"It was our pleasure," I assured him. "But, Michael, why *do* they allow these meetings?" The government was explicitly anti-religion.

Michael slowed, mulling his answer. "*Na, ja*, you must understand a little bit about the history—and the State's psychology." He took a deep breath. "Do you know the *Grundlagenvertrag*—?" he looked at me, expectant.

I wracked my brain. "The Basic Treaty?" I translated literally but had no idea what that was.

"*Ja, genau*. It recognized that we are a *separate* nation—separate from West Germany. This recognition was good for us."

"Oh—the Quadripartite Agreement," I recalled. "It made travel to the East easier and helped the economy because westerners bring hard currency."

"And provided for diplomatic relations. The U.S. embassy here opened in 1974," Amy added.

Michael nodded. "Yes, yes, and then, the rest of the world could better see inside, see how life here was. So, to better its image, the State had to make it appear—how you say?—looser? more loose—the life over here. For example, our leaders knew it was not possible to stop religion. And hidden religion is more dangerous because they cannot control it. So, instead, they decided to tolerate it. You understand? And so when we practice religion, we do not have to hide and, of course, anyone can participate. But, we are actually *accepting* the State's *authority* to grant this to us, so *they* keep control of it. You see? It is about power." By recognizing East Germany as a separate country, some restrictions had eased, but in another way, the State had gained more power. It was tricky. They were allowed these meetings so they did not have to meet in secret, but it also lured nonconformists out into the open.

We turned and walked single-file down a narrow sidewalk. I fell in sync behind Michael, lulled by his heavy, rubber-soled shoes—the kind you might find at a cheap market in the West. He was not hip, but totally endearing, his skinny legs lost within baggy, thinning corduroys, a belt cinching a narrow waist beneath a loose sweatshirt. It was true, I was drawn to him—or was it the *idea* of him?—yet at the same time, I knew that the barriers between our worlds were literally insurmountable. He was like a riddle I didn't want to solve.

37

The sky was still gray, but the clouds higher, less threatening. We walked past simple houses, close together, behind low walls. They looked distinctly German yet different from the houses in the West, less grand, less confident. Wan light penetrated thin curtains pulled across windows, so faint, it could have come from candles. Even the streetlights were dim. Few cars, mostly little Trabis, dotted the curbs.

It was fully dark by the time Michael stooped at a low, wrought-iron gate, opening it to let us pass through. A half moon gleamed down between clouds, casting eerie shadows over a simple, white-washed stucco cottage, thin wisps snaking from the chimney the only sign of life. An odd bump protruded from the middle of the small yard; as we passed by and my eyes adjusted, I could make out a metal door in its upper half, its base buried beneath decaying leaves and weeds littered with terra cotta shards.

We matched Michael's footsteps, landing on flagstones in the dark, around to the far side of the house where soft, yellow light glowed behind white curtains. Michael opened a door, calling inside, kicking off his shoes before entering. Anika appeared, pulling us into a cozy, warm kitchen where tinny music emanated from a tiny transistor radio set on the windowsill above a deep, cement sink. A white-clothed table and chairs practically filled the room. We kicked off our shoes while Michael hung our jackets and Anika pulled out chairs, indicating that we should sit.

The siblings scurried around like mice. They produced bread, opened a can of tuna—taken from what appeared to be an otherwise empty cupboard—and dished it onto a plate. Anika lit a flame and placed a heavy, black kettle on it, while Michael sliced the bread. They moved like a familiar, married couple, narrowly avoiding each other in the small space.

I stroked an embroidered sunflower sewn into the tablecloth, wondering where their mother was—and hadn't Michael mentioned a brother? It felt like no one else was home: the door to the rest of the house was shut—probably to contain the heat which emerged from the oven. The room felt still and contained, so unlike the dazzling modernity of our bright kitchen at home.

"Our mother sewed it," Anika said, softly. I looked up. She was pointing at the sunflower beneath my fingertips. The melancholy tinging her voice added to my inkling that their mother was not about to burst smiling through the door, armed with a basketful of groceries, cheeks flushed with the cold. Was it just the two of them then?

"They're beautiful," I smiled. There were sunflowers in each corner and on the hems of the curtains, too.

Anika filled a cloth strainer with tea and dangled it inside a pot mottled in a pine green glaze that matched all the dishes stacked on the shelf and the mugs and small plates she placed on the table. Michael set a bread basket down, then the plate of tuna, smiling as if he'd killed the fatted cow for us.

"Did your father make—?" I began, a mug resting between my hands. The rest of my question withered with an image of a gray-haired version of Michael in a dark cell somewhere.

"Yes," Michael replied reverently. "These are his design."

My finger traced the rounded, delicate handle. I liked how the dark green outside blended with a lighter shade on the inside. "It's beautiful," I said, appreciating its weight along with the heaviness of their situation.

"I am learning, also, to make ceramics," Michael explained. "When my father returns, together we will make more—to sell. We will get rich." He laughed, pulling out a chair. I imagined his long fingers oozing with moist, wet clay, spinning works of art out of blobs. "But first I must to do my military service."

"Military service?" Amy asked, surprised.

"Yes, for 18 months. It is obligatory. I declared myself—how do you call it? *Pazifist?*"

"Pacifist," I nodded, intrigued.

"Yes. So therefore, I will become a *Bausoldat*. I will not hold a weapon. We will build things." He was spooning chunks of tuna onto pieces of bread while he spoke, placing one on Amy's plate, another on mine. I hesitated before reaching for it, balancing being hospitable with the anguish of eating what little they seemed to have.

"And after that?" Amy asked. She bit into her morsel, so I lifted mine.

Michael turned to me, switching to German. He seemed tired. I commiserated with the effort it took to communicate in a foreign language. "He said that this alternative military service will separate him from the normal soldiers—making him even *more* of an outcast," I translated for Amy. Michael nodded, adding a shrug of acceptance.

Anika joined us at the table with the teapot. She began to pour us each a steaming mug of tea. "Your school in West Berlin? It is an American school?"

"Yes. It's for military children—but it isn't a *military* school," I said, realizing how confusing that might sound. Then Amy tried to explain how different it was from a regular American high school, but then got stuck describing what that meant. "Probably, the biggest difference between our high schools and yours is American football," she joked, giving up, and going on to explain how our sports teams travelled within the West German DOD school league, and how, during home games on Saturday mornings, the entire community came out to cheer for Berlin American High School. "Our cheerleaders have a lot of spirit," she added.

Anika, listening intently, her elbows on the table, hands cupping her chin, now sat up. "Cheer-leader? What is it?"

Amy pushed out her chair. "C'mon, Kate. Let's show them." I agreed, grinning, and stood up, though I couldn't help but think this was a weird aspect of our culture to be demonstrating—of all the things we could be portraying about the West.

"S! P! I-R-I-T! We've got Spirit! Let's hear it!"

Anika and Michael laughed and clapped, resisting at first when we tried to pull them up to teach them the moves that went along with the cheer. After a few attempts at it, we fell apart, laughing, and sank back down to the table.

A sweet silence filled the room, German folk music floating in thin waves from the transistor radio. I scrutinized a faded, black and white photograph hanging on the wall behind Amy. It was of their family: a little boy, maybe six or seven, with mussy, blonde hair—doubtlessly little Michael—standing in front of a tall, bearded man who could've been Abraham Lincoln's brother. He had one hand on the boy's shoulder, the other around a petite, pretty woman, her head tilted toward him, her hair draped over a shoulder. The woman's smile was identical to that of the leggy, teenaged girl sitting in the grass in front, Anika. And next to her was a lanky, teenaged boy, cross-legged, leaning back on thin arms, his eyebrows high, as if surprised by the camera. Michael and Anika followed my gaze, shifting in their chairs as if they knew what was coming. But I hesitated.

Amy, too, had followed my gaze. When she turned back, she asked, naturally, "Where is your mother?"

After a heavy pause, Michael replied. "She died," he said, his eyes on the photograph. "Seven years ago. Cancer."

"I'm so sorry." I swallowed. The echoes of our cheers that had filled the room evaporated into the shadows of the small kitchen.

"How old were you?" Not that I couldn't have done the math myself; it was something to say.

Anika responded as though reciting a tired script. "Michael, eleven; I, fifteen; Stefan, seventeen." She cast Michael a worried glance as if anticipating where the conversation would go next.

"Stefan?" Amy looked from one to the other, then me. Anika chewed a hangnail, stalling her response, her eyes sad and tired.

"Stefan," Michael began. He gazed at his big sister, as if pleading for her to take this one.

Anika let her hand fall from her teeth to her lap. Her words came out clipped, efficient, like that of a newscaster on the evening news. "Stefan tried to escape. He was shot at the Wall."

My stomach dropped. Murdered. Their brother was murdered by the State.

Amy's hand flew to her mouth. "What? When?"

"Almost two years ago," Michael mumbled.

"Why—I mean, was he just—trying—to leave?" Amy looked horrified, her eyes shuttling back and forth between Michael and Anika.

"Our father," Michael continued, "is paying the price for raising a son who did not cooperate."

My insides swirled: fury, hot and churning, wrestled with an icy, burgeoning fear. What kind of government shoots its kids for wanting to leave? That was why their father was in prison? I thought of how Peter, earlier, had been mocking escape attempts. He must have known about Michael's brother. Michael had said nothing, just absorbed the bullying.

"How long will he have to stay in prison?" I asked. My voice came out low and raspy.

Michael shrugged. "We don't see or hear from him," he mumbled, his fingers wringing the corner of the tablecloth into his fist. Anika reached over to lay a hand on her brother's knee.

All at once, I needed to go. I was squelching a simmering panic that we wouldn't be allowed to leave. I pictured the obstacles between here and home, pictured my parents, the stability and comfort of our lives, the American passport snug inside my back pocket. We would be allowed to go. But they couldn't. Not ever. I felt a shame spread through me as I wondered how quickly we could get out of there—recognizing the unfairness of it all.

Anika was quietly consulting with Michael, who nodded. In English, she said, "Amy, we can take you home, if you like. You can show us the way?" and to me, "And we can take you to the checkpoint."

"Oh, thank you. But I'm going home with Kate," Amy replied. "Wait, you have a *car*?" She dropped her eyes, embarrassed by her surprise.

"A little Trabi," Michael replied, his sparkle reemerging—though I couldn't imagine from where. "A luxury car!" He winked. "It is quite old, but it is faithful. *Ja,* come, Anika, it will make us happy to drive."

When arriving earlier, we'd missed the low, slanting wooden roof on the side of the house that covered a tiny vehicle. The Trabi reminded me of the little cars in *The Game of Life*. It needed a few decals over its baby-blue—some flowers, or maybe a psychedelic peace sign on the hood.

As I was about to climb into the back after Amy, something darted past me in the dark. "Hey, there's something over there!" I cried. Curious, I peered into the shadows.

"Ach, it's Flitvut." Anika said, wandering over to pick up a large, fluffy, gray cat. It writhed and mewed in her arms.

"Flitvut?" Weird name for a cat, I thought, stroking the soft fur.

"Flitvut Mac!" Michael grinned.

"Oh, Fleetwood Mac!" I giggled. "She or he?"

"We are not sure," Michael laughed.

Squirming to escape, the cat suddenly froze and for a moment that registered like a snapshot in my brain, the two of us stared directly at one another. Then, it leapt from Anika's arms and disappeared into the shadows. "The day after our father was taken away, she came to us," Anika said, pausing to peer in the direction the cat had gone. "We needed her as much as she needed us."

When the Trabi door shut with a sound more like a screen door closing than a car, all the Trabi jokes I'd heard at school began to come to me. *Did you hear? The new Trabi has two exhaust pipes, so that it can double as a wheelbarrow.* I smiled—keeping it to myself. Michael cocked his head low as he turned the key. The motor kicked in like corn popping and he nodded in satisfaction.

"No radio!" he shouted above the engine. "We will have to sing!"

Why are there no radios in Trabants? No point, because your knees cover your ears anyway.

Amy started to sing the song we'd belted out making pancakes that morning—a world and a lifetime ago—and I joined in. "We-e-e-ll, I got me a wife….and I got me a fiddle…Sun comin' up, I got cake's on the griddle…" Anika clapped while Michael tapped the steering wheel between his thumb and index finger, his hair—standing with static, reaching to the roof—dancing along. The dark, empty streets of East Berlin sped by, the car so low, my bottom tingled in anticipation of every bump. Before long, Anika caught on to the chorus and sang it with us, so we stayed with it, over and over until Michael stopped, killed the engine, and yanked up the parking brake.

What do you call a Trabi with brakes? Customized.

We stopped singing. Blinding spotlights illuminated the familiar long, gray expanse of the Wall. Graffiti-free on this side, its austerity sent a chill down my spine. A low hum of city sounds, I realized, was the West beyond it. I wondered where Stefan had been shot.

"*Na, ja,*" Michael said, pounding the steering wheel. "The end of *our* world! From here, you must journey by yourself." He jumped out and opened the door for Amy with a gentlemanly flourish.

Anika, her sweet head haloed by the spotlights behind her, swiveled to face me. "I hope we will see you again soon."

"Thank you, Anika. Me, too."

Outside, Michael and Amy were standing side by side, quietly gazing toward the checkpoint. On this side, no signs screamed that you were leaving the Russian Sector. Because, well, I reasoned, most weren't. I reached for Michael's arm, aching to connect. "Is it hard for you to call?"

"I sometimes can use the phone at the kiosk. They know, of course." He shrugged. "Please, come anytime. " He smiled. "Now you know where we live." When he pulled me in for a hug, my heart raced. I turned my face toward his, and we kissed. Anyone watching may have thought it just a good-bye peck—but I knew better. In the nanosecond that his lips held mine, something passed between us. He squeezed my shoulders before letting me go.

"You must be freezing!" I murmured, for an excuse to run my hand along his arm, his lean muscles taut beneath a thin sweatshirt.

"No," he whispered. "Now I am warm." A blush soared to my cheeks. We hugged each other once again, but then there was nothing else to do but go.

"Hey," Anika said, pointing at the Wall. "Wave to us!"

East German guards wished us a good evening as we passed them our documents. They stamped my passport and sent us on our way. So easy. Once in the West, we looked down the street that ran along the Wall, where wooden steps led to a viewing platform; the West had built them just for this purpose, and the East could do nothing about it. We climbed up and leaned against the railing, gazing up at the nearest concrete tower. Two young guards looked back at us, but their rifles were aimed toward the East. We weren't their targets.

Below us, the Death Strip consisted of a wide, barren path of finely combed dirt; a row of giant, concrete, 3-D jacks; and beyond them, two rows of chain-link fences—just for good measure. No wonder the rest of the East was so dim, I thought, squinting into the brilliance: all their electricity was concentrated on the Wall. "Imagine the minds that thought this up," I muttered.

Amy pointed down to where three bunnies munched on a tuft of dry grass at the base of the fence. An image of Stefan's lifeless, crumpled body flashed through my mind and I looked up, across the Death Strip, to where we'd left Anika and Michael. There they were, heads close, chatting, the Trabi like a plaything beside them. I nudged Amy and together, we raised our arms and waved. Anika nudged Michael, and they waved back. We waved harder, blew kisses, and waved some more until there was nothing left to do but stop and turn away.

38

On the drive home, Michael and Anika were quiet, still savoring their unusually social evening. When Anika began to hum, absentmindedly, the quiet tune they'd belted out on the way, Michael smiled. It had been a long time since he'd heard Anika laugh. It was bittersweet having met these American girls. They'd lifted them out of their sad situation—he hadn't worried about Klein all afternoon—but now that they'd gone—and who knew when he'd ever see them again—things felt more dire than ever. Still, he felt a strange sense of hope, of destiny, that he hadn't before.

Anika had stopped humming and was looking at her brother. "I could feel the connection between you and Kate," she said. "I'm worried. For your feelings."

Michael didn't respond. He was worried about his feelings, too, if he was honest. All afternoon, he'd been very distracted, imagining taking her hand and walking with her, talking for hours, just the two of them. Their kiss, however fleeting, had sent him soaring. But it was absurd, could lead only to heartbreak. He was torn—when Kate was around, he felt less alone, more alive. How could someone from such a different world feel so much more real than any girl he could meet here?

As if she'd read his mind, Anika said, "We aren't the only ones over here who think like we do. You'll meet someone, Michael. Once all of this is over, once Papa is home, things will feel different."

He wanted to believe her.

39

Mom was sitting in a warm circle of lamplight, her knees curled beneath her on the sofa, a growing sweater piled on her lap. She'd been knitting it for weeks right in front of Dad, knowing it would come as a complete surprise to him on Christmas day. In the adjacent den, a baby-faced soldier was reading the news on AFN: two GIs had been caught smuggling people out of East Berlin. They'd been court-martialed. Why the GIs should be punished for helping people escape, I didn't understand.

Amy was telling Mom about the Christian group meeting we'd gone to. We'd agreed to tell that much—omitting everything about it being in the East. "And they *made* us sing!" A part of me longed to tell my parents everything we'd been up to, but it felt like a betrayal to what Amy and I had created. I'm not sure we knew exactly why but it seemed imperative to keep our relationship with Michael and Anika to ourselves. Maybe we just needed a secret.

Mom was laughing, then dropped her knitting needles into her lap. "Oh! I almost forgot! Nadia called. She wanted you to come over as soon as you got home."

It seemed crazy that it was only just past eight.

"Not sure I'm up for Nadia and all her drama," I moaned a few minutes later, on the walk to her house. I'd been too emotionally drained to argue ourselves out of going.

"Maybe it's just what we need. A dose of reality." Equating Nadia with reality made us both burst out laughing. "We can just stay for a bit."

"Lavinia is always entertaining, at least," I noted. We were both fascinated by Nadia's mother and Nadia's strange relationship with her. It felt like forever since we'd all been together. We knew they'd done stuff without us—someone would mention something at lunch, then cast guilty looks our way before quickly changing the subject. "Think the guys are coming? Not that I care." Of course, I did.

I was nervous about seeing Will. At school, we'd developed a weird coping routine, but this would be different. I cared as much about him as ever—yet still felt I had to avoid him. Why? Nothing made sense. Michael's kiss—I had to admit my feelings for him. But Will was different. I needed him to understand, but what, exactly? What was I thinking?

"Katie." Amy walked ahead a few steps, then turned to block me. "I'll be gone soon."

I groaned. "I thought that was a taboo subject."

"I don't want to leave you like this. You're lost. Dazed. Confused." She shushed me. "I used to wonder if maybe you were pushing Will away because you're afraid of how close you were getting—which is natural. But today, with Michael, I saw—there *is* something…" She gazed off a moment, as if seeking an answer, then turned back. "For the record, I did see that sneaky, little kiss. But you know it's batshit-nuts, right? Even if you two fit like crazy socks—you gotta be real, Kate. Remember that little issue of a Wall? It's distorting your view—literally *and* figuratively." Her eyes narrowed and she crossed her arms, letting her words sink in.

But she wasn't done. "Here's what I wanna say. Tonight, if Will comes? Talk to him—just *talk* to him. Please? You two are…. And—the two of you pretending you don't care?—it's so fake." She sighed with exasperation. "Look. At the very least, Will will be your best friend here once I'm gone. You'll need him, one way or another. And I need to know—before I go—that you two will have each other."

My feelings looped and overlapped like noodles in a bowl. Amy was right. Will's friendship was invaluable. *Was* I shy about intimacy? Was that part of it? I didn't think so. Will, so tender and caring...and deep down, I knew a relationship with Michael was impossible. Didn't I? But something—a cosmic, magnetic force—kept pulling me to him—it was not just *passion*. But to grasp or define it was like trying to hold onto a fading dream, or relieve a relentless itch. If only Amy could get inside my mind and help interpret the turmoil. We were at Nadia's gate. "Amy. What *is* wrong with me? What is it with Michael?"

"I dunno," she acknowledged. "It is pretty intense." So she *did* recognize it. "Also, I can tell—for what it's worth—Michael feels it, too." She gave me a strange look, like she wanted to tell me something but couldn't, then shook it off. "Still, Kate. *Will!* Damn, he's perfect for you." She punched the doorbell and a moment later, the gate buzzed and the front door flew open. I braced myself.

"Oh, yay!" Nadia squealed from the doorway. As she pulled us inside, she glanced up and down the street behind us. "Willy and Ricky will be here any minute!" Willy. I moaned as Amy took my hand and tugged me forward.

Nadia's hair was in a puffy side-spout only she could pull off. She was wearing an emerald green, bellbottom pantsuit with sleeves that flared into butterfly wings when her arms went up. And up they went, the right and then the left as she danced around, taking our jackets, tossing them onto a chair with a flourish, flitting like a giant fairy. Behind her back, Amy was feigning a gag. My eyes rolled to the ceiling in agreement. How I'd miss Amy.

And then came Molly, trotting down the stairs in Nadia's clothes—at least, I'd have bet money they were Nadia's—leopard-patterned, skintight pants with a black turtleneck, a white, Isadora Duncan scarf flowing down her back.

"Gee," I whispered to Amy. "Looks like we overdressed."

Nadia dragged us toward classical music emanating from the living room to greet her mother. Sprawled across the couch in a cloud of musky perfume, her velvet muumuu, fingernails, and the wine swiveling in her glass a perfect burgundy match, lay the legendary Lavinia. Nadia shoved us in front of her.

"Girls," Lavinia began, beckoning with her wine glass eyeing us with charcoal-lined eyes peering out from beneath a shock of wild, black hair, "we were so hoping you'd come." Her voice husky, thick with seduction, left us dumbfounded.

"Hi, Mrs. Macomb," we mumbled in unison like cloyingly polite children in a TV sit-com.

"Dear *gawd*," she croaked, adding a startlingly high, mocking giggle. "Mrs. Macomb? *Please,* call me Lavinia. Do I look like I should be in an apron—baking *pies?*" Her final words were muffled from inside her wine glass as she tipped it to sip.

"We're waiting for the boys, Mummy, and then we'll be ready to go." Amy and I exchanged wide-eyed glances. It was the first we'd heard that we were going somewhere. It explained the outfits, anyway.

"Nadia, dear, you clearly haven't told *them.*" Lavinia used a pinky to hold back a disobedient tendril as she inspected our sweatshirts and jeans. She swung her feet to the floor. "We're going to Romy's," she announced. "You're my guests."

Behind us, Nadia clarified, "Romy—Romy *Haag's nightclub,*" copying her mother's unplaceable accent. "It's called *Chez Romy Haag.*"

"Wow. I'd better call my mom." I regretted it as soon as I said it and tried to save myself. "You know, to let her know we'll be late."

"*Absolutely,* darling. Ask her to join us, why don't you." A cluster of bangles danced and clinked as Lavinia dismissed us with a wave. "Nadia, darling, do find *some*thing for them to put on. Black. Stick to black. Always safe in a *pinch.*"

"Yes, Mummy, just what I was thinking." Nadia paused in the hallway to give me a gentle shove. "Phone's just there, Kate. Amy, you come with me."

As she took Amy by her elbow and led her up a back staircase, I found their phone in a nook just outside the kitchen, behind a beaded curtain. I dialed home, pulling the long cord through the beads into the kitchen for privacy. Mom made me promise to tell her everything in the morning. She sounded more excited about the evening than I did. I hung up as the doorbell rang, followed by footsteps pounding down the front stairs, the door flinging open with a rush of cold air.

"Finally! Get in here, you two."

I stepped out from behind the beads and dashed up the back staircase. "Kate!" Amy met me at the top. "Your outfit's waiting. Hurry. You gotta get dressed before you see *Willy*." I eyed her black bolero jacket. It had shiny fringe and clasped in the front with a matching, tassel thingy. Below, she had on black gauchos and high heels. "Hey. Don't judge. And I know—the shoes have to go. Nadia was acting so bossy and melodramatic, I'd have strangled her if Molly hadn't been there to witness."

I stopped short at the threshold to Nadia's bedroom. Clothes were draped over bedposts, flung over lamps, across seats and backs of chairs, wadded over every inch of carpet. "Holy smokes! Did her wardrobe explode?" Amongst twisted, inside-out, rejected items on the bed lay a black top with faint, silvery, vertical stripes and a pair of shiny, black pants.

Amy waved at the ensemble. "Simple, sleeveless, a touch of glitter—and *no buttons*." I shivered at the mention of them. Only Amy knew my secret button phobia. "Hip-huggers, super stretchy—though they won't be on you—haha. And you're welcome. You shoulda seen what *Nadia* wanted to put you in. Oh, and—!" She grabbed a short, black-leather jacket from the bedpost. "Nadia got it when she was twelve—can you imagine? It'll fit you perfectly!"

Riotous laughter downstairs shot me into action. Ignoring the fact that I was to wear Nadia's super-hip baby clothes, I yanked off my jeans. The pants bunched at my ankles and swam around my hips, but they'd do. "What about shoes?" I secretly adored the top.

Amy's voice came from deep inside Nadia's closet. "What do you think I'm looking for?" She emerged on her knees, a patent-leather go go boot in each hand. "How about these?" I tried them on and strutted around the room. If they hadn't gone up so high—namely past my knees—they'd have fallen right off me. "Lady, you look *hot*! A little make-up and you're set." She sat me on the bed, aimed a lamp at my face, and came at me like a mad dentist.

Molly was doubled over in reaction to a story Rick was regaling her with as we came down the front stairway. Nadia had an arm tightly wrapped around Will's waist. When she saw us coming, she made a show of pulling her arm away, the butterfly wing poised behind Will's back, while she puckered her face with knowing pity for me. It was worthy of a slap, but I was too busy focusing on avoiding eye contact with Will to care. He was doing the same with me.

Rick looked up at us and whistled. "*Smokin'!*" he cried, generously.

"It's all the black," I joked, hugging him before Will. "Hi, Will." He felt stiff, didn't meet my gaze. This was going to be painful. Rick launched in to retell his story, something about a kid tripping and spilling a coke on two annoying Mormon missionaries on the U-Bahn. I tried to laugh, relieved when Lavinia appeared in a floor-length fur, announcing it was time to go.

Their giant American station wagon was the kind Mom would see attempting to maneuver the narrow, old streets of Europe and comment, "What were they thinking, bringing that thing here?" But we all fit with room to spare: Nadia in front, Molly and I in the back; Amy made a thing of squeezing in the way back, giggling with glee, between the guys instead of sitting on the hump between Molly and me. It felt like a betrayal, somehow, to everything that had happened that day. And it hurt to see how natural she could be with Will. My throat clenched.

"A mix of Roxy Music and David Bowie," Nadia announced as she pressed in a cassette. She and her mother began to sway in sync to the cool beat, as did Molly beside me.

"We never drive downtown," I whispered to Molly, seeking an ally in my pique. "Parking is going to be a nightmare."

"You'll see. Lavinia will find a spot without one iota of sweat. She *oozes* good karma." I was annoyed with Molly now, too. Up front, Lavinia let out a howl, after Nadia told her about Amy and me, meeting Bowie in a hot tub.

"Did you?" She asked through the rearview mirror.

"Yep," I said, in no mood to expound. This was usually when I teased Amy about floating around without a clue.

"We'll have to ask Romy tonight what in bloody hell David was doing in the East in a hot tub," Lavinia laughed.

"Romy Haag *knows* David Bowie?"

Her eyes met mine in the mirror. "Oh, honey, they *love* each other."

40

Molly threw me an I-told-you-so look as Lavinia wheeled into a spot big enough for a jumbo jet a mere block from the club. "Remember where I put the car, kids," she called out as she sashayed away while we piled out. Rick locked and shut her door.

Furs—faux and genuine—quivered together like an excited skulk of foxes at a corner door. I joined the end of a long line squirming with anticipation in front of a ticket window flashing *Chez Romy Haag* in twinkling gold. But Nadia guided me away. "Uh-uh. Mummy doesn't use this door."

"What about tickets?"

She was hoping I'd ask. "Oh, no; *we* don't pay. They're *friends*, Mother and Romy. Brian Ferry introduced them in London *ages* ago." When harking back to her London days, Nadia's accent turned British.

She guided us around the corner where Lavinia was clutching the arm of a bouncer guarding an alleyway door, walkie talkie pressed to his face. He seemed oblivious to the cold, his bare biceps bulging beneath a black t-shirt. The door clicked open and, as he stood aside to allow us to pass, Lavinia leaned over and gave him a tongue-led kiss on the lips. Nadia turned to smile at me, clearly impressed with her mother's audacity. We followed her down a dark hallway, toward loud music that, even muted by walls, caused my chest to thump, and when a waiter tugged aside a heavy, velvet curtain for us, the music exploded into my ears. We wormed our way through the throbbing club beneath twinkling stars and florescent lasers flashing to the beat of the music to a table directly in front of a curtained stage. Lavinia directed Rick and Will to the chairs nearest the stage. Beyond that, her seating directions ceased—she didn't seem to care where the rest of us sat. Nadia scurried to sit beside Will. I pretended not to notice and draped her leather jacket over the back of a chair beside Rick.

The blaring music made it hard to converse, but we were distracted anyway. Outrageous costumes blurring gender distinctions spun our heads left and right. A red-sequined gown swished by my right shoulder. Treacherously high, stiletto heels bulged with fishnet stockings trapping long, black hairs on thick calves. To my left, green and gold eyelashes that would better have suited an elephant's eye waved and flitted, and someone with a Herculean physique floated by in a black leotard with beaded pink tassels and ballet slippers laced up chiseled legs.

The atmosphere buzzed with an infectious, may-be-no-tomorrow fever, a determined extroversion, as if channeling all the degeneration the East was purporting to deflect with their ugly Wall; as if the West was saying, "You fear freedom? Take this." I tried to imagine Michael sitting next to me, but couldn't.

Nadia was swiveling left and right, surveying the action, leaning on the back of Will's chair, her breasts bouncing inches from his face. He leaned away, clearly out of sorts. I watched as he tried to meet Rick's gaze, but Rick was too busy taking in the sights himself. Lavinia, meanwhile, was a social magnet, people popping by, greeting her. She ordered six cokes for us kids and a martini for herself, then shimmied off with a woman in a bow tie, disappearing into the crowd. Nadia's eyes followed her for a second, bouncing back to say something in Will's ear. He nodded, expressionless. Amy nudged my foot beneath the table, cupping her mouth against my ear. "Save him."

I shook my head. "Me? He can take care of himself."

A waiter deposited our colas in front of us and Lavinia wandered back, glowing. I raised my Coke. "To freedom!" In response, Amy grinned, clinking her glass against mine before shouting into the din, "Die Mauer muss weg!" We laughed at our inside joke.

From across the table, Molly leaned over. "Hey, what were you guys up to earlier? Your mom said you were at a *church* meeting?"

"Um," I stalled, kicking Amy. "Well, kind of." Music from the speakers faded into a live drum roll offstage, saving me from making something up.

The club went black, a cymbal crashed, and the curtain swept open to reveal a violet-lit fog creeping across the stage, a haunting, husky vibrato rising from the wings. "*Mein Herz ist leer…*"

"ROMY!" Nadia shrieked, clapping, knocking Will with her unbridled glee. Will sent Rick another desperate look, but Rick was entranced by Romy's tall, slender body rippling across the stage draped in a lavender gown. She headed for the platform just above Rick and Will, stepping on it, towering above us, so close, we could smell her perfume. Romy Haag was beautiful: sculpted cat eyes, high cheekbones, and shapely lips; had we not been where we were, I'd have had no inkling this ideal, feminine figure had been born a he.

The crowd was going wild, but at the start of the third song, the place erupted. Within seconds, a montage of gold and glitter, boas, slinky gowns, and skin-tight leotards was pulsing in sync on the dance floor near our table. Romy swayed above us, a spotlight beaming from her, over the crowd, and down, settling on Rick and Will who blinked into the brilliance. When they waved with shy reluctance, blindly into the light, the room erupted into another outburst of piercing shrieks and applause. Lavinia—cheeks flushed, eyes sparkling—jumped up and raised her glass to Romy who blew her a kiss. The spotlight moved on, sweeping the crowd, this time settling on two men entwined in a passionate kiss, each with a cigarette aloft. The smoke coalesced above them, dancing in the light like mingling spirits. Again, the room erupted.

One wild act followed another—duets, arias, a cappella, tap, and ballet *en pointe*—Romy herself returning a few more times in between. The dance floor pulsed and writhed like a giant, happy octopus. The six of us sat transfixed until the finale. After the curtain fell, recorded music pumped once again from speakers. My heart felt full with that kind of feeling you get from a joyful reunion, like a huge, all-consuming, group hug.

Romy Haag appeared at our table in an iridescent pantsuit, every bit as magnificent as on stage. She and Lavinia ambled away arm in arm, abandoning Nadia, just as she stood to embrace Romy. Undeterred, Nadia turned and pulled Will to his feet. Resigned, Will trailed her to the dance floor with an endearingly awkward lope. Amy and Molly bounded off after them, leaving Rick at the table with me. He ducked down, pulling the tablecloth over his head to hide, peeking out only to allege he didn't know how to dance. I curled my index finger at him to come out, and since Rick could never disappoint, he obliged. He stood up and bowed, linking his arm in mine. As we neared the dance-floor, before I knew it, my hands were slapped atop sweaty, rhinestone-studded straps in front of me, Rick's hands arranged on my shoulders, and off we went, a train growing behind us, the crowd whooping and parting in front of us.

"Hey, I'm gettin' this!" Rick shouted. He was kicking his legs out to the side perfectly off-beat. I couldn't breathe, I was laughing so hard. We snaked up onto the stage and waved at Amy and Molly dancing with wild abandon below. Interlocking arms, the line faced front and attempted a can-can that looked more like a caterpillar having a fit. Out of nowhere, a plastic bowler appeared on my head and a turquoise feather boa around Rick's neck. I thought my heart might explode with love for all of kooky humanity. My cheeks were stiff from smiling. *Different* defined *everyone*. Why not embrace it? I scanned the mosaic coherence surrounding me, like a vibrant, beautiful bowl of fruit. It was something to acknowledge, to celebrate, treasure.

And then, there was Will, his back to us. I called out. A head turned. It wasn't Will. I began to search the crowd, heart pounding. Where was he? Nowhere. Nor was Nadia. That left only dark areas in shadow. I told myself I had no right to be jealous, not even angry, yet an indefensible panic rose.

Rick was tugging me off stage. "Kate, come here." In the wing, he leaned down to my ear. "Look, I'm not gonna pretend to understand what's going on with you and Will, but, I just gotta say..." He hesitated. "Maybe not my place. But Will...he's hurting, confused. Says he's giving you space. But now I'm watching you and I'm thinking, shit, she still *digs* him!" He pulled back to look at me. "Tell me I'm wrong and I'll tell him to stop his moping, let you go." He laughed, but it was clear he was upset for his friend.

Everyone wanted an explanation from me: Nadia, Molly, even Amy. But I couldn't even articulate to myself what was going on. And I knew that whatever I said now would get back to Will. I rose on tiptoes to reach his ear. "I *do* care about him, Rick—you're not wrong. But...," I came down for a second before rising again, "Will and I have to figure this out ourselves." Swallowing a lump in my throat, I turned away from his questioning stare, his exasperation. He took my arm again and led me back toward the table without a word. God, I thought. Were high school romances always so dire?

The moment we sat down, Will and Nadia reappeared, sweaty, breathing hard. I focused in, on my breathing, as Will had taught me. Molly and Amy also returned, glowing, hair sticking to their foreheads. Nadia flopped against Will wiping her brow. "Oh, my! Willy sure can *move*!" Amy made a face behind her, hiding it from Nadia, but I couldn't laugh. I was about to explode with frustration.

The next moment, I was squealing, possessed. "That was a *riot*, huh, *Ricky*? And *this*—I mean, where—?" I wrapped the boa tight around his neck, twirled the bowler hat off my head, popped it onto Rick's, then sat back, laughing like a hyena before leaning in to smack him hard, on the lips. Rick's eyebrows shot up. He laughed, always a good sport, playing along, but at the same time, gently pushed me away. I was giggling like a madwoman, afraid if I stopped, I'd burst into tears. Beneath the table, Amy clutched my knee as if to stabilize me. And then, thank goodness, Lavinia appeared, announcing it was time to go.

I settled on the hump between Amy and Molly as Lavinia veered out of the parking spot. No one had said a word since my crazy outburst. From the back, Rick was tickling Molly's ear with the feather boa. She swiped at the side of her face a few times before realizing, then turned to stick her tongue out at him. Amy broke the silence. "Thank you, Lavinia. That was really amazing." The rest of us echoed our gratitude.

"You're *quite* welcome, darlings!"

"Romy Haag is stunning," Rick remarked, "for a man."

"Romy is a *woman*," Lavinia instructed, launching into the distinctions between transvestites, transsexuals, and drag queens. "It's about your *heart*, not your *body*." Between this evening and Amy's confession about her mother, it felt like I was emerging from a cocoon.

"Imagine how lonely—without clubs like that where you can discover others like you," Molly remarked. Was Amy right about her? I wondered what struggles she kept to herself. It made me feel like a bad friend.

"They're a *necessity*," Amy concurred.

"It felt like a celebration of differences," I commented, imagining Peter's disgust. No doubt, he'd view it as proof of the West's decadence—the need for the Wall.

"The fact that we're *different* is what we all have in *common*," Will mused from the back, echoing my thoughts. My throat clenched.

"Exactly." Lavinia agreed. "Our truths distinguish us." She maneuvered a tight street one-handed, unconcerned that her side mirror grazed a parked car's. "Why on earth waste our one life denying who we were born to be? Hiding our truths does not make them disappear. Untended, kept tight inside, they'll *fester* until—eventually—they'll damage us. A *sham* is not a healthy lifestyle." She gazed back through the mirror. "And yet, sadly, given how the world behaves, some find it easier. To my mind, children, what you witnessed tonight was *courage*."

The engine hummed, our thoughts drifting. Before long, Nadia's head was bobbing against the passenger side window, cushioned by her hair sprout; Molly's lay on my shoulder. It seemed everyone but Lavinia and I had dozed off. "In the East, they think it's weak to emphasize our differences—that strength comes from forcing people to be the same," I mused aloud, hoping only Lavinia would be listening.

She nodded. "Yes, Kate, I think that's true. They've confused sameness with equality. I understand the motivation to strive toward *economic* equality—but you won't get it by squelching human differences—which are irrepressible, anyway, and tenacious. Some day, that society over there *will* implode, like weeds bursting through concrete."

Would it? I wondered. Michael's family had chosen to remain true to themselves, but look where it had gotten them: Michael, trapped, no choice but to work at a kiosk until his obligatory military service, after which he'd be ostracized even more. Their father? In prison for his son's attempt to live free. Anika? Beaten down, ineffably sad. True, their lives were not shams. But *was* it worth it? The alternative was Peter's approach: lose your self, become part of the whole. What would I do?

Amy's head bobbed next to me. I turned to peer in the back. Will, arms wrapped around knees tucked up to his chin, was staring at the road rolling out from the back. He's right here, I thought, but may as well be on the moon. I snuggled closer to Amy. Only she understood my quandary, maybe more than I did.

And she was leaving.

41

Dr. Retter had kind, gray eyes behind rimless glasses, a thin veil of silver hair combed neatly above his forehead. Anika was relieved to get him—rather than the young, self-assured doctor who had sauntered through the waiting room earlier. "You are twenty-one," he noted, without judgment, "nearly twenty-two."

Her eyes focused on the beige wall behind him, then darted to the brown vinyl of the examination table—both too familiar. Her stomach constricted into a knot. "Car accident," she blurted. "The baby's father is dead." Her prepared lie sounded hollow, not convincing. He would not believe her. What then?

"Ah." He shifted in his chair, studied her face. Looking for tears? Impossible. "I am sorry." Indeed, he did seem so. She bowed her head with a token sniffle, ashamed to be lying to such a sympathetic man. "A sad situation," he added, kindly. "You have other family?—support?"

She nodded, her hands twisting the strap of her purse. "A younger brother."

He made a note, cleared his throat. "As close as you remember, I need the date of the onset of your last menses; I realize it is sometimes difficult—"

"Eight May," she replied, the date etched in her memory, how she'd stared at the calendar in the moonlight that first night, counting the days; Klein's timing had been perfect. He'd gotten his wish the first time, she was certain. She gripped her purse to stop the shaking, her eyes landing on the linoleum floor, marbled swirls of black, white, and green—reflecting her shame. She winced, not knowing where to look.

The doctor's brow knit as he turned to the chart in his hands. "Let's see then…you are…." Tilting to peer from the bottom of his lenses, he spun a dial until numbers aligned, then looked up."In your 26th week, Fraulein Streil. You have seen no doctor before now?"

"No. It has been—I've been—grieving." She hung her head, hands wringing the purse strap.

"I understand." He hesitated. "Again, I am sorry for your loss."

Anika fretted, weighing her options—what to say—how much was too much, not enough? He reminded her of her father—the thought made her eyes tear up. Seizing the moment, she looked up.

"Ah, my dear." The doctor placed a gentle hand on the top of her head as he stood, his voice soothing. "We will do what we can from now on to make sure both you and your baby are healthy." He removed a folded cotton sheet from a metal cabinet and lay it on the end of the examination table with a pat, instructing her to remove her clothing below the waist and cover herself, then left her alone.

Anika stood and removed her shoes and stockings, succumbing to the trembling—inevitable, now, whenever flesh met air. She folded her skirt across the back of the chair, and then, on three, pulled down her underwear and removed them quickly, flattening and tucking them out of sight beneath her skirt. Enveloping herself in the cotton sheet, she climbed onto the examining table and waited.

Two days before, Klein had waylaid her on her way home from work. She'd left early but it was already dark when he stepped out of the shadows, blocking her path. Startled, she'd cringed in fear, bracing for a blow. His voice dripped with disdain. "What is this? Have you no polite greeting for me? Ah, of course, you were raised by crude boors." He'd then launched into a fury over her irresponsibility at not yet having gone to a doctor and informed her of an appointment he'd made at the polyclinic on Klosterstrasse. "I will wait outside. Don't even think of not going."

"What am I to tell the doctor?" Anika asked him. "Who shall I say is the father?"

"Tell him you were careless with your boyfriend who then left you because of your stupidity. Keep my name out of it or you'll be sorry. I only need to know my child is healthy."

He *needed* her. The revelation had rallied Anika, allowed for a momentary semblance of control, unearthing a clarity she'd not had in months. He could not hurt her—not as long as she carried his baby. She'd snapped back. "I pity this child, its father a rapist." And Trudi, her mother's cousin? Was she unable to conceive? Was she in on this plan? "Why didn't you just *adopt*?"

Reddened with ire, he came within inches of her face. Anika stood her ground, despite his fury, the now familiar stench of his breath. "*Adopt*? This child," Klein pointed at her belly, "is my blood *and* Trudi's. You should be grateful for the opportunity to repay your family's debt."

Such delusion. Did he actually believe he was saving her? Guiding her back to the true path of the State? And she thought she detected a flash of bewilderment, worry. Could it be that he had not thought through this plan of his?

"I'd like to hear what Trudi thinks," she'd dared to say, watching his response closely.

He'd grabbed her wrist. "If you—or your brother—come anywhere near my wife or ever breathe a word of this to her, I will shred what is left of your family. Do you hear me?" With that, he'd twisted her arm behind her back until she'd crumpled in pain, more certain than ever that he alone was in on this nefarious scheme.

After a crisp knock, Dr. Retter entered, followed by a nurse. Not the sneering young nurse who had judged her when taking her vitals; this nurse, like the doctor, was older. She, too, smiled with kind eyes, extending her hand, "I'm Schwester Helga." Anika wriggled hers free from the mummy wrap to take it.

Something in Helga's gaze told Anika she'd been briefed by Dr. Retter. What had he said? If the doctor found out there was no accident—might he demand to know the real father? Anika was wary, watching for a hint to their suspicions. But Helga revealed nothing. She gently guided Anika into position while Anika focused on the tufts of gray hair coming from beneath her starched cap, guessing she was about the age her mother would be were she alive today. Old enough to have had a life before the Wall.

The doctor murmured, "A little pressure." His touch was careful, methodical, but the tremors began anyway. "Deep breaths," he encouraged, pausing to steady her knee. Anika squeezed her eyes shut, holding in a sob that threatened to burst from her. Despite her efforts, a whimper escaped.

The nurse took her hand, stroking it gently. "There, there, my dear, it will be all right." Her voice was her mother's, soothing, a blanket of calm. Anika began to relax.

42

Exams were upon us, books scattered all over the floor of my room. Amy was highlighting notes, tapping her pen against her knee, humming to the music playing in the background. I was staring at a trig problem, trying to focus. An ache, a sense of something amiss, dwelled in me all the time now. Amy was leaving in less than two weeks—the day after school broke for the holiday, the same day Jack was to arrive. I'd begun to eliminate her inside my head—like when we were in line at the cafeteria or walking home together, or even while home—to accustom myself to life without her, as if that would help when she was really gone. Having been both the one leaving and the one staying so many times, I knew to be aware of that impulse to cut off closeness early, as a coping mechanism. But, like bracing before a vaccination, it really just made it hurt more.

Despite that, Amy and I were growing closer—ignoring everyone else, talking feverishly late into the night. We walked to school slowly, sat separately from the others at lunch. We believed that the closer we grew, the better the telepathy when we were apart. I'd even lost track of Will. Nothing mattered but the dwindling number of days left with her. And no one else even knew she was leaving.

My mother's voice called from downstairs. "Katie, phone—it's Michael?" Pencil flinging, I bounced up and, taking the stairs three at a time—Amy right behind me—dashed past Mom.

"Thanks, Mom," I said, my hand tight against the mouthpiece. "Michael?" I gasped into the phone. Amy's eyebrows shot up.

"*Ja, hallo! Wie geht's?*" His voice spread inside me like honey hitting hot tea. He was wondering when he might get a visit from his dear Auntie? I covered the receiver to consult with Amy.

"My house?" she whispered with a shrug. "Let's meet at the clock."

I spoke using short, German phrases. "Friday? Same as before—six thirty? *Ja, genau.*" I hung up the phone, bursting with excitement before it hit me. "Oh! That's your last weekend!"

Amy nodded. "Yeah. I know. It's perfect, don't you think? I wanted a chance to say goodbye to them. It'll keep us from being too sentimental."

The rest of the week was a blur of studying, typing papers, memorizing stupid formulas. I moped around, impatient, short-fused. When Mom told me Amy had to go home for a couple of nights, I was incensed. "Oh my god, *why*? Don't you realize it's her last week here!?" Every second felt dire.

"It's her last week with her father, too, Kate."

I knew better than to protest. History and algebra exams still lay between now and the evening with Michael and Anika. Like it or not, I had to focus.

This time, Amy and I were early. We were sitting cross-legged against the pillar beneath the *Weltzeituhr* when Amy started in again. "So. About you and Michael…"

"*Amy*. Don't worry. Just friends. I can do it." I had convinced myself that anything more between Michael and me was ridiculous. 'Friends' would have to suffice. Once Amy was gone, I'd be too afraid to come over here alone anyway.

"Mmkay," Amy murmured, unconvinced.

People were giving us disapproving looks. It was cold and windy, the winter sun low in the sky. I'd seen those looks before; even West Germans thought sitting on the ground gave you kidney disease or some other dreadful ailment. I prodded Amy and we labored to our feet. "In a week, this will all seem like a weird dream," she sighed, trapping a scrap of trash fluttering in the wind with her foot. My heart sank. Soon *she'd* be a dream. "But I am excited to go back and see Alex," she said, forcing a smile. "Mom, too, of course." Her foot worked the scrap into a crack at the base of the pillar. "Honestly, I'm scared of seeing her. What if she reverts to how she was before? *Then* what?"

"Then she'll sober up *again*. Anyway, it won't be like before, Amy, because *you're* not the same. She'll see that, too. You can be there for her in a way you couldn't before."

She looked up thoughtfully. "True. I do feel like a different person from when I left."

"Moving does that. Gives you another piece to the giant puzzle of life."

"The Universal Truth."

The piece of paper disappeared inside the crack. I bent down to investigate. "Check this out. There's a big space down there. We could leave messages in here for Michael and Anika. Like a hole in a tree."

"You mean *you* could—though it's not exactly convenient for you."

A couple was crossing the square, heads bowed deep in conversation. It took me a moment to realize it was Michael and Anika. When they finally looked up, their smiles looked strained.

"Whoa. Something's up," Amy whispered as they neared.

Our hugs and kisses lacked the compatibility of last time. In an awkward attempt to brighten the mood, I pointed down to the crack. "What do you think, Michael? It could be our secret mailbox!" It sounded stupid, like I was mocking their situation. But he perked up.

"Ah! A good idea, Katie!" He nodded, not even joking. "Maybe, in case it rains, we should use a plastic." Those eyes—that cosmic pull. Maybe he was my destiny. My resolve and clarity disintegrated.

"We have chili!" Amy cried, holding up a bag. We'd made it after school before Mom gave us a ride to Checkpoint Charlie. "We're going to my house. We have stuff to make a salad, too, if you like?"

Anika seemed to relax a bit. "Sounds wonderful!" I'd been fretting they might worry about going to go to Amy's house. But they seemed unconcerned. We linked arms and started off, Michael toting the chili. As we approached the edge of the square, a man appeared out of nowhere, sun glistening off slick, black hair, his feet wide—as if bracing against the breeze whipping at his long, black coat. He looked like a comic-book villain and I nearly laughed, about to go around him, when Anika recoiled, her grip on my arm tightening.

The man sneered. "Such a happy little group." He spoke in English.

Michael leapt between us and the man. "Herr Klein," he said, then turned to introduce us, his tone flat, his eyes hard, guarded. "Kate, Amy, the husband of our mother's cousin." My spine stiffened. Amy and I exchanged anxious glances.

"Of course, I already know who you are," Klein scoffed, tossing his head back with a jeering laugh. "The two American girlfriends. I am overjoyed to meet you face to face." He looked at me, then Amy, his eyes registering every inch of us. I had the urge to run. But where? With the speed of a lizard tongue, his arm darted out and, shoving Michael aside, he grabbed Anika, ripping her from our linked arms to spin her around, pinning her against him. Amy and I shrieked, grabbing each other as the man slid his hand down Anika's body, letting it rest on her belly, where he patted it with that sardonic laugh. Amy and I were frozen together in shock, Michael buffering us from the man, poised to pounce, when Anika began to thrash, writhing until the man let her go, laughing all the while.

Then, he turned on his heel, an arm flying up over his head as if to bid us farewell. But before we'd even moved a muscle, he turned back, pointing right at Amy. "And for you, a *permanent* farewell!" He then retreated once more, his coat flapping out to the sides like batwings. We stared in stunned silence until we were sure he was really gone.

My body began to quake. I stared at Amy in shock before turning to Michael and Anika. "He *knew* about us?"

Michael's fists were clenched, his face rigid with fury. Anika gazed down, her arms tight around herself. She was crying. "I-I am so sorry," she sobbed, shaking her head.

"What? Why are *you* sorry?" Nothing made sense.

"Sorry for him scaring you," Michael said. His fists clenching. "He is someone we must—" he scrounged for the word, "must tolerate. We—we have no choice." He looked at Anika. " This man… He has power. He works—where he can help, or hurt us."

"He is evil," Anika interjected with a ferocity that made me shiver. I glanced around, half expecting the man to reappear, wondering what was really going on.

"We will explain more later. We go?" Michael's voice was low. He put an arm around his sister's shoulders and we resumed our walk toward the streetcar, dazed and shaken.

"Amy?" Michael asked cautiously. "Is this true? You are leaving?"

Amy stole a glance at me. "I was going to tell you tonight. I am going back to the States in a week. My mother wants me to come back."

"*Ach*, I am sorry. Bad timing for us. So soon—just now when we meet. Katie," he turned to me, "you will be sad, no?" I nodded, still trembling. While we trudged alongside, Anika began to speak to Michael in a hushed tone.

"What a monster," Amy whispered between clenched teeth. "The way he was pawing Anika? I wanted to kick him in the nuts."

"Me, too." That man had clearly meant to scare us. But why? "Something weird is going on." Amy and I quietly debated the wisdom of going to her house, until we realized that man already knew everything about us. At the S-Bahn stop, Michael and Anika turned to face us.

"Before we get on the tram," Michael announced, Anika blinking next to him, her lips pressed together, "we would like to explain."

Anika took a deep breath, pulling herself together, looking from one to the other of us. "I am going to have a baby. *Ja,* but, it—this baby—is not for me to keep."

Amy and I stared dumbly back at her.

"How do you say in English—? *Sie ist Leihmutter.*" Michael looked to me.

"A *borrowed* mother?" I translated, puzzled.

"Yes. Like for a woman who cannot have children—"

"A surrogate mother," Amy said.

I was stunned, full of questions, but none seemed appropriate. "When," I began, "is the baby due?" That, at least, felt nonintrusive.

"In March," Anika replied. All eyes turned to the belly hidden beneath her coat. One thing was clear: neither one of them was happy about it.

As we boarded the streetcar, the clues aligned in my head like a word appearing from a jumble of letters: why they'd told us now, his hand on her belly, their feelings of helplessness, their hatred of him. I felt nauseated, grabbed a wooden handle to keep from stumbling. The baby was *that man's.*

43

Max was out—no surprise—when we got to Amy's. We made a salad while the chili warmed in the oven, then ate in the kitchen, chatting about cooking and foods we liked, without once mentioning the creepy confrontation at Alexanderplatz—or Anika's predicament. But the topics hovered in the background like ominous clouds. Despite the stack of records on the stereo providing continuous background music, we spoke softly. After clearing the table, we sat back down with some tea. The flickering candle filled with wax. I pressed a match against the lip, letting the hot liquid that dribbled over flow onto my finger, when an image of Herr Klein behind the walls in headphones popped into my head, and I jumped up and ran into the living room to turn the music up even louder.

Michael managed to make us laugh with his imitation of his bumbling co-worker, Ingo. Ingo, knocking down stacks of magazines, falling asleep standing up, telling jokes that made Michael cringe, yet want to explode with laughter. But it was Ingo whom Michael trusted not to say a word when he used the phone to call the West, though it had to be assumed each call was monitored, Ingo who'd made up Michael's aunt.

"Tell us about Stefan?" Amy urged, gently.

I looked up from the clump of wax I'd molded into a teardrop. Both siblings were gazing into the flame with placid expressions. I wondered if they might just ignore Amy's plea. But then, Michael shrugged. "He was a hippie—long hair—tall." He went silent again. I sympathized—how would one begin to describe a sibling whose life was cut short for no good reason?

"After Berlin was divided," Anika's voice was barely above a whisper. We had to lean in to hear over the loud music, four heads too close to a burning flame. "Stefan respected our father, his faith. When he was older, he refused to join the FDJ. Instead, he went to the *Junge Gemeinde*."

"It was more dangerous in those days," Michael added.

A young body crumpled at the base of the Wall flashed into my mind as Elton John sang *Tiny Dancer* in the living room. I smoothed the wax teardrop between my fingers. Would they talk about their brother's horrendous ending? I wasn't sure I could handle it.

Anika continued. Stefan was fifteen. Their mother lay dying. He prayed, held her hand, stayed by her side, day and night, refusing to leave it. But when her breathing changed to a shallow, racing pant, their father had commanded Stefan to fetch Michael in from outside. The moment he left, their mother had passed away.

In the months following her death, Stefan changed. He grew despondent, then angry. Why had their mother's life been shortened so? He questioned everything: illness, injustice. War. Dominance over one's fellow man, totalitarianism. How could they believe in a merciful god? A god that expected—demanded—to be worshipped? Was that not the signature of a tyrant? How could you love such a god? What was the point? Despite their father's attempts to placate, Stefan had lost his faith.

Michael was watching his sister intently, rolling wax between his palms. I wondered how often they talked about their brother. "Stefan," Anika said, "was never truly content again." I shifted uncomfortably. Never again. She could say that, because she could see her brother's life in its entirety. Beginning, middle, end. "The

West became an obsession." Anika looked up, her eyes flickering in the candlelight. We fell silent. When she spoke again, it was clear. No more was to be said about Stefan. "Kate, tell us, please, what is it like to live all over the world?"

A question I'd been asked often, and had a ready answer for: Nothing broadens the mind better; it's traumatic to pack up and start all over in an entirely new country every few years, but, it's worth it—the more challenging, the greater the rewards. When people in America quizzed me about our lifestyle, they often emphasized the negatives: how hard it must be to lack a 'true' home or roots, create 'deep' friendships—how much I must long to settle down in the United States. Some became defensive if I offered an alternative viewpoint: sincerity and experience solidified a friendship, not time. And roots? Trees had roots, not people. People had eyes, minds, curiosity. I argued that giving so much worth to roots (when we didn't have any anyway) could lead to closed-mindedness and pointless fears of people and places unlike ours. I'd said it all before, to people who had no *desire* to travel—but never to anyone not *allowed* the freedom to travel the world. Yet Michael and Anika seemed to get it right away, to appreciate the lifestyle. Maybe it was because they didn't have the luxury *not* to contemplate what they were missing.

"Moving changes you," Amy added, her eyes on the flame. "I'm about to go back to where I lived before, but it won't be the same. *I* won't be the same." She looked at me and bobbed her eyebrows up and down. "I'm wiser."

Michael had worked his wax into a perfect, tiny vase. "I imagine travel also helps you to see yourself. Who you really are—when somewhere not familiar?" he kept his voice low. "Here, jobs, education, housing—you can have it all—if you agree to think the way they want you to." He looked up. "No travel. No choice. No perspectives. Really, who benefits?" He dropped his tiny creation back into the liquid around the flame. The melted wax overflowed, dripping down the sides of the candle.

We moved to the living room leaving the dishes piled in the sink. Outside, a heavy rain beat against the windows. Amy retrieved the candle from the kitchen and lit incense. Michael put on *Rumors*, stacking more records on top. We dropped cushions from the sofa onto the carpet and snuggled down so we could talk, heads close, music our cover.

Amy and I told them about the evening at the Romy Haag club. We talked about the human instinct to fear differences in each other and why, decided that overcoming the fears was the only way to harmony and peace. We talked about Amy leaving, where she was going. When a good song came on, we sang for a bit, then drifted back into chatting. Then it was too late for them to leave. At some point, Anika crawled up to lie on the couch saying she would continue to listen from there but, immediately, she fell asleep. The little hillock of her belly rose and fell, and I tried to picture the tiny, partial being curled inside her—cringing to think of how it had come to be.

When Amy, too, rolled over and fell asleep, Michael reached over me to grab a couple of pillows from a chair, and I snuffed out the candle. We stretched out on our sides, facing each other. "Michael," I asked, feeling braver in the dark, "is Anika…all right?" When he didn't answer right away, I worried I'd overstepped.

"Anika is strong," he replied, finally. He spoke in German—it felt more intimate, somehow, when he spoke in his own language. "But, it has been very difficult and stressful."

"How hard will it be…to give up the baby?" I stayed with English.

He propped himself on an elbow and leaned close, my question dangling, his lips brushing my cheek. He toyed with a tuft of my hair, then intertwined his legs with mine, drawing me close. Blood throbbed through me. I ached for a kiss. Instead, he began to whisper in fierce, short bursts. "We are afraid. It is so dangerous, our situation. Anika has been tortured, Katie. And I—I did nothing. I can do nothing. We talk to no one—only each other. I shouldn't talk, even to you. But, only you—"

His body tensed. I reached my arms around his shoulders, to steady him, as if to keep him from teetering over an edge. I wanted him to explain: why? What was so dangerous? But I knew—it was that demonic man. He was responsible. I held Michael tight, lay my head on his chest so I could hear his heart beating. When he spoke again, each word pounded with a quiet, frustrated rage. "She was forced, Katie. This Klein is a crazy man with much power. We are in no position to fight him. He could make it worse—much worse—for us. And for our father." He paused. "Anika *must* do what he says."

Herr Klein. That maniacal laugh. His hands all over Anika. I felt sick—the word 'rape' flying from news, books, and movies into my reality. Nearby, Anika's breathing seemed calm and peaceful. But what horrors returned the moment she woke?

"Anika is insisting she cannot give him the baby," Michael continued, his words edged with worry. "But, she must. She must."

The room that had felt so cozy swirled with unseen, sinister forces. I held him, stroking his feathery hair until I felt his body begin to relax. Even when it twitched in sleep, his breath rising and falling with an easy rhythm, I still held tight. I kept myself awake, as if to keep watch.

At some point, the music stopped. Max came home, his silhouette pausing in the doorway before ambling on toward the kitchen. I wondered what he made of the bodies in his living room, the dishes in the sink. When he climbed the stairs to his bedroom, Michael stirred. He hugged me, and began to kiss the top of my head, turning my face to kiss my eyes, my cheeks, my lips. I drank him in, pushing aside thoughts of Will, telling myself Michael and I needed each other right now. A sense of urgency took hold, a need to reject anything between us, and we lifted our shirts, clutching each other tight, skin to skin, staying that way, afraid to move a muscle. "Katie,"

Michael whispered. My mind swirled with emotions ranging from ecstatic to grief that seemed to come from eternity itself. This could not be, I knew it, yet at that moment, I wanted nothing less. Then we both were crying, our tears mixing between our cheeks. I buried my face in his neck and kissed it. Then, we fell apart and lay side by side, wiping our eyes, hands clutched tightly between us.

When Anika began shaking Michael and calling his name, I surfaced from a deep, dreamless sleep. Michael stirred beside me where I lay, a pea in his pod. He kissed my neck before peeling away, leaving behind an icy void. I sat up and rubbed life into my eyes. Amy lay beneath the coffee table, her hair fanned out behind her. I pushed away the table so she wouldn't bump it when she sat up, then nudged her awake.

The sky was luminous, that rare cobalt blue of predawn. Wordlessly, the four of us padded into the kitchen. We sat quietly while Amy made tea, setting the pot on the table. I yawned, craving more sleep. Anika yawned, too, smiling at me through it. My heart ached for her, wishing I had a way to help. As if sensing this, Michael took my hand beneath the table.

"We will miss you, Amy. I am sad our time was so short," Anika said. "You became a good friend very fast."

"You must write down your address," Michael added, "so we can write to you."

Amy pushed back her chair and darted from of the room, reappearing a moment later with the *Rumors* album tucked beneath her arm. "For you." She shoved it into Michael's hands and whirled to get out milk, spoons, sugar, pour tea. I could tell she was trying not to cry, and shut my mind to the other painful truth: Amy would soon be gone. "No. Please," she begged, as Michael attempted to press the album back into her hands. The red-glazed flowers on the teapot buzzed against the shiny, white porcelain as I stared and sipped, the hot tea a bulwark against tears.

A silence fell, our emotions talking without words. When Michael and Anika rose to leave, we moved slowly, solemnly. At the door, we exchanged hugs, Michael pressed my head to his chest. When at last he let me go, I thought the ache in my heart would tear me in half. The door closed, shutting them out into a biting, wintry air. We wandered back into the kitchen and slumped at the table.

"I'm not gone yet, y'know." Amy said, wiping away tears, her posture straightening. "So. What happened last night?"

I wasn't sure what to say.

44

The baby rolled over at three in the morning: same time every night now. The punctuality of a good German, Anika thought, shuddering against the specter of its father. She'd tried distancing herself, hating the baby, but her heart beat on beside it, her body continued to nurture it. When she found herself wondering if it was a boy or a girl, she stopped herself. It was not hers. She could become no more attached to it than a tumor, soon to be excised.

At work, eyes lingered and questioned and she knew that they talked; but she offered no explanation. Why should she explain? They were not her friends. Dr. Schmidt had called her into her office and handed her a form. She'd said it was clear Anika would need time off: she was allowed a month of maternal leave, longer by request. Anika had started to protest, deny she would need it, say she was not to be a mother—then thought, why not take it anyway, some time for herself?

Anika pulled herself upright, annoyed by the persistent need to pee, her feet searching for her slippers in the dark. When the baby pitched wildly, Anika clutched her belly, instinctively, as if to catch it. And like a beam of bright light bursting through the persistent fog of tortured thought, the truth flashed: she could not do it. Moment by moment, stronger, clearer this truth became. She would not give her baby to that man.

At her check up that day, Schwester Helga had lingered after Dr. Retter left the room. "Anika, would you let me buy you a tea?" she'd asked. "You are my last patient today and I am free in fifteen minutes. If you have time? There is a cafeteria downstairs. You could wait for me there." Reason had screamed at Anika to refuse, while her heart ached for kindness.

Anika had agreed. After she'd settled into a chair across from her, Helga had wasted no time. "You cannot hide it, dear," she'd said, firmly, though not unkindly.

Caught off guard, Anika had groped for her lie. "It's—the accident—his death. It's very painful. I'm so sad."

Helga's eyebrows had risen, her head cocked to the side as if to say Anika's lie was as see-through as a spiderweb. "Anika," her cup clinked down onto its saucer, "we both know that is not the truth. I'm sorry, dear, but you have not fooled me—or Dr. Retter. He is concerned. Knows you are not at peace. It is our job to protect you and your baby." She paused a gentle moment. "So, now, dear. The truth."

It was risky, perhaps downright stupid. But Anika was desperate. Helga's concern felt genuine. Either the Stasi had hired an incredible actress, or she was trustworthy. She'd glanced around, taking in the din surrounding them, then, emboldened, she'd nodded. The dam cracked, broke. She told Helga everything in a fierce whisper, swiping at angry tears until, unburdened, resigned to whatever ensued, Anika sat back.

Helga's lips had pressed together as though she had to control what might burst from them, and then she'd murmured, "You poor, dear child." Placing a hand atop Anika's, she'd nodded. "So. We will have to get a little creative."

Now, leaning against the wall in the dark hallway, Anika sighed. The catharsis had been short-lived. The truth was, there was nothing anyone could do that wouldn't jeopardize her family. She would have no choice but to give the child to Herr Klein.

And at the same time, she also knew she couldn't.

45

"Hey, kiddo, I'm official!" Jack waved his new Flag Pass in front of my face. "I wanna see the East. Let's get the car and drive on down to Checkpoint Charlie." He grabbed the *Life* magazine I'd been reading peacefully. "C'mon. No more moping around, pining for Amy, reading girlie magazines." Dangling the magazine just beyond my reach, he lowered it, then snatched it away the moment I reached for it. I gave up. Jack had been there two days and already was driving me nuts. It was Monday—the first with no school. I'd hoped to do nothing.

"*Life* is not a girlie magazine," I grumbled, attempting to rise from my bean bag chair.

After school let out early Friday, Amy and I had joined Nadia, Molly, Rick, and Will out front where we'd lingered in the freezing cold talking about vacation plans. Rick's family was going skiing in Austria, Nadia and Molly's families together to Mallorca; Will had relatives coming and they were going skiing, too, somewhere in Switzerland. Stomping to stay warm while Amy's secret boiled inside me, Amy and I had added nothing. Amy hadn't cared that I'd be stuck with explaining—didn't even care what I told them once she was gone.

"So do we get to meet Jack?" Molly'd asked.

I'd assured them they would but made no attempt to plan. The awkwardness had grown until Amy and I had wandered off with a vague "maybe" about meeting up at the Outpost later that evening for a movie. That was the last Amy ever saw of the gang. On the way home, she'd cried a little, but defended her reasons for not saying goodbye.

Later in my room, I handed her a wrapped package. "What's this?" She tore it open. I'd addressed envelopes, even put stamps on them.

"It's your starter kit. For writing me." Within the pad, I'd scribbled anecdotes, memories, stuff we'd done together. She'd find them later.

"I'll write the minute I land. Even on the plane." After she hugged me and put the box aside, she announced, "OK, so I have something for you, too. Close your eyes." Soft wool that smelled like Amy's Charlie perfume constricted my head, then fell around my shoulders. Her poncho. I opened my eyes. She was grinning.

"Really?" I hugged her and started to well up. "I'll pretend you're with me whenever I wear it."

"It's just a loan. You have to give it back to me after you leave Berlin. In *person*."

"Deal."

Then Max picked her up after dinner to take her home for a couple hours' sleep before departing for the airport at three in the morning, and she was gone. I'd wanted him to get her from my house on the way to the airport, but Amy rejected that idea as too depressing. When Jack pulled me up from the bean bag chair, I was counting in my head. Amy had been gone sixty hours.

"So, I'm going to need to get a Soviet belt buckle. And maybe an *eff-day-yot* t-shirt," Jack declared. I stared at him, calculating.

We could drive by Michael's house just to see if they were home. Would that put them in more danger? I couldn't see why. Not a day passed that I didn't think about them. "Did you even *ask* if we could take the car?"

The MP at Checkpoint Charlie explained that we had exactly two and a half hours in the East. After that, they would send out troops looking for us. When Jack's eyebrows shot up, it made me laugh. I was used to this stuff. We snaked our way around the barricades and stopped for the East Germans—the same guards I could chat with when walking through as a diplomat; now we had to pretend they weren't there. In our car with bright green U.S. military license plates, we were not to recognize them. We weren't entering East Berlin. We were entering the Soviet Sector.

I stared straight ahead and pressed my Flag Pass to the window, opening it when the guard indicated to, never meeting his eyes. He ambled around to Jack's side and Jack did the same. "*Jawohl!*" he whispered, eyes wide and front, stifling a nervous chuckle. The guard waved us on. "Man, talk about bizarre," Jack murmured. It was weird to be the one who knew the ropes. How far I'd come in accepting this strange game.

A few blocks into the East, Jack looked up, flipping the map around in his lap. "Turn left. No—right!" Too late. We'd missed the turnoff to Alexanderplatz. I grabbed the very next right, intending to make a u-turn. But the road ended abruptly at a three-meter high, chain-link fence topped with barbed wire plastered with blood-red signs warning, "*Eintritt Verboten.*"

"Oops." I started to back up when, as if we'd tripped an alarm, sirens began to wail. Out of nowhere, three *Volkspolizei* cars appeared, lights spinning. We were trapped. I grew frantic. Next to me, Jack shrugged, freakishly unperturbed.

"Relax, Katie. You've done nothing wrong. I'll explain. No biggie." With that, he hopped out and approached one of the police cars. His German was much better than mine, so I let him go. Until I remembered the rules. *Do not engage with East German authorities.* In the pocket next to the window, I grabbed the card that shouted: *I DEMAND TO SPEAK TO A SOVIET OFFICER*—in English, French,

German, and Russian. The moment I rolled down the window to wave the card at the policemen, they grabbed Jack and threw him against the hood of one of the *VoPo* cars.

I screamed. "*Hey!* I demand to see a Soviet Officer!" The police ignored me, twisting Jack's arms behind him. Keep calm, I told myself. Think. They must've understood Jack. His German was almost flawless—why weren't they listening to him? My mind churned. Then, as the Germans say: *der Groschen ist gefallen,* the penny dropped.

They thought he *was* German. In fact—they thought he was an *East* German—in my American car. They thought he was trying to escape!

I began to shout through the window. "Stop! *Er ist mein Bruder!* He's my brother! We demand a Soviet Officer!" *Do not engage with East German authorities!?* But—my mind raced—what if *they* engaged with *you*? A guard was pressing Jack's head into the hood with his forearm, shouting for his *Ausweis*.

"Kate! My passport!" Jack managed, between smashed cheeks. I ripped the key from the ignition and dove across the seat to unlock the glove compartment where we'd stashed our diplomatic passports before leaving home—just in case. Diplomats in a military car—it contradicted all security scenarios. My fingers flicked through the top passport to the photo: me. I tossed it aside and waved the other one out of the window. *"Er ist wirklich mein Bruder!"*

One of the policemen reached for it, but I held tight. I wasn't going to let it go. I opened to the picture, tapped it, then pointed to Jack—then flipped it to expose the cover: black with a golden eagle and the words Diplomatic Passport, United States of America, blazed across it. Then, just for good measure, I held up the card again, blowing up every one of the taboos. *I DEMAND TO SEE A SOVIET OFFICER.* We locked eyes for what seemed like an eon, and then he shouted over his shoulder. The policeman pressing Jack down backed away. Jack pushed himself upright, regained composure, and faced his assailants, eyes narrowed.

I was afraid of what he might say. "Jack," I urged. "Let's go."

Jack ambled over to the passenger's side. But then he paused and turned to the policemen and in loud, crisp German, announced, "I accept your apology." He climbed in and shut the door, an angry, red flush rising across his cheek. With trembling hands, I started the car and, palms sweating against the icy steering wheel, began maneuvering back and forth in the narrow street until we faced the way out. The two *VoPo* cars blocking us drove off, but the third, on whose hood Jack had been pinned, remained, the cops standing beside it, eyeing us with a steely gaze. As I carefully steered around them, Jack rolled down his window.

No, I thought. Oh, no. I tugged on his jacket, nearly driving into the chainlink fence. "Jack! What're you...? Don't, Jack, don't!" I slumped low in anticipation of whizzing bullets, torture, prison, maybe even death.

But Jack was already shouting. "*Danke für die angenehme Einführung in Ihrer Nation!*" Thank you for the pleasant introduction to your country. Jack rolled the window back up. "Just being polite."

We made our way to Alexanderplatz as though nothing had happened. But even after we'd parked and walked into Centrum department store, I was still shaking, bracing for a swarm of *VoPo's* to descend, assuming every pillar and corner had eyes. Jack, meanwhile, rummaged through folded piles on a table. "DDR flags!" He unfolded one, its red, black and gold stripes just like the West German flag, with the addition of a hammer and compass—adapted from the Soviet's hammer and sickle—adorning the center. "They're practically free. Five East Marks." Less than one West Mark with our black market money. "How many should we get?"

"Jack, shush! Fold it back up." I looked around nervously.

"Hey, relax, kiddo. We'll buy a couple, then whip by your friends' house on the way outta here. We've still got time."

He didn't get it. "We're not driving by their house in our car after what just happened! It'd light them up."

"Oh, come on, I'd like to meet them."

"No." I was adamant. "By now the entire Stasi is on high alert!"

"We just made a wrong turn," he said, brushing away my angst. In no apparent rush, he selected three flags and a handful of FDJ t-shirts, and headed to the cashier. I tried to adopt his mellow attitude, but it wasn't happening. One of us is naive, I thought.

Once outside again, we wandered past the ugly, modern fountain toward the *Weltzeituhr*. I'd told Jack all about how it was our meeting point—and about our secret mailbox beneath it.

"Let's check it," Jack suggested, beelining toward it.

"Jack, wait!" I hissed, grabbing his arm. "Don't just go straight there. No one can see us checking!"

"OK—then how 'bout I grab a bratwurst. Want one? Meet you there."

The square was brightly trimmed for New Year's, posters exalting the GDR's forward march into 1978. The green and red tinsel looked remarkably similar to Christmas decorations in the West. I sat on a low wall a few feet from the clock, glancing around warily, registering faces. Jack handed me a paper plate with a tiny wooden fork poking up from a steaming bratwurst. Munching, he read the names of the cities rolling around the clock as we walked toward it.

"You can't get there from here," I said.

Jack shook his head with a chuckle. "Dark."

"Here, hold this?" I handed him my plate and crouched down beneath the clock, pretending to tie my shoe. "Look—be subtle! Here's the crack." Stuffed down inside, I saw something. Certain it was just trash, I pulled it out, anyway. A piece of plastic bag. Inside it lay a neatly folded note. My heart flipped.

"Find something?" Jack wadded up his paper plate and started on my wurst, while my hands shook, fumbling with the plastic.

We ambled back to sit on the low wall. Jack flipped through a newspaper he'd grabbed at the kiosk. "Such blatant propaganda. Who buys this crap?" he grumbled through a mouthful of sausage.

I swallowed hard. The note was in German: cursive, small and neat, straight across unlined paper. *Liebe K—*, it began. My heart pounded. He'd been careful not to write out my name. I translated: *I wonder how you are, if you will find this. I miss you very much. We are worried. HK—* I whipped around in a panic, then focused again, my hands trembling. Herr Klein... *leaves luxury foods at our house. Make no mistake—it is not out of kindness. He controls us. Anika grows bigger.* The date at the top was 16-12-77. Five days ago. I brought the note to my nose, seeking Michael's essence, but whiffed only the coal-saturated air of East Berlin.

There was more. *Ich glaube, dass ich dich liebe.* I felt dizzy and looked up. Everything was painfully sharp and bright. I closed my eyes to control my breathing but—his lips, his body, his smell—for a flash he was there. I read on, translating, devouring his words. *I think about you and imagine being together. But—I know we both understand it is not possible. Who knows what would be if circumstances were different? We will never know. The moment we fell apart, I felt such love. That love will be there, no matter what. Your M.*

Ich glaube, dass ich dich liebe. I believe that I love you. A fat tear dropped onto the note, exploding the word *liebe* into a wet, black rose.

"You OK there, kiddo?" Jack was staring at me, his newspaper folded in his lap. I swallowed hard, tucking the note beneath Amy's poncho to fold it back up.

"Can we go home?" I sniffed.

Jack zipped up his jacket. "Sure, let's go. This place is beat, anyway."

We started off in the direction of the car, when I stopped. "Jack, do you have a pen?" My voice was screechy and pinched. "I have to write back." I pulled out Michael's note. There was space for a short reply.

"Sure, yeah, think so. Hang on." He fished around till he pulled a ballpoint from a pocket. "Here." He ruffled my hair. "Take your time, kiddo. We still have an hour."

I stuck to English, scribbling quickly, trying to keep it legible. *Dearest M—, I feel the same. We will never know what could have been. In our hearts forever...love, Deine K—.* Beneath Amy's poncho, I folded and tucked the note back inside the plastic as we meandered back toward the clock.

A few minutes later, we were driving back through Checkpoint Charlie. I sighed my relief. Jack laughed. "You give them way too much credit, kiddo," he said, tuning the radio to AFN, Casey Kasem counting down the *American Top 40*. We pulled up alongside the American hut. The same MP who had signed us out earlier strolled over.

"Everything OK? No incidents?" He motioned for us to climb out of the car. The *Top 40* was playing in his hut, too.

"Purchase anything?" He tapped his pen against the clipboard while peering through the back windows.

"A few souvenirs. Flags, t-shirts—propaganda, couple of bratwurst," Jack flashed his disarming grin. "Been on duty long? Racking up the overtime?"

"Hah," the MP chortled, scribbling on his clipboard. "In the wrong line of work if I'm about making money." He tapped the pen where I needed to sign.

Back safe and sound. I tried to breathe easier. But driving away, I got turned around and we dead-ended at the Wall. Twice. Jack thought it was funny while I pounded the steering wheel in frustration. He leaned back and kept quiet. Another wrong turn, and I was completely lost. I burst into tears. Jack ordered me to pull over. When we came to a stop, the whole story came out.

Jack parked the car in our tiny garage while I ran straight up to my room. I smashed my face into my pillow and bellowed until my lungs objected, my throat sore. Reason was saying, "Cut the drama, Kate." I ran water until it was hot, plugged the sink, waited for it to fill, then sank my whole face in until I came up gasping for air. Again and again. Between dunks, I glanced in the mirror. What. Dunk. Is. Dunk. Your. Dunk. Problem?

I needed Amy. I leaned against my *kilim* pillow armed with paper and pen, ready to write. Where to start? The empty sheet of paper glared back at me, Amy's absence settling around me like hardening concrete. It wasn't the same. She was gone. I was alone. I doodled a giant, elaborate *AMY!!!* across the top of the page. Self-pity pooled around me as Christmas spices wafted from downstairs.

The military phone rang. Mom's voice, "Merry Christmas, Will." I jumped up to hover at the top of the stairs to listen. "Haven't seen you all in ages.... Uh huh.... OK.... Hmm. Well, hang on, let me see...." I tore back into my room, softly closing the door behind me, heart pounding, awaiting a summons. What would I say? My mind raced, toying with my options. Seconds passed. Eventually, I opened the door. Music carried with it cozy, Christmas smells: pine, incense—and—was that *Glühwein*? Mom and Dad were laughing, Jack was telling a story. Was it about me—and Michael? Jack had promised; he would never betray me. Would he? Even if he had, they wouldn't laugh. Would they? Or was he telling them about our incident with the *VoPo's*? No, we'd sworn not to tell them about that. When had I started *not* telling Mom and Dad things?

Maybe Mom had called up to me and I hadn't heard. Maybe the receiver still lay on the desk, Will on the other end, waiting for me. I tiptoed downstairs and peeked around the corner. Both receivers lay in their cradles. More laughter, Dad now holding forth. I tore back upstairs, threw myself on the bed. Michael's kiss, his words, his touch, over and over, I could feel, hear them. It was hopeless. I couldn't stand myself any longer.

Mom looked up from the couch smiling. "Well, there you are!" Next to her, Dad held a rolled up *Time* magazine, poised for emphasis. Mugs were perched on a wooden tray next to my favorite Christmas platter, empty but for a few cookie crumbs. Across the room, lights twinkled on the fragrant tree we'd bought the frosty evening Jack had arrived, the day Amy had left, a few brightly wrapped presents beckoning beneath it.

Jack grinned at me from an armchair, one long leg crossed over the other, eyebrows raised. He'd come home looking more like a man, and I wasn't sure what to think about that. Just in case he'd betrayed my confidence, I scowled at him, regretting it when his expression turned hurt.

Dad pointed to the empty platter. "Christmas cookies, Kit. Where've you been? Also had some of your Mama's delicious *Glühwein*." He licked his lips. Goofball.

Pushing aside wet bangs, I forced myself to engage. "What was so funny down here?"

"I was telling Marvin stories. The guy's incorrigible," Jack said, shaking his head.

"Seems the roommate lacks some basic social skills. Your brother has an enviable capacity for forbearance," Dad intoned, the magazine tapping his palm. They laughed again, at what I'd missed.

Mom glanced up, knitting needles not missing a beat. "Honey, Will called. For his mom. She wanted Greta's number." Greta was the scary German woman who cut hair. A lot of the American women used her. "He said he didn't need to speak to you." She eyed me, her needles paused. "Everything OK with you two?" When I said nothing, she went on knitting. She was not one to pry.

"You had *Glühwein* and didn't tell me?" I leaned over and pressed a finger into the crumbs on the plate. "Any left?"

46

The first day of school after the winter break dawned, a gray fog lurking just above the treetops. To calm my nerves, I forced myself out the door for an early run. I imagined the pretty morning mist over the *Krumme Lanke*, and decided to head to the lake, despite being alone.

Jack had dubbed our holiday runs Jingle Jogs. He didn't like running. "…when I've got nothing to run *from*," he'd say, but he'd gone with me anyway—lest I got too mopey. On our last jog together over the break, I told Jack how, when we ran together, Will would set the perfect pace for me, and how I missed running with him.

"I like the sound of Will," Jack had said. "Patch it up, Kate. Plus, he lives in the West. How convenient." He'd thought my preoccupation with Michael was unhealthy, figured the romance of a forced separation magnified the attraction.

"Don't think so," I'd insisted. "If the Wall wasn't there, I know I'd be feeling just as conflicted."

"You can't know that, Kate. Anyway," Jack added, "the Wall *is* there."

The dirt path snaked through a tunnel of trees toward the lake, then meandered along the bank. Will and I used to run around the

Krumme Lanke every Thursday morning. One Thursday we'd run together and the next, we hadn't. Maybe we never would again. The murky sun reflected off the lake in a mushy blur. I began to relax, settling into an easy rhythm. I could handle anything after a run, I thought, hoping my worries about starting school without Amy would melt away.

The break had been filled with a flurry of holiday parties both with other Americans and with German friends, including a work reception at our house for Dad's local contacts. Jack and I had pitched in, making hors d'oeuvres and decorating the house. For New Year's, Mom, Dad, Jack, and I drove downtown to watch the competing firework displays—East vs. West. We'd parked on Bernauerstrasse where the Wall went right through the houses and climbed onto the roof of the car with a thermos of cocoa, passing it around. Jack and I snuggled under a sleeping-bag and watched the skies explode above us.

I'd managed to avoid the gang until two days into the new year, when Mom took me by surprise. "Time to call around to invite your friends to the Bashing Party!" Every year, we made a gingerbread house from scratch and then hosted a post-New Years' party to smash it. But—in my distraction—I'd forgotten all about it. I tried to persuade Mom to make it just family this year.

"None of my friends are around, anyway," I'd claimed. But Mom had run into Rick's mom at the PX and already had mentioned the party to her. When I began to whine, I got her no-nonsense 'that's-enough' look. "Snap out of it, Kate, she ordered. "We're doing it like we always do. Start calling your friends."

I called Nadia first, bracing in anticipation of her exuberance. She didn't disappoint. "Katie!" she screamed. "Happy New Year!" I groaned as she droned on: they'd all had so much fun in Mallorca—wait till I hear—and Ricky and Willy were back, too—perfect timing for a party. (Without Amy to do it, I had to feign a gag on my own.) "Oooooh, and we get to meet Jack!" When I mentioned that parents and siblings were invited, too, she practically swooned. She had a thing for Rick's five-year-old brother, a mini-Rick. "Mickey will loooove it!"

The day of the party, I was on door duty since we had no bell and over the din of music and voices, knocking might not be heard. Coats piled on my parent's bed, I ushered guests to the dining room where the gingerbread house adorned the center of the table, twinkling amidst numerous tea-candles surrounding it, unaware of its impending doom. Little ones swarmed around the table, begging to start smashing the house, plucking candy canes and chocolate kisses when adults weren't looking.

With each knock, my heart skipped a beat. Soon, everyone—except for Will and his family—had arrived. Still perched near the front door, I listened as Jack's charm and wit won over my friends. He complimented Nadia on her dazzling mid-winter tan that stood out against her white sweater, and Nadia sidled up to me to whisper. "I'm in love!"

Mom offered glasses of Dad's spiked, homemade eggnog and Dad engaged Molly's father in a discussion of the significance of Bophuthatswana's independence. Lavinia was raving about the eggnog between laments on the house's fate. "It's far too precious to demolish!" she proclaimed, bangles jangling, stunning in a black, pearl-encrusted flapper dress. Nadia's father sat in a corner, talking Rick's mom's ear off. She looked painfully bored.

"If it isn't smashed," Mom explained, "next year, there will be no Christmas." We held no such superstition. But she knew how to handle Lavinia.

Jack offered little Mickey the hammer for safe-keeping. "Here you go, li'l man. Later, you can take the first swing. But not until I give you the signal. Deal?" Immediately, Mickey began to hop up and down, the hammer aloft in precarious, baseball-bat readiness.

"Whoa." Rick intervened, deftly tickling his little brother until he was in a writhing, giggling mass on the floor and the hammer dropped from his grasp.

I had begun to wonder if Will's family wasn't coming after all, thinking I probably could desert my post, though appreciating the vantage point from which to observe the party, when Nadia had headed my way. "Hey, where's Amy?" she asked, popping a mint I'd seen her pry from the iced roof into her mouth. "Isn't she back yet?" So preoccupied about seeing Will, I'd forgotten to prepare my story. In retrospect, I thought now, confident and calm, jogging through the brisk morning air, I'd handled the Amy story pretty well. I'd simply explained that Amy had gone back to the States as planned for Christmas—and only *then* decided to stay, because her mother, who'd been sick, was better and wanted Amy there. A mix of truth and a little distortion—not quite a full-on lie—just enough to spare feelings.

Nadia, devastated, in utter disbelief, had pressed for details, of course. Sick? Had I known? What was I going to do? Was I *devastated*? She'd run off to spread the news when the anticipated knock came. I jumped up and pulled open the door, my knees jelly, hands trembling. Yet the moment I laid eyes on Will, a sense of tranquility had washed over me, the tight knots in my brain loosening for the first time in ages. Will. I knew Will. I sighed with relief. It was going to be OK: we'd work it out, get to the bottom of things. Smiling, I pulled him inside and offered to take his coat with exaggerated aplomb. He laughed, clearly relieved at my warmth. He, too, must have been nervous.

Behind him were his parents—plus a young woman—an older sister back for the holidays, I assumed. She removed a floor-length coat to reveal an emerald, cashmere sweater that matched a beret tilted over long, wavy blonde hair. She was nothing short of movie-star gorgeous. And then, this beauty snuggled against Will. She kissed his cheek. Her arm entwined with his, she addressed me. "You must be Kate! Will has told me all about you." Cool porcelain fingers, perfectly enameled in pink, slipped into mine. I could only stare in confusion. She was no sister. Jack and I would never behave like that.

Rick and Nadia came up to greet them with big hugs. "Miranda! Will! Happy New Year!" Chatting like old pals, Miranda draped herself around Will like a ribbon on a Maypole. My face burned with a campfire in my head, nasty sprites dancing around it, mocking: "Will has moved on! On! And *up!*" And apparently, I was the last one to know.

"Kate. This is…" Will had started to say.

My scrawny legs scissored beneath me, thudding against the dirt trail. My shame burned yet, remembering how Will had tried to meet my gaze. I'd turned away. I didn't want to hear. What had he ever seen in me? I sped up, rounding the far corner of the lake, trying to forget.

The rest of that evening had passed in a dizzying blur. I'd hidden in Jack's shadow, watched Greta's three-year-old twin hooligans, refilled drinks, played the too-busy-to-chat hostess. The gingerbread house had come crashing down to a formidable howl of "*shazam!*" from Mickey, and I'd passed out the ruins to adults who nibbled at the candies and gnawed at the stale gingerbread before wadding it into napkins to leave on the dining room table.

At one point, Nadia waylaid me on the way to the kitchen, my fingers clawing several, dirty eggnog glasses bound for the sink. "Hey, Katie, terrific party!" I'd mumbled thanks and attempted to move past. She blocked me.

"Um, Kate, you do *know* about Miranda, right?"

I'd stared back at her with a steamy burst of indignation. "Do *I know* about Miranda?" I scoffed. "Duh, Nadia. Look, I gotta…" I pushed past her into the kitchen.

Seeing Will with Miranda shed doubt on everything I thought he and I had shared. I didn't know anything anymore. And somehow, as though that doubt had triggered a love-sucking reality check, the magical aura of Michael had faded too. I was left with only numb, cold reason. And the harsh reality of school starting today. Without Amy.

The quiet thud of my feet reverberated with an echo. My ears pricked up. Not an echo. There was someone behind me. I slowed. The other footsteps slowed, too. Approaching a curve, I darted ahead to glance back through the bare branches. No one there. My heart began to pound. Legs, arms, and adrenalin pumping, I tore off in a sprint. In a flash, he was beside me, syncing his steps to mine. I screamed, stopping dead. "Will! You scared the crap out of me!"

"Sorry, Kate! When I saw it was you, I was afraid, at first. Afraid to catch up." He was flushed, his hair curling in the damp, morning air. "I didn't know what to do."

"Something like saying, 'Hi, Kate' might have been one, logical approach." Annoyed, I ran on. He kept pace, the familiarity of his stride tugging at my heart. He hadn't wanted to catch up with me because I'd made things so weird between us. I dropped my righteousness. "It's OK. It was just scary."

"Sorry. Really." He rested a hand on my shoulder for a moment before dropping it. We ran on without talking. I kept my eyes front, saying all of the things I wanted to say—in my head. Miranda's image appeared, as she had so many times since the party. Was she smart, too, or just bewitchingly beautiful? Where had they met? I'd find out at school. I'd have to find a whole, new crowd, if Miranda started hanging out with the gang. I wanted to move again. Now. We turned away from the lake. Will would run with me all the way home, just like old times. I fought back tears. No, nothing was like it used to be.

"Kate." Will reached for my arm. "Hey, hang on a sec—stop running, will you?" I stopped, but gazed past him. "God, Kate. I hate this. I hate that we can't even talk." I could feel his eyes intent on my face. "I miss you. I miss *us*, Kate. But you—you're so full of-of..."

"Of *what?*"

"I dunno—*hatred*? I feel like you *despise* me. It—it hurts. 'Cause I really, really do not hate you, Kate."

Stunned, my eyes met his before I could look away again. Hate? How could he think I hated him? Had I made him think that? I wanted to tell him how sorry I was, how much I still cared about him, how confused I was, tormented. But how—how could I just move on as friends—while Miranda adorned his arm? I wanted to form an honest friendship, love him, as a friend. But, now, Miranda—I couldn't. If he said nothing—or anything—I knew I'd cry. All I could manage was to shake my head. The words, "Oh, Will, I don't hate you," screaming, but only inside my head.

The sun had burned off the fog. We were going to be late for school. We turned to rush. As we neared my house, it came out of the blue.

"Take me to the East with you."

I tried to process his words. "What?"

"I want to go—with you. And—if it's OK—meet your friends," his words were halting, as though he was just coming up with the idea, "over there."

The request threw me. Will—meet Michael? It was crazy, inconceivable, there was so much he didn't—couldn't — know; and yet somehow, it made sense. I'd been dying to visit, but after that last fiasco with Jack, I'd been too afraid to go alone. Will's eyes searched mine.

"OK," I heard myself say. I'd think about it later.

He nodded and disappeared down the street with a wave. I brushed off an image of dazzling Miranda waiting for him, just around the corner.

47

Scrutinizing every detail, Anika went over and over the plan as she marched down the wet sidewalk towards the statue of Lenin. The gusts of wind invigorated her, bolstering her confidence. She veered off onto a path, slippery with dead leaves, meandering up a steep mound to the base of the granite pedestal. Double-checking that her blue scarf was knotted securely beneath her chin, she gazed up. Most of the statue had disappeared into a cloud; only a disembodied bronze hand beckoned above her.

The baby shifted. She caught her breath, palming a pointy bulge, an elbow or a heel, and pictured the tiny life curled up tighter and tighter inside her. He would kick his way out soon—very soon. Or she? Her eyes closed, allowing the wonder. This is for you, my baby, all for you. Today was the day. Footsteps drew her into high alert, her senses sharp. Stay strong, her inner voice commanded. Nothing to lose.

Klein had insisted on meeting her for a report following her recent checkup. She watched as he turned from the sidewalk to climb the hill. "Ah," he said, nearing. "There you are. So insignificant beneath the great man." He is completely deranged, she reminded herself. His insanity is our strength. That—Helga had concluded—was how we win.

"How is my child?" he demanded, looming over her now, his leather fingers black, stiff, twitching. She shivered, knowing their potential.

"Three weeks late. That is the doctor's best guess."

"Late?" The news upset him, as she'd hoped it would. "The baby is fully grown. No reason not to take it now! There are ways." His eyes darted, the gloved hands wringing with impatience.

So predictable. Anika took a step back. "Don't be a fool," she snapped, unleashing her contempt, knowing the force would surprise him. "You will do nothing to disturb the natural course of things."

Grabbing her chin, he twisted it, as though adjusting a car mirror, forcing her to face him. She smelled his hot breath and tried to wrench her face away, but he only gripped it harder, steering it back. "I am tired of you. I want my child."

Anika's cheeks contorted beneath his grip. She grit her teeth, strengthened her resolve. Through his fingers, she hissed, "*Your* child?" and jerked her face free. "I have decided something. I am going to speak to your wife—my cousin—and tell her exactly what you have done. She will see you for who you really are: a cruel, crazy, foolish monster." And then—kerosene on a flame—she spit in his face.

When his hand slammed into the side of her head, she shrieked, her feet sliding out from beneath her. Arms flailing, hands grasping at air, she tumbled down the hill, rolling, over and over, cold, wet leaves sticking to her, until she lay as still as the granite marker that had stopped her.

He stood over her mud-streaked body. Her eyes shut, her legs and arms askew. Falling to his knees, he whimpered and tugged and clawed at the mound of her belly, as though he could gouge out the baby. A leg twitched, she moaned. He leaned back on his heels, noticed the dark, scarlet stain oozing through the pale blue scarf and jumped up in horror. He stared, backing slowly away.

Through the fog, from between trees, a woman appeared. She began to run towards the scene. With a cry, she dropped down beside Anika. "What have you done?" she shrieked, screaming at his receding figure. "Go! Get help!" He scurried toward a black sedan, slammed the door, and sped away.

Anika opened her eyes to smile up at her angel. "He's gone, dear, he's gone. You poor, brave thing. Did he hurt you? Are you all right?" Helga helped her stand, gently removing the blood-stained scarf from her hair, brushing mud and leaves from her coat. She checked Anika's body and head for injuries. "You were magnificent, my dear. What a ghastly man." Arm in arm, the women walked away.

Two days later, Michael heard the tell-tale sounds: the car, the parking break. The door slamming. He ran to the kitchen sink, rubbed the heels of his moistened hands against his eyes. Footsteps. He pulled out a chair at the table. No time left to think things through. Just make it look real.

Klein barged through the backdoor. Michael cradled his head in his arms on the table. He killed my sister's baby, he told himself, over and over. There was a sharp rap against his head. "Sit up, boy!" He looked up, wet lashes blinking, his face crumpled in pain. "What's the matter with you? Pathetic." Klein strode through the door to the living room. "Where is your sister? I must see her. Immediately."

Michael pushed his chair back, his fists pounding the table."You dare ask where she is?" He spoke through his teeth, not having far to reach to find anger.

"She brought that fall on herself. Never mind. Where is she? She has served her purpose. My child must come out of her. Immediately." He roared, pounding one gloved hand into the other, as if he had something similar in mind for Anika.

Michael inhaled deeply, deliberately, then stood. He locked eyes with Klein. "Your child. Is dead." He waited for his words to register, a short pause, and then began his attack. He lurched, knocking over the chair, allowing months of pent up frustration to discharge. "Murderer! Get out of here." He raised his fists. "It is over. We have nothing left to fear, nothing! We will go to your wife, your superiors—you think you are indestructible? We'll tell anyone who will listen. You, mein Herr, have gone too far!" He pushed Klein to the wall, pinning his shoulders.

But instead of resisting, Klein wilted like a rag doll against him. Michael paused, off guard. Klein's eyes were squeezed shut, his face contorted. To Michael's horror, the pinched line of lashes began to glisten, his shoulders tremble. Michael dropped his hands and stepped back. The man squeaked like a rusty door hinge. "Dead? Dead?" His body crumpled against the wall, hands pressed to his face. Michael could discern a few words. "…failed you…for you, my love…ours….our baby." Fascinated, Michael watched as the whimpering mass slid to the floor.

Michael wanted him out. Out of their house, out of their lives. But there was one more thing he had to do. "Listen." He nudged the quaking heap with his foot. "You can be absolved of blame—of murder—*if* we go along. We will say it was a natural death. We will remain quiet. On one condition. Are you listening? No negotiations." He nudged him again. Klein, his head in his hands, nodded.

Revulsion drove Michael from the kitchen into the living room where he sank into a chair to wait. On the small table next to him lay a Death Certificate prepared by Dr. Retter. With the patience of one who knows he has finally triumphed after months of restraint, he waited for their tormentor to come, and grovel.

48

We parked in the West near the checkpoint since Will was a civilian and couldn't go across in the car with me. I asked him to leave his varsity letter jacket in the car, afraid to stand out any more than we already did. He smiled, obligingly, and tossed it in. We walked by the American MPs and on over to the East Germans. I passed my diplomatic passport to the border guard and Will handed over his regular passport. He had to pay five Deutschmarks for the one-day tourist visa and convert twenty-five West Marks one-to-one to East German Marks—though they were worth a tenth of that and could not be converted back. As we walked into the East, I saw it again as I had the first time, as Will might be seeing it now: buildings coated with grime and neglect, empty streets dotted with only a few cars that looked like toys—the feeling of it being frozen in time. Of course the weather was cold and gray, too, completing the stereotype.

"Well," he looked around. "If anything, you made it sound more...*alive*."

Will and I had been managing a cultivated civility, at least. Working on the school newspaper, *The Bearly Scene*, during lunch had become my excuse for evading the gang. Marny and Odele worked on it, too, and I'd gotten to know some other kids better.

But, still, I missed the gang. And still, Will had insisted he wanted to go to the East with me.

We were heading straight to the house. It had been months since that night at Amy's. What would we find? I wasn't at all sure this was a good idea, showing up unannounced. No matter what, the visit would be bittersweet. By now, Anika had to have given the baby to that horrible man. Since her due date in early March, I'd not been able to stop thinking about it, yet hadn't mentioned it to anyone since Amy left. I didn't want to jeopardize their safety by saying or doing the wrong thing—whatever that meant.

As we boarded the bus, I tried to imagine Michael and Will in the same room. It seemed impossible, worlds that could never merge. Just the thought of seeing Michael again made me dizzy. The tram jerked side to side. We stood, grasping straps, not bothering to sit, though there were several vacant seats. Neither of us acknowledged it when our bodies bumped. Will was wearing the long-sleeved t-shirt with our cross country logo, the one he'd worn beneath the wool sweater the night we'd gone to *Das Klo*. The sleeves had blotted all that blood—how had he gotten it out, I wondered? A lifetime ago. My helpless tenderness from that night rushed back. I turned to stare out the window, afraid to expose my feelings. Miranda didn't live in Berlin after all, which had been some relief; I'd overheard Molly tell someone she'd been here for the holidays, just visiting her family. But it didn't change things. I couldn't compete, even with a far-away Miranda.

After getting off the bus, it took me a moment to get my bearings. Will ambled silently beside me. I wondered if he had any inkling of my growing apprehension. The house looked the same, though the vines that had been bare now covered the walls with fresh, green leaves, and the hard, dirt yard was speckled with hardy clover flowers and buttercups. I bent to open the low gate, and moved aside, allowing Will to enter my secret world. Together we walked around to the kitchen door, my heart thudding in my chest, my face burning with the memory of Michael's lips, his soft hair against my skin. It was inappropriate to have brought Will. What was I thinking? I raised my hand to knock. Will smiled with a reassuring shrug. He looked adorable in his scuffed up Converses, his hands jammed into real Levi's. So healthy, so American. I smiled back. It wasn't easy for him, either. This was what I'd kept from him—what, somehow, had torn us apart. Yet he'd asked to come. Whatever happens, I thought, my knuckles rapping against the wood, I'll remember that.

Then, there he was. Michael, gaping in surprise—his hair longer, his eyes flooding mine with warmth. "*Mein Gott!*" He enveloped me in his arms, swung me around, pulled me into the house; he kissed both my cheeks and grabbed my face between his hands to direct a kiss on the lips, then hugged me again. Will followed us inside, tentatively. He closed the door behind him, then stood waiting, rocking slightly, toe to heel. I pulled myself from Michael's arms.

"Michael," I said, "this is my friend Will. Will, Michael. I am sorry we couldn't let you know we were coming…." I looked around, sensing Anika was not there. The house was very still.

Michael pumped Will's hand. "I am so happy to meet you." I had to pinch myself. There they were, side by side. I loved them. Both.

"Please, come sit. I'll make tea." Michael gestured toward the table pulling out chairs, unable to conceal his excitement. The familiarity of the kitchen filled my heart, made me miss Amy.

"I made cookies." I pulled a Tupperware container from my bag, relieved to have something to offer. "Chocolate chip. Hope you like them."

"Ach, wow, they look *echt lecker*! You made them? Katie, I was worried—that I would never see you again. It has been so long. So much—" he glanced at Will and smiled, swallowing whatever he'd been about to say.

I had so many questions, but arranged cookies on the unnecessary plate he offered, afraid to ask. Something had happened. I could sense it. Michael, fussing with tea preparations, focused his attention on Will. He asked how we knew each other, was excited to hear we'd run on the cross-country team together.

"Remember, Katie, how you and Amy made those cheeries for us?"

It took me a second. "Oh, the cheers!" I laughed, and recounted the kitchen cheering session for Will.

Michael continued, telling Will about us entertaining everyone at the *Junge Gemeinde* meeting. "The girls have many talents," he said.

Will just smiled, nodding, eyeing the two of us.

Pouring boiling water into the pot, Michael asked about Amy. I reported that she was well, that for now, she and her mother were living with Amy's grandmother, Enid. I didn't mention that her sober mother was having a harder time dealing with the years she'd lost than Amy, and Amy wasn't sure she and Alex clicked anymore.

When Michael brought mugs to the table, I told Will that Michael's father had made them. He nodded with appreciation, turning one around in his hands. Michael and I exchanged glances, the air thick with unmentionable subjects. Michael seemed to figure that Will had no clue. We sat, blowing across our teas, still too hot to sip. It was hard to know what to talk about. Michael grabbed the plate of cookies and held it out for each of us before taking one himself. "*Echt, lecker!*" he said after a nibble. He munched a moment, savoring the taste, then jumped up to turn on the radio which was playing a traditional folk song—anything would do. He sat again, grabbing another cookie. He seemed anxious.

I toyed with the handle of my mug, wondering if I should have explained more to Will, worried it was unfair to have put him in this situation. At the same time, I fretted about Michael's feelings, barging in on his complicated life with some strange guy. Will pushed back his chair and stood, stretching, casually asking where the bathroom was in a pretty obvious move to let us have some time alone. The moment the door closed behind him, I turned to Michael and whispered, "The baby? What happened with the baby?"

Michael glanced at the outside door, then back, worry spreading across his face before leaning in to whisper directly in my ear. I had to strain to hear him over the music. "It is a story, Katie. I cannot tell you now—it's too much, too dangerous." He leaned back, but then, his face brightened and he leaned in to whisper in my ear. "*Both*— Anika *and* her little girl—are safe. They are with a friend." He held a finger to his lips and winked.

My hand flew to my mouth, my mind whirling with the news. Anika had had a baby girl—what's more, she *still* had it. Michael, no longer whispering, changed the subject. He gestured towards the door. "He seems very *sympatisch*. I like him very much. Is Will—" he pronounced it like *vool*—" your boyfriend?" His tone was nonjudgmental, matter of fact.

"No." I smiled. "Just a good friend." It was the truth, if twisted. I gulped hot tea, my mind processing. Was Anika in hiding somewhere? What about Klein? He must be frantic looking for her—and the baby. The full extent of their dangerous situation sank in.

Michael's eyes twinkled. "Well, I can see in his eyes—he likes you very much. Of course, who wouldn't?"

I looked away. "He has a girlfriend." Now I sounded pouty.

Michael placed a palm against my cheek. I put my mug down and leaned over for a deep, tender kiss. "Your note," he whispered. He placed one hand over his heart and the other on mine. "Always." We kissed again, then pulled apart, anticipating Will's return. "I have a good feeling about Will," he whispered. A fat tear escaped, and I looked down to watch it drop on an embroidered sunflower. When I looked up, Michael was wiping his eyes, too.

Will announced himself outside the door with a loud throat-clearing, before entering. He sat, beelining for a cookie. "Phew. I was worried you guys would've eaten all of these!" We laughed, each reaching for another, and sat a moment, munching together. Sitting with both Will and Michael, a moment of perfect bliss washed over me. My first loves. And they seemed to like each other.

I jumped when Michael sprang up from the table. "How could I forget? I have a surprise! Come. Bring your shoes."

Shoes in hand, Will and I followed Michael through the tiny living room, down a narrow hallway. I peeked through an open door, inhaling Michael's aroma. There were twin beds: one covered with a crumpled duvet, the other stretched taut, not a wrinkle in the cloth. Stefan's bed. I sighed. Farther along on the opposite side, green light streamed through closed curtains in a small room, a flock of tiny, ceramic birds arranged on a glass-topped bureau. No sign of a baby. Just beyond it, a windowless room, like a large closet. Wooden shelves stacked with unglazed pottery lined one wall, and in the middle stood a wooden table with a circular platform in the center connected with a rod to another round board below: a potter's wheel. Breathing in the scent of wet clay, I wanted a demonstration, to watch Michael at work, but he and Will were heading through a door at the end of the hall. Slipping into my sneakers, I followed them, out to the carport where the Trabi was parked. Michael, a finger to his lips, tiptoed around it to a pile of wooden crates.

"You remember Flitvut?"

I smiled, turning to Will. "Their cat is named Fleetwood—after Fleetwood Mac."

Michael knelt by a large crate on its side. "Look what Flitvut has made." He stood to give us room.

"Kittens!" I gasped, crouching low, waiting for my eyes to adjust to the darkness, hearing the tiny mews before I could see them. Against Fleetwood's large fluff of gray belly lay a furry, writhing frenzy. "Four—no, five?" They were mostly black and white; one had gray socks and ears; two were all gray like Fleetwood. But only one had her fluffy coat.

Michael nodded, holding up five fingers.

Will crouched beside me to peek. "So tiny."

"Almost one month now," Michael said. "I came home one evening and heard *mew, mew*. She had them here, in this box. Perfect, yes?"

"Adorable!" I reached in to pet the mini-Fleetwood.

"In a couple of weeks, you can take one," Michael said. "If you want."

"I'd love one." I whispered, already choosing the one that looked most like its mama. "*This* one." I smiled. If I couldn't have Michael, I could at least have one of his kittens. It would be a part of Michael with me—in the West.

"You, too, Will?"

"No, thanks." Will grinned. "Atticus would probably eat it for breakfast." I laughed, knowing his old, gentle Lab would do no such thing.

"Who's the papa?" I asked.

"*Keine Ahnung!*" No idea. Michael laughed, as the front gate squeaked open.

"Kati?" Anika was as surprised as I was. She rushed over. "I thought for a moment you were Amy. You are wearing her beautiful cape!" She hugged me and peppered me with more questions than Michael had; and despite my dying to ask her what was going on, she had me talking about me, how I'd filled the void left by Amy by getting involved in the school paper. As I spoke, I was conscious of Will listening, wondering if he knew the truth: that my dedication to *The Bearly Scene* was more due to the void left by him—now that his loyalties lay with someone else—than Amy's departure.

Anika linked her arm in mine and pulled me behind the kiln, anxious and skittish, speaking in rapid German, her voice soft. "Four days ago, I had a beautiful baby girl. Katarina—it's our mother's name." She squeezed my arm. "And yours." I hugged her, bursting with questions about the birth, awed at her being a new mother. But it wasn't the purely joyous occasion it should have been. My question burned inside me: what about Klein? But I needn't have worried. Her fingers gripped my arm, her head shaking as though she herself couldn't believe what she whispered. "Klein believes the baby is dead." My mind reeled. "Such a story, Kati! For now, we are safe with a friend. Together, we have found a good family who will take her.

For Katarina, it is best. I know this, but—" She shrugged, sucked in air, swiped at her eyes.

It was too much to process. She was going to give her baby away. But not to Klein, who somehow thought that the baby had died. There was another family somewhere. It sounded unreal, dangerous. Anika was risking her own life to give her baby a better one. "Oh, Anika," I whispered. We clutched each other's arms, face to face. Tears were streaming down her cheeks. Beyond the kiln, we noticed that the boys had stopped talking.

"I came for some things," she said, dabbing her eyes with a handkerchief, her hands shaking. "I must go right back. I'm so excited to see you, Kati." She waved at Will, gave me a quick hug, and dashed inside.

"Will," I called. "We'd better go." He was watching Anika's hurried retreat; he hadn't even been introduced to her. But he nodded, no questions asked.

Michael lay his hands on my shoulders. "In two weeks you can come take your kitten. OK? Saturday?" A perfect reason to return. I hugged him close.

The bus pulled up as we rounded the corner. Without a word, Will and I broke into a sprint, leaping on a second before the doors closed. We sat, breathing hard. Will stared out the window so that I couldn't read his expression. It was a kindness, as if he knew: I didn't want to explain things, not yet, anyway.

Seeing them had calmed me. Anika and Michael were OK. She'd had the baby and both were safe. For now. I drew my hands to my heart to register Michael's love, where it now lived, forever. And the kittens, my kitten. And Will! He'd been wonderful. I glanced over at him, longing to tell him how grateful I was—until even these words were stifled by a flash of him entwined with the ravishing Miranda. Will kept staring out the window. Maybe we'd never really known each other at all.

Walking back into the West, my pulse quickened as it did, to sync with the other world. "Feel that, Will? The bustle, after the East?" He didn't reply, hadn't said a word since we'd left the house, his silence now a statement. At the car, I unlocked the passenger side before walking around to climb in behind the wheel. Will slammed his door as I jammed the key into the ignition, growing upset. He turned as if to speak, so I took my hand off the key and placed it in my lap. He shifted in his seat. I braced myself.

"I appreciate you taking me, Kate. There was a lot going on." His voice was thoughtful, calm. "Clearly, you and Michael have a—a *bond*. I have a pretty good idea of what's up, or *was* up. At least, I think I do." He raised his hand when I began to interrupt, which was good because I wasn't sure what I'd intended to say. "I needed to go, to understand." He paused again. "I also get that it's been...unusual. Hard—for you. I think I understand some of your," he scratched his head, fishing for the right word, "turmoil." He faced me. "So, thank you, for taking me."

Tears sprang to my eyes. It was everything I'd wanted him to comprehend, to say. He was not only empathetic but insightful. "That means so much to me," I managed to croak, knowing there was so much more to discuss—and now, finally, it seemed possible. But first, I needed an explanation, to understand, now or never. I cleared my throat, took a deep breath, and forced it out. "I want—need—to know—about Miranda. How—when did you two—?" I stopped, faced him, hoping for at least a trace of remorse. He owed us that much.

Instead, he looked confused. His eyes ballooned with disbelief. "What? Wait. You think—?" Falling back against his door, he shook his head. "Kate. Miranda is my *aunt*."

"Huh?" My head hit the window on my side. He was dating his aunt? The flaws in my thinking began to dawn. *No* one had actually *said* they were an item. "But—you—and she—" She'd wrapped around him like a hungry python at that party. "And Nadia said..." I couldn't remember what Nadia had said, only that she'd definitely *wanted* me to think they were an item. Hadn't she? "But—everyone—*knew*—*knew* her." Deflated, my gaze dropped to my lap, embarrassed. I felt like a fool. All these weeks, how could I have been so *wrong*?

"Miranda," Will explained, his words coming slowly, as if for him, too, a new understanding was dawning, how I'd been behaving, my distance since that day I opened the door to him at our party, "is my dad's younger—much younger—sister. It's weird, I know. She's in her twenties, I forget how old. She loves Berlin and comes every Christmas. The gang has met her before. Nadia is gaga about her because she's an *actress*—lives in New York—she's in a famous soap opera. Miranda's all about herself, getting attention. And whenever she visits, I'm stuck as her designated babysitter."

My mind whirred like a camera lens—zooming in, blurring, zooming out, not knowing where to focus. My finger traced the center of the steering wheel, around and around, the circle beginning to swim. Of course, it was ridiculous—Miranda and Will! Only someone blinded by jealousy would leap to the stupid conclusion I had. The streetlights were coming on against a darkening sky, shifting shadows inside the car, an evening chill seeping in. "Oh, Will. I'm such a dip-shit. You have every right to be furious, even hate me." I was unsure how to say what I needed to say. "The truth is, my feelings for you have been clearer—more *real*—than ever. I've wanted to talk, to tell you. But, I was so," I looked at him, flooded with shame, "jealous of Miranda."

"Katie." Will took my hand, laughing gently. "It all makes sense now. Look. I could've said something, too. But I was too busy acting like a dejected puppy. It's not all on you."

He gave a little tug, inviting me over. He took my face in his hands and kissed first one eye, then the other, then the tip of my cold nose, and finally, my lips. Together, we soared to that place, so familiar and wondrous, created only by the combination of *us*. And we stayed there a sweet, long time. Eventually, I pulled away. I had to get the car home.

"Your *aunt*," I groaned, turning the key. "I shoulda known. You're way too sophisticated for her."

49

Anika stared with wonder into the tiny, navy blue eyes of her daughter as they gazed back at her, as if, of course, she knew Anika from a different time and place and her birth was but a reunion. The setting sun was streaming in through a small window beneath the eaves, washing them in a cocoon of warmth as they rocked together. Anika could hear Helga fussing in the tiny kitchen, the scent of roasted potatoes wafting through the cozy apartment. Her heart overflowed with gratefulness. Helga had risked and endured so much to save them. What would Anika have done without her?

"Katarina," Anika whispered, reenforcing her resolve to do whatever necessary to keep her baby safe. "I promise you, your father's evil will never touch you. A kind family will love you, raise you with care, as though you were their own." She held her breath, blocking thoughts of all that was yet to come, from the dreaded image of handing her baby to someone else, for good. It was to happen tomorrow. Yet never had she been more certain that it was what she had to do.

Helga burst through the front door—so entranced with her baby, Anika had not even noticed her leaving the apartment—and began to pace, hands wringing, before sinking into the sofa. "Oh, Anika."

Her hands fell lifelessly to her lap, her face taut with her news. Anika's heart dropped. Something was wrong. The familiar panic returned. She clutched Katarina to her breast.

"The family have had a change of heart," Helga began. "They insist on knowing more, the circumstances, the risk. Which of course is impossible." She faced Anika. "So, they won't be taking the child." She stood, forced a semblance of calm. "We'll find someone else, of course. There are plenty of the right people who want to adopt." Helga's wringing hands betrayed her upset. "It will just take time."

Anika knew, however, that the 'right people' kept a low profile, and were, indeed, much more difficult to find. Time was precisely what they did not have. She'd reported the baby's death and must return to work soon. The baby began to fret, wriggling and fussing in her arms, as though she could perceive trouble. "I could ask for more leave—" Anika rocked faster as the baby's whimpers grew. "Psychological leave—for grief? Grieving takes time...." She stood, hummed, and swayed, shifting Katarina in her arms. "Shh, Katarina, shh."

But the risk of staying at Helga's grew by the minute. Thus far, the neighbors had dismissed the periodic crying, believing the baby belonged to a visiting niece, but the longer the baby stayed, the more suspicious they'd become. They could trust no one; anyone could be an informer. The sooner she and Katarina left, the better.

"If only...." Helga's voice came from the kitchen. She appeared a moment later, handing Anika a bottle. Anika watched Katarina's mouth work, sucking down the nourishment with a steady rhythm. Helga gazed out of the small window where the setting sun hovered like a tangerine over the horizon. Anika did not press her to finish her thought.

50

When I heard the jangle of the German phone, I ran to catch it. It was Friday evening. The next morning, I was to pick up my kitten from Michael.

"Psyched?" Will's voice warmed my heart.

"Yep." It was all I could do not to beg him to come with me. I had to be brave about going alone, but my stomach had been flip-flopping for days just thinking about it. Will was helping Rick assemble his new ping pong table today. It was an obvious excuse to get out of going, but I understood his reluctance. Will knew there was something I was keeping from him, but until I knew the baby was safe, I didn't want to divulge anything. It scared me to talk about it at all, as if just putting it into words could jeopardize them—such had grown my paranoia about being listened to. We both knew I had to do this trip alone.

"Let's figure out the timing, so I can meet you as you come back through."

"I'll leave here at ten, sharp. Thirty minutes to get to the checkpoint, fifteen or so to get across, and then—the clock starts ticking! I doubt I'll end up using all of the two and a half hours." It should be plenty of time; though I didn't think anyone would care about an escaping kitten, I felt better having it in a bag in the car than carrying it while walking through the checkpoint.

51

Michael was late for their rendezvous. Anika stood at their meeting place in the damp, evening cold, growing more despondent by the minute. Time had run out. Monday, she had to return to her job. On top of that, Helga's neighbors were asking questions; Anika had no choice but to take Katarina home where Klein could pop in at any moment. She shuddered with terror. It was only a matter of time before he found out that his baby was alive and well.

So upset was she, she did not notice Michael, until he was at her side, words tumbling from of him, his hands squeezing her arms in earnest. He'd dug out a box in their father's closet, full of old letters and photographs. One, of a gangly man smiling next to a tractor, his hair blonde and shaggy, like Michael's. "'Manfred. Kreischa. 1954.' That's what it said, in Papa's handwriting, on the back. Papa's uncle. Think, Anika! Do you remember him?"

"Vaguely," Anika searched her memory. "He was a farmer. There was something sad. Someone died, young, of a fever, maybe?" She shook her head. It was all she could remember.

But Michael nodded, excited. "Yes—in the letter, mailed from Kreischa in 1968—Manfred wrote that his granddaughter had died of Typhoid. His daughter—the mother—was inconsolable." He stopped talking, waiting for his idea to sink in.

Anika nodded, slowly, but her mind raced. They knew nothing about these people, but they sounded kind, were relatives. It was risky: the Trabi was unreliable; and if Klein found out they were away, he could get suspicious. "Yes," she whispered, searching for hope then shook her head, reality sinking in. "No, Michael. Even if they are safe, we can't endanger them. How would *they* explain having a baby? And Klein—what if he knows them?"

"Remember," Michael reasoned, "Klein believes his daughter is dead and that he is responsible." He paused, remembering how, when he'd shown Klein the death report, he'd fallen apart and agreed to everything to cover it up. "I have a good feeling about this. The Trabi can make it. Kreischa is just south of Dresden—four hours' drive, at least. We just need to get Katarina to them."

Anika's eyes welled with tears. It was a long shot, so dangerous, full of flaws, but it was all they had. She nodded. Michael put his arms around her. "One more night at Helga's. Tomorrow morning, Saturday—I don't have to work—I'll meet you and Katarina. We'll head home, get the Trabi, and leave—quietly."

52

My palms were sweating as I started the car, my mind running through what Dad called a pre-trip inventory: Flag Pass inside my shoulder purse beneath Amy's poncho; my diplomatic passport, just in case, locked in the glove compartment; my gym bag with a towel folded across the bottom on the back seat for the kitten—I smiled, imagined a tiny, whiskered face poking out, mewing. The bag also held a box of chocolate Easter eggs for Michael and Anika.

At Checkpoint Charlie, the MP went through his drill while I dutifully signed the clipboard, hoping he didn't notice my hand shaking. I supposed it was some comfort that they'd come looking for me if I didn't return in time. Then, I drove around the cement barriers, stopped to press my Pass to the window for the East German guard—eyes straight ahead—and finally, rolled slowly into the East. Deep breath.

Since our car stood out like a spaceship in the East, I parked it near the Checkpoint rather than drive to the house where it would light them up. On the S-Bahn, I sat near the door, prepared to jump right off when I recognized the stop where I had to transfer to the bus. It felt like a daring adventure, until I imagined everything Michael and Anika had been going through. By now, she'd have given up her baby—a scene and emotions I couldn't begin to imagine. Had they really fooled Herr Klein? Were they safe? I focused on the sway of the tram, trying to steer my mind away from thinking about their past few days. And Klein's cold, malicious gaze. That laugh.

The Trabi was there, though I knew they rarely used it, and by the time I knocked on the kitchen door, I was certain they were out. We hadn't set a time. Edging away from worrisome thoughts, I forced my mind to think of the obvious: I'd come too early or maybe Michael had forgotten and they'd gone shopping at a weekend market. When I moseyed back around to the little carport, I dropped my bag on top of the crate and crouched down low to peer in. Three kittens—including mine, the fluffy gray one—were left. Bigger but still graceless, they bumbled over a languid Fleetwood who yawned and leaned over to lick them, one by one, eyeing me with a steady, proprietary gaze.

"Yeah," I said, softly, reaching in to pet her, noting the parallel with Anika giving up her baby. "I am going to take one of your kittens, sweet mama. I'm sorry." My kitten wobbled and stretched before pouncing on a slumbering sibling. I reached in to pick her up. What must giving up a baby feel like, if this felt cruel? I pressed its soft fur to my cheek while petting Fleetwood between her ears.

It took me a moment to register the sound. So few cars drove down the street at all—but one had stopped. Curious, I peered over the hood of the Trabi. Directly in front of the gate, was a shiny, black vehicle. The license plate read PYU 7861: my birthdate in the European order: day, month, year. The door opened. A head rose.

Herr Klein. What was he doing here?

In a flash, I'd ducked behind a stack of crates, the kitten, still in my arms, writhing and clawing, its mews louder than a tiger's roar. The baby's dead, dead, I repeated to myself, hoping the story would hold throughout an interrogation. Not breathing, flattened against the stack, I covered the kitten with the poncho to muffle its cries. A claw dug into my wrist. Under no circumstances could I let him find me. And then I saw it: my bright blue gym bag, lying exposed on top of the crate. It was too late to grab it.

The gate squeaked open, slammed shut. Shoes tapped against the stepping stones. He was heading to the far side of the house, to the kitchen door, where no one would answer his knock. And then—if he walked back—he'd see me, plain as day. Without another thought, I bolted. Avoiding the squeaking gate, I climbed over the low brick wall, the kitten's protests growing from beneath the poncho. I tore down the street, sprinting all the way to the corner where I stopped for a glance back, my heart pounding: a bass drum next to the kitten's rolling snare.

Herr Klein was bending to open the gate. I whipped around the corner, my ears straining for sounds of his car starting. He'd parked facing the other way. Would he turn around or go around the block? He could come from either direction. Across the street, a bus pulled up to the stop. I ducked behind a bush trying to think, sheer panic fogging reason. When it pulled away, a man and woman began to cross the street. Michael and Anika. I stood and waved frantically, bouncing a finger against my lips. The kitten leapt from my grasp. Michael comprehended immediately, pulled Anika, and a moment later they were crouching next to me behind the bush. We crumpled against the ground just as the black sedan sped past.

"Klein!" Michael hissed. "What does he want?"

Adrenalin surging, my whisper came out a screech. "He came to your house. I hid—and then ran."

Heads together, the kitten bawling piteously somewhere beneath the bush, we waited, panting in fear. When the car did not return, we rose up to our haunches. Anika's coat swung open, and there, snuggled against her, lay—but for dark wisps coming from beneath a tiny, lavender, knit cap—a tight cocoon, not much bigger than a loaf of bread.

"Oh!" I gasped, the magnitude of the near-miss hitting me: here was the baby Klein believed was dead. Anika and Michael whispered frantically while I scrounged beneath the bush to grab the kitten and, together, we dashed toward a nearby, thicker, broader bush and crouched low between it and a brick wall. I struggled to follow their frantic German which had descended into colloquial idioms, their fear palpable and contagious.

The magnitude of their dilemma began to unfold. Anika could no longer stay hidden where she'd been. The family had reneged on their promise to take the baby. They hoped a relative might, but they didn't know him, he was far away; it was risky, but also their only hope. They'd come to get the Trabant. They had to leave. Now.

I stared at them, at the baby nestled against her mother, where she should be. "This relative—he doesn't know you're coming?" Anika shook her head, sinking into a well of sadness as though I'd just exposed how flimsy their plan was. They looked so alone and desperate. We were innocents caught in a giant, complicated web, so much bigger than all of us. I swallowed hard.

Michael whispered, his voice hoarse. "*Sonst, haben wir nichts.*" Otherwise, we have nothing. He put his arm around Anika protectively, as if to reassure her of the plan, then, as though shot with adrenalin, he flipped into high gear, planting his feet. "We must leave before he finds us." But he didn't move; instead, he crouched back down, rubbing his forehead. "What if Klein now sees the car is gone?" If they didn't go, it was all over, they couldn't hide a baby long. Yet they had no idea if their relative could—or even would—help them and Klein might catch them leaving. Action, inaction—both—were rife with danger. Then, Michael, decisive again took charge. "We must get out of Berlin, now. Wait here. I will get the car!" Anika was quaking, her arms framing her baby, holding on for dear life.

It came to me with perfect clarity. "Wait. I'll take her. My car—it's parked near the checkpoint. Help me. I can hide her—here. Quickly!" Just then, the hood of the black car slowed at the corner like a marauding shark. We dropped to the ground huddled together, peeking through branches. The car turned, picked up speed, and drove out of sight.

When we rose again, the three of us stared into each other's eyes, numb with shock. Then, moving as one, cogs turning together, Anika and I began to unwind the torn sheet from her while Michael kept watch, calming the hysterical kitten. Dropping the poncho to the ground, I reached for Katarina and held her to my tummy while Anika artfully wrapped the cloth around the baby and my waist, until Katarina lay cocooned against me. She knotted it at my hip with a final tug, made sure it was secure, then grabbed Amy's poncho. No one uttered a word. Thoughts flew at me: even if I got past the East German guards, the American MPs could arrest me—I remembered those GIs imprisoned for smuggling people out of the East—but, like pesky gnats, I swatted the thoughts away and focused on the baby's mouth pulsating like a tiny, pink anemone, the perfect lines of eyelashes quivering against smooth, soft cheeks—until the poncho dropped down, completely obscuring her. Incredibly, she did not wake.

"Oh," Anika covered her mouth as she stared. It was perfect.

Michael ran to get the Trabi while we crouched low. Two cars sped by sending shock waves through us. Anika gripped my hand so hard it hurt, yet I didn't want her to let go. After an eternity, we heard the distinct putt-putt and waited until Michael slowed to a stop in front of us, the engine idling in popcorn mode. Glancing right and left, still holding hands, Anika and I darted, crouching low, and climbed into the back.

"Stay down!" Michael ordered. He veered sharply, the Trabi choking into life as he accelerated, knocking us side to side. The kitten—I'd forgotten all about her—yowled, terrified, skirting between Michael and the passenger's seat. Muted little snuffles and intermittent cries began to emerge from beneath the poncho. Every neuron in my body woke, an icy panic washing over me. What the hell was I thinking? This was impossible, nuts. We hadn't thought this through. I opened my mouth to say I was sorry, I couldn't do it, it wouldn't work, but then Anika's trembling hand slipped from mine—to wipe tears—and when she let go, a dark isolation seeped through me, a taste of how worried and alone she'd felt all these months. The horrors that man had inflicted. The thought of him finding the baby. I closed my mouth.

"Kati, where is your car?" Michael fired, in English.

"Near Leipzigerstrasse? When you get close, I'll know...." I tried not to panic, assuring myself I'd know the street when I saw it.

"OK. We will find it."

Mumbling under his breath, Michael made an abrupt left, shifted, floored it. The Trabi whined with exertion while Anika and I braced against each other. At least Katarina seemed to have fallen back asleep. My legs ached, tucked into a low crouch, my body straining to keep from squishing her. After another, sudden wild turn, Michael slammed on the brakes and stopped, his arm reaching out to brace the kitten.

"Hide!" he rasped, his voice trembling as he cut the engine. Anika threw her coat over us. We hunkered down as low as possible, faces into the floor, and froze. Michael's door opened, shut. Outside, we heard muted voices. The kitten mewed frantically up front. Now and then, a tiny whimper emerged from my belly. I was afraid to breathe, quite certain one of the voices was Klein's. We tensed in sync, Anika's nails digging into my wrist. The door reopened, Michael's voice clear, oddly chipper. "*Ja, ja, siehst du? Das Kätzchen!*" The door slammed. Silence. Michael had grabbed the kitten. The door opened. The car heaved with weight, the door closed. The engine started. "*Ja danke, Herr Klein. Wiedersehen!*" The car jerked, the engine strained with acceleration. We remained in numb, petrified silence until, finally, Michael spoke, and we raised our heads, keeping them below window level.

"It was Herr Klein. He saw the car, followed us. I couldn't avoid him. He said he'd come to tell us..." His voice cracked. "Oh, Anika, I think it worked! Papa—he says Papa will be released soon! Can we believe him, this devil?" He drove on in silence for a moment, then shook his head, disbelief in his voice. "I think he is afraid—of us! He saw the kitten. I told him this one has found a home. He wants another—for Trudi. So, we will give them a cat! Instead of a baby."

Anika was bent over, her tears flowing. The baby, too, was wailing at the top of her lungs from my belly. The kitten, mewing, climbed up Michael's arm. Reason knocked at the edges of my mind, warning: flashes of Klein, of guards, prison, torture. What was I doing? Anika pulled up the poncho and offered a hysterical Katarina a bottle. I focused on Michael's yellow hair, remembering its softness, my hands running through it—back when I thought life was complicated.

Our eyes met in the rear view mirror. "Kati," he began, " I have no words...." His voice broke. Then we were all crying, a flood of relief and terror, hopefulness and dread. All except for the baby. The screams from my belly had transformed into contented, voracious sucking sounds, Anika's arm twisting awkwardly to hold the bottle in our cramped space. Gently, I placed my hand over hers and held it with her until she let go, nodding, a smile spreading between wet cheeks. We stared at each other in awe. Katarina's sucking slowed, became intermittent, and eventually stopped. She'd fallen back asleep, a pearl of milk on her bottom lip.

"She'll sleep for a while now. If she wakes, give her this." Anika pressed a pacifier into my hand. I leaned back across the seat to adjust my bloodless legs as Anika bent down to kiss her baby. Outside, buildings zipped past, dilapidated and dirty. A surge of longing for home made me vow: if I make it, I will never come back. I burned Michael's profile to memory, inhaling our crazy, last moments together. Terror, hope, but overall: love. I took a deep breath. It will work, I told myself. *I will make it work.*

Michael slowed and I kneeled, gripping his seat to peer out front. I recognized a street to the left. He turned and drove twenty meters before stopping, pulling up to the curb. Parked across the street, the car was obvious. I nodded, glancing up and down the road. A woman passed at a distracted clip. When she turned the corner, I readied myself. *It's OK. No one could guess there is a baby beneath my poncho.*

Anika tucked the empty bottle into a bag she'd packed for the baby that morning. "It's not much," she explained. "But, well, something." She shrugged, attempting a smile, and handed me the black-mesh tote. I took it, nodding. At least it didn't look like a baby bag.

"*Nein, Anika!*" Michael snapped. "What if they check—and see baby things? She can take *nothing*." He looked at me, his face contorted with worry, wet with tears. He wiped them, shaking his head. "It's not fair, Kati, what we are asking of you."

I shielded the baby's head to lean over the seat, my body trembling, tenderness pouring from me. "Michael," I insisted, my cheek pressing into his, "we have no choice. It will be all right. I know it."

Sitting back, I inhaled a few fortifying breaths. Anika lay one palm on Katarina's head, the other on my cheek. She kissed her baby one last time, then pulled the poncho down from where it was bunched around my shoulders. On wooden legs, I stumbled out and glanced down at the bulge between folds of poncho. Not too obvious, I insisted, forcing myself onward. Just get in the car. A man walking down the sidewalk glanced at me then took in the Trabant—no doubt more interested in the fact that a westerner had just gotten out of it than anything else.

Only after the key was in the door, did I remember the kitten and turned to dash back to the Trabi. But Michael had already rolled down his window and was holding out a wriggling, gray ball of fluff. "Maybe she is good luck?" he asked, in English. "Or, maybe you have enough?"

I reached for it, cradling the kitten next to Katarina, realizing only then that I'd left the gym bag on top of the crate. "At your house—my bag—inside, there are chocolates for you!" I could barely speak, for all my emotion and fear. Instead, I leaned in and kissed Michael one last time before standing back. "Happy Easter." And then they were gone.

I was alone in East Berlin.

No, not alone at all. I unlocked the car and climbed in. The kitten leapt onto the passenger's seat. "OK, li'l Fleetwood. Let's get this baby home and surprise the heck out of Mom and Dad, shall we?"

53

To accommodate Katarina, I had to push the seat back so my foot barely reached the clutch. But by the time we turned into Checkpoint Charlie, I had begun to get the knack of shifting gears in that compromised position. Li'l Fleetwood, mewing like mad, had jumped down to the floor by my feet. I managed to grab her and put her back on the passenger seat. "It's all good," I murmured, trying to believe it, on the verge of freaking out. We eased around the cement barriers.

In front of the East German guard hut, I put the car in neutral, and pulled on the emergency brake so I could reach for my Flag Pass in the purse that hung on a long, shoulder strap, so flat it hid under your clothes. In the fever of Anika strapping the baby to me, I'd forgotten all about it. I froze. It was trapped beneath the wrap.

A guard approached the window. I smiled at him, already breaching protocol, and called out, *"Eine Minute!"* while my hands fuddled beneath the poncho. I felt part of the strap and began to tug, careful not to nudge the baby, praying the wrap wouldn't loosen, that she wouldn't wake. Keep calm, I muttered, gritting my teeth. I had nanoseconds before the guard got suspicious and called a Soviet officer—or pulled a gun—shot me or…. I tugged and tugged. The guard peered in through the window. I grinned and twisted, pretending to scrounge around with one hand while the other dug and yanked beneath the poncho.

The guard turned and gestured to another who wandered over, curious. Now two guards were staring in. The jig was up. All was lost. My future was the Gulag. But then—a fluff of gray jumped up from the floor to the passenger's seat, and from there, to me, then to the steering wheel and right up onto the dashboard, where it paced back and forth, meowing in outrage. The guards began to point and laugh, the split second of diversion all I needed to grab ahold and wrest the purse from beneath the tight wrap.

I pulled out my Flag Pass, eyes front. It had all taken maybe twenty seconds but felt like an ice age. As I pressed the pass to the window, the guards stopped laughing at Fleetwood and, fun over, snapped back into military mode. My eyes drifted to the side and the guard raised his index finger to point at the kitten, then swayed it back and forth: a no, no. I swallowed hard, half expecting him to yank open the door and drag me out. Instead, he winked and nodded his chin toward the West. I was good to go.

The moment I put the car in gear, the baby let burst a loud wail— and I lurched. The clutch popped. The car stalled. The guard wandered the few steps back to the car to peer in. Ignoring him, I leaned over and picked the kitten up off the floor placing it on the back seat, praying he'd think it the source of the cry. The guard shook his head, fully laughing now at this uncommon, late afternoon entertainment. I restarted the car, put it in gear, and drove off.

After approximately three seconds of triumphant relief, I remembered the danger yet to come: the American MP. Glancing at the clock on the dashboard, I was relieved to see that though it had felt like a lifetime, I'd been over there less than two hours. Phew. But, the final gate to freedom in full view, the baby began to wail, really wail. I switched on the radio. AFN news—no. I searched for music, any music, anything to cover the baby's screams.

German polka pierced the air. "Crap-crapa-crap," I mumbled, rocking in time with the beat, "Crap-crapa-crap." But the baby kept screaming and there was nowhere to pull over, nowhere to go but right toward danger. The MP was inside the hut. I contemplated flooring it, tearing out of there, leaving Katarina hidden by the side of the road somewhere and then coming back, as if I'd just forgotten to check in. But the MP came out, motioned for me to pull up alongside. The cries grew louder; I turned up the music until the beat made the windows shimmy.

We were sunk. I was about to be arrested. What would they do with Katarina? Would they take her away? Send her back? I fell into despair. But then, at that moment, as clear as if she were sitting next to me, I heard Anika's voice. "If she wakes…"

The pacifier! What had I done with it? Adrenalin pumping, I closed my eyes. Calm, breathe, think back. Crouching on the floor of the Trabant, Anika handed it to me…my back pocket! I squirmed, felt back. It was there. I dug it out, found the tiny, wide open mouth. It gummed my pinky until I could maneuver the pacifier in. Immediately, her crying ceased. Magic. *Thank you, Mama Anika*, I whispered.

The MP was rapping on the window. Accordions wailing, I murmured "crap-crapa-crap," and rolled it down—a little. Skinner, I read his badge through the glass. Sergeant Skinner. I waved. "Hi!"

"You need to exit the vehicle, Miss."

The polka music still blasting, I got out and began to bop holding the poncho out like a dirndl skirt, a folk dancer's pose, my other hand beneath it, atop the pacifier, making sure it stayed put. Skinner eyed me, no doubt wondering if I was drunk. "I was born in Germany. This is my song," I reasoned, channelling Nadia's acting flair—as if, for me, this was perfectly normal behavior. Like I was one of those exasperatingly unflappable, happy types. Skinner sauntered around to the back, then glowered at me. I smiled back, stepped left (two three), and right (two three), like I'd been dancing this polka since I was born.

"What's so interesting over there that you'd go all by yourself, Miss?" I had to hand it to him. Considering my behavior, he was quite patient. We were this close to getting through—and Skinner was not going to stop us.

I stood still, looked directly into his eyes and released a heavy sigh. "OK. I'm going to tell you the truth. But don't get mad?" He had opened the hatch, lifted the floor, was shuffled through the spare tire. "A kitten."

He slammed the back shut. "Huh?"

One hand on the pacifier, Katarina's mouth pumping it like a beating heart, I leaned into the front and dragged the kitten out, claws splayed, mewing up a storm. "*This* little guy. I had to save him." I held the kitten up. "He was going to be drowned. In the Spree River. *Today*," I added, for dramatic emphasis.

Katarina stirred, I coughed, bopped a little, held the kitten even closer to Skinner.

Skinner's tough exterior dropped—right into his army boots. "Aw," he said, his voice rising an octave. And then, inches from where I sequestered a tiny human, the sergeant reached out to tickle the kitten. "He's scared," Skinner said, taking him from me. "You can feel his heart going a mile a minute."

"Yep. So, I'd better get him to his new home in the American Sector, dontcha think?" I seized Skinner's clipboard from where he'd tucked it beneath his arm, and scribbled my initials next to my earlier signature. He exchanged it for the kitten, and I climbed into the car, slipping behind the wheel as naturally as possible. Just for good measure, before driving off, I waved a kitten paw through the window. Skinner laughed and waved back with just his index finger. And then the three of us drove on into West Berlin.

Pulling into the same spot where Will and I had parked, just two weeks—and an eternity—ago, I cut the engine. The stillness hit like a brick and I felt myself crumble. I began to shake, sweat dripping from my forehead, gasping for air as though I'd just surfaced from too long under water. When finally the world began to focus, I stared down at my lap and lifted the poncho. A perfect, tiny face of a real, live, newborn baby stared up at me, blinking against the sudden light. The pacifier slowed until the miniature lips parted, releasing it. Katarina, for the first time in her life, breathed the air of freedom. I propped my head against the steering wheel and stared.

"Guess you're my sister now," I whispered, wondering how things would play out, realizing that from now on, much would be out of my hands. "I promise I'll do all I can to protect you. Always."

The tap on the window made me coil in alarm, dropping the poncho down over the baby, even after I'd registered that it was Will. He opened the door, laughing. "Sorry, didn't mean to startle you." I could only gape back at him. "Did you get it?" He peered in around me. My mind was blank. Get what? He opened the back door and reached in, emerging a moment later with the kitten cradled in his hands. "Pretty darn cute," he said, grinning down at me. "I came early, watched as you came through—what was all that prancing around the MP about?" His laugh froze on his face. "Kate? Hey, what's wrong?"

"Will," I began, my voice sounding far away, "there's something—." As if on cue, Katarina began to fuss and whimper. Fear engulfed me once again—before I realized it was OK for her to cry. We were safe. Katarina was safe for the first time in her short life. *We'd made it.* My mind swirled in a tangle of truth and dreamlike fantasy—until the reality of what I'd done crashed over me. I threw open the door, stumbled past Will, and threw up against a light post.

Will's free arm was around me, supporting me as I convulsed in tears, Katarina's cries competing with mine, the kitten clawing into Will's chest in terror. He put the kitten in the car, then came back, turned me to face him and gently lifted the poncho. Unmuffled, the baby's screams pierced the air. Will pulled me close—us—his face buried in my hair. He was shaking, too. "It's…a baby." It was as if he had to convince himself. "You smuggled out…a baby?" Katarina was wailing. I found the pacifier caught in the cocoon, and pressed it to her tiny lips. Her mouth leeched onto it, the wail became a whimper. I looked up, into Will's eyes, round with questions, and nodded.

"*Whose?*"

There was a sense of people walking by without even looking, scarcely interested in our little drama. Everything, so normal. Except: I looked down at the tiny face, the wet eyes, the undulating pacifier. Life, I knew, would never be the same. "Help me..." I yanked the poncho off, tossing it into the car. Will worked the knot loose, unwrapping the length of white that encircled me like a mummy. Finally free, I cradled Katarina, supporting her floppy head, and climbed into the passenger's seat.

Will got in behind the steering wheel, moving the seat back to accommodate his long legs. As he adjusted the side mirror, he stopped to stare a moment, then opened his door. When he climbed back in, he was holding an envelope. "Is-is her name...Katarina?" I nodded, incredulous. He handed me the envelope and I read, in a careful, neat hand on the front: *Katarina, auf Deinem Sechzehnten Geburtstag.* Katarina, On Your Sixteenth Birthday.

The envelope shook in my hands. It had almost been lost. How had I missed Anika tucking it inside the folds of the sheet? My chest pinched with her sacrifice. I imagined her writing it, aching to convey her love for her baby who may never know her. She must have written it thinking their relative would be handing it to her sixteen year old daughter. Instead, it would be me.

Snuggling into bed that night with li'l Fleetwood curled up at my feet, my mind refused to calm. Sleep seemed inconceivable. Mom came in and sat on the edge of my bed handing me a fresh bundle that smelled like baby shampoo. Katarina, swaddled in a new, flannel baby blanket bought after a frantic dash to the PX, was asleep, her breathing deep and peaceful.

"Quite a day, huh," Mom said, squeezing my knee where it lumped beneath my quilt, smiling at the understatement. "Kate." Her tone was somber. I looked up from the baby. "What you did was crazy, dangerous, not recommended—and *never* to be repeated." She reached over and gently pushed a curl from my eye. "It terrifies me to think about it," she sighed, "so I won't. But, your impulsive, extraordinary, selfless act may have saved more than one life." She knew the whole story now. "This certainly isn't how I imagined the next few years," she continued softly, "but, what an amazing challenge placed in our laps. We'll be a tag team, you and I. All of us will take care of Katarina. But"—she gazed straight into my eyes—"until the day she is reunited with Anika, I'm her mother. You have school, your life to live; and now you have a little sister to share it with. OK?"

"Oh, Mom," I said, my heart bursting, "I love you." She kissed my forehead and turned out the light. I leaned over to kiss Katarina as my mother's capable arms lifted her, and exhaustion defeated me. Mom left my door open two inches, exactly how I liked it. The last thing I remember was little feet walking up my body, and a ball of fur curling into the crook of my neck.

54

The next few days were a flurry of activity and clandestine excitement. Dad met with some lawyer at the Berlin Brigade. There was the question of protocol juxtaposed with the need to keep everything on the QT. I was petrified of them taking Katarina away, putting her up for adoption, or, worst of all, sending her back, but Dad repeatedly assured me nothing like that would happen.

Katarina, undocumented, unclaimed, with only the wild testimony of a teenage kid—me—to explain her provenance, was treated like a Cold War secret. The American Forces, worried about Stasi spies in the West putting Katarina in danger of being kidnapped, decided that in the interest of the child's security, the West German government would not be informed.

Two military officers, my father, and a lawyer gathered to hear my story—which I recounted in great detail. They asked questions, shook their heads, laughed in disbelief at the prodigious role li'l Fleetwood had played. Particularly interested in the fact Herr Klein was Stasi, they applauded when I gave them his license plate number, even went so far as to call in a sketch artist who drew him from my description. I shivered when I saw the drawing, so eerily did Herr Klein's piercing eyes stare back at me. I secretly hoped the CIA would lay some kind of trap to catch and imprison him. They promised me he would never be allowed to roam free in the West.

Tiny Katarina had an alias—plus two cover stories. One was her official document story. It was my idea: they'd say she was my illegitimate daughter, born in the American Military Hospital in Berlin. According to her papers, I had become a mother as a junior in High School (a *virgin*, no less, but that morsel was left out). She got a birth certificate and everything. And I made up her new name: Anna Kay Michaela Benton.

Of course, that story wouldn't fly to anyone who knew us, so we devised the "unofficial" story, a story to protect the story that protected the truth that had to remain hidden and considered Top Secret Confidential. Dad called it "sanctioned deceit," which he explained was "a fiction you must create to protect the innocent in life or death situations." That story, the one we told friends, was that Anna was the baby of Mom's-younger-brother's-wife's-sister who, along with her husband, the baby's father, had been killed in an awful car crash; that the baby had been left with a sitter at the time of the fatal accident and we were the only family members in any position to take her in. The relationship confused people enough to focus only on the "parents killed in a car accident" part—so traumatic, it silenced further questions.

Three days after her "unexpected arrival" (how we referred to that day so as not to slip up in front of others), Will heard he'd been accepted to the University of Virginia. Though it should not have been a surprise, the news knocked the wind out of me. After all those months of keeping him at arm's length, now he never felt close enough—and on top of that, we harbored an enormous secret. How could I let him go?

He told me as we walked home together after a movie at the Outpost theater on a day when, even after the sun set, the air retained some warmth. Stopping in the shadows beyond the circle of a streetlight, he pulled me to him. I sank my face into his chest, on top of his heart. The thought of it beating far away from mine felt like an impossibility.

"But, Will," I pushed back to look up at him, stunned with sudden comprehension, "I *love* you. I don't think I can stand you leaving." Tears stung my eyes.

He laughed softly, hugging me tighter. "I'm not worried, Kate. I'll be back for vacations and before you know it, you'll graduate and come join me. OK?" He began to whisper, kissing the top of my head. "Shh, it's months from now. We still have lots of time."

55

The next Saturday, Michael replaced Ingo at two. Anika walked with him to the kiosk, hoping the long, afternoon stroll would bolster her. Spring was in the air. The freshness helped clear her mind from thinking about Katarina. Today was the day.

"*Hallo*, Michael! Anika!" The moment they arrived, Ingo grabbed his jacket, slapped Michael on the back and took off, waving over his shoulder. Anika's pulse quickened. Michael let her precede him into the tiny hut open on one side where rows of newspapers and snacks lay in untidy piles. Michael removed a tied bundle of papers from the stool and gestured to Anika to sit. Standing close, he dialed, then held the receiver out between them so she could hear.

Someone picked up before the second ring. "Hello?" Kate. Anika's heart soared.

"*Ja, hallo!*" Michael did not give his name. "*Wie geht es euch?*"

Kate, controlling her voice, kept it short. "*Gut! Wir sind—Alle—völlig ok.*"

Michael pinched his eyes shut, allowing the relief to flow from him. Next to him, Anika cried softly, and Kate, on the other end, was crying too.

"That," Michael replied, choking on his words, "is good to hear." He added, "*Paß gut auf dich auf,*" take good care of yourself. Then he placed the receiver back into its cradle and took his sister into his arms.

EPILOGUE

Anna was a mellow, easy baby. She soon slept through the night—much to Mom's relief. "You and Jack were never this easy," she declared.

Who knew the truth? Will, me, Mom, Dad, a handful of government officials, and eventually, Jack when he came home for spring break—who, after hearing the whole story, revered me for a week.

Nothing, of course, could be put into writing. My letters to Amy carried the official lie. We didn't ever write about Anika and Michael at all, to protect them, just in case. But eventually, the day would come when I saw Amy again, to give back her poncho.

Anna's secret stayed close to our hearts for over a decade. Then, on November 9, 1989, hundreds of protesters in the East stormed the Berlin Wall—and, ultimately, tore it down. Stunned, I watched the breaking news at work and knew. The time had come to talk to Anna.

ACKNOWLEDGEMENTS

When my formerly "East German" friend Oliver Richter and his family visited us in Istanbul in 2014, our children bombarded us with questions. How did our friendship—separated by the Wall—prevail, let alone begin? I realized how anomalous that period was—and how much of it had already faded from memory. This story is written to rekindle those emotional days when I was a teenager, as a memorial to that strange chapter in history.

Encouragement came from so many, beginning with author Joie Davidow when I was living in Rome who pushed me beyond my harshest critic (yes, me) to get a first draft down. Those who honored me with crucial, critical readings of subsequent drafts include fellow Berlin Brats and lifelong friends Molly Moylan Brown, Suzanne Stovall and Gen. Richard Clarke (retired), and their lovely, compassionate daughter Madeleine; dear friends Laurie Caswell, Lili Lynton, Clarissa McNair, and Tim Rund; my dear cousin Carol Chapman Librizzi, and my inimitable little (never lesser) brother John Chapman, and scholarly niece Marguerite Chapman. I am particularly grateful to YA author Stephanie Bodeen—for her time, sage advice, and encouragement. And, while honoring her story as hers, this novel would never have materialized had it not been for my Berlin sister, Susanne Lowen, and all our exploits together. And last but by no means least, boundless appreciation goes to the patience and keen insights of my beloved daughter Nancy and husband Tim.

ABOUT THE AUTHOR

Sarah Brotherhood Chapman is an author, editor and mother, based in Munich, Germany. The daughter of a U.S. diplomat, she spent her childhood overseas in Germany, Afghanistan, Yugoslavia, Holland, and the USSR, graduating from high school in West Berlin. This enriching lifestyle continued when her husband, whom she met while attending the Radcliffe Publishing Procedures course, decided to join the foreign service. Sarah left her job at Smithsonian Magazine to raise their three children across seven countries while writing, editing, working as a personal trainer, and volunteering with incarcerated people and refugees. Sarah studied German linguistics at the College of William & Mary and creative writing at Goddard College. *Shadow of the West* is her debut novel.

NOTE FROM THE AUTHOR

Word-of-mouth is crucial for any author to succeed. If you enjoyed *Shadow of the West*, please leave a review online—anywhere you are able. Even if it's just a sentence or two. It would make all the difference and would be very much appreciated.

Thanks!
Sarah Brotherhood Chapman

We hope you enjoyed reading this title from:

BLACK ROSE writing

www.blackrosewriting.com

Subscribe to our mailing list – *The Rosevine* – and receive **FREE** books, daily deals, and stay current with news about upcoming releases and our hottest authors.
Scan the QR code below to sign up.

Already a subscriber? Please accept a sincere thank you for being a fan of Black Rose Writing authors.

View other Black Rose Writing titles at www.blackrosewriting.com/books and use promo code **PRINT** to receive a **20% discount** when purchasing.